U.P.S H.U.R

CHOCTAW GOLD

The secret in Devil Mountain

OTIS MORPHEW

iUniverse, Inc.

New York Bloomington

iUniverse books may be ordered through booksellers or by contacting:

iUniverse
1663 Liberty Drive
Bloomington, IN 47403
www.iuniverse.com
1-800-Authors (1-800-288-4677)

Because of the dynamic nature of the Internet, any Web addresses or
links contained in this book may have changed since publication and
may no longer be valid. The views expressed in this work are solely those
of the author and do not necessarily reflect the views of the publisher,
and the publisher hereby disclaims any responsibility for them.

ISBN: 978-1-4401-5969-5 (pbk)
ISBN: 978-1-4401-5970-1 (ebk)

Printed in the United States of America

iUniverse rev. date: 07/28/2009

"Dedicated to my wife, Connie, with all my love"

PROLOGUE

ONCE A MAN WITH A violent past tries to leave that past behind, he finds it almost impossible. Because there is such a thin line separating what he was, from what he tries to become,...and that line is most fragile.

Upshur, with help from friends and family, thought he had beaten the odds, and did for nearly three, happy years. He prospered without the tools of his begotten trade. Until that Sunday morning when the bank was robbed and his only son kidnapped. He was forced to use those tools again, erasing what he had become. But a gunfighter's past is hardly ever his own to discard at will, for without having once lived that past, he would not have gotten his son back,...or the bank's money.

When it was over, he redrew that frayed, thin line for the sake of family, friends and future. But, in bringing Willy home, he had gratefully given his word to a new friend, one he thought he would never be called on to keep. But to a man like Upshur, his given word was a part of what, and who he is,...and because of that, he would break that fragile line again. Because his new friend is in trouble and has sent for him,...and he has given his word.

Once again, the legally dead gunfighter would be resurrected in time, he hoped, to help those who had saved his son's life. Only this time, he would take an old friend back with him, both under the guise of a long overdue hunting excursion, not wanting to bring trouble to those who had put their own wellbeing on the line for him three years before....This time, only his wife and son would suffer his absence, and to William Upshur, that was quite enough.

But what choice did he have? He had none at all because this is the legacy of Upshur, the gunfighter that was once known as "The Reb" But what could he do against a small army of men with "Gold Fever", that an army of invisible warriors could not do? But what would happen on his third trip to the fabled mountain was almost more than he could handle, because now, another three years later, he was going back. Only this time, he and Rodney Taylor would take their families along, a sort of an outing, a vacation. But was that a good idea? Because Choctaw farmers had killed a giant bird in the Choctaw Nation, a flesh-eating, flying reptile that had been extinct for millions of years,...and both of them knew that the only place it could have come from,... was Devil Mountain. Was this the Evil White Buffalo had spoken of, the evil he said must be guarded, that if it should escape, it would terrorize mankind?

It would be up to them to stop this evil before it could spread worldwide, and at the same time protect the secrets in the valley. But they were not prepared for what they found in the tunnels beneath Devil Mountain,... or how to explain something so impossible.

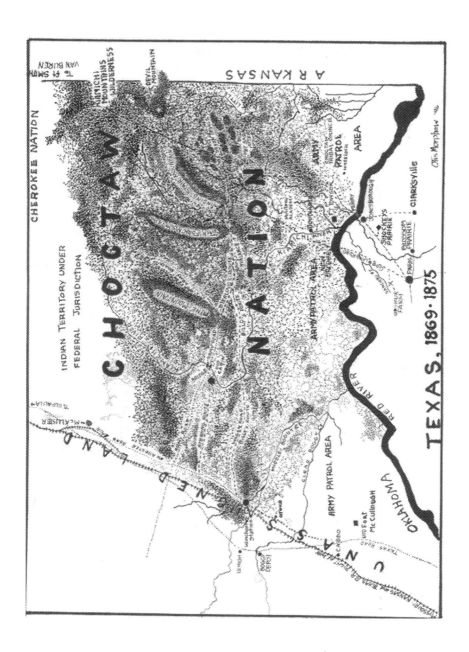

CHEROKEE NATION

CHOCTAW NATION

INDIAN TERRITORY UNDER FEDERAL JURISDICTION

To FT SMITH & VAN BUREN

WITCHITA MOUNTAINS WILDERNESS

DEVIL MOUNTAIN

ARKANSAS

ARMY PATROL AREA

Otto Momphew

Clarksville

ARMY PATROL AREA

RED RIVER

TEXAS, 1869-1875

CHICKASAW NATION

ARMY PATROL AREA

OKLAHOMA

TEXAS

NED LAND

To McALISTER

CADDO

Fort McCulloch

CHAPTER ONE

THE BLOWING ICE WAS STINGING his face, slapping at his eyeglasses with such force that he could barely see a thing. He couldn't even see the eyes of the thin gunman waiting to shoot him, he wiped at the eyeglasses with a gloved finger to clear them, but too late, he saw the killer draw and frantically clawed at the gun on his hip. But then he heard the terrible rumbling of the avalanche as the mountain of snow reached to engulf him. The killer held his fire, laughing as tons of white death rained down on him and all at once, he was in a black void of helplessness and unable to breathe.

Suddenly he was floating in the frozen darkness of a ravine, he knew this, because he could feel the clawing fingers of the ice-cold roots and sharp rocks that raked and gouged at his back. He couldn't remember how he had come to be there, or why, but he was buried in snow and blinded by darkness. So how did he get from the mountain pass, to the gully? It had to all be one and the same, because the tremendous weight of the avalanche was crushing the breath from his lungs.

He was helpless, unable to move his arms or legs, and his mind was screaming a mixture of frustration, fear and rage as he was forced to listen to the piercing laughter of the killer that still mocked him,…he could do nothing but wait, as the darkness swallowed him, screaming in rage as the void overtook him.

— —

Billy Upshur was sitting upright on the feather mattress, his screams still echoing in his ears as he wildly searched the darkness of the room, frantically dragging in huge gulps of the cool, pre-dawn air. He was sweating profusely as the vivid dream still clung to his consciousness, and he wiped the cold sweat from his face as he slowly returned to reality and was able to recognize the blurred furnishings in his bedroom, the pale glow of moonlight through the open window, however, made them easier to see in the shadows.

He was shaking badly as he wildly scanned the room, could even hear the beating of his own heart in his ears, and startled, he jumped in fear as Connie slipped her arm through his and sat up beside him on the bed.

"Sorry, honey...I didn't mean to wake you up." He uttered, then sighed and ran his hand over his damp hair. "I had a dream, that's all."

"The same one you told me about?"

"A little different version of it, but, yeah,...th' same one."

"Then, I'd say it's a little more than just a dream, wouldn't you?" Her voice was laced with concern as she peered at him. "You were fighting for breath this time,...and your arm is all covered in chill-bumps. Billy, I want you to tell me what really happened up there,...I know there's more to it, than what you told me."

"It was just a dream, honey, that's all,....I'm okay now."

"Well I think it's more than that." She insisted. "You had a nightmare,... and from what you've been telling me, it seems like they get worse as you have one." She hugged his arm against her chest. "I've got time, you know, if you want to tell me about it?...It might help,....and who knows, the dreams might even stop altogether?"

"I wouldn't know where to start, they're so jumbled." He muttered, and then leaned to kiss her on the forehead. "But you're right, I didn't tell you everything, and you know what?....We'll sit down tonight and talk about it, I promise.....I don't remember a lot about the dreams themselves,....but I'll fill in the gaps about the manhunt,...agreed?"

"Agreed." She sighed. "But right now, I'm worried about the nightmares. How long have you been having them, now,...a week,...two weeks?"

"About two weeks.....Hell, we've been home for three months,...it's over and done with!...I don't know." He sighed heavily. "Maybe it's just now catchin' up to me."

"Maybe." Whispered Connie. "But this is the first time you've woken me like this." She yawned mightily. "Billy?....If it's the same dream every time, then what makes it different,...you said it varied?"

"I don't really know, honey." He sighed. "But it all comes down to the same thing…..I'm supposed to be trying to help somebody,….but I never actually see anyone in th' dream. Anyway, I can't seem to get to whoever it is, because of that damn gunman,… whoever he is? And I don't think it's about Willy this time, but whoever it is, he needs my help……At other times, I'm in a blinding snow-storm, bein' run down by a herd of buffalos that I can't even see…..Everything's white, th' snow's white, and th' only way I know they're there is because I can see their red eyes. I don't even know how I know they're buffaloes,….I just know it."

Connie sighed. "Then don't try to figure them out right now, it'll just give you another headache, and I don't want you suffering like that. Lay back down, okay?" She yawned and lay back on her pillow. "Try and go back to sleep." She pulled the blanket up around her neck and became quiet.

He positioned the pillow and lay down again, but his mind was still on the dream and trying to understand what it meant. The gunman had to be Lance Ashley, the man he'd killed in Winchester Station nearly three months ago. But the man in his dream wasn't dead, and in the dreams he had no face. He could understand dreaming about the storm, and even the avalanche, but the gunman? Could he be someone he hadn't met yet?

He didn't know, but the buffalos could represent the chief of the Ancient Ones, as well as his warriors. But in one of his earlier dreams, a white buffalo had died, could that mean that something had already happened to White Buffalo,… or was about to happen? But if so, why would the warriors be trying to run him down, if that was what the herd represented?….Or were they just running away from whatever had killed their Chief,…or were they actually trying to kill him? What did it all mean? He sighed and turned over in the bed,….it would all come to him sooner or later, he felt sure of that.

He thought then of the Mountain, trying to visualize everything he'd seen while he was there,…anything that could tell him they might be in trouble, but there wasn't a clue. They were the most organized people he'd ever seen. Everything they did was so precise, and deliberate. A strong-willed people led by a powerful Chief.

CHAPTER TWO

IT IS LATE JANUARY OF 1870, and the Upshur Farm has continued to grow, from the first fifty acres to a little more than 450 acres of black-land in the first year, and by the close of the second year,...had grown to more than 600 acres, and three quarters of that was sown in cotton. Billy Upshur was a man of opportunity, wanting only to give his family the best that life had to offer. He had just closed on the last hundred-acre land deal before the bank robbery last October.

The rambling farmhouse and other structures stood a little less than twelve miles Northeast of Paris, Texas, and that was not a great distance. But it was much too far, he'd argued, for Connie to have to travel every day to open her Café. They no longer needed the Restaurant for their livelihood, but the argument, that she sell it had always fell on deaf ears. Even though his foreman had readily agreed to drive her and Willy to town every morning, he was still unhappy, and had only gone along with it because Sam went in to town every morning anyway for the mail, and the supplies they might need.

He was in a deep and frightening sleep. The dread of death from the thick, swirling snow was like a shroud settling around his head, smothering him as it crushed his lungs. But then he heard the birds and once again, he was in the mountains of the Seven Devils, with large, ebony crows circling overhead.

Their cries were loud, piercingly loud as more and more of them filled the sky above him. He stopped the roan to watch them as their shrill screams filled his mind and ears, and when they suddenly began to swoop down at him, it was as if his head would burst.

Billy woke with a start, gasping for breath as he sat upright on the downy confines of the mattress. The shrill cawing was still loud in his ears, and when he opened his eyes, was startled again by the bird's shrill noise,… and confused, he wildly began to search the moonlit room for the source,…..and that was when he saw the Crow.

The very large, blurry, bird was on the sill of the open window as, once again, it filled the room with it's loud, piercing song. The pale light of the moon was playing on its ebony feathers as the bird moved restlessly from one side of the sill to the other. Billy stared numbly at it as the agonizing noise continued, then swung his legs off the bed and covered his ears with his hands.

"I don't believe this!" He said loudly and turned for another look. A chill went through his body as he realized that his dream had just come true, that, or the Crow was the reason for the dream. The Crow cawed again and cursing, Billy fumbled on the floor for one of his work shoes and lobbed it at the window. With a fluttering of its large black wings, the bird scurried from the opening and flew away, cawing angrily in the distance.

"That was something strange.' He thought as he fished a match from a jar on the table and lit the coal-oil lamp, then yawned and pulled on his eyeglasses. He looked at the open window again as he stood and stepped into the Bib-overalls, then pulled on the clean shirt, Connie had put out for him, and still thinking about the bird he stared at the window as he buttoned it, thinking it strange that a Crow would come that close to the house.

He fished the straps over his shoulders and hooked them to the flap of the overalls as memories of circling Crows came to mind again,…but then he remembered that it had actually happened to him and thought back to when the Crow had dove at him, and it was at the same time that he felt he was being followed. Was it possible there was a connection?.....No, He thought and then quickly shook his head to rid himself of the nonsense.

'But it is damn strange.' He thought again, and shrugging, bent to pick up his shoe, then grabbed the lamp and went around the bed for the other one. Bending, he picked up the Brogan, and then heard the Crow voicing its opinion again,…prompting him to squat and peer out at the moonlit yard, placing the bird in the Pecan trees by the barn. Grunting to his feet, he shivered from the cold air and closed the window, then shook his head in disgust as he blew out the lamp and returned it to the night table,…and then turned abruptly and headed off through the house toward the kitchen where he knew there would be a pot of hot, strong coffee on the stove.

Billy heard the deep, gong-like chiming of the Grandfather Clock as he walked past it, and glanced at the time. Six o'clock, he noted. Thinking that Connie would be opening the Café about now, and the place would be crowded by the time coffee was made. He sighed then grabbed the coffee-mug from the table and poured if full from the pot on the stove as he wondered, one more time, how she could work all those hours in the Restaurant and still find the time to manage things at home? He replaced the pot on the old cast-iron stove and sat down at the table to sip at the hot liquid.

It was lonesome in the large house with her and Willy gone all day. He grinned then, remembering how he had enjoyed being with his own father. He was seven when his father offered him his first cup of coffee, and they had sat at the breakfast table and talked as they sipped the scalding brew. Those were special times, and an every morning's event after that. He would love having morning coffee with Willy, too, and would, had his mother not insisted he was too young. But his being in town all day with Mattie and Doc had severely cut into their special time together. In the last two weeks, since the dreams started, she had not even gotten him up when they left, said he needed his rest, and it was at times like that, that made him wish they lived in town. He raised a bare foot and pulled on one of his socks, then was startled by the flapping of large wings at the open window behind him. Twisting around, he leaned on the sill and moved the curtain aside in time to see the large Crow settle on the horse-trough where it began its insistent cawing again,.....almost urgently, it seemed.

"What th' hell is wrong with you?" He said as he watched the antics of the ebony bird, but watching it caused memories to stir once again.... Again making him wonder if this Crow might somehow be connected to the dreams he was having,...but how? He shook his head at the thought, wondering what possible connection a Crow in Texas might have with those in the Territories?....None, he thought,....absolutely none! He couldn't believe he was thinking that way.....It was crazy!

"Yeah, get out'a here!" He said angrily and watched it fly noisily away as Sam drove the buckboard across the yard to the trough, and then waved as the foreman jumped to the ground.

"Getting' a late start this morning, ain't ya, Boss?" Grinned Sam as he pumped more water into the trough.

"No,....you're just an hour early gettin' back....What's goin' on?"

Sam shook his head. "Missus Upshur was tryin' to hitch up th' buckboard when I got up this mornin',...so I got dressed and took 'em to town early.... Is anything wrong, Boss?"

"No, it's just them lousy dreams I been havin',….I woke her up last night,…guess she couldn't get back to sleep after that."

"That's what Missus Upshur said….Said they was gettin' worse, too. You figure what it's all about yet?"

Billy shook his head. "I wish to hell, I knew, Sam,… It's got me to where I dread goin' to sleep."

"Well, with what you went through up there, no wonder you're dreamin'……I wouldn't fret too much about it, though,…it'll pass." Sam looked toward the corral then. "What's with that big-ass Crow?"

"I wish I knew that, too,….damn thing woke me up this mornin'. It was on th' window-sill in my bedroom."

"You don't say?" Said Sam as he looked back at him. "Never heard th' likes of that before….Course I can't recall ever seein' one that big, neither….. Damn sight bigger'n any we got around here!...Louder, too,…must a come from th' Nations."

Billy lifted the window some more and leaned out to look toward the corral. "I think you're right, there was some bigger than that up there….Been wonderin' if this one didn't come from there, myself?"

"It's sure possible, I guess." Returned Sam, looking once again at the corral. "It ain't that far away."

"Well, its givin' me a bad feelin', wherever it comes from."

"How's that?"

"Can't figure that one out yet, neither……… But I'd almost swear th' damn thing was tryin' to tell me somethin', and with th' dreams I've been havin', that ain't too far-fetched."

"Well, we both know that ain't likely, Boss. Anyway,… them dreams could mean anything,…or nothin' at all. When I was a kid in Louisiana, I remember, there was an old woman livin' in th' swamps behind our house a ways." Sam chuckled then. "My Pop said she was a witch….Anyway, that old hag had Pop believin' that a dream was a look at th' future,…but I never did believe that hogwash."

Billy grinned then. "I hope it is hogwash….But there's somethin' goin' on with that damn bird, sure enough,… because I've got that tingle in my neck again and that usually means trouble of some kind."

"I hope not." Said Sam, reaching to scratch his head. "There's been enough'a that lately….It is damn strange, though." He came toward the window then and leaned on the sill. "I could shoot it, if you want?"

"Damn thing would be gone by th' time you got a gun." Said Billy, leaning to pull the other sock onto his foot. "Besides, a shot would just wake up the Hand's women-folk." He slipped his feet into the old worn Brogans and picked up the mug of coffee. "Everything's okay in town, I guess?"

"Same as always. Seen th' Missus inside and waited till she got th' lamps all lit,...then carried young Will in and put 'im to bed again....Little early for 'im to be up this mornin', I guess. Said she'd have th' Sheriff take 'im to Docs' later this mornin'."

"He does like to sleep," Sighed Billy. "Wish I could sleep that well.... We get any mail?"

"None, I don't think,...was a mite too early to wake up Luke, so I looked at th' mail-slot through the window and didn't see anything in it.....We didn't really need any supplies for today neither,... so I just drove on back."

Billy nodded and began tying his shoes. "hands in th' fields?"

"They was up when I was this mornin', I told 'em you wanted that West field plowed under today."

"Good,...I'm cold, Sam, come on in, will ya,... th' coffee's hot,...and I can use th' company."

Sam nodded. "Soon's I put th' rig away, Boss." With that, he went back to the trough and led the team and wagon toward the barn.

Billy took a swallow of the strong coffee and leaned out of the window again, watching as the large Crow lit atop the clothesline post, across the yard and began cawing loudly again. 'I sure wish that thing could talk.' He thought, then yawned mightily and dropped the curtain. His thoughts turned fleetingly to White Buffalo and the hidden valley in the mountain, and of the large Crows that always seemed to be there. Then he thought of his fight with Sterling and Lance Ashley,....and felt the chill in his bones. He'd watched the gunman die, so he couldn't be the man in his dream.

Billy shuddered and pushed the thought from his mind. Why was he still thinking about something he'd worked so hard to forget about? Willy had almost died in those God-awful mountains, everyone did. But yet,....he looked again at the window, hearing the insistent cawing from the yard, why did he feel that this Crow was a messenger of some kind, and if it was,.... from who,...White Buffalo?

Shuddering again, he lifted the linen cloth from atop the food on the table and folded it back, then went to the stove for more of the coffee. He stared at the windows fluttering curtain as he poured, then sighed and sat back down to wait for Sam.

— —

The sun was well up when Sam halted the wagon by the porch and nodded at Billy. "You look tired, Boss,...dream still eatin' at ya?"

Billy nodded and continued to watch the Crow fly back and forth between the corral and the trees along the road. The cawing had been continuous since its arrival and he'd been toying with the idea of shooting it.

"You okay, Boss?" Asked Sam again, also casting a glance at the ebony bird. "You don't look too good this mornin'?"

"What?" He looked at the Foreman then and grinned sheepishly. "I'm okay, Sam......It's that damn Crow! It's starting to get on my nerves some."

"I know th' feelin'" Said Sam as he turned to watch the bird again. "Wonder what's wrong with it,.....it ain't stopped that infernal noise since I got back?"

"Let me know if it comes to ya." Sighed Billy. "It don't make sense like it is." He shook his head, then reached tobacco and papers from his shirt and deftly rolled and lit the smoke. "You all set to go?"

"All set,....gonna be after dark when I get back,...so I guess you'll be goin' in after th' Missus today?"

Billy narrowed his eyes at him then blew smoke from his lungs. "Do me a favor, Sam,....if th' buckboard is still in th' barn when you get back, take care of things around here as usual, will ya?" He looked back at the trees again. "No, on second thought,...that's ok,....I'll go pick 'em up tonight."

"What's eatin' at you, Boss?"

"Sam, I don't really know....But whatever it is, its got somethin' to do with that Crow!" He sighed again and looked back at the Foreman's frustrated face. "It's just a feelin' I've got,....and it's probably nothin', so don't worry about it."

"Why don't you just shoot th' blamed thing and be done with it?"

"I'm thinkin' about that, too,....but in th' back of my mind, somethin's tellin' me not to." He angrily thumped the spent butt into the yard.

"You're beginnin' to sound like my old Papa, Boss." Grinned the foreman, looking back at the line of trees along the road. "You'll figure it out, though,... you always do....But till you do, th' last thing you'll need to worry about is this farm, or th' family...I'll see to that!" He picked up the reins then and looked back at Billy.

"You need me to stay here, Boss,...I can get one'a th' hands to go do this?"

Billy shook his head. "I'd rather you go, Sam,...I want to know its done right."

The foreman nodded. "See ya tonight, then." He slapped the reins on the horses' backs and turned them around in the yard. "I ought'a be back around sundown, somethin' don't bar th' way." He said loudly.

"See ya, Sam." He waved and watched the wagon leave the yard for the road, then sighing, stepped off the porch and onto the seat of the six-row bedding plow, Sam had left there earlier. He seated himself and clucked the team into motion.

It was almost noon when he stopped the horses in the settling dust. The Crow had followed him as he left the house and had been circling overhead for hours, and the constant cawing had frayed his nerves. He was ever closer to going back for his shotgun, because watching the plows and the bird at the same time had made his neck ache. He rubbed at his neck as he watched the soaring bird circle and then light on the unplowed ground in front of him.

"I'm running out of patience, Bird!" He said loudly. "You're walkin' on some mighty thin ice, I hope you know that." The Crow was motionless for a time as it watched him then suddenly, it looked off toward the trees, cocking its ebony head to one side,...and then to suddenly fly off in that direction where it lifted up to settle in the top of a tall Cottonwood. He watched it intently for a few seconds and then caught a flicker of movement in the shadows beneath the large tree,...and he was more than curious now as he studied the horse and rider. He pushed the eyeglasses higher on his nose and looked more closely at the shadowy figure on the paint horse,....and once again felt the tingle on the back of his neck. He looked up at the now silent Crow in the top of the tree and knew he'd been right. Relaxing for a minute on the iron seat, he rolled a brown-paper cigarette and lit it, drawing deeply of the relaxing smoke as he studied the horse and rider. Whoever he was, he'd not made a move to ride out into the open,....and that was strange in itself.

It was also strange that something was nagging at his memory, because the more he looked at the man, the more he looked familiar and sighing, he pulled the lever, raising the blades out of the furrows then locked them in place.

"Up to me, I guess." He muttered, and then wondered what was important enough to bring the little Choctaw all the way to Texas? He clucked the team into motion across the plowed ground and nearing the trees, slapped the lines across their backs, urging them up and into the shade of the Cottonwood. He grinned when he saw the emotionless face of the slender Choctaw.

"Didn't recognize you without your mule, Peter." He stopped the team and studied the tracker's face for a moment. "It's good to see you, man."

Peter nodded. "As well as you, Mister Upshur."

"How'd you find me?"

Peter shrugged his slender shoulders. "The Crow found you, I only followed."

Billy looked up through the branches of the Cottonwood. "I guess I figured as much." He shook his head and looked back at the tracker. "Damn bird came into my bedroom this mornin',.....been about to drive me crazy ever since.....I didn't understand it, but I had a feelin' it was connected." He looked back up through the tree again and nodded. "That's how they knew where I was all th' time,…it's how they know about everything that happens up there, ain't it?…They control th' birds."

Peter shrugged. "Only the Crow, I think….It is said that the Chief talks with them."

Billy pushed the hat back onto his head. "I find that kind a hard to believe."

"It is said he has many powers,…but I do not know."

Billy studied the Choctaw's face. "You know they saved my son's life?"

Peter nodded. "Every Choctaw knows."

Billy nodded and looked out across the plowed field before looking back at him. "What brings you all th' way to Texas, Peter?"

The tracker shrugged again. "A warrior came to me in the mountains, and he said that I must bring a message to Man-with-glass-eyes.….He said I must tell you to come to the mountain before it is too late."

"Too late for what?….Is White Buffalo okay?"

"I tell you only what was told to me,…that you must come."

"Peter,…nothin' goes on in them mountains that you don't know about. Now tell me what's wrong."

The tracker was silent for a time then finally nodded. "The Ancient ones would ask help from no one unless there was much trouble there. This warrior said that White Buffalo has trust for you only."

Billy stared at him, and knew he wasn't lying….He knew that Peter wouldn't say anything without thinking about it first, so he rolled and lit another smoke, inhaling the acrid relaxant while he waited.

"I have not been near the mountain." Continued Peter. "I will never go there, just as my people will not,….but something strange is happening in the mountains. My people have told me of hearing distant sounds of guns being fired,…and even I have heard echoes of gunfire, and it troubles me. Comanche warriors have been seen, and many white men, all of them heavily armed.….And all of this from the direction of the Devil Mountain….Marshal Thompson has not yet returned, and my people are afraid."

"Have you seen, or tracked any of these men yourself?"

Peter nodded. "I have seen Comanche warriors from a distance,… and signs of many passing horses in the Devils,…….and all moving to the North."

"Comanches?…Joseph told me they were too afraid to go there."

Peter shrugged again. "Maybe they are afraid no more, no one knows."

Billy sighed, inhaling more of the strong smoke. "Then we don't know if White Buffalo is alive or dead right now, do we?" And when Peter shook his head. "Couldn't you and your people help them,… surely there's enough of you to run these men out of the mountains?'

'The Ancient Ones would never accept help from the Choctaw in the Nations. Most do not even own weapons, except for hunting,…the Army forbids it. Anyway, most are too afraid to interfere, even if they are asked."

Billy nodded somberly, and felt the chill in his neck and spine again. Something was very wrong up there, he thought as he stared back at the plowed ground. They wouldn't have sent for him, otherwise. That means that the mountain itself must be under attack,…but from who,…and why? He knew that as much as he didn't want to go back into that wilderness,…he had to. He'd given his word,…and he owed White Buffalo his son's life. He sighed and looked back at Peter. "Tell 'em you found me, Peter" He sighed. "Tell 'em I'll come as soon as I can."

Peter nodded. "The warrior said you must wear the medallion,…for your safety. There is much fear in the hearts of my people, they will not trust a stranger."

"What about you, Peter?.....How do you feel about all this?"

Peter sighed this time as well. "I am troubled….The Ancient Ones have been protectors of my people for a very, very long time. We fear them,…yet we live in peace and safety because they are there. Life would not be so good without them, I think."

"Those are my thought, too." Sighed Billy, then he grinned. "Have you been well?"

"Yes, my friend. I am well."

"And Joseph?"

"Also well," He nodded. "But he has gone to stay with his family until the danger has passed…..They are unprotected."

Billy nodded grimly, then smiled at the Choctaw. "You look tired and hungry, Peter. If you're a mind to, you are welcome to rest at my home before you go back."

The Tracker shook his head. "Thank you, my friend,….but I do not wish to be seen. I must leave now, but I hope good luck for you in what you must do." With that, he reined the spotted pony around and started to leave, but stopped when Billy called out to him.

"Take care of yourself, my friend,….and please,… take that damn Crow with you, okay?"

Peter grinned for the first time since his arrival, then continued on into the trees.

Billy watched him leave, feeling the chill in his bones as he remembered the conversation between them. It sounded to him like there could be an army of men attacking the mountain, and if that was the case, what could he possibly do that an army of skilled warriors couldn't? They were unconquerable, like ghosts…At least, they were! Something very bad must have happened, something very dangerous. He sighed and mashed the spent butt out on the iron wheel, then clucked the team around in the shade of the Cottonwood, slapped the reins across their backs again and headed for home. He had plans to make, and thinking to do, about how he would tell Connie he was going back.

CHAPTER THREE

CONNIE POURED FRESH COFFEE INTO Rodney's cup as he finished eating, then looked up as the departing customer opened the door. "Thank you, Mister Clovis. Come back now, you hear?" She smiled as he waved and closed the door behind him.

"Wonder what Billy's doing here so early?" She said, having seen him drive up to the hitch-rail as Mister Clovis was leaving, and was instantly afraid that something was wrong at the farm,.....Sam usually came for her and Willy,... but not this early.

"Ain't nothing wrong with that." Grinned the Marshal. "Probably got lonesome stuck off out there by himself,....after all, he was gone for quite a spell."

She grinned at him and reached for a cup then filled it with coffee before taking it to their table by the window. "I can't wait till you get married, Rodney.... You'll understand a few things then."

"What's to understand?" He smiled. "It's plain to see the man can't stay away from you."

"You are way too early." She beamed as he opened the door, and tiptoed to kiss him on the lips. "Now,...what's wrong at the farm?"

Billy saw Rodney then and put his arm around Connie's shoulders to steer her toward the counter. "How are you, Rod?" He grinned as he took the lawman's extended hand. "Good to see you.... How's th' shoulder?"

"I'm good, Billy." Grinned the Marshal. "And it's been three months,… the shoulder's fine."

"That long?" He released Rodney's hand, his face turning serious. "I'll be back in a minute, Rod,….. I want to talk to you." He gripped his friend's shoulder and then ushered Connie over to the table.

She sat wide-eyed as he told her of Peter's visit, and of how his dreams must have been an omen of some kind. She began vigorously shaking her head as he told her of the message Peter had brought, and then gasped loudly when he finished by telling her of his decision to go back and help the ancient Indians.

"Billy, no!" Tears filled her eyes quickly then. "Damn it, you almost died up there!….Our son almost died up there! I won't go through that again!…I can't go through that again,…You're not going back!"

He took both her hands in his. "I'm not going because I want to, honey,…I have to. If it wasn't for them, Willy would be dead now. We owe White Buffalo and his people more than we can ever pay back. Don't you understand that?….. He needs my help now, and I can't turn 'im down.…..I'm sorry, honey,…I just can't,…I gave my word."

"But you said there were hundreds of Indians there to help him, Billy, what can you do that all those Indians can't do themselves?"

"I won't know that till I get there."

"Oh, God!" She moaned, knowing the futility of trying to change his mind once it was made up. "Okay," She sniffed, laying her hands palm-down on the tablecloth. "We do owe them a lot, I know that. I just,….I'm afraid I'll lose you, Billy! I couldn't live if I lost you.…I don't think I'd even want to!"

He squeezed her hands then. "You will never lose me, I promise.…You ought a know by now, that I can take care of myself."

"But we need you here, and besides, you have a choice this time,…you didn't before!"

Billy shook his head. "No, honey, I don't have a choice.…If you know me at all, you know that…. I'd hate myself if I didn't go. White Buffalo's a great man, a man of truth and honor…. He could have killed me any time he wanted to up there, but instead, he gave Willy back to us.…..And because of that, I promised him that I would come if he ever needed my help.…..I gave my word, honey,…do you really want me to break it?"

She covered her face with her hands then wiped the tears away. "When are you leaving?" She sniffed.

"Tomorrow mornin' early.…I'll be gone a week, two at the most."

"Okay." She nodded, then wiped at her face again. "I know you're going anyway,….and I do understand. It's just that I'm terrified of you going back up there alone again,…can't you take someone with you this time?"

15

"Yes." Said Rodney as he walked up to the table and pulled out a chair. "He can...This time, I'm going with him." He sat down and smiled widely at them, then sipped at the coffee he brought to the table with him.

Billy shook his head. "I appreciate th' offer, Rod,... but you've got no part in this,...you've got duties right here."

"Oh, but that's where you're wrong, old son, I do have a part in this,....a big part." He reached and gripped Billy's arm. "I owe that man about as much as you do, he saved my Nephew's life.....and he didn't kill you.... Besides, it won't be you who has to see what it does to your family if you don't come back,....and it sure ain't going to be me this time!" The lawman met Billy's stare for a minute, then nodded his head. "Because I'm watching your back on this one.... You can't stop me, you know,...Cause I'm the law,...and I've got some time off coming to me,...and if you say no,.......Well,....I'll follow you anyway."

Billy opened his mouth to speak, but grinned instead.

"Good." Said Rodney, smiling broadly again. "I'm glad that's settled."

"You're th' only man I'd even trust to go with me." Nodded Billy. "But you don't have any idea what you're getting yourself into. Those Indians are not like anything you could ever imagine,...and they're dangerous. And if they're askin' for my help,...it's likely a lot worse than both of us can imagine."

"All the more reason, I go. Look,...if anybody else had told me a story like the one you told, I'd have thrown them in jail for being drunk and disorderly. But I believed you when you told it, cause I know you don't lie.....If you're in trouble, my friend, I'm in trouble, too!"

"Okay, Rod!" Laughed Billy. "You made your point,....thanks."

The lawman scraped back his chair and got up. "I'll go make arrangements right now....I have to fill Jim in on a few things"

Billy nodded. "Stockwell's a good enough man.......I'll come down to your office in a bit, we'll need to make a supply list."

Rodney nodded, then picked up Connie's hand. "Try not to worry too much, okay? I'll bring him home,.....and that's a promise."

— ⸺

Rodney waved at Willy as Sam stopped the buckboard at the hitch-rail and went to lift him down from the seat. "Man, you're getting heavy." Grunted Rodney playfully.

"I'm almost all growed up, ain't I, Uncle Rodney?"

"It's, I'm almost grown up, William, not growed up?" Fussed Connie as she allowed the lawman to help her down also.

16

"Are you okay, Connie?" Asked Rodney as he felt the tenseness in her arm.

"I'm fine, thank you, Rodney." She took Willy's hand and ushered him up the steps to the boardwalk.

Sam tied the horses and hurried up the steps to open the Café's front door for her, coming back only after she had lit the kerosene lamps along the wall. "Missus Upshur's a mite testy this mornin', Sheriff." Sighed the Foreman as he came down the steps. "Didn't say a word all th' way in."

"She's got a right to be, I guess." Nodded Rodney. "How are you, Sam?" He shook the Foreman's outstretched hand.

"I'm good, Sheriff.....I got a say I'm a mite worried about all this, though, sounds dangerous as hell to me!...Th' Missus nearly went plumb crazy, th' last time he went."

"To tell you the truth, I'm worried about it, too....No telling what we'll be riding into up there,...but I damn sure ain't letting him go in there alone again!"

Sam nodded. "I hear ye, you men take care a yourselves up there....From what th' boss told me, it could get a little rough....I'm glad you're goin' along, Sheriff."

"Tell you what, Sam....I will do my best to watch out for him,... if you'll stop calling me Sheriff? I'm a Marshal now,...and there's a big difference."

"A badge is a badge to me." Grinned the Foreman. "You been Sheriff for as long as I can remember."

"Rodney shook his head and grinned then looked back down the dark street. "Wonder what's keeping Billy, I thought he'd be right behind you?"

"He'll be along. He was still getting his gear together when we left." Sam turned to look also, and then nodded. "Looks like it might be him comin' yonder."

Rodney watched while Billy reined the nervous Roan up to the hitch-rail and then walked around the animal's rump.

Billy dismounted and leaned across the saddle to stare at the lighted window of the   restaurant, then nodded his head in greeting as the lawman stopped beside him. "I hate this, Rod....I really hate it!"

"I didn't think she was all that upset yesterday."

"Not upset, as much as hurt,....and a lot scared!...And you know what? So am I." Sighing, he tied the mare then went toward the packhorse. "Stout lookin' horse,...you get everything on th' list?"

"I think so." Returned Rodney, slapping the lumpy canvass. "Brought a few extras along just in case."

"Like what?" Grinned Billy.

Rodney grinned also. "Well, like two extra rifles, two handguns and a thousand rounds of ammunition."

"We goin' to war?"

"Might be, from what you told me,….and preparation is half the battle, you know. Got this, too." He pulled the long, thin telescope from beneath the tarp and gave it to Billy.

"I wouldn't have thought of this. Good thinkin', Rod, it could come in handy."

"You got everything, Boss?" Asked Sam as he walked in beside them.

"I think so, Sam….You be okay with handlin' things till I get back?"

Sam nodded. "I got it covered, Boss….And don't you go and fret none about th' Missis and young Will. I'll see they're okay."

"I don't worry when you're there, Sam,….and thanks, it means a lot to me. Oh yeah,…I never did finish that patch this mornin'."

"I'll put Ross on it today…Want them supplies on th' packhorse?"

"Might not be room, with all that extra ammunition." He reached to slap the grinning lawman on the shoulder. "I'm just kiddin', Sam, Go ahead."

Sam nodded. "Oh, yeah, Boss,…just so you don't get surprised….I took it on myself to trade you my Henry rifle for your saddle-gun. You just might need a gun with a little more kick and range to it up there."

Nodding his thanks, Billy watched him go to the wagon, then breathed deeply of the morning air as the Foreman removed his Winchester and slid the long rifle into the boot on his saddle. "It's getting' late, and I'm cold." He said as he looked up at the Café. "Lets get us some breakfast,…be a while till we eat again…Hurry it up, Sam, let's eat!"

Billy and Rodney in front of Café before leaving.

They began passing empty shanties and boarded-up, dilapidated shops as they neared the river port of Jonesboro, having to move off the narrow road and into the tall grass and weeds a time or two to allow loaded wagons to bounce past.

"Looks like a few of 'em are movin' on." Commented Billy as he urged the roan back onto the rutted road. "Place looks a lot different than it did three months ago."

"It's about outlived its time." Returned the lawman. "And that suits the hell out of me. I spend half my time in this hell-hole,....and my Deputies are here the other half."

"Railroad's puttin' a stop to about all th' river trade hereabouts,...and you better hope none of these outlaws wind up in Paris when it does."

"Be a while before I'll have to worry about that. I figure this place to die on the vine in another year or two....I've got at least that long before I'll need to worry about any more vagrants in town."

"More,...they already a problem?"

"Yeah," Nodded Rodney. "Rail yard's crawling with hobos and tramps... we deal with them every day......Well, looks like we're here,....and there's the Ferry."

They turned the animals down the grade to the river, seeing the Ferryman come out of his tired, old tarpaper shack and wave at them. They dismounted and waited for the old man to open the gate, then led the horses onto the worn planking of the listing barge.

"You know." Sighed Rodney as he watched a small steamer being poled away from the dock in the distance. "As much as I don't like this place,...I sort of hate to see it die....Hell, its been here forever, and now look at it..... It was crawling with people a few months ago,...a dock full of boats, and more waiting to dock. My deputies were over here every Saturday night, bar none....I guess Fort Towson landing will get the trade now."

"A lot can happen in a month." Breathed Billy as he checked the mare's cinches.

"Well, I hate that, too." Sighed the lawman. He leaned against the rump of his horse and stared gloomily at the distant, rolling hills to the north of them. "Just where is this Devil Mountain of yours anyway?" He asked, bringing his eyes to rest on the dozen or so shanties along the road on the other side of the river. "I mean,...how are we going to get there in time to help these Indians?"

Billy gazed at the hills then, too. "By usin' the roads as much as possible,... if they look safe enough.... Anyway, our mountain's right in th' middle of th' Kiamichi Wilderness,...and callin' that place a wilderness is too tame a word." He sighed and dropped the stirrup before leaning across the saddle. "But no

matter how we go, it's a good four day's hard ride from here, maybe five…..
and you're right, We might be too late to help 'em."

"Well then,… why not go to Fort Towson, maybe we'll get an escort?"

Billy shook his head. "We'd lose another day. Besides, th' Army don't
know they're up there,….and even if they did, I doubt they could get us
through that country any faster than we can do it ourself."

"Then we got it cut out for us, don't we?"

"I'd say so." Sighed Billy. "Rod, ain't there a settlement up that road, on
th' other side there, I recall hearin' music off yonder somewhere?"

"Wheelock." Nodded Rodney. "I went through there with Douglas Henry
once after a load of rock. The Comanche were on a rampage, and he insisted
I could guarantee safe passage,….my ass was scared, Too, I hope to tell you.
Anyway, Wheelock's nothing but a couple dozen shacks and a grungy saloon,
it's mostly a hangout for the cavalry."

"Then we'll be bypassin' Wheelock. We don't need to be stopped and
questioned by th' Army, if we can help it…..Come to think about it,…might
be a good idea to avoid any Choctaw cabins, too,…and that could mean
stayin' off th' roads completely."

"Why, Billy? So what if we're seen, the Choctaw are friendly?"

"You don't know, I guess,… but white men are supposed to notify th'
Army when they go to th' Nations,… answer a few questions, give good
reasons for goin',….and then, if they're in a good mood, they'll give us a
written permit….And as far as th' Choctaw bein' friendly,…well, they're
also friendly with th' Army. Besides, with what Peter said was goin' on at th'
mountain right now, they ain't liable to be too friendly with anybody."

"I guess you're right,…and I did know that, by the way."

Billy grinned. "We're gonna be seen anyway, sooner or later,…but I'd just
as soon it be later."

"It would help if we knew for sure what was going on up there."

"It's not knowing that scares me." Returned Billy as he looked around
him. "And where's that old man?"

"Hold your horses….I'm a comin', I'm a comin!" The Ferryman stepped
onto the barge and locked the chain across the entrance. "Where you off to,
Marshal? Lookin' for somebody, are ye?"

"Might be we're just going fishing,…might even do some prospecting."

"Uh-huh….You cleared that with th' Army, I reckin'….White men ain't
supposed to be up there, ye know,… not without permission."

"The law goes where it wants to go, old timer. I don't need permission
from the Army."

"Yeah, well that's okay by me….Keep them horses still now, you hear?….
Planks are rotten on this old tub. Wouldn't want one of 'em fallin' through."

He stopped on his way to the front of the raft and peered up at Billy. "Ain't seen you in a spell." He went past him to the rusty bell that dangled from a pole at the front of the raft and hit it hard with the hammer that hung below it.

Both of them quickly reached to calm the startled animals then watched the man on the opposite shore lead the team of mules down the high bank of the river.

The Ferry creaked loudly, then lurched and began to groan as it moved out into the fast-moving current of Red River.

"You fellers' had come yesterday mornin', you couldn't a crossed,...damn barge was froze in solid. Had snow in th' Ki'michi again, too." He grinned toothily at them as he grabbed the large towrope and began guiding it through the iron rings. "Won't be long, though, I won't need this old tub anyway..... Yess'ir, Jonesbora's a dyin', gents,...all be gone another year or so,......and so will I, I reckin."

"Why's that?" Asked Billy as he watched the Steamer round the bend of the river.

"Progress!" Cackled the old man. "Least it's what th' Army calls it. Says they're gonna build one'a them there Span-bridges across here,....already buildin' one West'a here somewhere. Said a man'll be able to drive a train a loaded freight wagins across it easy as you please....Reckin a bridge'll get a lot a that Clarksville traffic then, since it'll be openin' up th' Nations for business trade"

Grinning, Billy reached into the saddlebags and recovered the two medallions then went around the packhorse to where Rodney was watching the other shore. He gave one to the lawman then removed his hat to pull the rawhide loop over his head.

"What's this?" Quizzed Rodney as he examined it, and the polished metal glistened brightly in the afternoon sun.

"A gift from White Buffalo to me and Willy,....Peter said we should wear them. Might keep us from getting' shot by a scared Choctaw."

"This thing's made of gold!" Exclaimed Rodney as he pulled it over his head. "What's its purpose?"

"It's supposed to guarantee us safe passage,....providin' we're close enough for th' Choctaw to see it......But it'll keep the Ancient Ones from mistakin' us for a couple'a them white men up there."

"And once we're there, what then?"

I wish I knew." Sighed Billy.

CHAPTER FOUR

THEY LED THE ANIMALS OFF the barge and waved to the old man as they mounted, then Billy led off up the narrow, rutted road and almost immediately spotted one of the dreaded army patrols coming toward them. Stopping their horses, both of them breathed a sigh of relief as the dozen or so blue-coated cavalrymen left the road in the general direction of Fort Towson before moving on.

They rode side by side on the uneven clay as much as possible, nodding, or waving at the half-dressed Choctaw children at play in the front yards of the remote shanties along the way. A few women were washing clothes near one or two of the decaying shacks and stared at them as they passed. They were also chased by mangy dogs at times, having to hold the frightened animals in check as their legs were nipped at. But by keeping the horses at a fast walk on the gnarled and pitted road, they began eating up the miles in a slow, but sure fashion, ever alert for any sign of hostility.

Waist-high grass and thick brush crowded the old wagon road on both sides of them. Mesquite and wild Pecan trees were numerous, but they were beginning to see more and more of the tall Pine trees as they came closer to Wheelock, then leaving the road altogether when they saw the settlement ahead of them.

Billy led the way through the tall grass and thickets and soon entered a dense forest of those pines, where they would be out of sight from anyone that might be traveling the road. He was constantly working the mare around large rocks and fallen timber as they continued northward into the foothills, of which were fast becoming taller and more thickly populated with trees and rotting debris. Mesquite brush and pricking vines raked at their skin and snagged their clothing in an effort to slow their progress.

It was late in the day when they made their way back to the road, only to find several more cabins dotting the landscape. Billy stopped the roan and shook his head at the lawman, then shrugged and led the way back into the trees, continuing northward into the ever-taller foothills of the Seven Devils Mountain range.

It was sundown before they started the upward climb toward the Devils, the trees were thick and the rocks and rotten timber were pretty well hidden in the tall dry grass as they continued slowly in the ever-deepening shadows. Then at long last, and having had enough for one day, Billy decided to stop for the night and dismounted in a grouping of large rocks, surrounded by stunted Mesquite. He set about gathering dry wood for a fire as Rodney dismounted, then got his attention and nodded at the rocks.

"Good place to camp over there, Rod,....no tellin' when we'll get to stop again, and besides,....I can't tell North from South as dark as its gettin'."

"I've been lost since we left the barge." Commented Rodney as he loosened the cinches on his horse. He then went to the packhorse and undid one corner of the tarp, bringing canteen, coffee pot and sack of coffee back as Billy struck a match to the handful of grass and dry wood. The fire took quickly, and he added more wood to the flames as it began to crackle and sputter.

"How far have we come already?" Asked Rodney, looking back at the trees.

"Not far, a few miles, I guess,...and With another four days or so, to go." He stood and also stared back the way they had come. "Providin' we don't hit any snags along th' way....I saw unshod pony tracks back there a ways,.... some wagon-ruts, too."

" Yeah,...I saw 'em, too....Choctaw, you think?"

Billy shook his head. "I sort'a doubt it....Except for the Ancient Ones, Most Choctaw ride shod horses,...and most of 'em are mules, at that. No, I don't think it was Choctaw,...Peter said armed Comanches have been seen in th' mountains,...but I can't figure why they would be this far South, with th' Army so close,.....unless there was a large bunch of 'em,......anyway, I doubt they'd be pullin' a wagon."

Rodney poured a handful of grounds into the water and placed the pot on the fire. "That wouldn't make a whole lot of sense, sure enough." He said, looking once again at their back-trail. "All I seen was a handful of tracks, six or eight horses, maybe."

"Eight was my count." Returned Billy. "Not countin' th' wagon team. We best keep our eyes open from here on, because I got a feelin' this country is gonna get a mite rough before this is over. Th' Comanches are dangerous right now, 'specially Quanah Parker's bunch,…but then again, I don't think Quanah Parker could be influenced by no white man, he hates us."

"You saying they're not Comanches?"

"Billy shook his head. "If they are Comanches, they're renegades,… probably broke out on their own,…and according to Peter, they were all headed North."

"No doubt, to join up with whoever is attacking the mountain!"

"White men!" Nodded Billy. "Come on, lets get th' weight off that packhorse."

Both of them were busy with their own thoughts as they tended to the animals, and once back at the fire, placed the night's provisions on the ground where Rodney immediately began preparing the meal. Billy sat back against a large rock and reached tobacco and papers from his shirt then deftly rolled and lit the cigarette, drawing deeply of the acrid smoke as he watched the lawman turn the meat in the skillet.

"Wouldn't hurt to fry all that up tonight,…we might be eatin' in th' saddle from now on…….I got a feelin' we ought to hurry, too."

Rodney twisted around to look at him. "You're really worried, aren't you?"

Billy stared into the crackling flames and nodded. "Peter said he heard shooting in the direction of the mountain,…a lot of it! And if these Comanches have joined up with white men to attack White Buffalo,….then I'd say it's enough to worry about. Yeah, I'm worried,….a lot more than what I let on to Connie."

"Thanks, that eases my mind." Grinned Rodney as he reached to stir the beans into the frying meat. "Now I'll worry enough for both of us…..It's getting cold, too,…now, I guess I'll freeze while I'm worrying."

"Bein' worried ain't necessarily a bad thing, Rod."

➤ ➤

Mid-day found them well into the Seven Devils Mountains as they maneuvered the horses up the side of a tree-studded slope. Footing was treacherous on the loose rocks, causing the horses to falter in their attempts at keeping their legs beneath them. Once on the crest, Billy stopped to rest the animals and to get his bearings,…and shifting his weight in the saddle, he stared briefly down through the trees, then at the mountains above them.

"You see something?" Asked Rodney, as he urged his horse up beside him.

"Cause I can't see nothing but trees and rock. It's too God-awful quiet up here, too, and cold!….So,…why'd you stop,… what's wrong?""

"Nothin's wrong,…not a hell of a lot to see, neither" Returned Billy, shading his eyes at the sky. "Just thinkin' we're lucky, it could be blowin' snow right now….. Must not a snowed much up here, since th' blizzard….And you're right, it is quiet,….too damn quiet, no birds, no smoke in the air,…it ain't natural." He clucked the mare across the rocky crest and down through the trees on the other side, and an hour later they were in a narrow valley with the mountains rising high on either side of them.

Billy followed the rock-infested glen for a ways, then saw it begin to widen some and decided to follow it. The trees and brush were thick in the valley, however, making it dark and quite cold beneath the foliage. He reined the Roan around a large, dead limb, having to lean out of the saddle to avoid the reaching branches and was surprised when the trees suddenly gave way,… prompting him to stop on the bank of the water-filled ditch and stare at the tree-studded thicket on the other side.

"I feel like a pin-cushion!" Complained the lawman, riding in beside him.

"It'll get a lot worse." Breathed Billy, looking back down at the water. "Let's give the horses a drink." He urged the mare down the slick embankment and into the clear, fast-moving current where he stopped again.

"You got any idea where we're at?" Asked Rodney as he studied the tall trees above them. "Cause I sure don't!"

"Seven Devils Mountains." Answered Billy as he reached for tobacco and papers. "And God only knows why they call 'em that, too!" He rolled and lit the Durham before looking up at the mountain. "Look at it up there, a mean-looking Son of a bitch, ain't it?" The mountain loomed tall and grotesque above the trees, made more sinister-looking by the thick pines along its slopes.

"Well, it's a hell of a lot meaner down here." Sighed Rodney. "Cold, too…. Ain't there a road around here anywhere?"

"Probably." Said Billy as he blew smoke from his lungs. "But there's cabins all along them roads." He twisted in the saddle and scanned the area above the creek-bank. "And as scared as the Choctaw are right now,…I expect they'll be barricaded up in them cabins with a rifle in their hands, if they have one." He sighed and looked at the lawman. "They'll shoot at anything that moves, Rod,…and I wouldn't blame them." He pulled out his watch and checked the time. "But we've been makin' good time so far, considerin' we been stayin' off th' roads,….at least we ain't been shot at."

"Then I take it, this is about as good as it's gonna get?" He said distastefully and then, when Billy suddenly held up his hand. "What?" He whispered urgently.

"Didn't you hear it?" Returned Billy then cocked his head to one side as he listened.

"Gunfire!" Nodded Rodney. "There it is again." The sharp retorts were muffled by distance as they echoed through the mountains, but were quite distinct. "Six, maybe seven shots....You tell where they're coming from?"

"Sound travels a long way up here,....somewhere North of us, I think. Come on, Rod, we're gonna climb a mountain." He nudged the mare out of the water and up the steep embankment into the trees, and was soon leading the way up the slope of the unpredictable mountain.

Footing was treacherous as the loose shale shifted dangerously beneath the hoofs of the shod horses, causing a sound like hammers striking an anvil as the iron shoes struck the loose shale. Each time one rock shifted, several more would shift, creating small rockslides as they tumbled down the slope.

They were constantly fighting the nervous animals in their effort to help them keep their balance along the side of the rocky hill and for hours, continued to move in a Northerly direction. The horses were close to exhaustion by the time they smelled the smoke from burning wood, and an hour later, the smoke had drifted all through the mountainous terrain, creating a blue haze along the slopes. They had spotted several rundown shacks through the trees along the way, but none showed any signs of activity, and none of them had been on fire. Stopping once again, they sat their horses on the side of the sloping mountain and listened intently to the sounds of what appeared to be bouncing wagons and running horses from somewhere below them. Both men strained their eyes through the trees as they watched the dry creek bed, then suddenly they saw them, several of them as they bounced along behind teams of terrified mules. The wagons were careening precariously along the bed of a dry, rutted creek as men whipped the backs of the straining animals in an effort to make them go even faster. The wagon-beds were crowded with cowering women and small children, all watching behind them in obvious fear, while at the same time trying to keep their meager belongings from bouncing out of the wagons.

"They appear to be scared of something." Breathed the lawman. "Now, these are Choctaw, right?"

"Two or three families of 'em, looks like,....and they're runnin' from something, that's for sure."

"Look in that last wagon, Billy, that man's losing blood. Hell, he's soaked in it!"

"I see it." Nodded Billy as they watched the wagons disappear around a bend of the creek, and he was about to urge the mare down the slope, when he saw Rodney dismount, and curious, he slid off the Roan and made his way down the unstable shale to where the lawman was kneeling beside the trunk of a large Pine, and quickly squatted down beside him when he saw the Indians.

"What do you think?" Asked Rodney as they watched the armed warriors walk their decorated ponies along the bed of the creek.

"Got a be Comanches!" Breathed Billy as one of them slid off his horse and began to study the mud in the creek. "Better get your rifle,."

Rodney looked at him, then got up and slid the Winchester from the boot. "What are we planning to do here?"

"See for yourself." Said Billy. "They're trackin' them wagons and they'll kill them folks if they catch 'em,… and that leaves us with only a couple of options….We can let it happen, or we can stop it…. If they are Comanche, they'll have to stop them wagons,…else th' Choctaw could go to th' army."

"I see your point, Billy….But I can't hit him from this high up, not shooting through these trees,…..I can barely see him."

The Comanche tracker got to his feet as Rodney was speaking, said something to the others and pointed at the bend in the creek, then quickly mounted and kicked the skittish pony into a hard run, followed closely by the others.

"We got a stop him now, Rod,… shoot th' Bastard!"

Rodney raised the rifle to his shoulder and squeezed the trigger, The shock of the explosion was deafening in the jungle of ancient pine, and the Comanche was forcibly lifted from the back of the running pony and thrown into the Mesquite thicket alongside the creek. He quickly levered the Winchester and fired again, knocking another Indian from his pony's back, and causing the others to fearfully slide their horses to a stop and then to retreat at full gallop back the way they had come.

"Think they'll be back?" Asked the lawman, once the concussions had died away.

Billy shook his head. "Maybe,…but I think they'll high-tail it back to whoever's behind all this and report what happened……Damn good shooting, Rod."

"Are you still convinced there's a white man behind this?"

"You asked me that already, Rod……But th'Comanche wouldn't be here at all, if there wasn't…..They're too afraid of White Buffalo."

Rodney nodded then. "Whoever this man is, he would have to convince the Comanche that he was more powerful than White Buffalo,…he'd have to make them believe he could protect them."

"Looks like he succeeded." Nodded Billy

"From what you've told me,....the man would need an army to defeat White Buffalo's warriors in their own stronghold."

"Yeah." Agreed Billy. "But I can't figure why the Comanches are out here killin' unarmed Choctaw?....Why ain't they at th' mountain with th' rest of 'em?"

"That would be good to know....You think this bunch might stick around to see who shot at 'em?"

"Probably not,...they might have been partly convinced they'd be protected,...but down deep, they're still afraid."

"Well, I hope to hell you're right." Said Rodney, getting up to slide the rifle back into the boot. "Smoke's getting stronger, you notice that?...The source can't be too far from here, neither, so let's find out where its coming from."

Billy made his way up to the Roan as the lawman mounted. He stepped aboard the groaning saddle as Rodney led the pack animal up behind him then clucked the mare into motion and led the way up toward the crest of the mountain.

An hour later, they were sitting their horses on the downward side of that mountain and staring down at the smoldering remains of a cabin and what used to be a barn some five or six hundred feet below them. Thick, towering trees were blocking most of their view of the tragedy, but they could make out the carcasses of dead animals in the rickety corral. The bodies of a woman and two children lay sprawled in front of the cabin's burning remains, their bodies tinted a crimson red in the sunlight.

"Ohh, man!" Gasped the lawman as his face drained of color.

"Yeah." Sighed Billy and cautiously urged the roan down through the trees toward the road below them. Another hour of dodging trees and slipping on the loose rock, found them sitting their saddles and staring at the gruesome sight.

"They raped the woman and th' little girl first." Commented Billy as he surveyed the yard.

"They even killed the chickens!" Choked Rodney. "The dogs,...everything! What kind of savage would do something like this?"

Billy nudged the mare forward and rode slowly around the yard until he found the tracks, then rode back to stop beside the lawman. "Found tracks of four shod horses, over yonder, and six or eight unshod....Looks like they came in from the North."

"There's about that many unshod tracks leading into the road here, too," Said Rodney hoarsely. "At a run, it looks like, and coming in from the direction of the creek."

"Th' same bunch." Nodded Billy then rode out into the road to study the ground. "And you're right, here's where they came into the yard and stopped, then rode on again, still in a hard run...... You can see where th' shod horses joined 'th' others."

"The same bunch all right!" Sighed Rodney. "God damn it, Billy,...a white man that would take part in something like this!!.....Well,...killing would be too good for him!" He sniffed, then wiped at his eyes with a coat-sleeve. "We gonna bury these folks?"

Billy shook his head. "No time for that. These tracks are fresh, and it's gonna be dark soon.......We follow 'em, we could find th' Bastards who did this!"

"I hope to God, we do!" Choked the lawman as he looked back at the bodies, then he made the sign of the cross and followed Billy down the hard, rutted road.

They followed the narrow road for an hour with drawn pistols, keeping the horses at a fast walk as they continuously searched the surrounding trees and hillsides. Smoke was still hanging like a shroud in the trees, the blue haze making it harder to see anything in the shadows along the tree-shaded road as it blocked out some of the sun's light.

They were both silent, each one harboring his private thoughts as they continued along the deeply rutted wagon road, and it was well after dark when the stench of burning flesh filled their nostrils again, and a short time after that, Billy held up his hand and they stopped the horses in front of the smoldering debris of what once was a Choctaw family's home.

"Son of a Bitch!" Muttered Billy, and pulled his bandana up to cover his mouth and nose. He was completely aghast at the savagery of the murders.

"Where are the bodies?" Gasped the lawman, trying to talk through the hand he had clamped over his nose.

"Still in th' cabin." Gagged Billy, suddenly prodding the Roan on up the road and up-wind from the blunt of the smell. "They either burned 'em alive, or dumped 'em back in th' house after they killed 'em." He said as Rodney rode in beside him, and at that moment, gunfire shattered the stillness, causing both of them to jerk at their horse's reins as they wildly searched the tangled brush and dark trees around them.

"Where th' hell did that come from?" Gasped Rodney breathlessly.

"From farther up th' road, I think." Gritted Billy. "Th' shots were muffled some,....come on!" He prodded the mare's flanks again, sending her at a half-trot down the dusty clay road, with Rodney and the packhorse close behind him.

A half-hour passed before they saw the large, black bulk of the wagon and mule-team,...and the dark shape of a man could be seen sprawled half on and half off of the wagon seat, his arms dangling over the side of the wagon. Billy stopped the Roan to check the body as Rodney rode on past him, but then looked up as the lawman struck a match.

"Oh,...man!" Choked the lawman as he stood in the stirrups and peered over the wagon's tall sideboards.

Billy rode around him and looked as well. The naked and spread-eagled bodies of a woman and young girl lay side by side in a river of blood. They had been brutally raped, and then their throats were cut. The body of a small boy was under the seat of the wagon and had been shot in the head.

Rodney dropped the spent match, reined his horse away from the wagon and dismounted in the road. He was still bent over and heaving as Billy stopped the mare beside him. "Rodney,...this was a revenge killing. Guess they thought it was the Choctaw shootin' at 'em back there....You gonna be okay,?"

The lawman straitened and breathed deeply of the cold air. "How do you know that?"

"They didn't burn th' wagon,...they wanted th' Choctaw to see it as a warnin'."

"God, we have got to find these Bastards, Billy!" He blurted, then turned and shakily found the stirrup with his boot, causing Billy to have to grab his arm and help him into the saddle.

"You gonna be okay?" He asked again.

Rodney looked at him then and nodded. "I will be." He gritted. "When we find these Sons of Bitches!...Let's go do it!"

Billy nodded grimly in the darkness, then led off at a gallop up the narrow road. They were silent for the better part of an hour before the road intersected with another one. The one they were on veered more to the west and Billy chose to stay on it. 'At least', He thought, 'until the moon gets high enough to track by'. He shifted his weight in the saddle and tried to relax, but the images of what they had seen was like a devil in his heart. Had the same bunch done all of these killings? He wondered, or were they just one of several groups out to murder the Choctaw? They had seen a lot of carnage along the road this day, and that much savagery would keep several men awful busy. But then again, these were not men......They were animals of the worst kind.

Billy sniffed at the air again, still able to smell the drifting smoke in the trees along the road. But he noticed something else also and stopped the Roan to let the lawman pull alongside.

"What's wrong now?" Whispered the lawman, glancing nervously around at the trees.

"What do you hear?"

"I don't hear anything,....why? What am I missing?"

"A half-hour ago these woods was full'a noise." He twisted around in the saddle for a look behind them as he spoke. "But now, they're not......Ain't that a little strange?"

"Come to think about it,...yeah. What do you make of it?"

"Somethin' scared th' birds away,....and not too long ago, neither." Billy searched the trees again as he spoke then looked back at the lawman. "Keep your eyes open, Rod,...we could be gettin' close." He reined the mare back to the center of the road and led off again at a fast walk.

It was close to midnight now, and very cold. The moon had climbed high into the star-studded sky, showing patches of pale light on the road where it filtered through the pines. Billy had just turned in the saddle to check on Rodney when the Roan snorted,...and instantly alert, he pulled the Colt from it's holster and stopped. There was the unmistakable odor of burning wood in the air again.

"You smell it?" He Asked.

"Billy, I've been smelling smoke all night, it's everywhere....what do you smell?"

"I smell burnin' wood,...and it's somewhere just ahead of us. I think a fire has just been set."

"I don't see any smoke."

"Maybe it ain't drifted this far yet, Who knows.....But we're close, Rod, I can feel it. Come on, they can't be too far ahead of us now." And after another quick, visual search of their surroundings, he nudged the Roan into motion again. It wasn't long, however, until the smell of smoke became very distinct, and became steadily stronger the farther they went and for the next two hours, both of them nervously watched the darkness on both sides of them.

They had just pushed aside several sagging pine branches when they saw the smoke. It lay thick and heavy across the road, some ten yards in front of them and by all appearances, seemed to be drifting toward them from somewhere north of the road.

They looked at each other worriedly then pulled their weapons and nudged the horses up an incline of thick trees and brush, having to lean almost out of the saddle to avoid the low, twisted limbs of an ageless Oak. After several long minutes, they saw the burning cabin just as the roof gave way, showering sparks and burning splinters high into the cold night sky as it crashed onto the cabin's floor, and the flames lit up the entire area of trees and yard with its brilliance.....It also highlighted the bodies in the yard.

"Dear, God, Billy!" Groaned the lawman as they dismounted, then closed his eyes tightly when he saw the nude bodies of the twin girls. Both the children lay pinned to the hard clay by the shafts of long arrows through their bodies,........and both had been mercilessly raped. The Mother and

Father had their hands tied behind their backs and had also been killed with arrows.

"Sons of bitches made em watch first!" Choked Billy as he jammed the Colt back into the holster. "God damn their sorry hides!...This was no revenge killing,...this was..."

"Sadistic!" Interrupted Rodney and wiped his eyes dry on a coat-sleeve. "It was pure, uncalled-for evil!" He went to the packhorse and pulled the short-handled spade from beneath the tarp. "I'm going to bury these folks." He said as he glanced at Billy, then moved to a spot under the limbs of another Oak Tree along the edge of the yard and began digging in the soggy earth.

Sighing tiredly, Billy slowly began searching the area around the burning cabin for sign, slightly nauseated, as well as thankful that he hadn't eaten anything. He walked around the darkening yard, searching the outer fringes for a good half-hour before finding where the men had crossed a small creek at the rear of the cabin and then followed the tracks in the light from the fire until they disappeared into a dark ravine a dozen yards away.

Coming back across the yard, he went to the packhorse and worked two blankets from beneath the canvass and then went back to spread them on the ground next to the girls. He carefully broke the ends off the arrows then lifted each girl's body up and off the bloody shafts before wrapping them in the blankets. He then carried them to the gravesite where Rodney gently took their bodies from him and placed them in the ground.

He helped Rodney carry the other two bodies to their graves, and then filled in all four with the wet sand and clay. Removing their hats, they backed off and stared at the small mounds of earth for a moment, then silently walked to the horses where Rodney retied the tarp over the spade.

"You find tracks?" He grunted, as he pulled himself into the saddle.

"Six sets." Returned Billy, just seating himself in the cold leather. "Four shod, two unshod,...leavin' two Comanche Indians unaccounted for."

"Maybe they went back to the mountain, or struck out on their own."

"Well, lets hope they did....It's two less we'll have to deal with."

"We're going after those six, though,...right?"

"Damn right!" Billy reined the mare across the yard and splashed across the shallow creek. Rodney looked back at the graves, made the sign of the cross again then leaned from the saddle to grab the packhorse's halter rope and followed Billy across the creek at a walk.

Two hours of treacherous footing in the dark ravine found them working their way down a steep clay embankment toward a much wider gap between the small hills. Once they were in the broken area of rocks and Pines, they pulled up to scan the moonlit area of grass and tall rocks between them and the trees ahead of them.

"I smell smoke again…..Think its another cabin fire?"

Billy stared at the trees across the small meadow then shook his head. "It's a campfire,…..and it's comin' From them trees off yonder…..Come on, Rod." He led off at a walk through the waving grass, depending on a lot of luck to get them there undetected, because the moon's light made them prime targets for anyone that might be watching their back-trail. But they made it, and once they could see the flickering fire through the trees, He stopped the Roan again, dismounted and made his way back to Rodney.

"We been lucky so far, Rod." He whispered. "But they're sure to have a guard out,….prob'ly somewhere in th' edge of them trees…..Think you can work your way in there on foot, th' grass ought a cover you?"

Rodney nodded and dismounted in the tall grass.

"If you find 'im, bring 'im into camp alive,…if you can."

"Don't worry about that." Growled the lawman. "What'll you be doing?"

"I'm gonna give you ten minutes and then ride right into that camp… ..I've got a few hard questions for these Bastards!"

"Sounds good to me, how's your gun-hand?"

"A mite stiff tonight, why?"

"Just thought I'd ask." Muttered Rodney. "Watch yourself." He touched his hat in a salute, then crouched and disappeared into the waist-high grass.

"You, too, my friend." Whispered Billy, then he took the horses and slowly led them to the edge of the dense stand of timber and stopping once he was able to see the men around the fire. It appeared they were already pretty drunk, or were close to it, he decided as he watched the Comanche Indian stagger between the outstretched feet of the other men. The four white men were seated with their backs against large rocks and were passing a bottle back and fourth between them and laughing as they kept the whiskey just out of the reach of the Indian.

The heavily bearded men were laughing and cursing at the same time as they used their feet to push the drunken Comanche away, and the Indian was yelling back at them in his native tongue each time they did. Billy looked beyond the fire at the gray bluff, counting six horses in the pale light from the moon, but only five men around the fire.

He felt he had given Rodney enough time and silently wished the lawman luck as he pulled himself into the saddle. He leaned and tied the packhorse to a branch, then felt the telltale tingling on the back of his neck again.

He heard the yell then and looked up in time to see one of the men shove the Indian backward into the fire, sending cinders and burning wood skyward as he kicked himself free of the flames amid the laughter of the white men.

He chose that moment to ride through the trees, pulling the Colt as he rode into the fire's flickering light.

One of the men saw him then yelled a warning to the others as he reached for his gun, but then stopped his draw when he saw the gun in Billy's hand.

"That's a smart move!" Said Billy loudly, holding up the gun for all of them to see. The man moved his hand back to his lap as the other three just sat and glared hatefully at him, but all were careful not to move toward their weapons. The Comanche had started to move himself away from the fire. "Tell your Indian friend to sit down." He warned, and one of the men said something to him. The Comanche glared drunkenly at him then dropped to the ground on the far side of the fire.

"What do you want?" Growled the man closest to him. "And who th' hell are you?"

"Never mind that!" Grated Billy. "Who th' hell are you, and why are you here?"

"Well God damn!" Voiced the large bewhiskered man farthest from him. "I know who this is, fellers, look at 'im!.....He's a fuckin' School Marm, spectacles and all." He laughed nastily then and looked gleefully at the other men. "Come on, Shorty, look at 'im!.....A fuckin' School Marm with a gun,... well kiss my ass!"

Billy ignored the sarcasm and looked steadily at the bushy face of the man called Shorty.

"Don't mind him, Mister, he's drunk." Said Shorty shakily. "Who are you?" He asked again. "We ain't got no money, if that's what you're after."

Billy grinned tightly and glanced at the large man. "I'm a School Marm, ain't you heard?" And when the large man guffawed again, he held the Colt up. "And this is my gun.....I'm very good with my gun, you know.....I'm so good with it, in fact, I don't think I really need it, there's only four of you. So, why don't I just put it away and trust you men to keep your hands right where I can see 'em?....Unless you just have to see how good I am?" He eased the hammer down on the gun and slowly slid it back into the holster. "And if that's th' case,...just reach for a gun....Well, do you want a know?"

"No?....okay then,...you all know who I am, thanks to horse's ass over there." He nodded his head toward the large man. "Now,...as to what I want." He stared at the man called Shorty, causing him to blink and look away. "I'm gonna ask you a few questions, Shorty, and I expect a truthful answer from you......Am I gonna get it?"

"Yeah,...I re...I reckin so." Sputtered the frightened man. "Wh....what is it?"

"To start with, you can answer my first question,...who are you, and what are you doin' here?"

"We, ah….we're miners, by trade….We're just doin' a little prospectin'…..just passin' through, ya might say."

"The Comanche's your guide, I guess…Okay,…if that's th' truth,…Then maybe you can tell me why you murdered that family a Choctaw back yonder?"

"We didn't!" Blurted the man, his lips beginning to tremble. "It weren't none of us done it, I swear." He looked nervously at the other men.

"Don't look at them, Shorty, God damn it, look at me when I'm talkin' to you!" And when Shorty faced him again; "You're lyin' like hell to me, Shorty,…and I hate liars. I tracked your sorry asses all th' way from that cabin back yonder, and there ain't no two ways about it!….Now don't tell me you didn't do it, because I know better!"

"Why, God damn, Ma'am,…Sir!" Laughed the large man tauntingly. "They was there and we kilt 'em, so fuckin' wh….."

The explosion was deafening, and the rock behind the large man's head turned red as he was slammed against it, changing the smirk on his face to one of disbelief as he slumped to the ground.

Billy held up the Colt and stared at it, then grinned. "Weren't bad for a School Marm, was it?" He trained the gun back on the ashen face of Shorty. "Now,…why did you murder those people?"

Shorty quickly glanced at the large man's body, then back at Billy. "We was tryin' to make 'em tell us about th' mine." He shrugged. "They wouldn't."

He studied Shorty's frightened face for a moment as he fought down the urge to shoot him then motioned with his gun. "Throw your gunbelts and guns over here on th' ground, come on,….all of you, right now!" He watched them disarm themselves then holstered the Colt again.

"Now then." He grinned. "Why'd you do it?"

"I done told you, man,…they wouldn't talk!…That's th' God's truth!"

"Okay then,…tell me about this mine that seems to be so important?" And when Shorty hesitated, he drew and fired again, the explosion once again shattering the stillness as the slug splintered large chips of rock from the boulder at the man's ear. Shorty covered his face with his hands, and yelling, threw himself into the man next to him.

"Wait!" He yelled. "Wait a fuckin' minute, man!"

"Tell me about th' mine." Repeated Billy.

"Th' mine's North of here!" He stammered. "Back in th' hills somewhere!….It's supposed to be a whole mountain of gold and it's rich, man, real rich!"

"He's talkin' th' truth, Mister, and that's gospel." Said the man beside him. "It's supposed to be real rich."

"Then why ask these innocent Choctaw about it, they're farmers, not miners…..Who told you there was a mine up there?"

"Th' Boss did." Said the second man quickly. "Th' Boss told us."

Billy caught the movement in the trees then, and looked in time to see Rodney push the Indian into the firelight, his knife at the Comanche's throat, then grinned when he saw the others staring at them. "What's wrong, Gents, you think I was alone?" And when they looked back at him; "Let's get back to that mine business, but first, tell me about your Boss." He leaned forward, placing his arms across the horn of his saddle then waved the barrel of the gun at them. "Come on, one of you better start talkin'."

"Mister, we don't know who th' hell he is!...he never told us his name,... he only showed us a map, he said he found in Mexico City."

"When did you join up with this,....Boss man?"

"Two, three months ago, over at Fort Arbuckle.....We was waitin' out a blizzard there. He said if we helped 'im find it, we'd all get a share."

"If he's got a map, why are you out here killin' Choctaw?"

"Cause somebody stole th' God damn map before we found th' mountain,....that's why....And he said it had to be th' Choctaw, seein' as how they're th' ones live here."

"Th' Boss thinks he's found th' right mountain, though." Blurted Shorty. "We just can't find th' way in without th' map,.....so he sent us to find out where th' entrance is."

"And these innocent Choctaw, you keep harpin' about." Said the second man. "Is jumpin' us when we go lookin' for th' way in......They're killin us, man!"

"And I guess you know it's th' Choctaw, cause you seen 'em, is that right?" Snapped Billy.

The man shook his head. "Nobody's sees 'em,...we just find th' bodies with arrows stuck in 'em."

"He tell you to murder these farmers?"

"Yes, Sir, he did,....said to have th'Comanches do it. Said it wouldn't do to have th' Choctaw go to th' authorities."

"Jeesus." Whined Shorty. "We answered your questions, what more do you want from us?"

"I only got one more, Shorty." Said Billy evenly. "And you Son of a Bitch, you better answer it true, cause I won't ask it twice!" He saw fear leap into Shorty's eyes as he quickly nodded his head.

"Who raped and butchered all them women and little girls?"

Shorty stared fearfully at him then quickly jerked his head at the Indians. "They did."

Gritting his teeth, Billy jerked his eyes at Rodney in time to see him slit the Comanche's throat, stifling a gurgling scream as blood gushed from the gaping cut. At almost the same instant, the other one leaped to his feet to run, but before he could clear the rocks, Billy shot him and then looked back at Shorty.

"Who else?"

"You done killed him, man…..Rest of us never touched them womenfolk, I swear it!" The other two men quickly voiced their innocence.

"You didn't try to stop it, neither!" He snapped. "And that makes you just as guilty as they are!" He took a deep breath then waved the gun at them. "What I want to do is shoot ever fuckin' one a you!" He sighed then. "But that wouldn't be good enough, and murder's against th' law, even in th' Nations…..My friend here is a Federal Marshal, and if he weren't here, that's exactly what I'd do!"

Rodney moved his coat aside to reveal the badge as he came to stand in front of them. "Just so you'll know." Said Rodney, looking each one of them in the eyes. "The authorities know all about this now,…and I am the authority. And what I'd like to do is hang every damn one of you from the nearest tree…..But to make that legal, we'd be forced to bury you,…and we don't have the time. So,…..I'm going to let Deputy, School-Marm here decide your fate." He grinned as all three men looked worriedly at Billy. "They're all yours,… Ma'am." He said, and almost laughed. "I'm gonna go collect the hardware from their horses." He tipped his hat, then turned and walked between the rocks into the darkness.

"This is what you three brave men are gonna do." Said Billy, still fighting down the urge to kill them. "You're gonna ride out of these mountains,… all th' way out of th' Nations,….and you ain't comin' back!…..Cause if you do,… we'll hunt you down and kill you,…..and that's gospel!"

"What about th' mine?" Asked Shorty. "Part a that gold's our'n."

"If there's any gold up there, it belongs to th' Choctaw Indians." Snapped Billy. "And we're gonna go find this Boss man of yours and explain that to him, too."

"With only th' two of ye?" Came the second man. "You ain't that good, Mister. You ain't fast enough to take th' Boss."

"We'll see…..Now, listen up,….th' Choctaw are friendly people, and they're also friends of ours,…so you better steer clear of 'em!….You don't, I'll find out! Now get th' fuck on them horses and out of these mountains, damn you!"

The three looked at each other, then got to their feet and abruptly walked out of the firelight toward the horses, giving Rodney a wide berth as he passed them.

"I thought you'd probably go on and kill 'em." Sighed Rodney as he dropped the rifles and saddlebags by the fire.

Billy dismounted tiredly and walked around the Roan, stooping to pick up the half empty bottle of Bran as he neared the rocks. "I prob'ly should have!" He said and threw the bottle against the rocks as he watched the three men ride away in the darkness.

"Why didn't you, then,....they damn well deserved it?"

"I couldn't." He said, turning to look at the lawman. "No matter what I've done before,... I've only deliberately shot a couple a unarmed men, and it didn't sit right." He looked back into the wake of the outlaws then. "But, I wanted to, Rod,...I wanted to!"

"I thought about it, myself." Replied Rodney. "And you know what?.... There's more than a fifty-fifty chance all three of 'em lied about not raping those girls."

"I know." Sighed Billy as he turned back to the fire. "At least, they won't be doin' any more of it around here." He stooped then and gathered up the holstered guns, hanging them around the horn of his saddle. "See what's in them saddlebags, Rod." He went to pull the gun and belt from around the dead man's thick paunch as the lawman emptied the saddlebags onto the ground.

"Nothing here but soiled clothing and a box or two of ammunition." Sighed Rodney as Billy went to stuff the other belted gun into his saddlebag. "You think they told th' truth about that mine?"

Billy was frowning when he turned around. "I don't know.....I was there for a week, and I never saw nothin' to make me think there was one......But, why else would th' mountain be under attack, and why else would there be a map that says so?......This is bad, Rod, even worse than I thought."

"You don't think they might be talking about that cave, you told me about?...You know, the one with the pit?"

"I wish it was,.....but Peter said th' mountain was bein' attacked. Besides, I doubt there's a map to that other one,.....everybody was killed. I'll go get th' horses, Rod." He said and mounted the mare. "You put out th' fire."

When he came back, Rodney was just scattering the last of the coals, then he gathered up the rifles and came over to the packhorse. "We turning north again?" He asked as he slid the guns beneath the tie-down ropes and retied the tarp.

"That's where th' mountain is." Sighed Billy, and when the lawman was mounted, he led off back the way they had come.

40

CHAPTER FIVE

THEY SPENT THE REST OF that night using the stars to travel by, fighting rocks and fallen timber as they skirted around patches of thick, prickly brush and ancient Pines,....and they had just climbed out of one of the many gullies when Billy stopped.

"I hope you know where the hell we are?" Breathed Rodney as he nudged the horses up to level ground. "Cause I ain't got a clue.....This is the most damnable country I've ever seen. How much farther we got a go?"

"Another couple a days, at least.....Want me to lug that packhorse for a while?"

"No, I'm used to it.....We still headed North?"

"Accordin' to th' stars, we are. At least in that general direction,... I can see Winding-Stair Mountain off yonder.....You can just make it out over th' trees there."

"And that's where we're going?"

"A little bit East of it, yeah."

"We're close then?"

"It means we're goin' in th' right direction, give or take a mile.....Let's go." He grinned and led off through the trees again.

By sunrise, they were out of the foothills on the far side of the Seven Devils, and in a maze of broken country known as the Kiamichi Wilderness. The area was dangerously cluttered with ground-debris, dozens of ravines and dry creeks, and the rotting trees were sprawled everywhere. Fallen tree-trunks, limbs with up-thrusting branches that could stab or cut a man and his horse badly, were a never-ending nightmare. Giant Firs and towering Pine Trees grew so thick in places that a horse couldn't get through, and all of these were studded with half-stripped Pecan and Burr-oaks,....and all growing amid large outcroppings of sharp-edged boulders.

After several miserable hours of riding in and out of gullies, detouring thickets of brush and dead trees, they breathed a sigh of relief when they climbed out of one of the deep canyons and onto more rolling terrain again. But that relief was only for a few minutes as they had to stop once again to rest the horses and get their bearings.

"I hope you ain't lost." Breathed Rodney as he pulled alongside. "Couldn't we have found an easier way to get there,.....I feel like I've been at war with a Bobcat?"

"I didn't want to chance bein' seen by any of them rovin' Comanches." Returned Billy as he stared above the treetops at the Winding-stair. "Anyway, I don't know any other way to get there,...I don't even remember the way I brought Willy home, we followed two of White Buffalo's warriors when we left......But it makes no difference, ain't none of th' ways, easy......And we're in for more of th' same, look's like,....you ready?"

"Lead on." Sighed the lawman.

Grinning, Billy clucked the Roan into motion, once again finding themselves in very dense pines. Broken limbs and thrusting branches gouged at them, Mesquite thorns stabbed at both them and the animals for hours. Until finally it was mid-afternoon and that's when they began seeing the circling Crows through the treetops, and could hear their faint cawing in the cold stillness of the trees. Billy kept them in the protection of those trees as much as possible as they continued North toward Devil Mountain.

It was now two days since leaving the outlaw camp, eating and sleeping in the saddle when they could. They were in and out of dozens of gullies and creeks, having to detour for hundreds of yards around dense thickets of briars......And they were exhausted.

On the morning of the fourth day, they were sitting just inside the line of tall pines overlooking a downhill slope of trees and rocks, and were silently watching the twenty-odd Comanche Indians maneuver their painted ponies through the brush below them.

"That's the third bunch today." Said Rodney as the Indians disappeared in the trees,....and they're all headed North."

"Yeah." Breathed Billy. "Wonder how many of 'em are up here?"

"More than enough, I'll wager." Sighed the lawman. "You think the Army even has a hint of what's going on up here?"

"I asked myself that question three months ago,…and I still don't know. Maybe they don't, though. According to Peter, th' Army hardly ever comes into these mountains." He held his hand up then. "We're gettin' close, Rod,….hear that?" The faint sounds of gunfire echoed toward them, then suddenly, a much louder explosion jarred the stillness.

"What in the hell was that?" Blurted the lawman. "Was that dynamite?"

"Sounded more like a cannon."

"A cannon?....Hell, the war is over! There's supposed to be Federal Marshals all over the Nations up here,…..how could they not know about this?"

"Not all lawmen are law-abidin', Rod,…not even Federal Marshals."

"You saying they're in on it?"

"Wouldn't surprise me too much, th' price bein' right…..Let's go." He led the way down the rocky slope, and had started another upward climb when he saw the clearing in the trees and got Rodney's attention.

Devil Mountain rose to an enormous height above the giant pines, looking hideously foreboding to anyone seeing it for the first time.

"Easy to see how it got its name." Muttered Rodney, just as the cannon fired again, this time much louder.

A short time later, they stopped the horses in a rock-littered stand of Pine Trees to search the debris and timber below them, but seeing nothing, continued on down the perilous grade.

They were almost to the mountain now and the shooting was more frequent, coming in volleys, much like the military would do in a battle. An open gully-infested area lay before them and after dropping down into one of the erosions they dismounted in the shelter of the wooded ravine, able to see the wide expanse of grass through the trees atop the embankment.

"Grab your spyglass, Rod." Billy leaned across the lip of the gully and stared at the meadow through the trees. He could see several tents along the tree-line on the far side of the grassy prairie, and there were men moving about everywhere. He knew he was looking at a small army here, and could feel the chill run down his neck,…a dreaded, ice-cold chill that made him tremble. Then sighing, he took the glass and trained it on the center of activity. "Got a be more than a hundred men down there, Rod,….countin' th' Comanche." He then moved the glass again just as the cannon fired, immediately feeling the tremor as the shell exploded against the mountain.

"They're firing exploding shells at it!" He looked through the glass again. "And there it is." He gritted then watched as one man breached the slender weapon, while another shoved another shell into the chamber. He turned and gave Rodney the long glass. "Ever see a cannon like that?"

Rodney scanned the encampment until he spied the gun, watching it intently as it was fired, reloaded and fired again. "Yeah." He sighed then leaned against the bank of the ravine. "In a newspaper from back East." He looked at Billy and shook his head. "It's a new gun made for the Military,... and if it's the one I saw pictured, its called a Howitzer, made somewhere in Europe, I think......That thing is bad news!...And also brand new,...how did they get it, I wonder?"

"If you think about it, it'll start makin' sense." Sighed Billy....."Remember me tellin' you about th' wagon tracks, that first night out?"

"Yeah,...so?"

"That wagon was pullin' somethin' with two wheels on it.....Them extra tracks didn't make sense to me then, so I forgot about 'em."

"It was pulling the Howitzer!" Breathed Rodney, once again raising the glass to look at it. "And It has two wheels,." He scanned the camp again. "There's the wagon that probably pulled it, up against one of them tents." He lowered the glass again and sighed.

"I don't like where this is going, Billy....Because right now, I'm thinking that the Comanches, or maybe some of these outlaws stole it from one of the Forts in the area......But, if they didn't....."

"Somebody at one of them Forts is in on this treasure hunt." Said Billy quickly.

"Yeah." Nodded Rodney. "And they're gonna tear that mountain apart with it! What'll we do about it,?...What can we do about it?"

Billy shook his head. "You see any soldiers out there?"

Rodney quickly searched the encampment again and shook his head. "I don't see any uniforms,.......unless they're in civilian outfits?"

Billy nodded. "Somebody has to fire that cannon,...somebody that knows what they're doin'." He looked toward the campsite then. "Can you see th' th' remuda?"

"Yeah, in a small canyon North of the camp there,...Comanches are camped there, too."

Billy nodded then searched the trees that surrounded them. "I need to talk with White Buffalo......Maybe we can figure out somethin'."

"I'm all for that,....you do know the way in,...don't you?"

"Yeah, but th' tunnel ain't two hundred yards in front of that cannon there.....We can't use it,... and they can't find it."

"What's gonna happen when that cannon finally caves it in?"

"We'll be outside,.....and White Buffalo'll be trapped inside."

"I don't believe that!" Said the lawman. "From what you been telling me, these people are smarter than that....There's got to be another way in."

Billy took the long glass and studied the impregnable heights of the mountain fortress, but couldn't see much along the base of it due to the trees and rocks. "Can't see anything." He sighed. "Lets walk the horses in closer to the mountain, see if we can see somethin'......And keep your eyes open."

He led off down the cluttered ravine, warily watching the trees for any sign of a roving guard,...and almost an hour passed before the trees were thick enough to chance climbing out of the gully and by this time, they were within a stone's throw of the mountain. Huge boulders littered the knotted terrain, and the giant firs completely hid the base of the towering cliffs.

"I guess we could work our way around it." Sighed Billy. "If there is a way in, its hidden somewhere behind all them trees......and again, keep your eyes open, White Buffalo's likely got somebody out looking for us right now."

"What makes you think he knows we're here?"

"Rod, he knew it when we crossed th' Red.....Come on, our luck's not gonna hold out forever." He looked around again. "And I ain't up to walkin' in this mess neither." He moved back beside the mare and swung himself into the saddle.

They had not gone a hundred yards when they heard the Crow. The large ebony bird almost took Rodney's hat from his head as it swooped down out of the trees, causing the lawman to yelp in his surprise. Billy stopped to watch as it lit atop a large boulder a few feet in front of them where it began cawing shrilly, its eyes darting from him, to Rodney, then back at him. Then suddenly it flew off toward the Firs, another hundred yards to the right of them and settled atop another rock, still voicing its loud opinion.

"Let's go." Said Billy quickly and clucked the Roan up and out of the ravine.

"Where you going?" Returned Rodney as he nudged his horse out of the gully behind him.

"I know where the entrance is, come on."

"Where?.....Wait a minute, Billy."

Billy stopped to wait on him, still watching the Crow's antics atop the rock.

"What's going on, Billy,...what are you doing?" Breathed the lawman as he stopped beside him.

"Followin' th' path of th' Crow, Rod." He grinned and pointed at the bird. "He's showin' us th' way in,....come on." He didn't wait for Rodney's confusion to continue, and clucked the Roan on up the slight incline.

Several minutes of threading their way through giant trees, rotting limbs and boulders found them at the base of the steep, rocky, tree-studded slope of the mountain. Fir and Juniper brush was tall and thick here, and completely hid the mountain's base.

"Where to now?" Breathed Rodney, then turned to search the way they had come,…and it was when he looked back at Billy, that he saw the Indian.

"Look out!" He yelled, pulling the pistol at almost the same instant. He was bringing the gun in line to fire when Billy grabbed his arm.

"That ain't th' enemy, Rod,….put it away." He quickly pulled the medallion free of his coat and held it up for the warrior to see.

The Choctaw turned his pony and motioned for them to follow and they quickly urged the horses up the steep incline of shale and grass and eventually found themselves at an almost invisible opening to a large, narrow fissure, well hidden behind the large Firs then followed him into the murky darkness of the damp cave. It appeared to be a natural cavern, and took several long minutes before they saw the light at the other end. But at last, they were riding out of the darkness into the deep, gray shadows beneath the giant Spruce and Pines in the valley. They were out of the trees almost immediately and passing the roughly hewn log fence of the corral.

"This is unbelievable!" Exclaimed Rodney, looking up at the towering inner cliffs of the mountain. He was grinning widely when he looked at the trees again. "These trees have got to be a thousand years old, Billy,…they're huge!"

"Could be." Agreed Billy then pointed at the pony enclosure. "See that cavern behind th' horses there?…Well, you ain't seen nothing yet."

They followed the Indian through the tall grass for another fifty yards before turning into the trees and into the gray darkness for most of a quarter hour before seeing the larger cavern with its many Wickiups, and they could finally see the extent of the trouble at hand. The floor of the cavern was teeming with activity as Medicine men, aided by the many women, tended their wounded on the smooth rock floor. The thick robes, they were laying on were soaked with blood.

They were completely free of the trees now and could see the mounted warriors at the cavern's entrance, as well as the tall, robed Indian standing before them. Suddenly, the warriors raised lances and rifles in salute, then turned and galloped past them into the trees. The warrior they were following held up his hand to stop them then rode on alone toward the cavern.

"That must be White Buffalo." Said Rodney as he pulled alongside.

"You'd be right." Nodded Billy. Watching as the Indian dismounted to converse with the Chief. The faint, muffled sounds of exploding shells against the mountain could be heard in the valley, and it caused him to tremble with dread, and helplessness.

"I don't know how to help him, Rod."

"We can still send for the Army,…Fort McCullough's to the South of us."

"It would take a week to get soldiers up here." Sighed Billy. "And we don't know who's involved in this…..Look around you, Rod,…these people have been here for over a hundred years and nobody even knew about it!...Hell, besides me, you're th' only white man to ever see 'em this close, let alone see this valley….We ain't got time to go for help." He sighed again and leaned his crossed arms on the saddle-horn.

"What would we tell 'em, anyway?... That a secret tribe of ancient Choctaw Indians are under attack by treasure hunters and needs their help?" Billy shook his head then and looked at his friend. "You said yourself, you'd throw a man in jail for a story like that."

"I did say that, didn't I?" Sighed Rodney. "Besides,…as far as I know, it's not illegal to hunt for gold up here,…even with a hundred men." He heard the Crow then and they both looked up as the large, ebony bird glided toward the two men.

"Want to know how he knew we were coming, Rod?...Just watch th' Crow."

They watched the large bird fly in and heard its urgent cawing as it neared White Buffalo and the warrior. The Chief turned to watch it, dismissing the warrior with a wave of his hand as the Crow settled on a lower branch of a pine, then walked toward it as it continued its loud message. He stopped within a few feet of the bird and listening intently for a few seconds then nodded his head and waved his arm, sending the Crow off toward the mountain again.

"What did I just see?" Marveled the lawman.

"Damned if I know." Returned Billy. "But, according to Peter, them birds are his eyes and ears in these mountains."

"Can he talk with all the birds?"

"Just th' Crows,….But I'd say, that's enough."

The warrior watched his Chief until the Crow flew away, then leaped astride his pony and came back toward them, and with his hand held palm up, gestured toward the cavern, and the invitation was evident. The warrior dismounted then and waited for them to do the same, then left the pony and led the way on foot toward the cavern. Billy dropped the mare's reins, and on seeing this, Rodney did the same and they both followed the Choctaw through the waving grass.

Once they were on the cavern's stone floor, the warrior stopped and pointed toward the rear walls, then abruptly left them. They continued on toward the rear of the cavern, past where a Medicine man was chanting over the wounded, and the wounded were everywhere. Most, it appeared had been hit by falling rocks, and others had been hit by random gunfire. Billy paused several times to shake his head sadly before continuing on to the rear wall where yet another warrior ushered them into the council chamber.

Nodding, Billy removed his hat and stepped into the lighted chamber of the elders, then turned to watch Rodney walk around the awe-inspiring room.

"Good, God, Man!" Exclaimed the lawman. "Look at all this!"

"I've seen it."

"They've recorded their entire history here….Every battle, death, birth,… my God!" He was wide-eyed when he finally looked at Billy, and seeing the hat in his hand, quickly removed his own. "This is just,…unbelievable!" He looked back at the walls again. "We have got to help these people. They're being destroyed over a God Damn gold mine that might not even exist!" He looked back at Billy then.

"Those men out there don't even know they're in here,…or that they're killing them."

Billy nodded. "They only know that Indians are tryin' to stop them from findin' a gold mine….And th' fact, that they haven't seen any Indians, don't mean a thing to 'em."

"Maybe if they knew?"

Billy shook his head. "You already seen the kind a men they are,…I don't think it would make a difference."

"Damn!" Muttered the lawman. "Then it's all gonna be up to us."

"And it's gonna take some thinkin',…and planning." He sighed. "And right now, I can't think of a damn thing we can do!"

White Buffalo's presence was felt immediately. He was dressed in the ceremonial skin of the White Buffalo, decorative moccasins and leggings, and his face was expressionless as he studied Rodney for a moment then came forward to grip Billy's arm and hand in friendship.

"It is unpleasant to welcome Man-with-glass-eyes in such sad times. I am happy you have come,…but too late, I think."

"Too late?" Billy could see the indecision in the Chief's usually stern features. "Why is it too late?"

Looking down at the floor, White Buffalo moved to his place at the head of the feasting robe, crossed his legs and sat down, inviting them to join him there, and once they were seated, raised his eyes to look sadly at Billy.

"Thirty of your days past, six white men entered these mountains…. They came here,… to our mountain. I sent warriors to warn them away, but not to kill them, as they had not committed any crime….But only five men left." He paused as a woman placed food and water before them then waved her away.

"One man was brought before me." He continued. "He had been bitten by a serpent and later died." He reached under his robe and brought out a folded piece of brown paper of which he passed to Billy.

"He carried the paper in his clothing…. Our mountain is there."

Billy unfolded the grimy, faded map and stared at it. It was crudely drawn, but it clearly showed a direct route across Indian Territory, all the way to Devil Mountain. It also showed a very large entrance tunnel, and he saw what could be the main cavern and several smaller ones, and on the paper also was a hastily scrawled, and unpronounceable word. He looked quizzically at White Buffalo while passing the map to Rodney.

"We was told about this map by men in the mountains,…is it true?"

White Buffalo nodded. "My great Grandfathers knew of the great doorway with its strange markings. When the spirit wolf brought them here, they found many bones, many iron shirts, and strange weapons everywhere. Head-wear, with many colored feathers, and more strange weapons were found among many other bones in the valley….My Grandfathers found the great doorway open and placed all the weapons and iron shirts inside. There was much wealth behind the great door, and so my Grandfathers closed the doorway,…and being afraid of the unknown, never opened it again."

Billy took a deep breath, taking the map back from Rodney and passing it on to the Chief. "White Buffalo, that map shows a gold mine on it….They might not know about th' treasure cave at all….But either way,… we're here to fight with you."

"And to die with me?"

"If it comes down to it,…yeah."

"Man-with-glass-eyes is a warrior, greater even than my own warriors, and he honors me with his presence." He looked across at Rodney then. "Is this man also a warrior?"

"Yes." Nodded Billy. "He's a man of th' white man's law, an honest man and much respected….He is my friend, and uncle to my son."

White Buffalo's dark eyes softened then. "Forgive me,…is Little wolf well?"

"Very well, thanks to you and your people." Nodded Billy. He saw a flicker of sadness on the Chief's face as he stared past him at the wounded.

"I have failed my people." He stated sadly. "I have let death walk among us."

"That map brought these men here, White Buffalo, not you. Their lust for gold makes them this way. They're killing your people without knowing it."

"It would make no difference." Returned the Chief. "I also know they are killing my brothers outside of the mountain. They burn the homes and abuse the women." He looked at Billy then. "It would make no difference."

"Yes it would, because they don't know you're here."

"And they must never know." White Buffalo said sternly. "They shoot at the mountain, and the unseeing bullets find my warriors. The thunder gun strikes the mountain, and falling rocks find my warriors,...I cannot fight such weapons,...I do not know how."

"We do." Said Billy quickly. "We know how to fight that weapon, because we've dealt with men like this before.....Let us try, White Buffalo,...at th' very least, we can even th' odds."

The Chief's dark eyes bored into his for several long moments, and then he nodded. "First, you must eat." He said, rising to his feet. "And I must think on it....I will return with my answer." He walked slowly out of the room and continued on toward the wounded.

CHAPTER SIX

THEY WATCHED THE ONCE PROUD Chieftain as he walked among the suffering, seeing his broad shoulders slump in his sadness.

"If I hadn't seen this place, and met this man." Breathed Rodney. "I still wouldn't believe it,….and you know what? Until a minute ago, it never crossed my mind that we could die up here….I hope you've got a damn good plan working, man!"

Billy nodded. "I do,…but it's a bit gutsy,…and it's th' only thing we can do. I'm still thinkin' on it." He took some of the charred meat from the bowl and began eating.

"I can't stop thinking about that map, and what the Chief told us about it." Said Rodney as he also began eating. "You remember that word that was printed on it?"

Billy nodded as he swallowed. "I couldn't make sense of it?"

"I've seen it before in a book,…and if I'm right,…it's the name of an Aztec God."

"You talkin' about Aztec Indians?"

"Aztec Indians….The Chief's name was Montezuma, and he was King of all of Mexico three hundred years ago, give or take,…that is, until the Spanish invasion."

"Mexico's a far piece from this mountain, Rod."

"I know that,…but according to the book, the Aztec were being slaughtered, and hordes of them escaped into this country ahead of the Spanish. Now, listen to this,....The Aztec Priests, from all over Mexico, fled the country with great treasures of gold, precious gems, golden statues and,.... well, you get the picture. Anyway, legend has it, they went to New Mexico territory and Arizona, and some as far North as Utah...But what if some didn't? What if some of them came here instead? After all, those men said the Boss found the map in Mexico, and it could only have been left there by surviving Spaniards."

"Thanks, Rod." Sighed Billy. "I like th' story,...but I think you're catchin' gold fever....Makes you wonder how th' man who wrote th' book, knew about all that."

Rodney shrugged. "Well, the treasure's here, ain't it? Got to be truth in it." He sighed then. "At least it took my mind off dying. And besides, I'd like to see what's behind that door,...and so would you."

"You better eat, Rod." Grinned Billy. "If White Buffalo lets us help 'im, you're gonna need it,...besides, that map never mentioned th' rock door,... just that word."

— —

They were still viewing the wall pictures when the Chief returned, and Billy tried to determine his answer by looking at his stone-like face,... but failed.

"I have decided that I must try and save my people." Began White Buffalo. "Even now, I have dead warriors, and many wounded,...and my people mourn for them. I must also protect our mountain and its great secrets.....I must not allow entry to the valley."

"Why, White Buffalo, you have the map? Once these men are gone, th' mountain will be safe again."

The Chief moved toward the wall and the pictographs, then turned to face them again. "Not only because of the map....More than two hundred of your years past, my ancestors told of a legend,...this was never written on our wall of life, instead, it was passed on to each Chief, by that Chief before him. In this legend, it tells of a great evil that will befall the people of this world, if it is set free. It is said that this warning came to them from the skies, from a winged God on a fiery horse that descended from the stars." He came to stand before them then.

"It must not be set free!" He said with determination. "You have one day's time to help us,...if we fail, all will be lost. Then we must close the mountain forever."

Billy nodded. "We'll need your help, to tell the warriors what needs to be done, but first we need to bring everyone back inside the mountain,...so that they'll know th' plan."

Nodding, White Buffalo left the chamber, and shortly afterwards, the sounds of Crows could be heard, along with the flapping of wings in flight.

"You believe that stuff about the legend?" Asked Rodney.

"I believe that White Buffalo don't lie.....He believes th' legend and that's all that counts here."

"But,...do you believe the legend?"

"Legends are stories that somebody tells to somebody else, and each time somebody else tells it, it gets stretched a little more out a shape....I believe in what's happenin' here and now, Rod. What's real to me is what I can touch, or see."

"Never knew you to be so skeptical." Grinned Rodney. "It's said that every legend is based on fact,...did you know that?"

Billy shook his head. "One fact at a time, okay?...Now come on, let's go tend to th' horses, and I'll tell you what we have to do."

A hundred warriors were at the timber's edge as they accompanied the Chief across the polished rock.

"White Buffalo." Said Billy as they walked. "Till now, your warriors have not been aggressive in tryin' to kill these men."

"Until now, we have killed only to protect our mountain and our lives,... or to avenge our brothers."

"I know that,...but that has to change. We have to take the fight to them. We have to hit 'em hard and fast,....and when they least expect it. We got one thing workin' in our favor,...they don't know that you're here. I ain't worried none about th' Comanche, cause when they see the Ancient Ones chargin' at 'em, they'll scatter and run for home. But it's different with these treasure hunters,...they'll have to be treated like they've just committed a great crime against th' Choctaw.... They'll need to be killed, all of 'em."

White Buffalo stopped at the edge of the polished floor of the cavern and turned to Billy. "Will this plan work?"

Billy nodded. "If me and Rod can silence that cannon, it will."

"How do we do that?" Came Rodney quickly.

"With so many men out there, they won't know that we're not one of 'em....We just walk into that camp like we belong there."

"And the cannon?"

"It can't fire without shells, Rod,...and that's why we're goin' in first."

"Is this the part you couldn't think of before?"

"It just came to me." Grinned Billy and turned back to the Chief. "I'd like you to send three or four of your best warriors out. Tell 'em to isolate as many white men as they can and kill them quietly. Men away from camp already, won't be missed....Tell 'em to take all th' white men's clothing, boots, guns and all then hide th' bodies. We're gonna need to dress as many warriors as we can in those clothes."

White Buffalo studied his face for a moment, then turned and gave the order, and when the warriors had gone, he turned back to Billy. "What is next?"

Billy shrugged. "We wait till it gets dark. We can sneak into their camp easier that way. Chief, there's guns and ammunition on our packhorse, please feel free to arm your warriors with 'em."

White Buffalo nodded. "My warriors will need food and rest for the battle."

Billy nodded and watched as he walked among the small army and dispersed them.

"Now what?" Breathed the lawman.

"We clean our guns and get some rest."

They watched as the Chief came past them to move among the wounded again.

"That man's hurting." Sighed Rodney.

Billy nodded somberly. "Let's move out under th' trees, I can't stand to look at all this." The lawman nodded in agreement and they walked away from the cavern's stone floor then sat down in the tall grass to lean against the huge trunk of an ancient Pine.

"You given any thought to dying, Billy?"

"A thousand times." He breathed. "And it still scares th' hell out of me.... Let's just not get careless out there tonight and we'll make it."

"You can count on that, my friend."

Billy ejected the cartridges from the Colts and cleaned the guns as he absently watched the activity in the cavern. He was both afraid, and worried about the outcome of the coming fight then sighing, looked across at the lawman. "Look at 'em up there." He said and nodded at the cavern. "Its hard to believe, that in three short months, it could come down to this....Them prospectors were already on their way while me and Willy was here."

"It was in the works long before that." Returned Rodney. "I just wonder if he knew they were coming?"

Billy shook his head. "I think he likely did, but was a little preoccupied at th' time, besides,...they hadn't committed any crime at that point....He likely kept an eye on 'em,...but by th' time he found th' map, it was already too late…..I'm wonderin' why th' Comanches didn't tip 'im off, they had to have been with 'em?"

"Probably wasn't with them yet,…probably only recruited them after the map was stolen?"

"You could be right." Sighed Billy, putting the guns away again. "It don't matter now anyway,…they're here,… and these people can't hope to fight the weapons they brought with 'em."

"It does make a mess." Sighed Rodney.

"Yeah,…and if th' Army's involved, th' odds are really stacked against 'em."

"If they are involved, they're keeping it quiet enough…. Wonder who they approached with it?"

"It would have to be a man of rank." Grunted Billy and pulled his knees up under his chin. "Somebody that could arrange for that cannon to be stolen, and make it stick. Be real easy to blame th' Choctaw for it, if it goes wrong…. Either way, the Son of a Bitch, they call Boss, will be in th' clear, no matter what happens."

"There'd have to be some recruits in on it, too,…he'd never get it out of the armory alone, too many guards….In my thinking, there's got to be at least one, maybe two noncoms firing that gun out there."

"Maybe." Nodded Billy. "But I doubt they'll be able to break through anyway, th' mountain's too high and solid."

"Maybe they're not trying to break through."

"Well, its damn sure a waste of shells if they're not!...What made you say that?"

"It's just a thought." Sighed Rodney. "But if it was me, and I was to chip away at the outside of the mountain in just the right places,…I might be able to scale up the face of it,…you know, come in over the top."

Billy narrowed his eyes at him. "You think that's what they're doin'?"

"Well, you don't think they hope to knock the mountain down, do you?... That would be impossible."

"Whewwww." Breathed Billy. "If that's what they're doin', they're whittling down the opposition at th' same time."

"I sure hope you got a good plan working for tonight, because I sure don't."

"Th' only thing we have to do is silence that cannon,…and it's th' how part that I'm working on,…but I'm thinkin' we play it by ear when we get there….Either way, once these warriors attack in force, White Buffalo's lost some more men."

"And we're going to have to eliminate the man behind it, else he's just gonna come back again."

"Look at 'em, Rod." Said Billy, still watching the women tend to the wounded. "There ain't no tears, no cryin'. They're just doin' what's expected of them....We got a pull this off, man."

"We will." Assured the lawman as he looked toward the end of the valley. "Say, Billy,...I wonder what he was talking about, when he said there was evil here?"

"We done been over that." Grinned Billy. "And I still don't have a clue.... But then again, half th' world is shrouded in mystery anyway, and th' other half is shrouded in legends,...and there's an awful thin line separating th' two. White Buffalo don't lie, I know that.....And if he says there's evil here, I believe him. Anyway, there's a more present danger at hand right now,...th' evil will have to take care of it's self."

"Amen to that."

Billy watched as Rodney pulled the old Walker gun and checked the loads. "Why don't you get rid of that thing, Rod, it takes a God awful long time to reload it?"

"You gave me this gun, and I like it." Grinned the lawman. "It suits me just fine, besides, I've got three spare cylinders already loaded and ready."

"You'd be a lot faster with a lighter gun."

"Maybe too fast,...might even earn me a rep like yours."

Billy shook his head. "Best get some sleep, Rod." He scooted down on the thick padding of needles, pulled his hat over his eyes and was soon in an exhausted sleep, and he hoped, a dreamless one.

There were a total of twenty-three warriors dressed in the dead men's clothing. Some were stuffing long hair beneath soiled hats, while others were cutting their long braids from their heads completely, and some were just walking around scratching.

"Think they'll pass for white men?" Muttered Rodney.

"In th' dark, they will." Billy tied the length of large white beads around his hat as he spoke, then gave a strand to the lawman.

"The warriors have the beads in place." Said White Buffalo as he approached them. "They will not fire on those wearing them."

"Then I guess we're ready." Nodded Billy. "Give us one hour's time, then send in those warriors in white men's clothes,...send them in two at a time so they won't be noticed.... Do they know what to do?"

White Buffalo nodded. "They are to greet all who see them by lifting a hand, or nodding with their head, and when they approach these men,...to act friendly, then use the knife."

"It's th' only way." Sighed Billy. "Those men out there won't quit till they get th' gold they're lookin' for....Now,... after the hour is up, tell the' warriors goin' in first to split up, half on each end of camp, and work toward the middle." He looked at the Chief then.

"And try not to worry, Sir,...these men would kill everyone in here to get what they want."

"I am convinced of this." Nodded White Buffalo. "My warriors are very good at killing their enemies....Until now, we have not needed to kill to survive." He breathed deeply of the crisp night air and nodded. "They will succeed."

Billy nodded and swung into the saddle. "If we do our job, you'll hear an explosion or two...When you hear it, send half of your warriors to attack the Comanche camp and to scatter the horses,...th' other half to attack th' main camp. Tell them to kill quick, them exploding shells will have those men so rattled, they won't know what hit 'em." He nodded at the graven-faced Chieftain and reined the Roan through the tall grass and into the trees.

— ~

Almost an hour later, they were dismounting in the trees above the encampment and kneeling down to study the activity around the many fires that danced in the night's stillness. There was limited movement in most areas of the camp, but they could hear loud talking and a lot of laughter and cursing.

"Suppertime." Breathed Billy.

"At least the shooting's stopped." Whispered Rodney. "My heart, too, I think."

"You okay, Rod?"

"Don't worry about me, I'm armed and rearin' to go."

Billy nodded. "We have to check out every one of them tents,...we find any explosives, we blow 'em up. Just be sure to give yourself enough time to check the other tents before they blow. Now, there's six tents there, and I'll take them on th' North end. You got matches?" And when the lawman nodded. "Okay,...you work your way down to th' South end and work toward me,...I'll go in right here, and Rod,....don't be no hero. When that stuff blows, get your ass away from th' blast and start killin'!...Work your way back here to th' horses,...I'll meet you here."

Rodney nodded and moved silently into the gully below them. Billy watched him fade into the darkness, then slid down into the gully and up the other side toward the fires. Fifteen minutes of feeling his way over and around large rocks, he pushed his way through some pricking thorns of Mesquite brush and found him-self at the edge of the encampment.

"Halt and be recognized!" Demanded a surly voice from the rocks in front of him. He had drawn and cocked the Colt as the man called out, then watched as the burly man got to his feet and holstered the weapon.

"God damn it, man, it's me, Billy…Put that fuckin' gun down!"

"Billy Womack,…that you?"

"Why, fuck yeah, it's me!" He blurted nervously. "Can't a man take a dump without bein' shot around here?"

"Well, they's Indians out there some'eres, by God! You could'a been one of 'em, far as I knowed!"

"Well, I ain't, so get that God damn rifle out a my face, okay?…Jesus Christ!"

"Where'n hell'd you come from anyways, I been here all night, and you damn sure didn't come past me?"

"Up th' gully a ways." Returned Billy. "Everybody in th'fuckin' camp must a took a dump down there,…enough to make a man puke….You gonna put that fuckin' gun down or not?"

"You go to hell!" Growled the sentry. "Next time let somebody know where you're goin'." He lowered the rifle then. "Go on, get on out'a here."

Billy breathed a sigh of relief as he moved on toward the camp and soon found himself among the most unlikely mix of humanity, he had ever seen. The stench of unwashed bodies was almost nauseating as he was jostled by some, greeted by a few, and cursed by others. He made his way slowly over the rock littered terrain, spying the three large tents against the Mesquite-covered bluff. The wagon that had pulled the cannon stood beside one of them. All three tents were near the center of camp, and right in the middle of the activity.

There were two guards in front of one of the tents, and he quickly turned toward the nearest fire when one of them looked in his direction. "Damn it." He muttered, and tried to calm his ragged nerves. He believed the exploding shells were in that tent and now knew that getting to them would be impossible from the front. He would need to find a way to get behind them without being seen.

He saw the Howitzer then, all sleek and shining in the fire's flickering light and walked toward it, noticing that several of the slender, bullet-like shells were stacked on the ground beside it, and spent casings littered the ground around it.

Startled, he wheeled suddenly when he felt the hand on his arm then pushed the Colt back into the holster as he looked at the man.

"Mite touchy, ain't we?" Growled the man, and his foul breath was almost too much for him,…but he managed to grin at him anyway.

"Couple months of this'd make anybody touchy." He said nastily.

"Well, just don't get too close to that there gun, Touchy."

"What's that to you?"

"Never mind that!" Said the man, looking back toward the tents. "You hear anythin' from th' Boss yet?"

What?"

"Get th' shit out'en your ears, boy,...when's he want us to start shootin' again?"

"I ain't heard nothing, God damn it!...Just wait like th' rest of us do."

The man glared at him for a second, then stared at the tent again. "Guess he's still piled up in that God damned tent, th' Son of a Bitch!"

"Well, go see, why don't you!" Spat Billy, wanting to get away from him. "I ain't his God damn keeper!"

The man glared at him again then sat back down by the fire. "Just stay away from that gun, ye hear?"

"What did he say Sarge?" Asked the man next to him.

"Nothin', God damn it! This Son of a Bitch don't know shit from chinola!"

With another look at the cannon, Billy turned back toward the tents again, staring down the surly stares at the fire as he left. He pulled the watch from his pocket. It had been more than an hour already, and he knew he had to get into those tents,...and he couldn't get behind them from where he was without the guards seeing him. He would have to go farther South and work his way back.

He put the watch away and scanned the encampment, knowing that the disguised Choctaw would already be infiltrating the camp, so he had to hurry. He was both nervous, and scared and silently cursed himself for the weakness.

He was jostled and cursed by several foul-tempered men on the way, and could see the eyes of the guards on him as he approached them.

"You know th' rules here!" Growled one of the men. "Keep movin'!"

"Get your ass back to th' fires, boy!" Snapped the other man.

He stopped a few feet in front of them then reached for the Durham sack, turning to watch the milling men as he rolled and lit the thin cigarette.

"Are you deaf, man?" Snapped the guard again.

Billy turned around to look at them and held up the smoke. "No, Sir. I'm just rollin' a smoke."

Well, smoke it somewhere else!"

Billy shrugged then motioned toward the cannon. "Sarge said to find out if th' Boss was still in his tent?" He saw the guard's eyes flick slightly toward the other tent, and knew they were guarding the one with the exploding shells.

"That ain't none a th' Sarge's business,…your'en neither,…now get goin'!"

"Well, God damn it, man, tell us somethin',…we ain't a damn bit closer to that gold than we was a month ago! We're gettin' a little tired a waitin'!"

The guard lowered the rifle from his shoulder and leveled it at Billy, and the bore of the sharps, fifty-caliber was a menacing sight. Billy raised his hands in a gesture of good intentions and moved on past them.

He knew that time was becoming his enemy and began walking faster, and once far enough from the tents he flipped the butt away and looked back. The guards were both looking the other way, and with one last look at the encampment, he quickly made his way into the dark area of the bluffs.

He slid down the crumbling bank of a gully that ran parallel to the camp and worked his way back. He was soon directly behind them, and after intently searching the darkness both ways along the gully he climbed out of the shallow ditch and crawled to the rear of the guarded tent, slid the knife from his belt and after searching the area for movement again, made a long slit in the tarp and crawled inside.

The interior was dimly lit from the partly open flaps in front, and he stared at the stack of open crates,…they were all filled with the brass shells. Alongside were several wooden kegs of gunpowder and an open crate of rifle cartridges. He could barely see the wooden box of dynamite sticks in the dim light of the flaps and worked his way over a few of the shell crates toward it.

His heart was beating like a drum in his chest as he gathered up several sticks of the explosives, and spotting the coil of fuse and box of blasting caps near the open flaps, worked his way over to them. He could see the legs of both guards, and they were less than a foot away from him as he deftly grabbed the coil of fuse then quickly cut off a length of it and tied four sticks of the dynamite together with it. That done, he cut a much longer piece and a couple of shorter ones then nervously worked the fuses into the blasting caps and inserted the caps into the explosives. Then, taking a second to calm his nerves again, he repeated the process on the two single sticks.

By now, he was sweating profusely and marveled at it. It had to be close to freezing in the tent. He was about to start back to the rear of the tent when the explosion shattered the stillness. 'Rodney' He thought as he settled back down by the open flaps to wait for his nerves to settle once again, and was about to gingerly step over the shell crates a second time when he heard the loud, excited voices from outside the tent, and could distinguish the guard's voices from that of another man. At that point he froze, afraid of exposing himself, and listened as they talked.

"Who the hell set off that charge, Leonard?"

"Damned if we know, Boss." Returned a guard excitedly. "It was at th' other end of camp down there!"

"Well, don't just stand there, God damn it, go see who it was, and bring the Son of a Bitch to me!....Go!"

Billy moved closer to the opening as the guards left, and could see the angled profile of the man called, Boss,...and at that moment, felt the tingling in his neck as something about the thin man stirred a forgotten memory. He studied the lean features and thick mustache, letting his eyes travel down the man's wiry frame to stop at the claw-like gloved right hand and once again, his memory stirred.

It wasn't until the man looked directly at the open flap of the tent, that it came to him. 'Snake' He almost said it aloud as he had flashes of the fight in the saloon at Rhone Springs, Texas. But then again, it wasn't that long ago, he thought....But why wasn't he dead?....The Army was going to hang him? He took another deep breath of the cold air and shook his head. He wouldn't even guess as to how he got away?"

He should have killed him that day, but a sudden show of conscience had made him render his gun hand useless instead. The man moved from his line of vision then, and remembering why he was there, he quickly stepped backward over the shell crates and made his way to the rear of the tent. He placed the four sticks of dynamite on the ground between the casks of black powder then uncoiled the fuse along the ground as he backed out through the slit in the tent. He paused again to listen to the excitement, as men began yelling wildly and running toward the far end of the camp. He heard the second blast then, closer than the first and hoped that Rodney was okay. The deafening blasts had started fires in the surrounding brush and trees, and he began hearing erratic bursts of gunfire as he played out the fuse and dropped back into the gully.

He quickly struck a match and held it to the end of the fuse and then, getting to his feet, searched the immediate area for movement and hearing even more gunfire as he crawled out of the ditch and walked around the wagon in the direction of the howitzer. He was walking at a half trot as he crossed the open area of prairie, then stopped long enough to light the fuses on both sticks of dynamite before converging on the cannon. He quickly dropped one stick down the barrel of the gun then dropped the other one next to the exploding shells and hurried toward the ravine, a dozen yards away,... and once there, dropped out of sight to watch the fireworks.

Both explosions sounded as one, shattering the stillness and causing the ground to tremble beneath his feet and then all at once, the entire camp lit up, and the night sky turned bright orange as the much larger explosion rocked the mountainsides, and he knew the shells and other explosives had blown. He moved farther down the ravine then, quickly stepping over the large branches and other debris as he went.

Several more explosions sounded then as the dynamite and rifle cartridges began to go, and the popping of the ammunition was more like the sound of an all-out attack from an army of cavalrymen, and was lighting up the night sky like some fourth of July celebration. Men were being hit, and some even killed by flying lead and fragmentation as they tried to find cover.

Then, suddenly there was havoc in the camp, and he raised himself above the crest of the gully to watch the white-robed Choctaw race by toward the Comanche camp, an eighth of a mile away. Then came the screaming and war-cries as the rest of the Choctaw warriors charged the encampment from the South end of camp, with bows strumming and war-axes swinging, they were relentlessly felling the treasure hunters as they desperately tried to escape. Those that tried to fight back were overwhelmed, and the gunfire was a constant thing in the arena of death,...but in reality, the attack had become more of a massacre, than a retaliatory raid.

Billy watched it for a few minutes, having to duck at times to avoid falling debris, then turned and made his way down the ravine. He was entering the area where they had left the horses by the time the explosions had echoed away. He climbed out of the gully then and crawled into the dark of the trees, and breathless, rolled onto his stomach and looked back at the melee.

It had become quite dark in the camp with the only light coming from the many fires that were still burning. Men were screaming as they died, while others were yelling and shooting at anything and everything, even at each other. Many had been killed outright by the explosions, and others just trying to crawl away with their lives, while many others had run screaming into the treacherous Kiamichi Wilderness in their efforts to escape.

After a while, Billy got to his feet, and hiding in the trees, began moving toward the horses only to suddenly freeze when he heard the challenge.

"If your name ain't Billy Upshur,...you're a dead man!" Came the voice he recognized.

"It's me, Rod, don't shoot me, okay?"

"Glad to hear it." Rasped the lawman. "Where the hell, you been,...you scared the devil out of me?"

"I'll explain later." Returned Billy, going past him to the Roan. He pulled the Henry from the boot then quickly raised his hand for silence, and both of them moved behind the trees again. More of the Choctaw were emerging from the rocks like ghosts as they converged on the encampment to join the conflict.

"Whoa!" Whispered the lawman.

Yeah,...White Buffalo's quite a war-Chief, ain't he?"

"What?"

"He held this bunch back, then sent 'em in to mop up. Those men that made it to safety will see 'em coming and think they're bein' attacked by a thousand, instead of a couple hundred."

"I see what you mean,...two groups coming in from each end, and one up the middle to do in the stragglers."

Billy stepped up to the tree and levered the rifle, took aim and fired, seeing one of the distant treasure hunters pitch forward in mid-stride. "These men don't know why they're dyin', Rod." He said, levering the rifle again.

"From what I've seen down there." Returned Rodney, cocking the hammer back on his saddle-gun. "It wouldn't matter if they did." Then he also began firing at the running figures in the firelight.

An hour of fighting had passed and then suddenly, it was over. Only sporadic gunfire could be heard in the distance as more of the raiders were flushed out of hiding. Scores of men lay dead and dying in the light from the fires, and only a few had gotten away to scatter in the surrounding wilderness. Those that were lucky enough to snare a stampeding horse, was quickly knocked from that animal's back by an ancient Choctaw. And then there was silence as the mounted Indians began to mill around in the empty campsite before quickly dismounting to retrieve the bodies of their dead and wounded.

"We better hang back for a while." Whispered Billy, and for the next several minutes, watched the warriors lift the dead to the backs of ponies and slowly make their way back toward the mountain. Some entered through the tunnel in front, while others came toward them to go in the other entrance.

"Why are we waiting?" Whispered the lawman.

"Somebody might be watching and try to follow 'em to th' valley."

"I doubt that, ain't nothing but bodies out there."

Billy shook his head "One or two could still be out there, besides,...we get too close, they might mistake us for two of 'em."

"That would not be good, would it?" Sighed Rodney, leaning back against the tree. "I want to tell you, Billy,...I was scared to death out there. I was never involved in anything like this before....I actually thought I was going to die, a time or two."

"You never stop bein' scared, Rod,...no matter how many fights you're in, and them that say they're not,...are liars."

They watched as yet another group of warriors began putting out the fires in the brush along the bluff, as well as a few farther out in the trees, caused by flying debris from the explosions. But, at last, even the campfires were extinguished.

"It's almost like they were never here." Commented Rodney as they watched the warriors file toward the front entry tunnel.

Billy nodded. "Except for th' bodies, a man would have a hard time figurin' out what happened here."

"Well, I know what happened." Breathed the lawman. "And I'll never forget it!"

"We never forget any of 'em, Rod,...we just learn by 'em, if we're lucky."

"Yeah,...you think they got the Boss-man?" He asked as Billy moved past him to slide the Henry back into the boot.

"I hope they did,...cause I know th' Bastard!"

"You know him?" Rodney shoved the saddle-gun into the boot and stared at him. "How?"

"I seen 'im just before I blew th' tent....His name's Snake, least that's what they called 'im.... I shot 'im a few years back."

Rodney grinned as he pulled himself into the saddle. "I find that a little hard to believe."

Billy swung astride the Roan and stared at him. "What's so hard to believe?"

"That you shot him,...how could that be?"

"What are you talkin' about?"

"I'm talking about you shooting a man, and he suddenly turns up here alive....It's got to be a ghost, or somebody that looks like him."

"Well, I didn't kill 'im, Rod!...A minute of weakness, I guess. Anyway, he's th' Boss of this outfit."

"He's got to be dead now, if he was anywhere near that tent when it blew." He stared back at the darkened camp again and sighed. "Guess it'll be up to me to report what happened here."

"Why?...You ain't th' law up here....You ain't got jurisdiction, remember? Besides, who would you report it to, there was two soldier-boys shootin' that gun.....At best, you'd get both our tails in a crack." He turned the mare and reined her through the trees. Rodney clucked his horse in behind him and they worked their way back toward the cave.

"It ain't over yet." Said Rodney from behind him. "This whole country's gonna blow up when the Government does get wind of this...Heads are gonna roll at one of those Forts, too, and the Choctaw will be caught right in the middle of it,...especially when them that got away start talking."

"It's out of our hands now, Rod, stop thinkin' about it, we won this one. Let's save th' next one for another day, now come on,...I'm tired." He clucked the Roan up through the tall grass and rocks, then under the giant Firs and into the freezing darkness of the cave.

CHAPTER SEVEN

THEY RODE OUT OF THE cave and into the lush valley, and several seconds later turned into the dense forest of ancient pines toward the large cavern a quarter mile away. They could see the flickering fires as they exited the trees and continued on toward the cavern's polished stone floor.

"Wonder how many they lost out there tonight?" Sighed Billy, looking at the half-dozen or so robe-covered bodies.

"I count seven." Returned Rodney. "And about a dozen wounded over there...But, if them treasure hunters regroup and come back, there'll be a lot more."

Billy nodded. "Lets leave th' horses here, Rod." He dismounted tiredly, and when the lawman joined him, both of them stood and gazed at the bodies for a time.

"I'm still worried, Billy,...I don't think this is over yet."

"Rod, th' only thing on them gents minds right now, is getting' as far away from this mountain as they can. There ain't that many left anyway,... and they're on foot. Th' warriors'll track em down,...and if there's still a threat after that, they 'll deal with it."

"I hope you're right, Billy, I really do....What are they doing over there?"

Both of them were frustrated as they watched the wickiups being dismantled along the inner edge of the floor, and the skins and furs tied into bales and packed onto litters. Women and children were chanting woefully as they mourned their dead, but there was no crying.

"Looks like they're packing up to leave." Commented Rodney.

"That's exactly what they're doing." Said Billy, dropping the mare's reins. "Lets find White Buffalo." He walked toward the stone floor then stepped onto the polished rock to stare at the activity. The women worked silently, packing away food, pottery and other personals onto travois. Warriors stood along the walls of the cavern, silently watching as preparations were being made to leave their life-long home.

White Buffalo was standing near the old man at the rear wall of the Council Chamber when they entered, and turning, the Chief's features softened when he saw them.

"You are safe." He nodded. "The spirits smile on us once again."

"A few of 'em got away." Sighed Billy. "No more than a dozen or so, I think."

Rodney had gone directly to the wall when they entered, and was watching the old man record the events. "Maybe less." He added as he turned to look back at them.

White Buffalo turned and looked at the lawman, then nodded. "It was to be expected." He said, turning back to Billy. "They will leave Choctaw land now,…and the Comanche will never return to this mountain." He dropped his eyes to the floor in thought for a minute then raised his head to look Billy in his eyes. "There has been enough killing." He smiled tiredly then and nodded, as if making up his mind to something. "And now there is something Man-with-glass-eyes must see,…come." He moved past him then and exited the room.

Puzzled, Billy looked at the lawman. "Rod?" He said, then followed in the wake of the Chief,…with the lawman close behind him.

They were led deeper into the cavern, then into another large cave that had water cascading out of its upper walls. White Buffalo was using two pieces of flint to ignite an ancient torch when they entered, immediately throwing the large cave into a bright, flickering light as it flared to life.

"Will you look at that." Breathed Rodney as he stared up at the natural falls then at the deep, clear basin below it and was shaking his head as he followed Billy.

They followed the Chief around the natural basin to another opening in the wall, but this one had obviously been made with picks and shovels,…and very long ago. White Buffalo stooped and entered the tunnel, then straightened and held the torch above his head, illuminating the cave's interior,…and the brilliance was blinding in the torch-light.

"Good Lord!" Exclaimed Rodney, not quite believing what he was seeing.

The roof, walls and much of the floor it's self were of pure gold, and extended the entire length of the deep tunnel. Chunks of the precious metal literally covered the floor, some as large as cannonballs.

They followed the Chief deeper into the mine where the walls were even richer with the yellow metal, and it was also rich with human bones, a lot of them.

"The Iron Shirts came here long before my people came." Reflected White Buffalo, his voice a loud echo in the cave. "My Grandfathers found the bones as you see them,…they had been butchered."

"By who?" Breathed Billy, still in awe at the piece of history he was witnessing.

"Perhaps by those who constructed the ancient door." Said White Buffalo gesturing at the bones again. "The spirits of these Iron Shirts have guarded the yellow iron for a great many moons,…and much of it was removed and hidden behind the ancient door in the valley, perhaps, also by the ancient warriors that were here before us. The great door was sealed long ago."

"They were Aztec Indians." Commented Rodney. "And they must have hidden it there,…but I don't understand why they would leave a place like this,…it's a paradise?"

"They were already gone when my Grandfathers arrived." Returned White Buffalo. "Perhaps they encountered the evil that is hidden by the mountain and were destroyed by it,… or perhaps all were killed as they destroyed the Iron Shirts, many weapons and headdress were found among the bones in the valley.…We will never know what happened."

"I saw some soot marks on the wall outside there." Said Billy. "They likely smelted the gold right out there."

"Yes." Nodded the Chief. "My people removed the stones long ago."

Billy nodded. "And by th' size of this mine, I'd say they took a boatload of gold out before they died…But what's all this got to do with you packin' up to leave th' valley,…you're safe now?"

"It will be made clear to you soon,…come." He abruptly moved past them toward the entrance.

They followed him back toward the ceremonial chamber, seeing him call to several warriors, who quickly came toward him. He conversed with them and they immediately left, then the Chief stopped, and waited for them to walk with him.

"I have known for many moons that we cannot kill, what cannot be killed." He waved his arm to take in the valley. "All is lost here…Our time here has passed. We have protected the mountain, and in so doing, have protected the secrets it hides.…I have shown you one secret, because you are Choctaw, a warrior, and now I will show you another.…But I will not show you all the secrets, because the evil hides them….We have this night, killed many who would destroy the mountain, and that is as it must be…. But my people are few now,…and the white man is many,…and so, we must leave." He raised his hand when Billy started to protest.

"Man-with-glass-eyes has worked his magic once again…Our sacred mountain has been spared….Our women and children are now safe. It is because of this, I show you the secrets. This honor, you have earned, as warrior and friend to the Ancient Ones." He turned then as two mounted warriors brought their horses then he swung aboard the white pony and waited until they were mounted before leading off toward the opposite end of the valley.

They rode in silence for some time, and it was nearing dawn when they came to a part of the mountain that was completely hidden from view by thick patches of Juniper, climbing vines and giant Fir. Here, the Chief dismounted and gave the order to clear away the foliage.

They sat their horses in the icy dawn and waited as the giant rock slab of a door was uncovered, and the strange markings revealed to them, showing a large feathered serpent and other figures of Gods in feathered headdress and tail feathers. There were other markings as well, that could have been some form of ancient writing, but was too weather worn to tell.

More than another hour passed before the straining warriors began forcing the great rock slab to move. Crude pry-bars of long hewn poles were used to move the stone outward and at last, there was an opening large enough for them to enter the room.

With lighted torches, the warriors entered the ancient cave ahead of them, throwing the hidden contents into sudden brilliance.

"Good God!" Gasped Billy when he entered.

The warriors moved deeper into the room and held the torches high, revealing an enormous pyramid of gold ingots that reached almost to the twenty-foot height of the cave's roof.

"That answers one question." Said Rodney as he stared at the gold bars.

There were tall, large clay urns, decorated with faded markings, and figures of plumed Gods. Several of the urns were filled to overflowing with minted Spanish coins, priceless jewelry of braided gold neckwear, raw turquoise and emeralds, jade, rubies and countless other gems. There were golden idols and statues, and tankards of pure Jade, inlaid with gold and emeralds. Another half-dozen urns contained nothing but large, priceless gems, some the size of a man's fist.

On the uneven walls were ceremonial masks inlaid with gold and gems, made into the likeness of Gods. Against the walls were dozens of Spanish weaponry, including lances and war-axes, swords of tempered steel, braided breastplates and headwear.

Billy stooped and picked up what appeared to be a wolf's head atop a length of polished ebony. The face of a man was embedded in the wolf's open mouth and he was awed by the weight of the solid gold head. The outside of the piece was overlaid with shells from the ocean and the shells were inlaid with gold. It appeared to be some sort of a walking stick. Sighing, he put it back and picked up one of the many heavy necklaces that lay draped over the coins in the urns, and wondered how it might look around Connie's neck. Putting that back, he scanned the walls of the cave, seeing brightly colored, plumed paintings of the Aztec Gods and at last, coming to rest on the feathered serpent, the same as on the door of the cave outside.

He breathed deeply of the ancient air and watched as Rodney dipped his hands into one of the urns of coins, letting them fall through his fingers, and he grinned, thinking he was like some little boy that had just opened what he wanted for his birthday.

White Buffalo came forward then and his face was expressionless. "All of this was here." He waved his arm as he spoke. "Before my Grandfathers came, and it is this that brings the white man to the point of madness...I think, perhaps, that it was wise for them to close the great doorway forever."

"I can't argue with that." Breathed Billy. "It's, ahhhh,...it's..."

"Beyond belief!" Said Rodney quickly. "That's what it is, it's way, way beyond my belief! A man could dream about gold every night for a lifetime, and still not see as much gold as I've seen today." He grinned and stared at the walls of the cave, then back at Billy. "I told you they was Aztecs, Billy, I....."

"Well, fuck!...I could have told you that!" Interrupted a raspy voice from behind them, causing them to quickly turn toward the doorway.

As Billy turned, his hand was snaking the belly-gun from the holster, across his stomach.

"I wouldn't do that!" Snapped the voice, stopping Billy's draw. "I'd like to do this quietly and without anybody gettin' hurt...But then, it's strictly up to you."

Billy slid the Colt back into the holster and saw Rodney do the same. He looked across at the two warriors then, seeing their hands on the hilts of the long knives in their sashes, but otherwise staring expressionless at the intruders.

"Now, this is doin' it th' smart way, Gents." Grinned Snake. "I'd hate like hell to bring all them Indians down on us by shootin' you good old boys.... Now, go ahead and drop them pistols because I will shoot one of you if I have to, and take my chances with th' Indians,...go on, drop 'em!"

Billy had recognized the thin gunman's voice immediately, and was now staring at the two men with him as he dropped the Colts in the dust of the treasure vault.

Snake grinned as they dropped their weapons, then waved his pistol to move them farther into the cave while he edged closer to the overflowing urns. "Jesus Christ!" He gasped loudly. "What did I tell you boys, huh? Th' fuckin' map didn't say anything about all this, but hey!…Who cares,…I'm a fuckin' rich man!"

"We,…are rich men!" Snapped one of the others. And that was when Billy saw the partially concealed badge on the man's shirt.

"Hey-y, Tom, that's what I meant, man!…We're all rich!" He grinned widely and stared greedily back at the treasure-trove.

Rodney moved closer to Billy and was also staring at the man with the badge, "You're a Federal; Marshal!" He blurted loudly. "What's going on here?"

"He sure is." Laughed Snake as he waved the Indians farther away from the urns. "I couldn't have pulled this operation off without 'im." He came to stand in front of Billy then to stare up at his bespectacled face. "You blew up my gun, didn't you?" He grinned then looked back at the Choctaw warriors. "And them Peckerwoods nearly killed us all out there,…I wasn't expectin' that…Hell, I didn't even know they was here!…What kind of Indians are they anyway?…I never seen none like 'em before,…and everybody knows Indians don't fight at night!" He glared at Billy again, then at the hate-filled face of Rodney and grinned again.

"Oh, well, hell,…I ain't mad about it." He looked back at Billy. "Th' minute I saw you two gents out there in th' trees, I knew you was behind th' whole thing. That's why we followed you,…and you know what?…Was me, I'd a done th' same thing you did.…Yes'ir." He looked back at the treasure then.

"Just look at th' pay-off!…Okay, Gents,…counting yours, we got nine horses outside there, and you are gonna load five of 'em with as much of this stuff as they can carry. Then, you five are gonna walk across this valley in front of us, and we're all going through that tunnel together.…Oh,…and we're gonna be real quiet about it, too. Hope I said that plain enough." He laughed again and gazed greedily at the treasure.

Billy had been watching White Buffalo as Snake talked and had seen him close his eyes,… and he thought he knew what might be coming.

"Okay, Gents, hop to it.…Let's go,…move it!"

Rodney had started to comply, but stopped when Billy gripped his arm, and as they heard the Crows, he moved closer to the lawman.

Suddenly, the narrow opening was filled with the flapping of ebony wings and ear piercing caws as the birds swooped into the treasure room.

Billy quickly pulled the startled lawman to the floor as the Crows entered, and they both covered their faces to escape injury from the birds' sharp beaks and talons.

The Crows attacked without mercy, clawing and pecking at the faces and arms of the intruders, their loud songs drowning out the curses and screams of the gunmen, and suddenly they began firing their guns wildly as they flailed at the attacking birds. A dozen shots rang out in the confines of the cave, deafening explosions that seemed to pierce their minds, causing them to cover their ears from the pain it caused.

And then it was over when the three men managed to escape through the doorway, still screaming as they ran for their horses. Billy scooped up the Colts as the Crows departed in pursuit, then moved quickly through the narrow opening in time to see that there had been a fourth man with the horses. The horses were already in motion when Snake and the other two ran outside, and Billy was just in time to see them swing astride the running animals and flog them mercilessly through the tall grass.

He dropped the hammer down on the pistol as he watched the Crows finally break away from the chase and fly into the pines. The men were well out of range as he holstered the weapon, and then they both watched as a dozen warriors raced out of the trees in pursuit of the men.

"Bastards had us cold, Billy." Panted the lawman as he holstered the Walker.

"No they didn't." Gritted Billy. "They were up against somethin' they knew nothin' about!"

Rodney nodded, and with a last look toward the disappearing riders, followed Billy back into the treasure vault.

"Jesus!" Cried Billy when he saw the dead warriors. White Buffalo was kneeling beside the bodies, quietly chanting and dusting them with powder from a deerskin pouch.

Billy bent and retrieved a fallen torch from the musty floor, and it wasn't until White Buffalo stood up that they saw the blood. "God!" Groaned Billy and started toward him, but he stopped when the Chief raised his hand and came toward them.

"You must leave now." He said sadly then moved past them and exited the cave. The Chief was already astride his pony when they emerged from the vault.

"Come." He said then reined the pony back toward the great cavern and galloped away.

They were very much concerned when they mounted their horses to follow him, and he was already giving orders to several old men by the time they dismounted at the rock floor. Women and children were gathering around him as the old men moved off toward the rear of the great cave.

"You think he's hurt bad?" Muttered Rodney.

"Looks bad to me." Sighed Billy as he idly watched several women as they began strapping heavily loaded travois to the backs of waiting ponies.

"Guess they're really leaving." Sighed the lawman.

"Yeah." He saw White Buffalo turn then and motion for them to follow him. "We may be about to find out,...come on, Rod."

They stopped again when the sounds of the returning warriors came to them and in looking, counted only six men as they pulled to a sliding halt beside the cavern's stone floor,....and they had brought their packhorse with them.

"Where's the rest of 'em?" Muttered the lawman. "Think they might have caught up to 'em?"

Billy shook his head. "Weren't gone long enough, likely left some guards at th' tunnel....Let's go." He sighed and continued on to the Council Chamber.

Rodney watched the warriors dismount and knew that Billy was probably right,...they had given up the chase. 'But why' He wondered, then shrugging followed Billy toward the Council room.

CHAPTER EIGHT

White Buffalo was seated at the head of the feasting robe when they entered. A woman was placing food and water for them then hurried away when they came to be seated. Another woman was cleaning the blood from a gaping wound in the Chief's side, and they watched as she applied the wound with an ointment and sprinkled it with a white powder from a small clay jar,… and then he waved her away.

The food was eaten in silence and when they were finished, the woman returned to clear away the pottery.

White Buffalo grimaced slightly as he straightened and looked at his guests, and then his features softened as another woman entered with the long ceremonial pipe, holding a small, lighted tallow-stick to the strong tobacco as he puffed. She left the room then, and the Chief passed the pipe to Billy, and after Rodney had passed it back to him, he waited for the woman to return and take it away.

"You have questions that I must answer." Began White Buffalo and looked intently into the eyes of both of them. "I am honored that two such good friends have come to defend our sacred mountain,…once again, you have shown your skill and bravery.….Myself, and my people will be grateful to you both for evermore."

"Man-with-glass-eyes, and Man-of-the-law will forever be remembered in our hearts, and in our songs." He looked sadly at them then grimaced again.

"But our time is over here." He quickly raised his hand when Billy started to speak.

"I have given this much thought,...and we must leave the valley. The paper, that you call a map will someday bring others in search of the hidden treasure,...and they, also, must never find it. It brings death and destruction to those who seek it, just as it did on this day." He stared through the doorway at the now almost deserted area of polished rock.

"We have dwelled in this, our valley for many, many of your years, and it is hard to leave our homeland." He took a deep breath and looked intently at them again. "The mountain must be sealed....There must not be an opening for them to find,...and as long as we are here, this cannot be done. This Devil Mountain hides much more than the yellow metal, or the treasure of the ancients,...it hides an evil that must never be set free,...men would not know how to fight it."

"Chief?" Blurted Billy, hunting for the right words, and then both of them got to their feet when the Chief once again raised his hand.

"Your concern is for my wound." He said, almost smiling at them. "I have been wounded many times....Do not be concerned. My word is law here, and I have spoken it....Your ponies have been readied with skins of food and water, and your belongings have been loaded on your pack animal. All is ready for you...Please go in peace, my friends,....I am grateful." With that, White Buffalo got to his feet and left the Council Chamber.

"My, God, Billy!" Sighed the Lawman.

"Yeah.....Lets go, Rod." He said and moved toward the door. "It's all we can do."

The horses and pack animal were loaded and waiting at the line of trees. White Buffalo was astride the white pony, and mounted warriors waited patiently behind him. The Chief nodded as they mounted, then led the way into the trees.

They had just entered the darkness of the trees when a ground-trembling rumble came to them.

"Guess he meant it." Said Rodney from the shadows behind him.

"He meant it." Returned Billy with a feeling of gloom in his heart.

They rode the rest of the way to the tunnel in silence and when they neared the opening, White Buffalo reined to one side to wait for them then urged his pony alongside the Roan and gripped Billy's arm in friendship.

"Remember us to Little Wolf." He looked deep into Billy's eyes, then nodded and reined his pony around the mare to take Rodney's arm in his firm grip,...then he faced them both and nodded. "You must go now,....and we must prepare for our departure as well. We will not meet again, my friends, but the spirits of my ancestors will ride with you always.....'Yokoke'

Billy nodded grimly as he stared at the great man's expressionless face, then puzzled, looked past him at the stream of white sand pouring from the rocks beside the tunnel, then dismissing it, he raised his hand to White Buffalo. "Yokoke" ...Good luck to you and your people, White Buffalo,...I won't ever forget you." Then, with bowed head, he clucked the Roan into the freezing tunnel.

They were through the tunnel in a matter of minutes and in sight of last night's body-strewn battlefield, and at the rim of the shallow gully, Billy stopped and twisted around in the saddle to stare back at the tunnel, then up at the battle-scarred face of the mountain before sighing again. He stared back at the battlefield to watch the large circling vultures light atop the bodies of the dead. "They ain't wastin' any time, are they?" He commented, then thought of something and turned to look at the lawman.

"Did you see th' sand comin' out'a them rocks in there?"

Yeah,...and it reminded me of something else, I read once...The Egyptians used sand like that to hold up giant stone doors in the Pyramids. When they wanted to seal off a tomb, they'd just let the sand run out,....closing the tomb forever."

Billy stared at him then they both heard the rumble inside the tunnel. "God damn it, Rod!" He jerked the startled Roan back toward the tunnel and kicked her hard in the flanks.

"Billy, stop!...Stay away from there!" Rodney reined his horse in between Billy and the Fir Trees, and at that moment, Dust and rock-debris belched out of the tunnel as it collapsed completely. The ground began to tremble again and the shale was moving beneath the animal's hoofs as the mountain shifted to compensate for the empty space. The horses reared and tried to pitch in their frenzy, almost unseating them, so they swung from the saddle as the rumbling subsided and eventually calmed the animals. Billy then leaned against the Roan and held on, suddenly too weak to stand.

The lawman quickly tied his horse to a branch and moved to his side. "You okay, man...You hit by a rock or something?"

Billy looked blankly at him. "They killed themselves, Rod!...Why'd they want a do that?...It makes no sense!"

"Maybe it did to them, Billy,...if that's what they done? And maybe they thought they couldn't survive outside of that valley, who knows?...Come on now, let's sit a spell." He steered Billy to a nearby rock and sat down across from him,... then they sat for a time, both staring at the giant Firs, that once hid the tunnel.

"There was no other way out of there, Rod."

"Well,...you're right about one thing." Sighed Rodney. "It wouldn't make any sense to trap themselves in there,...and I don't think they did."

"What?...You heard that other tunnel cave in, Rod,...that was the only other way out!....Nawww, I think they stayed behind to die,...and I should have known it when I saw that sand fallin'."

"Well I read the book, and I didn't know...Don't beat yourself up about it. If that's what they really did, you couldn't have stopped them anyway."

"He was dyin', Rod,...you seen that wound! No,...they killed themselves on purpose,...I'm convinced of it."

"Then tell me this, Billy?....Why go to the trouble of taking down their tepees, packing all their possessions on travois, then strapping the travois behind their ponies, if they were going to commit suicide?"

"I don't know, Rod!...All I know, is that my gut tells me they stayed behind to die,...and my gut-feelings are hardly ever wrong!"

Rodney sighed heavily. "Look, Billy,...Maybe they did plan to die, I don't know...But, if they did,...they're warriors, maybe they thought it was the only choice they had. Maybe they thought that, by dying,...their spirits would be free to protect the mountain forever."

Billy stared narrowly at him, then grinned and nodded his head. "I knew there was some reason, I liked you...Thanks, Rod.,,, Listen, I hear Crows,... guess life won't be th' same for them now, either."

"I guess not." Sighed Rodney. "Now, don't you think we ought to get out of here? It ain't gonna smell so good around here before long, and I'd just as soon put some distance between us and this place,...what do you say?"

Billy nodded and got to his feet, looking skyward again when he heard the cawing. "Every time I hear a Crow from now on, I'll think about this, Rod." At that moment, the flapping of large wings caused them to look toward the mountain to watch as the huge bird cawed shrilly at them, and they were both in awe as they stared at the monstrous Crow, and its almost totally white head was out of contrast to the rest of its inky blackness.

The Crow watched them in silence for several long seconds, then suddenly cawed piercingly and flew straight up the sheer side of the mountain.

Rodney slowly shook his head and looked wide-eyed at Billy. "No way, Billy!" He blurted. "Do not even think something like that."

Billy nodded in agreement, then walked to the mare and pulled himself into the saddle where he sat and stared up toward the top of the mountain. "White-headed Crows are a common sight in these mountains, Rod,... everybody knows that."

Yeah." Commented the lawman as he mounted his horse. "I bet we could find a lot of these Choctaws that can talk to 'em, too,...if we tried." He grinned then. "Ain't nothing strange about that!"

"Nope." Sighed Billy, looking back at the body-strewn camp-site. "Nothin' strange at all."

"You know." Sighed Rodney, also looking at the battlefield. "Sure is a lot of hardware laying around out there,...think we ought'a collect it?"

"If the authorities was to see them bodies, and there was no weapons layin' around,...they just might try to charge th' Choctaw with murderin' a bunch of unarmed prospectors....and they're gonna have it tough enough as it is,... don't you think?"

"I can see that happening...You had something on your mind a minute ago, what was it, White Buffalo again?"

Billy shook his head. "I was thinkin' about Snake.....As long as he's out there, this mountain ain't safe, Rod....He knows what's in there now,...and if it takes th' rest of his life, he'll try to get at that treasure again."

"Well,...like you said,...ain't a lot we can do about that...Unless you want to try and track him down?"

Billy shook his head and sighed. "I found out th' hard way that I ain't no tracker."

"That leaves me out, too....You never know though,... we might run into him again, who knows?

Chapter Nine

THEY WERE SEVERAL HOURS AWAY from the mountain and in some of the roughest landscape possible. Winding-stair Mountain loomed tall and silent in the west as they battled through the fallen timber and gouging, up-thrusting branches, rocks, waist-high grass and ancient Pines. The uncaring, unforgiving Kiamichi Wilderness was making their progress an almost impossible task again.

Billy led the way through the snaring vines and dead wood, reining the mare down into one twisting gully after another. But the dead wood and rocks, that totally littered the beds of those gullies was a nightmare in it's self. Raking branches sought to stab them in passing, forcing them to either try and push them aside, or to break them off before going by. The horses were scratched and bleeding in dozens of places, and the only thing that saved the heavy sacks of supplies, was because they were made from hand-tooled animal skins.

It was late in the day and they were still in the rugged foothills of Winding-stair Mountain. Billy was trying to keep them off the loose shale by riding in the valleys between the sloping hills, but at times they were forced to climb the tree-studded swells to bypass impossible tangles of brush and dense briar thickets,...and it was almost full dark by the time they rode out of a twisting gully into the tall, waving grass of more open terrain.

The large, jagged rocks were more numerous here, and harder to see, but they continued to steer the animals around those obstacles and through the dense groves of wild Pecan, Burr-oak and towering Pines,…and it was becoming harder to determine if they were still riding toward the South. Another two hours found them once again in a wide expanse of broken, dead trees and twisting ravines, but by this time, they had a moon to see by when finally dropping down into one of the deeper ones.

Billy stopped the mare amid the clutter and stared up the steep wall of red clay, seeing nothing along the crest, but rocks and Mesquite brush. The floor of the ravine was thick with the stunted shrubbery, and there were fallen tree limbs everywhere along with a large assortment of sharp rocks, making it an ideal place to camp he thought as he dismounted in the shadows of the moonlit embankment.

He leaned on his saddle and watched the lawman dismount. "I don't know about you, Rod, but I'm dog-tired,…and hungry."

"That makes two of us." Groaned Rodney. "I thought you said there were roads up here somewhere? I feel like I've been in a fight with a porcupine,… and lost th' fight."

"Yeah,…well, I thought I remembered th' way me and Willy went home, but it all looks different now,…hell, I don't know where we are."

"Well." Sighed Rodney, reaching to untie and tug the blanket roll from beneath the skins of heavy supplies. "Think we can chance a fire down here?"

"Long enough to cook with." Billy retrieved his own bedroll and dropped it against one of the large rocks. "Besides,…it's gettin' cold, and I can hardly keep my eyes open."

"Me, too,…but I'm still a bit worried. I keep thinking about that man, Snake. He could be around here somewhere. And like you said,… he will be going back for that treasure… I've been trying to figure out where he might go to recruit more men?"

"One of th' Forts'd be my guess,…there's always a few men hangin' around."

"Yeah,…maybe." Returned Rodney, slapping his hand against one of the heavy skins. "You know, they must have given us half of all the food they had left."

"Guess they figured they wouldn't need it." Sighed Billy sadly then went about gathering wood for a fire.

"You want to use some of it tonight?"

"No….I wouldn't be able to eat any of it,…we'll leave it with a Choctaw family somewhere."

"Good idea….You know, in spite of how all this turned out,…I'm glad I came with you. I'll never forget those people, especially White Buffalo,…he's everything you said he was, and I believe that's putting it mildly."

"Yes, sir." Grunted Billy as he stuffed dry grass under the dead wood and lit it. "He was a hell of a lot more than that…I'll never meet a greater man, Rod."

The lawman nodded in the darkness and slapped the heavy skin of food again, and was suddenly surprised at how hard it felt,… and curious, he untied the leather strap that was holding the skins in place behind the saddle and pushed them over the rump of the horse, letting them drop to the ground behind the animal.

He squatted and untied the rawhide strap from the top of one of them and allowed the contents to tumble out onto the ground. "Billy," He gasped loudly. "You might want to take a look at this!"

Billy looked across at the lawman and then, also curious, grunted to his feet and walked toward him. "I might want a see wha…" His voice caught in his throat, and his breath left him at sight of the large nuggets. He quickly scanned the tops of the dark ravine, then removed his hat and squatted down beside the breathless lawman.

Rodney handed him a large chunk of the precious metal. The nugget was as large as his fist and quite heavy as he hefted it. "Son of a Bitch, Rod!"

"Yeah!" Grinned Rodney. "There must be over a hundred pounds in this sack alone, not counting what's in the other one!"

Billy turned to stare at the bulging skins behind his own saddle and swallowed. His heart was pounding as he looked back at the gold on the ground. "No wonder th' horses are winded,…they've been carryin' double all this tine!" He looked back up at the rim of the gully. "Better tie it back, Rod,…we'll move it against them rocks by th' fire till we leave…Never know who might be watchin' us."

Rodney nodded and quickly replaced the nuggets then tied the strap around the top again. It took them both to move the heavy sacks into the rocks at the clay wall of the gully, then they quickly went to where the Roan was tethered.

"White Buffalo was not only a great man." Grunted Rodney as they lifted the heavy skins from across the mare's rump. "He was damned appreciative!" They pulled the heavy sacks along the ground and placed them beside the other two. Then they both straitened and stared down at them.

"There's a ton of money there, Billy." He sighed, and then also searched the rim of the ravine. "Sort of changes things a little, don't it?"

"It changes things a lot!" Breathed Billy. "Snake and them three could be anywhere out here."

"And that's not counting your average, everyday outlaw." Grinned the lawman. "This country's full of them, too."

Billy nodded, still checking the high rim of the wide ravine. "We'll let th' packhorse tote it when we leave here, we can carry th' supplies on our horses."

Rodney nodded, then turned and went back to the packhorse. Billy watched him leave, then went to unsaddle the Roan, dropping the saddle beside the skins, then used the blanket to rub down her sore back. Once done, he went and did the same for the lawman's horse as Rodney stripped the supplies from the pack animal.

The fire was crackling when Rodney placed the beans and pork on the flames to heat and then, with a cold biscuit in his mouth, he moved back against the rocks with Billy and sat down. He studied Billy's bearded face for a moment, watching as he rolled and lit his thin cigarette.

"How are we gonna explain all of this?" He asked then bit into the cold bread.

Billy blew smoke from his lungs and looked at him. "Been thinkin' about that….Couple of weeks ago, you told everybody we was goin huntin'….Who's to say we didn't happen on a cave full a gold?"

"We got too much gold for that, Billy,…God, nobody would believe it!… We're talking about maybe four hundred pounds of pure gold here! We lay that much gold on 'em, folks would be flocking up here by the thousands looking for it!"

"Then we'll just have to be smart about it." He blew smoke from his lungs and stared up at the opposite rim of the ravine. "We'll have to hide it." He looked back at the lawman then. "Sell it off a few pounds at a time,…and not in Paris, neither."

"Where we gonna hide that much gold, Billy, with our luck, sombody'd find it?"

"We can figure that out later." He thumped the spent butt at the fire and grunted to his feet. "Right now, we have to worry about keepin' it." He went to the fire, grabbed a tin plate and spooned beans and meat from the skillet then made room for Rodney as he went back to sit down.

"I got me a feeling." Grunted the lawman as he sat down again. "That once them bodies are found, there's gonna be another explosion in these hills,…and it'll be a lot louder than that one last night."

"Far reachin', too." Nodded Billy as he swallowed. "If th' Army's involved,…and we both know they are. I got me no desire to be here when them bodies are found."

"Amen to that!…What do you think might happen to the Choctaw up here?"

"They been survivin' for a long time, with next to nothin' to show for it." Said Billy as he forked more food into his mouth and chewed it. "Only difference is." He said as he swallowed. "They won't have their guardians around to protect them anymore,...and that's gonna make it a little rough for 'em."

"That's the worst part of it." Sighed Rodney, hearing the remorse in Billy's voice. "You do know we did everything we could up there, don't you?"

Billy nodded. "Except for not makin' sure that Snake was dead!...It was just such an unnecessary loss of life for somethin' good not to come of it,... and nothin' did!"

"Yeah, well, I don't have an answer for that one."

They ate in silence then, and once the food and tins were put away, they rolled out their bedding and set about dividing the supplies from the packhorse into canvass bags cut from the large tarp.

"I hope the packhorse can carry all that weight." Sighed Rodney as he got to his feet. "We still got the shovel and the pots and skillet to go on there."

"We can carry them, too....We'll just have to travel a little slower,...and hopefully stay out of too many of these damned ditches....She'll tote th load okay. Anyway,...I think we might ought'a take turns sleepin' just in case."

"It pays to be cautious." Nodded Rodney. "I'll take first watch,...I'm too rich to sleep anyway."

They were in the saddle again by daylight and urging the animals up out of the ravine and into the uneven foothills, and several hours later began seeing remote cabins in the lower and more level areas. But even though they were still in the clutches of the Kiamichi Wilderness, they thought it might be a bad idea to purposely let the local Choctaw see them,...especially now, so they gave the cabins a wide berth. They continued traveling in the wilds, fighting the raking brush and fallen timber. Deep gullies and twisting creeks that were still full from the storm's massive runoff, and each filled with limbs and branches from the wild Pecan Trees along their banks.

Billy continued taking the lead through the obstructive underbrush and thick stands of Pine Trees, breaking off the gouging branches before they could stab the horses in passing, and having to move aside the slapping, needle-laden limbs of the giant trees. Deadly shale, stones were dangerously hidden beneath the blanket of tall prairie grass and dead needles and several times, he had almost decided to take one of the roads that twisted southward below them, but because of their cargo, decided against that, also.

They had seen even more of the rundown shacks alongside the roads, but a lot of them had appeared deserted, and some had been burned and once, Rodney had spotted six white men walking on one of the roads, and after discussing it, thought it best to leave them be, as they were still headed away from Devil Mountain…. and considering them lucky to have gotten away with their lives.

It was late that day when Billy decided to rest the horses again. They were almost out of the worst of the wilderness at this point, but looming in the distance were the grim-looking Seven Devils Mountains. Billy dismounted beneath the heavily needled branches of a tall Pine and tied the mare's reins to one of them before going back to the drooping packhorse.

Rodney joined him there as he was inspecting the animal's back. Even with the thick padding of blankets, the wide leather straps had rubbed it's back pretty raw,…and Billy shook his head as he held the blankets up for the lawman to see.

"What do you suggest we do about it?" Sighed Rodney.

"I don't know,…remember what th' old prospectors used on them donkey's backs,…it was made'a wood, and they hung their supplies on both sides of it?"

"Think we can make one?"

Well, there's plenty of dead wood around here,…we can give it a try….If we don't do somethin', she's gonna give plumb out on us."

Straining tired muscles, they hefted the dead weight from the animal's sore back, then set about finding the strongest and shortest branches they could find in the tall grass and once they figured out how to construct the crude device, tied it together with several long pieces of canvass cut from the tarp.

"What do you think, Billy?"

"If we use all th' blankets, it might work." He nodded then looked around them at the maze of trees. "What say we stay right here for a spell, eat a cold meal and leave when th' moon comes up?"

"Sounds good to me." Groaned the lawman, I'm tired of being poked in the ribs anyway….Never saw so many limbs on the ground."

— ⁓

The moon was full, and high in the sky when they loaded the gold and then, mounting their cold saddles, headed south once again under a yellow orb that was full and bright, making travel in the unforgiving terrain a little easier, and made the trees and rocks stand out a little eerily in the shadows,… and those shadows were already playing their usual tricks on their eyes.

But after studying the surrounding landscape, Billy reined the Roan into and through the tall grass with its loose shale, having to maneuver around the many sharp rocks and prickly Mesquite with the only sounds being that of groaning saddle leather, the pinging of shod hoofs on the loose rocks and the occasional huffing and snorting from the animals. They made their way slowly across the high, uneven ground for the better part of an hour before finding themselves on a downhill slant again, and yet another hour of picking their way through large rocks and trees found them about to enter a thick grove of tall Pines,... and it was at that point that Billy saw the mare flick her ears forward in the moonlight and raised his hand for the lawman to stop.

He watched the Roan intently for a time, as she had raised her head and was staring at the trees below them.

He sat and searched the dark trees and then looking back at Rodney, dismounted and went to stand at the Mare's head.

"You hear something?" Breathed the lawman at his elbow,

"She did,...and I've learned to pay attention to it. I think we ought a walk on down through them trees, Rod....And keep your wits about you,...you hear th' mare whinny, you stop."

They carefully descended the hill and entered the stand of Pines, painstakingly working their way through the thick underbrush, leading the animals behind them ever deeper into the darkness. For several long minutes, they slapped at the large mosquitoes and pushed aside needle-sharp nettles as they moved through the jungle of trees,...and bleeding from their wounds, were nearing the edge of the grove when the Roan snorted loudly, the familiar sound stopping both of them in their tracks to listen intently for any sound that would tell them someone was there. Billy draped the reins over a branch and made his way back to Rodney.

"What time do you think it is, Rod?"

"I don't know,...maybe three,...why?"

"I don't like walkin' into somethin' I can't see....Let's tie up here and go on alone." Then, with the lawman behind him, they moved silently past the Roan and through the underbrush, enduring frequent slaps to the face from probing branches before finally coming to the floor of a small canyon.

Stopping well within the trees, they slowly scanned the moonlit expanse of the canyon's rocky floor and at last, spotted the small flickering fire in some rocks at the base of a tall bluff, and then were able to make out the dark forms of sleeping men in the deeper shadows.

"How many?" Whispered Rodney.

Billy shook his head. "Can't tell from here." They heard the stamping of restless horses then, placing them somewhere off to the left of the sleeping men. He moved to the edge of the clearing and went to his knees to peer around the trunk of a large Pine before moving back with the lawman. "Six horses, I think." He turned and studied the canyon floor again, then stared at the large rocks in front of him. A lone Pine Tree stood next to the rocks, casting it's shadow from there to where they were standing.

"There's got to be at least one guard out there somewhere,...and it's prob'ly a Comanche, one of them horses was an Indian pony, couldn't see th' others that clearly."

"What do we do then?"

Billy studied the terrain again, then nodded at the rocks. "Them rocks there ain't ten feet in front of us....If we take it slow, and stay in th' shadows, we could make it." He looked at Rodney and saw him nod, then slowly moved to the edge of the clearing and went to his hands and knees, and then slowly crawled toward the rocks, careful to stay well within the shadow of the tree. Huge rocks and broken timber were everywhere along the uneven ground, and he knew there could be a guard behind any one of them. It briefly occurred to him, that he was a rich man, and should just go back to the horses and leave, but then he remembered that Snake had eluded the warriors, and it could be him in those rocks.

He crawled in behind the rock's protection and waited while Rodney moved in beside him and then, using the tree for cover, he stood up behind it to study the campsite again before holding up four fingers for Rodney to see. There were six horses and only four men accounted for, and his heart was racing as he sat back down beside the lawman.

"We got us two guards out there somewhere." He whispered, then raised slightly above the rocks to search for them, straining his eyes at every rock and dead tree-trunk, but it was only when he looked back over Rodney's head that he saw the Indian.

The Comanche raised himself from behind a boulder, his rifle lowered as he silently watched them.

He felt the chill on the back of his neck then. "Don't move a muscle, Rod." He whispered. "There's an Indian with a rifle lookin' right at us,...and I don't think he's sure about who we are. But if he raises that rifle, I'm gonna kill 'im....So,...when I tell you, man, fall over sideways fast.."

The Comanche raised the rifle then. "Duck!" Hissed Billy, making his draw as he said it, and the impending shot shattered the pre-dawn stillness with an explosion that rocked the confines of the small canyon. The Indian grunted as he was pitched backward, and in that same instant, he saw the other Comanche and fired again, knocking him from the top of the rock, then breathless he dropped back down beside the lawman as the echoes rumbled slowly through the canyon.

More shots rang out then as bark and rock fragments stung their faces. The men were awake and had taken cover in the rocks where they slept.

"That worked out well, didn't it?" Breathed Billy as the shots died down.

"Leaves us in a tight spot, too." Blurted the lawman. "You think it might be Snake and that crooked Marshal?"

I don't know,….but they came from th' mountain, all right,…them was Comanche Indians."

"I hope we live long enough to find out, ain't much cover out there….. What's the plan now?"

"I'm fresh-out a plans, Rod."

"Then we're in real trouble….Even as cold as it is right now, that sun's gonna get pretty hot out here in the open like this,…and we left the water on the horses."

"They can't get to their horses, neither."

"Well, that makes me feel better." Muttered Rodney as he slowly raised himself above the rock for a look, but quickly ducked down again as a bullet took a portion of the rock away.

"That was a rifle!" He panted.

"We could sure use one about now." Returned Billy.

"Who th' hell's out there?" Yelled a voice from the bluff. "Stand up and show yourself, we'll hold our fire!"

"That's awful big of you, Snake!" Shouted Billy as he recognized the voice. "But I'd rather you come out!"

There was silence for a time as the morning sun began turning the sky to a crisp brilliance. But they were still in the shadows of the tall bluff, and the air was still quite cool.

"How do you know me?" Came the voice again. "I ain't used that name in years!"

"I met you once, a long time back."

"I doubt that,…if we had met, you wouldn't be here!"

"You think too much of yourself, Snake,…cause I'm still here. You could say I've been given a second chance!"

"For what, to die?"

"To correct my mistake…By th' way, you still fast on th' draw?"

Rodney watched Billy's face as he pushed fresh cartridges into the Colt pistol, thinking he was seeing a look that he hadn't seen since the raid on Sycamore, years before….The look of a gunman.

"You can find out easy enough!" Came the voice again. "Just step out from behind that rock and we'll see."

"Naww,…come to think about it, you weren't really all that fast anyway…. But tell me,…you been back to Rhone Springs, Texas lately?"

There was a pause while he thought about it, then."Never heard a Rhone

Springs!...What kind a game are you tryin' to play anyway? Who are you, God damn it?"

"What are you up to, Billy?" Whispered Rodney urgently.

He looked at the lawman. "I'm tryin' to bait 'im, Rod,...make 'im mad enough to come out a them rocks. Like you said,...it's gonna get hot out here before long."

"What's goin' on out there?" Yelled Snake. "Talk to me! Come on out where I can see you, hell, let's talk about this!"

"How's your gun-hand, Snake?...You know,...th' one you used to shoot with?" There was no immediate response from the rocks, and he looked at Rodney. "Keep an eye on their horses, if they try for 'em, we'll have to rush 'em."

"Have to, is right!" Breathed the lawman. "Be a hell of a shot with a handgun."

Grinning slightly, Billy raised up for a look at the bluff. "Hey, Snake!...It was me that crippled your right hand, don't you remember?...It was th' day I Beat you to th' draw?"

"Yoy're a fuckin' liar!" Snake's voice was laced with anger now.

"Come on now, Snake, you remember th' saloon at Rhone Springs, don't ya?...I sure as hell do!...They used to call me Th' Reb, Snake,...course that was in th' old days. I ain't used that handle in a long time, neither....But what's in a name, right?" He grinned at Rodney then.

"That name ring a bell, Snake?...It jar your memory any?"

"It don't mean a fuckin' thing to me!"

"It meant somethin' to Jason Ryker!...Course, he weren't all that fast, neither. He's dead now, you know,...I killed him!"

"You Son of a Bitch!" Yelled Snake.

"Might be, Snake!...But I'm th' best you ever went up against, and you know what?...I still am!"

"Come out from behind that rock and we'll see about that!"

"That wouldn't be too smart, Snake,...not with three rifles pointed at me....You send those three out without any hardware and I'll oblige ya!"

You got men with you, too,...send them out first!"

"There's only one man with me, Snake,...and he won't interfere. You ain't got much choice here, ya know, you try for them horses and we'll kill you!...On th' other hand,...if we try for ours, you'll prob'ly kill us!...So what we got here is a good old-fashioned standoff,...so what do you say?...Send those men out unarmed and we can settle this?"

"You go to hell!"

"Okay, Snake,...but th' only way you're ever gonna ride away from here, is to kill me!...And while you think about that, think about this, too,...You'll never get your hands on that treasure while I'm alive!"

"You that Bastard from th' cave?"

"That, I am, Snake,...But I ain't no Bastard,...I had a Mother and a Father,...till you helped kill 'em....And you know what else?...This man here with me killed your other Boss,...what was his name?...Oh, yeah, Ben Lang,... you remember him, don't you?"

Billy's face was red with anger as he sat back down against the rock. The sun was clearing the bluff now, and the crisp morning air was already beginning to heat up. Billy leaned forward and shrugged out of the long coat then folded it and placed it on the ground beside him.

"Do you know what you're doing, Billy?"

Billy shrugged. "He's th' last one, Rod,...he raped my mother and then killed her!" He sighed then, and looked at the lawman. "You know a better way?"

Rodney shook his head. "can you beat him?"

Billy shrugged. "He had to learn to shoot left-handed, hell,....I beat 'im handily once, no reason I can't do it again."

"I could try and get behind them,...I could use the rocks for cover?"

"They've got rifles, Rod....It ain't worth th' risk."

"Well, what's to keep one of them from getting up on that bluff there,... they could see us real good from up there?"

"We'll just have to take our chances and hope they won't think about that."

Suddenly, loud voices caused them to chance a look over the rock, then more angry voices came to them.

"It's th' only way, Buck!" Argued Snake as Buck got to his feet.

"Well, you can go to hell!" Shouted Buck. "I ain't about to go out there without my gun,...you're crazy!" He backed up and pointed his finger at Snake. "I was crazy for joinin' up with you in th' first place, so I'm quittin',... I'm gonna get on my horse and get away from th' likes a you,...and you can't stop me!"

"Come on, Buck." Argued Snake, suddenly standing up. "I can beat that Son of a Bitch, trust me."

"How?" Yelled Buck. "He done beat you once!"

Snakes voice was too low for them to hear what was said, but then Buck suddenly yelled and went for his gun. Snake drew and fired as Buck's weapon came up, pitching him back into the rocks and out of sight.

"Looks like you're a man short now, Snake!" Yelled Billy and sat back down against the rock. "I'm gettin' to 'im." He grinned, looking at the lawman.

The morning was passing slowly as they waited, and already getting quite warm in the canyon. Billy was leaning against the trunk of the Pine and watching the bluff, and for the next half-hour, there wasn't a sound from Snake, or his men and he was beginning to think they had made a run for it on foot, when…

"You still out there, Reb, or whatever th' hell your name is?"

"Why?" Yelled Billy. "You make your mind up?…Hell, I'd done thought you ran out on me!"

"My mind's made up,…but it ain't gonna happen your way!…And I never run from th' likes a you!"

"Okay,…what's your plan then?"

"The two of you against th' three of us….You don't go for that, you can kiss my ass!"

Billy looked at Rodney then. "You up for this?"

Rodney nodded. "That's why I'm here."

Billy nodded, then raised above the rock. "It's your call, Snake….We'll come out when you do, cause I sure don't want a kiss your nasty ass."

"We're standin' up right now, you Bastard!" Yelled the gunman.

Billy nodded at Rodney, and they both stood up as the three men came out of the rocks, and then moved out into the open area to meet them. The two men with Snake moved out several feet on either side of him.

"How's your gun hand?" Breathed Rodney.

"A mite stiff today, why?"

Rodney stared at him. "You let me get killed today, and you'll answer to Connie for it."

Billy grinned tightly at him. "Watch yourself."

"That phony Marshal's all mine." Said the lawman as they moved a few yards closer to the men and stopped.

"Well," Nodded Snake. "It was you in that cave,…how come them fuckin' birds didn't attack you?"

"God damn, Snake!" He laughed.…."They cut you up pretty good, didn't they?

"Fuck you!…What th' hell was you doin' up there anyway?"

"We came for th' gold, like you did,…except that we got it!….The Chief's a friend of ours." He was still watching Snake's unblinking stare, and the thin man's eyes were hard and unforgiving as he looked from Billy, to Rodney, then back again. "Well, I don't think you got any of that gold." Said Snake thinly. "But I'm gonna have me that treasure,… right after we kill you, because I'm gonna blow that fuckin' mountain apart!"

Billy only grinned at him, further infuriating the gunman as the tension mounted between them. The seconds ticked away as they waited, and it was then that they heard the dull, loud thump, followed by a crisp yelp of pain,... and all this before the crack of a rifle echoed toward them.

All five of them stared up at the bluff in time to watch the man called Buck fall into the rocks behind Snake, his rifle falling into the dirt between them. And already startled, Billy almost missed the signal. He drew and fired as Snake's gun was clearing the holster, the slug driving the thin gunman into the Mesquite brush behind him. He then shot the second man as he was thumbing back the hammer on his gun, these explosions blending with that of Rodney's as both men fell. The noise was deafening inside the small canyon, but only for an instant as it echoed away in the distance.

"You're a damned sudden man, Billy Upshur!" Breathed Rodney, still staring at the dead Marshal's body. "I was almost worried."

"You had a right to be,....old Buck there had a bead on one of us."

They holstered their weapons and walked the twenty yards to where the would-be sniper had fallen. Buck lay grotesquely in the rocks, one leg bent unnaturally beneath his body, his head crushed, bludgeoned against the rocks as he hit the ground.

"Had us completely fooled, didn't they?" Sighed Rodney, and it was then that they heard the Crows, but when they looked, failed to see them. "Guess they're still keeping an eye on us."

"Maybe." Nodded Billy as he scanned the canyon's distant walls. "But I'm wonderin' who fired that shot?"

"Well, it came from a long ways off, I know that." Returned Rodney. "I heard the bullet hit him, well before we heard the shot." He stared at the distant rim also and shook his head. "But nobody could make a shot like that,...that's got to be more than eight hundred yards away, maybe a thousand."

"No,...but Peter could,...and he did!" Grinned Billy, suddenly pointing at a high crag of wind-polished rock above the pines, where the slight figure of a man was holding a long rifle above his head with both hands. Billy raised his arm in the air as Peter lowered the gun and disappeared from sight. "Thank you, Peter." He sighed, then turned back to look at the dead man again. "That was a hell of a shot."

"So, that was Peter." Grinned Rodney. "How'd he know where to find us?"

"You, yourself said th' Crows were keepin' an eye on us, Rod."

"The Crows brought him?...Well, I'll be damned!" Rodney shook his head and looked questioningly at Billy. "Who is Peter, anyway?...I've heard you talk about him, but,...just who is he?"

"Peter's a man-hunter,...used to track for that crooked lawman over there. He's just a trail-wise little Choctaw Indian tracker,...and a damned good man that just saved one, maybe both our lives." He turned then and walked toward the bodies. "We got us six men to bury, Rod,...come on."

"I'll go get the horses." Said Rodney and headed back to the trees.

Billy watched him jog past the rocks, then automatically reached for the Durham sack, and as he fumbled for the book of brown papers in his shirt, he squatted down next to the body of Snake and spotted the slender cigar in his vest-pocked, and grinning, put the tobacco sack away.

"Thanks, Snake, I don't mind if I do." He slid the long cigar from the vest then dug a match from his shirt and lit it, inhaling the strong smoke as he stared at the hateful, blank face of the gunman, and at the same time,... wished fervently that he could kill him again. He had led the raid that killed his mother and father, and he was responsible for every man that died at Devil Mountain, inside, and out.

He blew smoke at the bloodless face and remembered that day in Rhone Springs, Texas. The day he had spared his worthless life. One time, one fleeting moment in time, he had grown tired of the killing and turned away from it,...and in so doing, allowed this piece of worthless garbage to live,... the very man that would someday destroy a whole race of people, and one of the greatest men he'd ever met. He pulled again on the strong smoke, briefly wondering if it had been his own decision to let him live back then?

"Well, whatever it was, you paid th' price this time, you miserable piece of shit!" He grunted and got to his feet. "You made me pay for it, too, damn you,...so, rot in hell, you Son of a Bitch!" He clamped the cigar in his teeth and began collecting the weapons and gun-belts, buckled them together and draped the holstered pistols over a large rock before collecting the rifles. He went through all of their pockets and placed what money he found atop the rock also,... but he pocketed the two half-empty sacks of smoking tobacco, as well as the silver Marshal's badge from the shirt of the dead lawman.

He had just dragged the second of the two Comanche in beside the others when Rodney led the horses out of the trees and came toward him. "Took you long enough."

"I hadn't herd the mare's greeting, I might never of found them."

"Well, pitch me th' spade and I'll start diggin'." He searched the high walls of the canyon as Rodney untied the shovel and brought it to him. "Thanks,,...you might tie them rifles together and hang 'em from your saddle-horn,...hang th' gun-belts on mine....Oh yeah, I saved you that Marshal's badge, you might want a send it to his boss."

"Yeah, I'll do that very thing....But tell me why we're gonna bury this trash, none of them deserve it?"

"That's a fact." Said Billy, looking again at the canyon's high walls. "But them shots would have been heard for miles,...and besides, he was waitin' here for somebody.....Maybe this was where they planned to regroup if somethin' went wrong, I don't know,...but if they don't find anybody here, maybe they'll leave th' Nations."

"No markers then?"

"Nope,...flat ground's all they're gonna find."

It took the better part of an hour to bury all six men, and between filling the graves with the red sand, and watching the trees and bluffs, both were exhausted.

"It's too damned hot for this!" Breathed Rodney, going to replace the shovel on the packhorse. "And a hell of a lot better than they deserve."

"Yeah." Agreed Billy as he scattered dried branches over the flat surfaces of the graves. "There's enough dead bodies in these hills.....But these six won't be leavin' any more of 'em...Better go turn their horses loose, Rod, and make sure you run 'em out a th' canyon, I want it to appear like Snake didn't wait for whoever comes lookin'."

Rodney nodded and mounted his horse, dropped the pack animal's lead rope and galloped off toward the tethered horses.

Billy took the cigar butt from his mouth and looked at it, then tossed it away and rolled and lit another Durham before checking the cinches on the Roan, then went to check the heavy skins on the packhorse and was satisfied that the makeshift rack of dried sticks were doing the job they had hoped for. He looked again at the crag of rock where Peter had stood then shook his head as he went on to retrieve the coats they had left in the rocks.

— —

He was in the shade of the bluff and smoking when he saw Rodney returning then walked across to the Roan. He was in the saddle when the lawman rode in beside him to take the halter rope and Mackinaw from him.

"I thought all the Comanche had left?' Said Rodney as he draped the heavy coat across his saddle and searched the canyon's rim. "Wonder how many more are still up here?"

"Some, maybe...But with Snake dead, they won't have anybody to lead 'em, so they'll all prob'ly go home now." He looked one last time at the gravesite. "And Snake was a leader, Rod,...we got a give th' Son of a Bitch that."

"Yeah, that was obvious." Sighed Rodney. "I'm still worried about what the Army might do to the Choctaw over this....I know we've already talked about it, but I can't get it out of my mind."

"Ain't a hell of a lot they can do to 'em,…they put 'em here….Gonna confuse th' hell out of 'em, though,…th' Choctaw ain't armed."

"What about Peter,… he was?"

"I think they all might be armed, Rod,…they just keep 'em hid when th' Army's about,…and as for Peter,…he worked for that Marshal. I'm sure he arranged for 'im to have a permit to keep one."

"Well," Sighed the lawman. "I hope you're right about all this, cause I'm sure tired of being here….Let's go."

"I'm all for that." Nodded Billy. "Oh, I found papers in that Marshal's shirt….Name was Thomas Leroy Thompson,…worked for Judge Isaac Parker over in Van Buren, Arkansas,…and I wish to hell I could tell th' Judge how he died, too,…and why!"

"I'll take care of that." Returned Rodney. "From what I've heard, Judge Parker would have hung him himself, if he knew about this."

"I guess th' Marshal took one look at that map of Snakes' and decided he was in th' wrong business." He twisted around in the saddle to scan the canyon again before looking back at the lawman. "I think we ought a get away from here now,…I've got that tinglin' on th' back of my neck again,…felt it when we was buryin' Snake,…and it always means trouble."

Rodney quickly looked toward the rim of the canyon again. "The Crows are back." Both of them watched the large birds as they circled above the cliffs.

"Wonder who they're bringing this time?" Commented Rodney.

"Maybe they're tryin' to tell us they're already here…let's go." He prodded the Roan into motion past the gravesite and on through the broken terrain toward the eastern end of the twisting canyon, and a half-hour later, they were leaving it behind them completely. But then, feeling the chill again, he stopped the mare to turn and stare at the timber along the canyon's walls behind them.

"What's wrong?" Asked the lawman, also looking back. "You see something?"

"No,…but we're bein' watched by somebody." He reached up to rub his neck as he spoke.

"How do you know,…I don't see a thing?…Oh, yeah,… the tingling again."

Billy ignored him. "They're either not close enough yet,…or they're keepin' out a sight,…but they're there."

"Maybe it's Peter."

"It ain't Peter's way." He continued to search the distant, rocky floor of the canyon, but couldn't see a thing out of place there.

"We gonna wait 'em out?"

"Not here." He reined the mare back to the task of climbing to the crest above them and at last were entering a forest of giant Pines as they continued southward in the welcome shade of the trees. It was already quite hot now, and they kept to the trees and picked their way through them carefully so as not to have to fight the tangled underbrush.

The tingle in his neck was still there, however, and it worried him. Whoever was tailing them were staying out of sight and keeping their distance. They continued along the tree-lined ridge for another hour before he made the decision to wait for whoever was there, and reined the mare into a cluster of large Firs to wait for the lawman to join him.

"You still got that feeling?" Asked Rodney as he twisted around to look behind them. "I still don't see anything."

"They're there." He said and looked at the tree-lined slopes ahead of them. "And we're due to run out of open ground." He dismounted and leaned against the Roan. "You got that telescope handy?"

"Yeah, right here." Rodney pulled it free of the saddlebags and passed it over the mare's back. "What's on your mind?"

"Stayin' alive to spend my gold." He grinned, then rested his arm across the saddle and raised the glass. "I want to know who I'm dealin' with, too."

Several minutes passed before he shook his head and turned the glass over to Rodney, then rolled and lit a smoke, drawing the relaxant into his lungs as he idly watched back the way they had come. His mind turned to White Buffalo and the stronghold then and he shook his head to rid himself of the thoughts. Instead, he looked at the bulging skins of gold on the packhorse. He was a very rich man now, and the possibilities of his family's future was unending,...thanks to that great man. It was just too much to comprehend and sighing, he shook his head again and looked at the lawman.

"Anything yet?"

"Nope,...wait a minute!...Yeah, I saw something move just then." He gave the glass back to Billy and pointed. "Just in the edge of the trees down there,... about a thousand yards out."

Billy quickly searched the area along the distant line of trees.

"You see 'im?"

"Yeah,...it's a Comanche Indian,...and he's readin' our sign." He paused then and searched the trees behind the tracker. "One, two, three, there's six men sittin' in th' trees behind 'im." He lowered the telescope and looked at the lawman.

"What do you want'a do?" Urged Rodney. "Think we can outrun 'em?"

Billy shook his head. "Not with that Indian trackin' us....This must be who Snake was waitin' for back there."

"Then they must have seen us leaving the canyon."

"Didn't have to see us, with that damn Indian along….But I got a think they likely did,… and when Snake wasn't there to meet 'em,…they got curious….Especially, if they found th' blood." He lowered the glass and pulled himself back into the saddle.

"Okay,…what's the plan?"

"We have to find better cover to fight from,…come on."

It was late in the day when, scratched, bruised and mosquito bitten, they rode out of the worst of the underbrush and thick trees and into the waist-high prairie-grass of a large clearing. The ground was broken and slightly rolling, and crisscrossed with wide cracks and even deeper gullies,…and large rocks protruded tauntingly above the waving grass. But still Billy led the way toward another thicket of Pecan and giant Fir, some six or seven hundred yards to the South of them.

Finally arriving, Billy moved several yards inside the grove, then dismounted and moved back to the edge of the trees to use the telescope again. Rodney tied off the animals and joined him there with rifle in hand, and they watched the distant trees intently for a good half-hour before seeing the Indian. The Comanche had stopped his pony just inside the trees on the far North side of the prairie.

"Persistent Son of a Bitch,…I'll give 'im that!" Said Billy and passed the glass to Rodney. "Have a look." He knew they would be overtaken sometime after dark, and then likely ambushed. And with that extra weight on the packhorse, they had no chance to outrun them. He sighed heavily then and walked back to the Roan to slide the long-barreled Henry Rifle out of the boot, pushing fresh cartridges into the magazine as he rejoined the lawman.

"How are you at long range shooting, Rod?"

"I'll do, why?...We gonna fight 'em here?"

"No,…but we're gonna get rid a that Indian before he gets close enough to smell us,…if he ain't already. Those men might turn and run without 'im."

Rodney nodded then took the rifle from him and levered a shell into the chamber, and then, bracing his arm against the tree, he placed the barrel of the rifle across a lower branch, adjusted the sights and took aim down the length of the long barrel.

Only the Comanche's head was visible over the waving grass and only then, when he moved, but the shadows of the trees, and the distance involved made him a questionable target at most.

"I can't see enough of him to chance a shot." Breathed Rodney.

"It's too far anyway." Said Billy quickly, still watching him with the telescope. "If he ain't already spooked, he'll come closer,…he knows this is a good place for an ambush, and he'll wait till he thinks its safe."

The Comanche sat his pony in the shadows for several minutes then finally he leaned from the pony's back to study the tracks in the grass before coming out.

"Here he comes, Rod,...get ready."

The Indian's progress was agonizingly slow, his eyes were constantly moving from the tracks in the grass, to the land around him and back again.

"Cautious Bastard, ain't he?" Whispered the lawman. "How far away is he now?"

"Set your sights at five hundred yards, he's about a quarter-way across,... and make it count, Rod,...you won't get a second shot."

The lawman sighted down the octagonal length of the barrel and waited for several long seconds before he was able to see the Comanche's upper torso and the pony's bobbing head above the grass.

"Any tine you're ready, Rod, and remember,...if he smells an ambush, he'll hightail it so fast, you won't get a chance at 'im."

Rodney got a firmer grip on the rifle, and when the Indian stopped again to check the tracks, he fired.

The sudden explosion of sound in the clearing was deafening, and rolled like thunder across the hills. Still using the long glass, Billy watched as the Comanche was lifted from the back of his pony and thrown over its spotted rump to disappear in the grass, then continued to watch the trees on the clearing's far side for several more minutes.

"You see anything?" Asked Rodney, a little breathless.

Billy shook his head as he continued to watch the trees and then, after a few more minutes of seeing nothing but trees, he lowered the glass. "I can't tell if they left or not,...there's nothin' moving out there....Let's get out a here, Rod,...they might have pinpointed our location by the sound of that shot." Billy took the Rifle from him, and after the lawman retrieved his own, they walked back to the horses and mounted.

"That road with th' burned-out cabin should be due South of us somewhere,...I think its time we found it and got th' hell out a these mountains."

"I'm right behind you." Said the lawman. "But what about those men,... you think they'll come after us?"

"I ain't got a clue,...we'll just have to deal with it when it comes." He reined the Roan into the trees again, with Rodney and the packhorse behind him. The travel was slow in the dense growth of brush and rotting timber, having to skirt around those obstacles many times while in and out of the deep gullies and fast-running, rock infested creeks.

It was still steaming hot in the low areas of the thickets, and even though the sun was almost down, it wasn't cooling off very quickly,… and the large mosquitoes were swarming badly, causing both of them to continually slap at them with their hats. Billy replaced his hat as they came to the rim of a deep, narrow ravine, and after seeing no way to go around it, urged the Roan down the embankment into a foot or so of trickling water, then continued along the rocky floor until he found a way out again. He urged the tired mare up the steep embankment into the trees again, glad to find himself on an upward climb toward higher ground. It was almost an hour later when he stopped on the crest of the wooded hill and twisted around to check on the lawman.

"How you makin' it, Rod?" He asked as Rodney pulled up behind him.

"I ain't got any blood left, if that's what you mean,….and I'm cold." He shook out the fleece-lined coat and pulled it on.

"What say we find us a place to stop for th' night?…Maybe on high ground, so we can watch our back-trail?"

"That never sounded better to me, Man,…let's do it!"

Billy led off through the trees again and it wasn't long before he found a good spot for a camp, deciding on a cluster of large rocks at the base of a high, clay bluff. He got Rodney's attention and pointed at it with a swing of his arm, then reined the mare up the fifty yards or so of incline to dismount in the rocks.

"Good place." Commented Rodney as he dismounted. "I'm a tired little cowboy, too, I hope to tell ya."

Billy was already scanning the trees below them with the telescope. "At least we got th' advantage of high ground here."

"Think we might have lost them,…it's been a while now?"

"If we didn't, we'll know soon enough." Returned Billy as he lowered the glass. "Lets us unload them animals tonight, Rod, maybe rub 'em down, they need it."

"I'd say so." Returned Rodney. "I take it you didn't see anything down there?"

Billy shook his head. "In a way, I'd feel better if I had." He went to the Roan and slid the long glass into the saddlebag, then lifted the supplies and weapons from around the saddle-horn and dropped them at the base of the bluff. He then released the cinch-strap and pulled the saddle from her sore back, saddlebags and all and placed that against the bluff before using the blanket to briskly rub her down.

Once Rodney had his horse unsaddled, they lifted the heavy skins of gold from the back of the packhorse and pulled them along the dry ground to rest against the bluff as well.

"If I had to load them up again, right now, I couldn't do it." Gasped Rodney. "God, that's a lot of gold."

A short time later, they were sitting against the large skins and silently chewing on cold bread and dried pork as they strained their eyes at the dark trees below them. The night birds were out and loud as darkness descended full upon them. The gray killers were also on the prowl,… they could hear the pack's mournful howling.

"That's an eerie sound." Shuddered Rodney as he took a drink from his canteen.

"Nothin' eerie about a pack of wolves." Returned Billy. "But I think we ought a move th' horses in here under th' bluff." They grunted to their feet and went to where the animals were feeding on the lush, dry grass, gathered the reins and halter rope and led them under the bluff, tying them to the heavy skins there. "This won't stop 'em if they're hungry enough." He said as he sat back down. "But at least we can fight 'em off easier."

"The damn things scare me." Shuddered the lawman again.

"Wolf won't hurt you unless he's cornered."

"No,…but he could make me hurt myself!…I don't know what it is,… they just sound so,…haunted."

"Haunted?"

"Well, yeah,…for the lack of a better word….They remind me of those men at the Mountain, wolf-lean and mean as hell!…Makes me wonder how many of those fellas actually got away?"

"Well, there was six, we saw walkin', six at th' canyon, and the six that was trackin' us….Eighteen got away, that we know of and we killed seven, countin' th' tracker….That leaves eleven that got away clean."

"You think you're funny, don't you?" He chuckled. "That ain't what I meant."

"I know what you meant….I just hope we don't see any more of 'em."

"Amen to that!….This, my friend,… will be one hell of a messy cover-up."

"That's for sure." Sighed Billy. "Washington's gonna have to get involved in this one, and when it does,…I'd sure hate to be th' guilty soldiers….But you know what th' worst part is, Rod?…I could a prevented this whole damn thing, four years ago, if I'd only killed that Bastard in Rhone Springs."

"That's one of life's greatest mysteries, Billy,…none of us knows what the future will bring,…and I don't think I even want to. If it hadn't been Snake that found that map, though, it might a been somebody else….It wasn't your fault."

"Yeah, well,…it don't help a hell of a lot, but thanks anyway….You want first watch?"

Rodney laughed. "How'd I know that was coming?"

"You're th' one too rich to sleep, remember?" He started to grin then, but suddenly waved his hand at the lawman for silence as the telltale clink of iron on rock sounded again. "Shod horses." He whispered and quickly got to his feet. The Roan uttered a low whinny then also, causing him to stare down at the trees where she was looking.

Rodney was on his feet now, and both of them moved in close to the animals to keep them quiet.

"Can't see a damned thing in th' dark." Breathed Billy. "Keep your eyes peeled at them trees on th' right there."

The seconds ticked slowly by while they waited, but they couldn't hear the clink of iron anymore and knew that whoever was there had heard the Roan. The mournful howling of wolves came to them again, causing the horses to snort restlessly and paw at the ground and prompted Billy to quickly grab the mare's nose to keep her quiet,... and that's when he was startled by the muffled voice.

"Heloooo, th' camp!" Came a gruff voice from the darkness of the trees. "Anybody up there?...We mean you no harm?"

Billy looked at Rodney in the dark then moved away from the Roan.

"What are you doing?" Whispered Rodney.

"They know we're here,...and we don't know who they are, or where they're at....Just be ready." He moved out of the bluff's deep shadows, his eyes still on the trees, then pulled and cocked the Colt.

"Show yourselves!" Called Billy Suddenly. "And state your business here." He stiffened then as the vague figure of a man stepped out of the trees and climbed the grade toward him.

"Name's Slade." Said the man. Clifford Slade." He came up to stop a few feet in front, and below Billy. "You can put away your gun, Mister,...we ain't lookin' for any trouble."

"We?"

Slade nodded his head back down at the trees. "Got three men with me,... down in them trees there."

Billy studied the man in the darkness, wishing he could see his face. "What is it you want, Mister Slade?"

"I don't know,...some company, somethin' to eat, maybe,...some directions?"

"Directions to where?"

"I'd rather discuss that over some supper, if you don't mind,...it's been a while since we had anything to eat?"

Billy glanced toward the bluff and then back at Slade. "Okay, Mister Slade,...I never turn a hungry man away,...call 'em in."

"We do thank you kindly." Said Slade as he turned toward the trees. "Bring th' horses in, boys, we're gonna eat." He climbed the last few feet to level ground, hesitated to look at Billy, then walked ahead of him toward the bluff.

Rodney, having heard the sketchy conversation, already had a small fire in preparation and was watching as Slade came into the rocks, then watched as Billy moved on to stand in front of the bluff.

Slade turned to look at Billy as he squatted down by the spreading blaze, then grinned up at Rodney. "I sure hope you got some strong coffee, Mister,... th' stronger, th' better?"

"I guess we can handle that." Said the lawman, getting up to fetch the pot, coffee and canteen of water from the supply sack. Coming back to the fire, he kept his eyes on Slade as he poured water and grounds into the pot then placed it in the fire to boil. "Beans and pork is all we got, Mister Slade."

"Ohhhh," He laughed. "That sounds damn good to us, man!"

Billy watched him in the fire's flickering light and could see the hard, unblinking eyes, eyes that didn't grin at all when the mouth did. Slade was a hard man, he decided, and one to watch closely. He looked then as the other three men led their horses into the light, stopping to tie them to a dead branch before walking on in to the fire. He nodded at them as they came on to squat down next to Slade, and then sighing, he turned and moved closer to the horses. Stopping in front of the skins of gold, he met Rodney's eyes and nodded slightly,...warning him to be on his guard.

Rodney nodded and looked across the fire at Slade as he sliced four thick slabs of dried pork into the skillet, then opened two cans of pre-cooked beans and poured them in with the pork. "Where you men headed?"

"Well,...I was sort a hopin', th' same place as you." Slade grinned and looked up at Billy. "We heard somebody up here was hirin' men to help find a mountain of gold,...but we got lost in these damn hills. Hell, you're th' first white men we've seen in a week."

Billy stooped to retrieve the tin cups and plates from the sack then watched the men closely as he walked the few feet to the fire. "If that's why you men are here." He said evenly. "You came all this way for nothin'." He gave Rodney the tins then watched Slade again. "Truth is,...we just came from up that way."

"And we couldn't wait to leave, neither!" Added Rodney.

"Why's that?" Asked Slade with narrowing eyes.

"Well,...I don't know about any mountain of gold." Shrugged Billy. "But we come on to about a hundred dead men some thirty miles North a here, bodies with a lot of arrows stickin' out of 'em." He shrugged again. "Nothin' up there, but buzzards, mountains and trees, Mister Slade,...and if there was any gold, we didn't see it."

"God damn it!" Cursed Slade and looked down at the fire. "What do you think happened?" He peered up at Rodney as he spoke.

"We were hoping you might tell us." Said Rodney. "But seeing as how you just got here, I guess not."

"You th' law, Mister?" Asked Slade, his eyes boring into those of Rodney.

Rodney moved his coat aside and nodded. "Federal Marshal out of McAllister....We heard the shooting up there from a long way off, but by the time we got there, dead men was all we found....And not a single dead Indian among 'em,...figure that one out."

"No bodies?" Stammered one of the other men.

"None,...a hell of a lot of unshod pony tracks, and some unused arrows layin' around." Rodney sighed loudly. "We're on our way now to report it to the Army at Fort Towson."

"That's why we had a cold camp here." Added Billy. "Been somebody tailin' us th' last couple of days....figured they might not want us to reach th' Fort."

"Jeesus, Slade,...maybe them stories we heard was truth!"

"God damn it, Sidney!" Snapped Slade. "I told you they ain't no such thing as ghost Indians. Ghosts don't kill people." He shook his head and grinned up at Billy, then jerked his head back at Sidney. "He's a superstitious Son of a Bitch!" He shook his head again, then grew serious. "Don't guess you found a map on any of them bodies, did ya?"

"A map?" Rodney shook his head. "I'm sorry, friend, we didn't search any of the bodies,...that's the Army's job.... What kind of map we talking about?"

"The man that wrote to me said they had a map to that gold mine."

"That would be strange." Said Rodney. "I don't recall anybody ever finding any gold in these mountains,...not that there ain't none, mind you."

"You are aware that th' Army's got a ban on white men comin' into these mountains?" Said Billy as a matter of fact.

Slade shook his head. "No,...I guess we didn't,...why is that?"

"Don't know why, exactly." Returned Rodney. "But when the Army finds out about that massacre up there, the Choctaw Nation will be closed tighter than old Dick's hatband,...at least till they get to the bottom of it."

"Them that done it are still in these mountains somewhere." Added Billy, still watching the men closely "And I think it might be in your best interest to trail on back out of here,... while you can."

"He's right as rain about that." Said Rodney, "Whatever those men were hunting up there, they shouldn't have been doing it,...because it got 'em killed. Ghost Indians or not, they're still dead,...and the only suspects we got are Indians."

"If you men just got here." Said Billy. "Mind tellin' us which way you came in?"

Slade stared at him narrowly then shook his head. "Don't mind a'tall.... We came down from up Arkansas way,...but we went too far South before turning North." He grinned then. "These mountains are a nightmare, my friend,....I do not envy a Marshalin' job in this wilderness, no'sir..... But ah,... why do you ask?"

"No particular reason." Shrugged Billy again.. "You see any activity around any of th' farms along th' way?"

"No,...Didn't see any farms a'tol, why?"

"Just curious,...we passed several cabins North of here, and some had been burned, and th' rest deserted....I'm thinkin' them Indians are killin' more than just white men up here. Because we buried a couple a Choctaw families at them burned out cabins."

Slade looked at Rodney then and grinned. "Would you mind showing me that badge again?"

Rodney hesitated a moment, then shrugged and moved his coat aside.

Slade nodded. "No offense, Marshal." He grinned. "It's just easier to believe a Federal Marshal, when he tells a wild story like this." He grinned up at Billy then. "And it is wild, you got a admit that."

Billy nodded. "It is that,...but so is yours....There's Choctaw farms all over the area you came through."

Slade grinned, then nodded. "You're right,...we seen the same thing you did, but none that was deserted, or burned....We even hailed a few, but they wouldn't come out."

"They're too scared to come out." Returned Billy. "And with good cause."

"You know something?" Grinned Slade. "I think you two are tryin' to accuse us of something....That what you're tryin' to do?"

Rodney shook his head and chuckled. "Nothing like that, Mister Slade.... We're lawmen,...we're just trying to determine how wide-spread this thing is, and all we've got, so far, is a lot of questions with no answers....By the way,...I've got to tell you, you're very perceptive,...where you from anyway,... if you don't mind my asking?"

Slade laughed out loud then, as did the other three men. "I don't mind a'toll, Marshal,...I'm known pretty well up around Cheyenne, so's Sidney there,..., Ben and Caleb, a little further North....That answer your question."

"Hope you brought your own plates and cups, Mister Slade." Grinned Rodney as he pulled the skillet away from the fire. "That answer yours?"

"Sure does." He grinned, then turned to the man behind him. "Go get 'th plates and cups, Sidney."

Rodney put food on Billy's plate and passed it to him, their eyes meeting once again in cautious understanding, then he filled his own plate and backed up to one of the rocks and sat down.

Billy moved back against the bluff and watched the men fill their plates and wolf the food down. He didn't believe any of Slade's story, except for the part about going to join up with Snake. He also knew they were not treasure hunters, and he knew they didn't give a damn about the possibility of Rodney being a Federal Marshal,....he also knew they were not planning on leaving empty-handed. He watched Slade's darting eyes as he ate, and they were everywhere, from Rodney, to him, to the horses,...and especially at the large, heavy-looking rawhide bags of gold.

"That was damn good!" Grinned Slade and wiped his bearded mouth on a coat-sleeve. He placed his plate on the ground and grinned again. "We're much-obliged to you gents." He looked across at Billy, then at the horses and waved his hand at them. "Good lookin' Roan,...she yours?"

"She's mine." Said Billy, bending to put his plate on the ground. "Who was it you was supposed to meet up here, Mister Slade,...to join up with this treasure-hunt, I mean. Can you give us his name?"

Slade stared at him, and his eyes were cold, and hard....But then he suddenly shook his head. "He's just th' man with th' map, that's all we was told."

Rodney put his plate down and went to the fire. "Coffee's done, Gents." He said, looking across at Billy again. "You men help yourselves." He poured Coffee into his and Billy's tin cup and got to his feet to watch as Slade and the other men poured theirs, then went to take Billy's to him. He dropped his hand down and moved the leather loop from the Walker's hammer before going back to sit down again to watch as the men sat back on their haunches to sip at the scalding liquid.

"There's good reason to believe the man you're looking for is dead, Mister Slade." Said Rodney, breaking the momentary silence. "And, like I said, The Army's going to shut this whole territory down when they hear what happened up here,...be a long time before they open it again, too....So, what do you plan on doing now?"

Slade stared up at him for a second, then shrugged. "Ain't decided yet, Marshal,...but tell me something. Do you really think it was Comanches killed those men up there?...I mean,...couldn't it have been somebody makin' it look like Indians done it? I thought all th' Indians up here was supposed to be on friendly terms,...peaceful, I mean,...on reservations and th' like?"

"They are." Returned Rodney. "All except Quanah Parker's bunch,...he's still raising hell like always….And to answer your other question,…white men don't ride unshod horses,…not in this wilderness."

"And you think they're still loose up here?"

Rodney nodded. "Dangerous as hell, too."

Slade shook his head in apparent disgust then looked across at Billy, paying close attention to the guns on his hip. "You a Marshal, too, are ye?"

Billy shook his head. "Farmer….I help th' Marshal out sometimes."

"Like in, Cotton, or potato Farmer,…or is it your name?"

Billy shrugged. "Just Farmer."

"You're mighty well-heeled for a farmer,…but I do like your set-up. You any good with 'em?"

Billy shook his head."Not very,…are you?"

Slade grinned. "Fair,…just fair."

"Okay!" Said Rodney suddenly. "Mister Slade, we got us enough outlaws loose in these mountains already,…and with the trouble we've got, we don't need anymore….You may, or may not be outlaws, I don't know,…but if you men are smart, you'll head right on back to where you came from."

Slade's eyes turned hard again as he stared at Rodney. "That wouldn't be a threat, would it, Marshal?"

Rodney grinned slightly. "Not yet, it ain't….As far as I know, you men aren't wanted anywhere up here….No, Sir, it's just some damn good, free advice."

Billy watched Slade intently, suddenly realizing that the man had a plan, he was too damn sure of himself. He glanced at the man called Sidney when he heard him snickering, and felt himself tighten up inside. They were obviously playing some sort of a game. 'Sitting us up for the kill' He thought, again feeling the chill on his neck. He knew also, that whatever was going to happen, would happen soon and he slowly moved the tin cup to his left hand and lowered his right arm to his side.

"You always travel that heavy, Marshal?" Slade jerked his head toward the bulky skins behind Billy. "That's a lot of supplies."

"It's a hard country, Mister Slade." Returned Rodney, casting a quick glance at Billy.

"You're right about that." Grinned Slade, "Some of th' worst we've been through. So, tell me somethin'?…Just where, exactly, did you find that hundred dead white men?…I'd like to go see 'em for myself,…not sayin' you're lyin' or anything, don't get me wrong….I'd just like to look for that map before th' Army gets here."

Rodney shook his head. "It's against the law to tamper with evidence…. But it is a free country, Mister Slade,…and since I can't legally stop you from going,…short of arresting you, it's about thirty miles, due North…The smell will lead you right to the spot....But I'm warning you again,...whoever done it is still loose, you won't have a chance if they find you."

"We do appreciate the concern, Marshal, but we'll take our chances." He looked over at the partially exposed skins again and nodded at Billy. "And since you're both goin' to th' Fort anyway, I'm sure you won't mind us takin' half of your supplies with us....Since you won't be needin' 'em. I mean."

"But, we do mind." Said Billy calmly. "You should a brought your own.... Like you said,...it's a rough country up here."

"Well, Golly-mollies!" Gummed Sidney shrilly. "That weren't no friendly request, Mister Farmer!....That were a God-damn fact!...And if you reach for that fancy gun a your'en, he'll kill ya, fore you can spit!"

"Shut your mouth, Sidney, you ass-hole!" Growled the man next to him, who until now, had not spoken.

"You can kiss my ass, Walt!" Sidney grinned and looked back at Billy again. "Black-Jack Slade just said we was takin' your supplies,...now what are you gonna try to do about that?"

"It will be a chore!" Stated Billy, still watching Slade intently.

"I don't quite know what's on your mind, Slade." Said Rodney, quickly getting to his feet. "But, whatever it is,...Don't!... You can't beat him!"

"Don't pay no mind to Sidney, Marshal." Grinned Slade, looking up at Billy, then back at Rodney. "I don't want any trouble, and neither does he. Truth is, we been out of grub so long, that we're desperate." He looked back at Billy then. "I apologize, Mister....For Sidney, and myself." He nodded and looked back at the blackened coffee pot, and then up at Rodney. "Marshal,... if I could just have me th' rest of that coffee, me and th' boys'll be on our way."

"That would be a very wise decision." Grated Rodney. "I'd really hate it if you forced me to arrest you."

Nodding, Slade leaned and took the pot from the fire then drained it into his cup. He got to his feet then and looked around the campsite, then raised the cup at Billy in what appeared to be an attempt at a salute before bringing the cup to his lips. He gasped loudly when he sloshed some of the scalding liquid onto his chin and shirt.

"Ahhhhh,...Shit!" He gasped loudly. "God damn it!" He took the cup in his right hand and turned his back to Billy as he bent forward to place it on a rock, and in that same, fluid motion, Slade dropped his right knee and whirled as he drew his gun.

Billy was ready, making his draw as Slade's weapon came up, and firing as the gunman thumbed back the hammer. The force of the slug caused Slade's shot to go wild as he was thrown back over the rock and down into the brush and rotting timber below them. It had happened in the fraction of a heartbeat.

Billy fired again as the third man drew his gun, pitching him into the rocks behind him, that shot blending with Rodney's, and hearing Walt yell as he was knocked head-long down the slope into the tangle of Mesquite-brush. Then they both turned their guns on Sidney.

"Noooooo!" Yelled Sidney as he flailed his arms wildly in front of his face. "Don't shoot!...Don't shoot!...I ain't no gunfighter, Mister Farmer,.... Please?"

Billy let the air out of his lungs and stared at the trembling man. "Drop th' gunbelt!" He ordered then holstered the Colt as the whimpering man complied. "Now just sit right on down on th' ground there, Sidney, and don't move....You do, I'll kill you!"

Rodney had quickly moved to quiet the horses as the echoes of gunfire died in the hills.

Breathing deeply of the crisp night air, Billy walked to where the man called Slade had fallen and squatted on his heels to stare down at him. "Who was he, Sidney?" He asked, looking back at the wide-eyed, would-be outlaw.

"Black," He swallowed then as he almost choked...."Black Jack Slade!" He blustered. "He's,...he was a gunfighter....Killed thirteen men in Cheyenne,... all of 'em fair fights, too!"

"How long you been tailin' us?" Asked Rodney, coming to stand in front of him.

"Ain't been,...and that's th' Gospel truth....It was all truth, what Slade said."

"Then who told you about that gold mine?" Asked Billy. "Who sent th' letter?"

Sidney shrugged. "Weren't no letter,...a man in th' saloon at Fort Towson's all I know. I was drunk, man,...I don't know who it was!"

"Describe him then." Said Rodney, going down on one knee. "Was he wearing a uniform?"

"A uniform?"

"Was he a soldier?" Snapped Billy.

"I don't know,...they was soldiers all over,...th' saloon was full of 'em!"

"Guess we'll never know." Sighed Rodney, getting to his feet. He looked down at Sidney and shook his head.

Billy sighed, then rolled and lit a smoke before pushing to his feet. "You sit tight, Sidney, I ain't through with you yet." He went to stand beside the lawman then. "What's eatin' you, Rod?"

Rodney looked at him. "How in hell did you know what Slade was going to do?"

"I didn't, I just knew he was up to somethin', and I was ready."

"Well, he sure fooled me, hell, I thought we had him buffaloed!...How the hell am I ever going to be a good lawman, if I can't see through things like that?...Shit,...I thought he had you beat!"

"Slade pulled that same trick a couple weeks ago." Blurted Sidney. "Worked, too,... man was a Sheriff."

"Look, Rod." Said Billy, dismissing Sidney's comment.. "Before three months ago, you never came up against men like these...Hell, you ain't hardly been out a Lamar County,...not in three years, anyway....But you done good,...real good, and I couldn't ask for a better man to side me....But you know what?...If you had a lighter gun, you might a got both them other men."

"Thanks." Grinned Rodney, then nodded at Sidney. "What do we do with him?"

"You're th' Federal Marshal,...from McAlester." Grinned Billy.

"Yeah,...right!" Nodded the lawman, looking over the fire at the spot where Slade had fallen. "Lang told me you were the best he'd ever seen."

"You never told me that!...He really tell you that?"

Rodney nodded. "I figured it best to let it lay after what happened."

"He talk about me much?"

"At first,...all the time." Nodded Rodney. "But then, he became so infatuated with Connie, that it changed him." He sighed then. "But, if he hadn't, we'd never have known what he did." He stared out at the blotches of rock and timber and shook his head. "Lets not talk about that anymore, okay, Billy?"

"Sure,...if that's what you want."

"You think those men are still behind us?"

Billy looked down at the trees also. "Well, a lot a folks prob'ly heard those shots, a while ago....Lets just hope it don't bring us anymore of this kind a company."

"Amen to that....Want I should put out the fire?"

"Why?...If they're out there, they've seen it already,...be better to just go about our business and keep our eyes open....Besides, th' Roan will let us know if they're about."

"Ummm,...Ha,...hey,...can I go now, Fellers?" Asked a fidgeting Sidney. "I promise, I won't never come back, and that's th' Gospel truth."

"He's th' Marshal." Grinned Billy as he moved toward the horses. "Ask him."

"Well, Marshal,...can I?"

Rodney stared at him. "I'm thinking I might just go ahead and shoot your sorry ass,...save us the trouble of taking you in."

"God damn, Marshal, you can't da,...you can't do that,...you're th' law!... That'd be murder,... wouldn't it?"

"Tell you what, Sidney." Said Billy. "Why don't you go unsaddle them horses and let 'em loose,...all but yours, then bring all th' rifles and saddlebags back over here, including yours.... Collect all the gun belts and guns from your friends there and put them on th' ground in front of me here." He looked at Rodney then. "Anything you want a add?"

Rodney nodded. "You've got three bodies to bury after that!"

"You heard th' Marshal, Sidney,...now you listen to me real good.... When you get done with all a that,...I want you to get on that plug of yours and get th' hell out a these mountains....And Sidney,...if I ever lay eyes on you again, I'll shoot you graveyard dead,...and that's th' Gospel truth!"

"You do understand all of that,...don't you, Sidney?" Asked Rodney with a grin on his face.

"Yeah." He stammered. "Yes, Sir, and that's,...Gospel."

They grinned as he clumsily made his way to the horses and began to strip them.

"He might not stop till he gets back to Wyoming." Grinned Billy as he rolled another smoke.

"You know we just made you another reputation, don't you?" Grinned Rodney. "You're the Farmer now,...and you just outgunned the fastest gun in Cheyenne."

"Speakin' of such." Said Billy, thumping the match away. "Old Snake had himself a right, good-lookin' pistol." He went to where he had dropped the holstered guns and pulled the bone-handled Colt pistol from the holster and brought it back to him. "Why don't you hang that old Walker gun on th' wall above your desk, when we get back,...and try this one instead?...Pick out one a them holsters you like, too?"

CHAPTER TEN

"CA,…CAN I PLEASE GO NOW?" Stammered Sidney, gently placing the shovel on the ground beside the gun belts. "I done ever'thin' you said?" He nervously looked from Rodney, to Billy, then back at Rodney, his beady eyes still wide with fear.

Rodney looked down at his boots, then up at Billy. "We did tell him he could leave,…what do you think?"

Billy nodded. "You're a lucky man tonight, Sidney, I hope you know that,…so, you'd best remember what I said about comin' back here."

"Yes'ir, you won't see me no more, ever,…I swear it!"

Billy nodded. "Then get out a here!"

"And don't stop till you're out of these mountains." Added Rodney as he watched him run for his horse.

After several hasty stabs at the stirrup, Sidney finally mounted the skittish animal and then, looking fearfully back at them, kicked the horse in the flanks and sent it down the grade and into the maze of trees.

They laughed then and could still hear the hasty departure in the underbrush.

"That takes care of that, I guess." Grinned Rodney. "Poor Bastard will be afoot by morning." He shook his head and looked at Billy. "Do we get some sleep now,…or do we leave, too?"

Billy began gathering up the gun belts and buckling them together, then shoved the pistols into the holsters before dropping them next to Rodney's saddle. "I don't know about you." He said as he watched Rodney pick up the rifles. "But I could use an hour or two of shut-eye."

"Suits me." Yawned the lawman, pulling his pocket-watch and checking the time. "I'll wake you in three,…or four hours,…if I'm awake." He grinned and went to put out the fire. "Just kidding, Billy."

Rodney was already snoring, and Billy couldn't seem to fall asleep,…and although groggy from the lack of it, he couldn't shake the events of the night long enough to even doze off. Slade had been a gunman and reasonably fast on the draw, but he relied on trickery to win his fights. He hadn't wanted to kill the man either, he would rather have let them ride away,…if only they hadn't tried playing that silly game of surprise. He sighed then, realizing that Snake had inadvertently caused the deaths of another three men. He swatted at the buzzing of large mosquitoes and found himself retracing the events of the past two weeks, especially those at the mountain.

He was almost sure that White Buffalo's wound was bad enough to kill him, but then again,…he wasn't so sure,…he was, after all, a powerful and strange man. He was not like other men, even Peter said he had mystical powers,…he had even witnessed one of them. It certainly wasn't normal to communicate with Crows. And Rodney was right, too,…they wouldn't have packed all they had on travois behind ponies if they did not have another way out of the mountain. If they did leave, and White Buffalo did survive,… then where could they have gone? And why had they let him believe that they were going to die there? But then again, White Buffalo never actually said they were going to stay in the valley,…he actually said they were leaving to find a new home.

Billy sighed heavily. None of it made any sense to him. Maybe they did have another way out,…but if they did, wouldn't they be traveling in these mountains somewhere, and wouldn't they have seen some sign of them? A party of Indians that large would surely stand out in this wilderness, especially ponies with travois attached to their backs, because that would definitely be a rare and forgotten sight.

He shook his head and tried to push the thoughts away. There were just too many questions, and no answers to any of them. He sighed tiredly then and reached back to rub his tingling neck, then realized that he had not noticed it until now. He sat up quickly to stare into the darkness, searching the dark rim of the campsite and surroundings intently as he reached to slide the Henry rifle from the boot at his head. He rolled over and placed his hand over Rodney's mouth, causing the lawman to wake up suddenly and blink his eyes wildly in surprise.

"We got company." Whispered Billy as he took his hand away and let the lawman up.

"You see 'em?" Whispered Rodney as he threw the blanket off.

"Not yet, but somethin', or somebody is out there....You stay close to th' horses and be ready,...I'm gonna be in them rocks there." When the lawman nodded, he crawled across to the rocks, past the ashes of the fire and then raised himself up to observe the trees at the bottom of the slope.

The moon was high overhead, and it was full and bright, but not enough of that light was filtering through the trees to see by. He was cold, too, and realized he'd left the long coat rolled up against the saddle. Several minutes passed before he caught the flutter of movement in the brush below him and peered at it. The shadow moved again and he could just make out the shape of someone slowly crawling up the slope toward him. He moved around the large rock to be in a position to watch his progress, waiting until the man had almost made it to the rock before he spoke.

"You can stand up now, friend." He said evenly, hearing the man's gasp of surprise. "Do it now,...and do it slow....Both hands empty and where I can see 'em. Do it,...or I'll blow your stinkin' head off!"

"Okay,...God damn it!...I'm gettin' up!"

Billy watched him get to his feet. "Now, climb your ass over this rock, and keep your hands where I can see 'em." The man's unwashed body reeked of sweat and grime as he came up to stand in front of him.

"What made you think we wouldn't be on guard up here?...Never mind that,...Who th' hell are you?"

"Name's Gabe Turner."

"Okay, Mister Gabe Turner, what are you doin' here?" And when the man didn't answer him, he jabbed the barrel of the rifle hard into his midsection, bringing a swift grunt of pain from him. "I won't ask you again!"

"We followed you here." He growled. "You killed a friend of ours."

"Which one,...that fuckin' Comanche,...or Snake!"

"Fuck you,...That Comanche weren't no friend, and I don't know no Snake!"

"Who was your friend then, Buck,...or that ass-hole Marshal?,...Speak up,... Cause when I knew your Boss-man, his name was Snake,...don't know th' other one."

The man glared at him in the darkness and began inching his arms slowly downward.

"Ray." He said quickly. "His name was Ray Mallory, not Snake."

"And what makes you think I killed Ray Mallory,...you see me do it?

Turner stared at him in the darkness. "Th' Comanche saw you leavin' th' canyon,...and we found blood in th' rocks, so we know he was there....We was supposed to meet 'im there if somethin' went wrong at th' mountain!"

"There was six of you behind us, where's th' rest?"

"Down there in th' trees, and they got rifles trained on you!...We want what you got in them packs over there....You give it to us and we'll leave."

"Ain't nothin' but supplies in that pack, Gabe,...and that leaves you shit out a luck, th' way I see it....Now, if you men are hungry, you should have said so."

"Don't hand me that shit, Mister." Growled Turner. "That Comanche, you shot, saw you two at th' mountain th' other night....So, we figure you got gold in that pack, and we want it!"

"You keep lowerin' them hands like that, and you will get it!...Now, come on up here in th' clearing,...and move real slow."

"I'm warnin' you." Snapped Turner. "They'll start shootin' if they can't see me."

"Come on up here, you piece a shit!" Said Billy angrily. "As dark as it is, they start shootin', it'll be you they hit, not me.....Come on, move your sorry ass." He removed the pistol from the man's holster when he moved past him, and stuck it in his belt. "Where's your rifle?"

"I dropped it down there when you called out."

Billy turned as Rodney came toward them with a length of rope then nodded. "Put your hands behind your back, Mister Gabe Turner." He ordered then moved aside to make room for the lawman. "Tie 'em real tight, Rod, and while you're at it,...meet Gabe Turner....He's a good friend a Snakes'.... He also thinks we got gold in our packs."

"Talk about being wrong!" Sighed Rodney, tying the man's hands securely. "You are now under arrest, Mister Gabe Turner."

"Arrest?" He stammered. "You can't arrest me,...you ain't th' fuckin' law!"

"Then why am I wearing this badge on my shirt?" He turned him around and then hooked his thumb in his shirt to push out the badge, shirt and all in front of his face.

"Okay, God damn it, I see it!....If you're th' law, what th' fuck was you doin' at that mountain?"

"Trying to find out what you ass-holes were up to,...till the Indians showed up and started killing everybody. We work these mountains, Mister Turner,...and there's a law against white men even being here,...and that law, by the way, was ordered by the Government when the war ended....Now,... do yourself a favor and call your friends in."

116

"You call 'em in yourself, you want 'em?...But when you do, they're gonna start shootin'!"

"If they start shootin', I'll shoot you." Said Billy.

"You're a real tough man, Ain't you, Gabe?" said Rodney. "So, tell me this,...do you know what the penalty is for committing murder on a Government Reservation?...Or the attempted murder of a Federal Marshal?"

"We ain't murdered nobody!"

"There's at least a dozen dead Choctaw families in these mountains,... and that makes you a fucking liar!" Grated the lawman.

"It weren't us that done it."

"Sure it was....Everybody at that mountain had a hand in it, because every damned one of you worked for Snake,...and he ordered it done!...In my book, Mister Gabe Turner, that makes all six of you guilty of murder."

"And since th' rest are all dead." Drawled Billy. "You six are gonna pay for all of it....And on a Government Reservation, ta-boot. Th' penalty for that alone, is th' firin' squad."

"Uh-uh." Said Rodney. "Firing squad's too good for them....They're gonna stand before Judge Parker."

"They won't have a chance, Rod, he's a hangin' Judge."

"What's the difference,...they're gonna die anyway. Now, call those men in before I decide to save the expense of a trial!"

Turner pulled out of Rodney's grasp and moved back to the rocks, then stopped and looked back. "If I call 'em in, will you let me go?"

"Not a chance!"

"Okay, Okay,...I'll call 'em in." He looked down at the trees then. "Hey, Luke." He yelled. "Can you hear me?"

"We hear you, Gabe,...you get 'em?"

"No,...they got me!...Shoot 'em, Luke!" He threw himself headfirst down the brushy slope as he yelled.

Billy shot him as he jumped, the slug driving the breath from the man's lungs with a loud grunt as he fell limply into the dead timber below.

They quickly dropped to the ground as bullets began thumping dully into the rocks and upper half of the bluff behind them. The men were shooting blind, unable to see in the darkness.

"Shoot at the flashes, Rod." Shouted Billy as he fired back. He saw the flash of orange then and quickly fired again, hearing the man yelp as he was hit and then suddenly, the shooting stopped.

"Hey, you, Luke!" Shouted Billy then. Gabe is dead, and I just plugged somebody else. You men are shootin' at Federal Marshals here, and that will get you dead."

"There ain't no gold here, neither!" Yelled Rodney. But, what is up here, you ain't gonna get!...So here's something for you to think about....If the rest of you men want to go on living, get the hell out of the Choctaw Nation,... and stay out!"

"If you don't, we're gonna kill you!" Added Billy. "It's up to you?"

They waited breathlessly for several minutes and then were startled when a voice called out to them.

"Don't shoot, Marshal, we're leavin',...and we won't be back!"

They got to their feet when they heard horses crashing through the brush.

"Let's pack up and leave, Rod." Sighed Billy. "We ain't gonna get no sleep anyway."

"Suits me, I'm give plumb out.....I never lied so much in all my life." He sighed. "You must be a bad influence."

"Whatever works." Returned Billy. "Let's pack up."

"Right behind you." He said and followed Billy to ready the animals, but that's when they heard the Roan whinny, and the other horse answer.

"We could use that other horse, Rod,...our packhorse is about played out."

"I'll go get it." Said Rodney and went back to the rocks then down the dark, cluttered slope and into the trees.

At last, the gold and supplies were packed onto the two horses, and their own mounts saddled and ready, when Billy turned to stare at the terrain again.

"These hills won't be safe for anybody, for a long time, Rod." He said as he dropped the stirrup. "Damn shame it had to happen."

"It'll be policed pretty good from now on, that's for sure...But it's either that, or give the Choctaw back their guns....They'll need protection, especially if the Comanche come back." He looked at the spot where Turner fell and sighed. "We gonna bury ol' Gabe before we go?"

"Yeah,...we need to find his rifle anyway."

— —

Dawn found them still fighting the rocks and timber, and the dead limbs and thick brush was fighting them back, making their southward progress a nightmare as it tried to refuse them passage. Several times during the morning, they were forced to detour as much as a quarter-mile to bypass thorny thickets. But at last, mid-day found them descending out of the forest of trees and onto a narrow, rutted wagon road, passing what was left of the cabin where they had buried the twin girls and their parents.

Billy set a faster pace after that making twice the time on the dusty road, but was keeping his eyes open, not knowing who might still be following them. The air was once again free of smoke, and the wildlife activity was back to its usual loud normality as they continued to keep the animals at a fast walk along the uneven road, each lost in their own thoughts as they continued to watch the trees. It was late that afternoon when they rounded a bend in the road and once again stopped the horses.

"Somebody came back and buried them." Sighed Rodney, staring at the graves a few yards from the burned-out cabin.

"Choctaw most likely. "Nodded Billy. "Good for them." He looked around at the steep, tree-studded slope of the mountain, and then at Rodney. "We're comin' into the Seven Devils now,…and folks could still be a little jumpy….We might ought a take to th' hills again,…I'd hate to get shot this close to home."

"Lead off,…I've had enough of this myself."

Nodding, he reined the mare into the tangle of trees alongside the road and, tugging the extra packhorse behind him, urged her up the loose shale of the tree-studded slope along the side of the mountain, and almost along the same route they had used coming in, and by sundown, were dropping out of the foothills again and back onto another road where they continued the faster pace between the knee-deep ruts of hard, dry mud, but at last they were descending out of the Devils and Billy urged the mare to a steady gallop as they followed the twisting road down out of the mountains where they, once again began seeing more and more activity around the many cabins and farms.

They were within five miles of Wheelock when they heard the galloping horses on the road ahead of them, and quickly leaving the rutted trail they urged the horses up the brushy embankment into the trees above the road to watch the troopers ride by and waiting until they were around a bend in the road before speaking.

"In a hurry, weren't they?" Breathed Rodney. "You see the Indians?"

Billy nodded. "Scouts, I guess, they were wearin. Army coats."

"Most likely Kiowa,…army uses 'em as Scouts. A civilian was with 'em, too"

"He must a come for help." Mused Billy. "But I didn't think there'd be that many troopers in on it."

"I think they probably don't know what they're riding into up there."

"Well,.. we know where they're goin….And we know what they're gonna find." Billy clucked the Roan out of the trees and down to the road again. "And I don't want a be here when th' shit starts to fly."

"I wonder just how the Army did get involved in this?" Said Rodney as he pulled in alongside the mare.

"It only takes one man in th' right position." Grinned Billy. "Think about it....You're an officer at Fort Towson, earnin' forty, fifty dollars a month,.. doin' a job that nobody else really wants. Then, in walks Snake one day, all dapper-like and shows you a map....And you bein' a educated man, you'd know all about them Aztec Indians and their legends....Make a man's future look pretty bright, havin' all that gold."

"Well, whoever the Bastard is, he's as much to blame for this as Snake was,...and he needs to pay for it. Maybe I'll just pay me a little visit to the Fort in a week or so."

"And tell 'em what?...And who would you tell,...the commanding officer might be th' one involved?"

Rodney sighed. "Well, using that logic, they're gonna get away with it."

"I wouldn't say that." Returned Billy. "You are an eye witness, and them telegraph wires do reach all th' way to Washington....And there's th' mail, too,...a nice long letter to th' Justice Department just might do th' job....Not that I'd try to tell a Federal Marshal from McAllister how to do his job."

"Thanks." Grinned Rodney. "But I like that. A nice lengthy letter just might work,...and please,...feel free to tell me anything, Mister Farmer. But while you're at it, you got any ideas on how to go about not involving myself?"

"Yeah, don't sign your name....Give th' letter to th' Engineer on a train to Dallas or somewhere,...let him mail it when he gets there."

"I could have figured that out for myself." Laughed the lawman.

Billy grinned. "Wheelock's just up ahead a ways, ain't it?"

"Couple of miles,...why?"

"We don't need to be seen,...somebody might remember us to th' Army. We're not gonna make it home tonight anyway, so lets cut southwest a ways and find a place to stop,"

— ~

It was almost dark by the time they rode down out of the timber. They were at the bottom of the hill and in belly-deep prairie grass, on land that was almost completely level and with low, rolling hills on either side of them. Billy stopped the Roan and dismounted to lean stiffly on her rump to watch the last vestige of crimson sink below the skyline in the west.

"This place looks familiar." Grunted Rodney as he swung down beside him. "We ought to be home by tomorrow night sometime." He lifted the stirrup and loosened the cinch strap. "You all right, Billy,...you ain't said hardly anything since we left the road?"

"Just thinkin', Rod, I'm okay." He lifted the Roan's stirrup and loosened her cinches. "I'm hungry, too." He saw Rodney about to remove the saddle from his horse's back then. "leave th' saddle on, Rod, just in case....Don't want a get too careless this close to home."

Rodney nodded and loosely buckled the strap again. "What about the pack animals?"

"Them. Too,...we just got another day or so to go, they'll make it."

Nodding again, the lawman went to heft the sack of supplies from the packhorse while Billy gathered wood for a fire,...and by full nightfall, they were sitting against the rocks and sopping their plates with cold biscuits, after which, Rodney grabbed the pot from the fire and refilled their cups with the strong coffee. "Now,...you can tell me what you were thinking about?" He grunted as he moved back against the rock again.

"When?"

"When we got here,...you said you'd been thinking."

Billy nodded. "About th' past two weeks mostly."

"Me, too....It's sure something I'll never forget. And I'm glad I got to meet White Buffalo and his people, even though the people weren't all too friendly,... but I guess I can understand that.....It's gonna be tough, though, not being able to tell anybody about them." He looked across at the packhorses then. "All that Gold." He muttered. "Can you believe it?...And I'll still be dreaming about that treasure cave when I'm an old man,...and I can't even brag about it. Hell,...nobody would believe me anyway."

"Don't forget the mine." Added Billy. "There was more gold there than in that Aztec cave."

"I don't think I'll have any trouble there, neither."

"You ought a be rich enough now to ask that gal to marry you."

"Thinking about that, too." Grinned Rodney. "Hell,...I might just ask her and her sister both to marry me, I can afford it! But then again, it might not be enough, neither,...hell, I don't know how to be rich!"

"Every man was born to be rich, Rod,...it's just that most don't have th' time to do it." He flipped the butt of the smoke at the fire and sipped at his coffee.. "You'll figure it all out, though,...just don't get too greedy."

"Greedy,...what do you mean?"

"I mean, greedy,...like we talked about....Don't try sellin' it all at once, or you'll start a gold-rush. Don't sell too much in Paris, neither, we got to live there."

"That brings up another problem." Said Rodney, turning to look at him. "Where to hide this much gold while we sell it off?"

"Oh, that's th' easy part,...tag th' two sacks you want, and we'll keep it at th' farm. In fact, we'll make that our first stop on th' way in,...how's that?"

"Rodney nodded. "And you know what?...When that runs out, we'll know where to get some more." He grinned and gathered up the tin plates and cups and stacked them, then poured the coffee grounds on the fire. "And don't give me that look,…I know you think there's no way back into that mountain,… but,….I think you're wrong about that."

"But, I'm not, Rod, so forget about it….I have no real desire to ever go back up there,…well,… I don't want to go back, lets put it that way."

"I don't believe they killed themselves, Billy, no matter what you think. It's too much to comprehend, let alone, believe,…nobody would purposely do that."

"There's lots of ways to die, Rod,…let it go, will ya,….It's th' way they wanted it, and that's th' way it was….But I do agree, somewhat,…and I do hope you're right."

"I know I am,… cowards kill themselves, not the Ancient Ones….You'll never convince me they didn't have another way out….White Buffalo knew this day would eventually come, and he was prepared for it….That's what I believe."

"To tell you th' truth." Sighed Billy, reaching for tobacco and papers again. "I've been thinkin' that myself,…but don't you really think they would have closed that escape route behind them when they left?"

"Now you see,…it's logic like that that keeps me guessing all the time…. But, I'd still like to know for sure."

"Me, too, Rod,…and maybe someday, we'll go back and see what we can find….After it calms down some up there."

"You know I'm all for that!" Sighed the lawman. "I do like a mystery, that's for sure."

"It is that." Agreed Billy, putting a lighted match to the smoke. "And as it stands right now, you and me are th' only two people alive that knows what's in that valley,…and I think it's better that way. Because, aside from the treasure,…if there is somethin' evil in there, th' damned thing is better off left alone,…and you can believe that….Good night, Rod."

CHAPTER ELEVEN

THE DAYS AND WEEKS PASSED slowly at first, and with not a lot of news about the episode at the mountain. But what happened there was ever present in Billy's mind, and for a long while, was as if it had taken place only yesterday.

They had gotten away with the hunting trip story, and their side-venture in prospecting, and everything was back to normal again. Another harvest was behind him, and as the weeks dragged into months, he was able to put the sadness into a private part of his memory, hidden there, but not forgotten. Because not a day passed without his thinking of the mountain and of White Buffalo,...and of the unsolved mystery that surrounded the whole affair.

Hundreds of unwanted questions plagued his mind in the fields during the day, and again at night, causing sleep to be slow in coming. He was tired, and restful sleep had become a stranger to him, and when it did come, it was a fitful one. But otherwise, he was just grateful to be home, and after selling off some of his gold, used his new-found wealth to acquire more land, and the tools to work it with,...and that meant adding more hired hands, too. He was now raising wheat and barley, along with potatoes, corn and peanuts. He had also purchased nearly five hundred acres of grassland along the Red River, north of, and adjoining the farm where he built a low, rambling ranch-house before giving Sam the deed to it all,... along with the money to start his Cattle Ranch with.

He kept himself busy with the farm, his family, and his friends in an effort to find closure. He attended Church regularly with his family, and that included their latest addition, a daughter, Angelina. Connie had been pregnant when he left to help White Buffalo, and had since presented him with yet another question. Would he have gone, if he had known?

— —

It was now more than a year since the attack on Devil Mountain, and the questionable disappearance of White Buffalo and the Ancient Ones, and even now,…it was still very hard to understand why it happened. Billy understood the reasoning behind it, but he couldn't help thinking it didn't have to be that way.

If Rodney was right, and he felt sure that he was, and they did have an escape plan, why hadn't it been shown to them? He had wondered about that almost every day since, and the only conclusion he could come to, was that it was for their own protection. But what were they being protected from?…The evil, White Buffalo had spoken of,…or the danger it might have put them in, if they were told about it?

He had never met a man like White Buffalo before, the man some said was a spirit, and not a man at all. But man, or spirit, he had definitely been a powerful force. A ghost-Chief, who could talk with Crows, and the large, black, birds seemed eager to do his bidding. He was a spirit who ruled his people with an iron hand, his very presence commanding respect, and instilling fear in the hearts of his enemies. He was a man who had become his friend,…and he missed him.

Devil Mountain was sealed forever now, along with its secrets. Gold hunters would never find the vast treasure of the Aztecs, or the endless veins of pure gold in the walls of the Spanish mine. He was convinced there was no way back into the hidden valley, and if there were, its secrets were guarded by the ghosts of ancient warriors,…at least, he hoped they were.

It had taken the Army most of the past two years to clean up the mess at the mountain. The bodies of the treasure hunters were buried close to where they had died. However, they never found the damaged cannon, the Howitzer that had been reported stolen from the armory at Towson, thus beginning an investigation that lasted for months,…an investigation that terminated with the arrests of three Noncoms and a Captain at the Fort, charging them with treason and the oppression of a docile people.

Those treasure hunters, that were lucky enough, or smart enough to escape with their lives that night, were never found, and were presumed to have left the Nations. But the best part was that the Army had found nothing that would suggest there was a valley inside the mountain at all, or a gold mine, or anything else, for that matter,...and therefore had no legitimate reason to even try to get inside, finding no proof in the testimonies of the soldiers involved, and so, aiding and abetting the enemy was then added to their list of charges. If there was any talk, or speculation of the treasure in the mountain, it never made the papers, nor did any mention of the informant from Texas, who started the whole investigation.

The renegade Comanche were slowly rounded up, and some stood trial for the murders of Choctaw families and then hung, while still others were sent to a prison up North somewhere, their ravings about being attacked by ghosts was laughable and ultimately ignored at the Court-martials. The Courts believed that the Comanche had staged the massacre of the white men themselves, even to using arrows with no markings to cover up the facts. But this, also, was not completely provable, and was not pursued any further.

There was calm again in the Choctaw Nation and the murders all but forgotten. The vast Aztec treasure in the mountain of the Devil became just another myth, a mystery that couldn't be explained, or proven. Not a word had appeared in the papers once the trials ended, or about anything else having to do with the trouble in the territories. Even the trials themselves became a thing of the past as the Government quietly swept it all under the rug.

Rodney had watched the papers eagerly during those two years, including those from Shreveport Landing, Dallas and McAllister, but the National news traveled slowly and usually was received by local papers by means of courier, by stagecoach, or by train, becoming old news. He had also spent many hours with Billy during that time, perusing the news items, and reliving the experience at the mountain. Connie and Willy were always present, and were, in fact, infatuated by the talk of the Ghost Tribe of Choctaw Indians. Even Melissa, his pregnant bride of a year now, was there and usually wide-eyed, especially when they described the treasure cave and its contents. But no one spoke to anyone else about any of it, especially the treasure,...it would have been useless anyway, because no words could describe the beauty and wealth that was hidden there.

Paris, Texas, in May of 1873, was a town about to burst at the seams,... and was still called the Cotton Center of northeast Texas,...but even more so, now that more and more farmers had settled on the rich blackland in Lamar County. New streets were being graded weekly, and the land inside the town limits was being laid out in blocks, and the blocks surveyed into individual lots, on which homes were continuously being erected. More and more people were moving into the town and County to work on the farms and ranches, as well as the many new business places opening up. The Citizen's Bank had been repaired after the robbery, but had recently been torn down and a new one of red brick had just been reopened.

Billy sighed and placed the ledger on the table beside his chair while looking along the L-shaped front porch of the sprawling farmhouse. He thought again of the ancient Choctaw but then, almost immediately, wondered why? He hadn't thought about any of it in a while now, and was finally sleeping all night, every night, without the nightmares. He watched the Crows over the barn across the yard from him, thinking they must be why as he watched them circle above the trees. The large birds seemed to have adopted the farm since his return from the mountain. Or maybe he had just not noticed them as much, before now.

He sighed again and thought of Rodney, then checked his Samuel Colt pocket watch and thought that him and Melissa were due to arrive at any time, and putting the watch away, his thoughts turned to the large skins of gold, still hidden in the tool-shed in the barn. They had brought back a combined four hundred and ten pounds of the precious metal, the purest ever found in those mountains. He smiled as he thought of the lies they had told the two weeks they were gone, and again, to explain the small amount of gold they had cashed in at the bank. That had been some outstanding prospecting trip,…to say the least, but both of them had been content to leave it that way. It was as if a cloud had been lifted, making their lives better for it.

Now, if he could just convince Connie to sell her Restaurant, things would be perfect, Angie was three now, and Christopher almost two, she needed to be home with them. He had to grin at that thought however, because it was an impossible wish. His thoughts returned to Rodney then, and of his wedding, the year before. Melissa had been a pretty, young, blond-headed bride, and they seemed to love each other a lot, because both of them sparkled as they were pronounced man and wife. Rodney had built her a large home on the hundred acres he had bought just South of the farm, and only a mile or so from town and his job there. He had enough gold to retire on and live the life of leisure, as most of it was still locked in the tool-shed along with his. Both him, and Rodney had, of course, sold several pounds of it on business trips to Dallas and Shreveport Landing, but he said he liked being a lawman and refused to quit.

He was actually glad he hadn't quit, because as long as he was Marshal, the law was his ally. It was a selfish way to look at it, he knew, but he also knew that even though the Reb had been declared dead, the Federal Government could, and would reopen the files if someone should recognize him.

He looked at the screened-door then as the muffled screams of his daughter came to him, followed by Willy's high-pitched laughter and Christopher's crying because he couldn't play with them, and Willy did love to play with Angie. He heard her screech again and grinned widely. Unlike her brothers, she was the most energetic baby he'd ever seen, and lived to be tricked by her big brother, and for a two and a half year-old, she had a set of lungs that could fracture glass....He grinned again when he heard Connie fussing at them.

"William Upshur!" She scolded. "Leave Angie alone and come here,... your Uncle Rodney and Aunt Melissa will be here in a few minutes....Now wash up for supper,...Scat!...You've got your brother crying, and I've got to finish supper!...You hear me, young man?"

He saw the buckboard coming up the road then and watched as it drew closer, then wondered who their passenger might be? He could tell it was Rodney at the reins though, by the sun's glint on the Marshal's badge. He got up and walked across the porch and down the steps to the yard, and was standing there when the lawman stopped at the hitch-rail.

"Good to see you, Rod." He grinned. "You, too, Melissa." He shook the lawman's outstretched hand and then took the reins from him, going to tie the team to the hitching rail at the porch.

"And who's this young man with you?" He grinned, coming back around the horses.

"Billy, meet my Nephew, Benny,...Benny, this is your new Uncle Billy."

"Hi, ya, Benny." He grinned. "And how old are you?" And when the boy held up four fingers, he laughed then took the tiny hand in his and shook it. "It's very nice to meet you, Benny, welcome to th' farm." He looked back at Rodney then. "Get on down from there and come in, Rod, vittles are about ready." He walked around the rear of the buckboard then to help Melissa down.

— ⁓

As usual, the meal was noisy with four children at the table, but soon it was over and the two men retired to the sitting room, leaving the women to clean up in the kitchen. The kids took off through the house to Willy's room just as they were easing themselves down into the downy chairs.

"How's things in town, Rod?" Asked Billy, leaning to put a match to the coal-oil lamp on the table between them, then immediately rolled and lit a Durham, and holding the lighted match to Rodney's after-dinner cigar before shaking it out. "Anything goin' on?"

"Nothing major ever happens in Paris." Grinned the lawman. "Nothing too major, anyway....I spend about as much time at home now, as I do at the office,...not much need in it, with Jim there, and what with Sheriff Gose's deputies in th' County."

"Stockwell's turned out to be a good lawman, ain't he?"

"As good as any I've seen." Returned Rodney. "Town's growing too fast, though, I've had to hire a couple of new Deputies. But Jim's teaching them the ropes, so they'll do....I plan on using them at the depot, mostly to help the railroad-dicks, and to keep an eye on things there."

"Bums?"

Rodney nodded. "Panhandlers and hobos are becoming an epidemic,... begging at the back door of every house close to the rail-yard. That's about the only complaints I get here lately, and I don't know what I can do about it, hell, I can't lock 'em all up."

"Even bums get hungry, I guess." Agreed Billy. "It's prob'ly that way anywhere there's a railroad, though,... and I guess there's no stoppin' it. Some men just never got over the war,...or can't."

Rodney nodded. "Heard you bought the Ellis property?"

"Yeah." Sighed Billy. "Thought I'd raise Soybeans on it, there bein' a sizeable market for Soybeans back East....Anyway, I ain't decided, yet."

"You've already got the biggest farm in several counties." Grinned Rodney. "When you gonna slow down? There's more to life than working all the time?"

"As a matter of fact, I'm thinkin' about that, too....My ambition ain't what it used to be,... and I've got enough hands to run th' farm for me."

"About time, Man....So,... how's Sam doing?...That was a grand thing you did for him,...I thought he was gonna have a heart attack when you gave him that deed."

"Sam's got th' best head on his shoulders, I've ever seen when it comes to runnin' a spread....I plan on buyin' our beef from 'im, and you should do th' same....But what about you?,...Things okay at your cabin in th' woods?"

"Billy,...I am the happiest man alive, I think. Can't wait till the baby gets here, neither."

"When's it due?"

"Can't you tell? He grinned. "Doc Bailey said we could look for it any day now,... he also said that good things come to those who wait."

"I'm livin' proof of that, Rod." Grinned Billy.

"Yes'ir, you are." Grinned Rodney then quickly glanced toward the kitchen before leaning closer to him. "Billy,...I damn near couldn't wait to get here tonight, because I've got something to show you that's damn bizarre." He pulled the folded newspaper from his hip pocket and opened it on the low table between them. "Have you thought about the mountain lately?"

"Today, for some reason." Nodded Billy.....".What have you got there,... some news about th' mountain?"

"Not directly....But I think it does concern it....I found something you won't believe in the McAllister paper yesterday,...just wait." He opened the paper to the second page. "You ever see anything like that?"

Curious, Billy turned the paper around to see the picture on it, then held it up to the light of the lamp and frowned. "It's a picture of three Choctaw Indians holding up a giant bird of some kind." He mused aloud. Two men were holding each of the bird's outstretched wings, while the third man seemed to be struggling as he held up the very large, anvil-shaped head. Then frowning, he peered closer to read the small print in the caption. "Says here, that several farms had been mysteriously losin ' Fowl and livestock for weeks before one of them spotted the monster-bird taking a milk-cow from his corral and flyin' off with it. Says the three farmers joined together and hunted it for two weeks before finally shooting it down....That's some big bird, Rod!"

"It had a wing-span of close to thirty feet from tip to tip." Blurted Rodney excitedly. "It also says they don't know what it actually is, except that it is not a giant bat, like first suspected,...but said it could be a bat's ancestor. Anyway, the Journal plans to send the picture to one of the more prominent Universities back East, to let the historians figure out what it could be." He grinned wider then....."But, I already know what it is, Billy,...and it's unbelievable!" He took the creased page of a book, from his shirt pocket and unfolded it.

"I found this in one of the books, Melissa's dad gave me,...just look at that!" He gave Billy the paper and waited while he looked at it.

"It's just a drawing of that same bird, Rod,...with a name under it, I can't even start to pronounce,...so,...what th' hell is it?"

"It's a damn good drawing of a Pterodactyl, Billy,....see the comparison in the paper there?"

Billy nodded. "They look th' same all right." He frowned then. "But, I'll ask you again,...what is th' damn thing,... I've never seen nothin' like it?"

"The Pterodactyl was a giant, flesh-eating, prehistoric, flying Reptile,... and it lived more than sixty million years ago....It's been extinct for that long, too."

"Extinct?....These farmers just killed th' damn thing, Rod,... It don't look extinct to me."

"I'm serious, Billy,...look at the picture. There's not a bird in the whole world, that even comes close to that,...read the last part of the story there."

Billy nodded. "It says, that farmers were hunting for it in it's last known direction of travel, and when they neared Winding-stair Mountain, they saw it flying toward them from out of the northeast, and when it attacked them, it became entangled in Mesquite brush and they were able to kill it." He put the paper down and reached for the tobacco sack again as he stared at Rodney, then meticulously rolled and lit the smoke, dragging the drug into his lungs as he glanced back at the picture.

"Well?" Asked Rodney, leaning even closer. "Does anything in that story ring any bells?"

"Like what?"

"Like where it might have come from?"

"Not a clue." Said Billy, blowing smoke at the ceiling. "But if this thing is one a them,....things, you called it,...it ain't been dead for no million years."

"It was coming at them from the northeast, Billy,...and Devil Mountain is northeast of the Winding-stair!...Now,...given what you know about the valley and it's secrets, and the evil that White Buffalo spoke about,...couldn't this be the secret he didn't show us?...Maybe this is part of the evil, that he didn't want to escape."

"Rod, are you listening to yourself?...Because you're talkin' plumb crazy!"

"That might very well be,...but I'm telling you again,...I don't believe the Ancient Ones intended to kill themselves at all. I believe they had a way out, and this Pterodactyl ties into all of it....That valley is hiding a hell of a lot more than was shown to us, Billy,...and this creature had to have escaped from there somehow....I think it's real, and it shouldn't be ignored."

"What makes you think it's real, Rod?...I mean, really, everything you just told me is circumstantial, as far as I'm concerned."

Rodney shook his head and then, sighing, struck a match and re-lit the thin cigar, somewhat aggravated that it had gone out. "What if it's all true, though, Billy,...what White Buffalo said, I mean?...And what if this thing did come from there?...There was nobody there to keep it from happening,...and if it is true, then this bird might not be the worst thing that could escape from there!...We're gonna have to find out, Billy, you and me,...because there's no one else to protect those secrets."

Billy sighed heavily. "I'm not sayin' you're right, Rod,...but what could have happened that would let this thing out,...It never happened before?"

"I don't know,...maybe it was the cannon-fire,... that mountain was bombarded pretty good, you know."

"And you think this thing crawled out of a hole in th' mountain, or something?" He grinned then. "I think I know where you're going with this, Rod....The Ancient Ones somehow traveled back into th' distant past, right?...A million years into th' past,...and when they did, they left th' door open and this thing crawled out." He smiled widely and shook his head. "The past is th' past, Rod,....we can't go back, and it can't come forward."

"Then you tell me where it came from,...because it is definitely a pterodactyl,...you just looked at the proof."

"You know I can't tell you where it came from!....But what you're sayin' is impossible, Rod,...th' past has already come and gone,...think about what you're tellin' me."

"I know it sounds crazy, okay?" Returned Rodney as he puffed on the cigar. "Hell I know it's impossible, too,...but the truth is,... that Pterodactyl is a prehistoric reptile, and it was killed on April the fifteenth, eighteen hundred and seventy-three.....And if an extinct flying, reptile can come back through time like that,...who's to say what else could do it? This is real, Billy,...there's no two ways about it." He tapped the picture with his finger then. "And right there's the proof, whether you want to believe it, or not."

Billy reached up to scratch his head, then dropped the half-smoked butt into the can by his chair before looking at the lawman again. "This is just too much to think about right now, Rod,...it's too far-fetched to seriously believe."

"But it's true, Billy. That is a Pterodactyl, and it didn't fly back from sixty-five million years ago. It had to have come from somewhere inside that mountain,...think about it,...it excites the hell out of me!...Don't it make you want to know for sure?"

"Now we're getting' to th' heart of things." Grinned Billy.

Rodney sighed. "I'm just saying that we should go back to make sure, that's all....If a Pterodactyl can come back from the past,...what else could come back? Some of those monsters back then, were as big as a house,...and all of them were meat-eaters....Think of what an animal that big could do if it got loose,...or several of them?"

Billy nodded then leaned forward to rest his elbows on his knees. "If it's true, you'd be right,...we'd be in a hell of a lot of trouble.... But to me, real is what I can see and touch....That bird is real, I can see that,...but it couldn't have come from th' past, Rod. There's got to be another explanation for it being here,...and I ain't got a clue to what that might be. But either way, it scares th' hell out a me!"

"Want to know what scares me?" Returned Rodney. "Number one,... There's not a weapon anywhere that could bring down one of the larger reptiles, outside of one of them Howitzers,...but that would be a maybe! Number two,...if another one of these Pterodactyls happens to show up, the Government could get involved again,...and they will surely trace it back to that mountain, and if they do?...No more secrets."

"You're giving me a headache, Rod,...take a breath, you've convinced me....I don't believe any of it,...but I'm convinced." He rolled and lit another cigarette as he stared at the picture. "Truth is, I've been hunting an excuse to go back,…been thinkin' about it a lot lately,…mostly just to see if it's changed any. Who knows, th' Army might have already looted it anyway,…nobody would know it if they did!…But then again, maybe not, too….I still don't think there's a way in."

"I just want to be sure." Sighed the lawman. "So, what do you say?…If we don't find a way in,…we'll go fishing, simple as that?"

"You sure you ain't got th' gold-fever, again?…Because you still got well over a hundred pounds of it in th' tool-shed."

"I wouldn't mind bringing back another sack full." Grinned Rodney. "And neither would you….So,…are we going?"

"God, Rod,…I don't know." He sighed and dropped the cigarette-butt into the can. "It's just impossible to believe all a this, hell, I couldn't even imagine it!"

"It was impossible for a tribe of ancient Indians to live in a hidden valley for hundreds of years undetected, too,…but they did,…and it was impossible that their Chief could talk with Crows,… but he could."

Billy nodded. "I believe you, Rod,…I see th' picture there."

"Then let's go back,…let's be sure. The Nations are open to white men now, and the Choctaw are friendly again…And they all know who you are,… so we'll be safe enough. What do you say,…we could take Connie and Will, Melissa and even Benny….It'll be like a holiday,…a chance to get away from it all for a couple of weeks. It'll be fun, and the boy's will love it."

"I don't know about takin' th' family, Rod,…it could be too dangerous."

"I don't see how?…Ain't nothing up there, but a few snakes and a Panther or two, and they won't be a problem. Come on, Billy,…one way or the other, we have to go."

"I guess Melissa's in there talkin' Connie into this, right now, ain't she?… And that also means that if we go, it'll have to be after th' baby is born,… that right?"

"Well,…yeah, but it won't be more than a couple of weeks, Doc said the baby could come at any time."

"You just told me those monsters were as big as a house." Grinned Billy. "Do you really want to take the family into somethin' like that?"

"If they were already out, no,…I just want to keep them from getting out….Now you know that if the Government takes notice of this bird, they could destroy any chance we might have of preventing another escape, They might even set those monsters loose on us, …who knows?"

Billy laughed at him then. "You could have been a lawyer, Rod,…you missed your callin', I think….I'll tell you what,…if Connie goes for this,…

we'll go back. But only if you send a wire to Peter,…we'll need a good guide to th' best fishin' holes."

"No problem." Grinned Rodney. "Where do I find him?"

— —

Billy blew out the lamp and lay down on the downy mattress, turning his head to look at the outline of Connie's face against the light from the window. "Are you really sure about this trip, Honey?"

"Of course." She said softly. "I admit it's a little frightening, after what you've told me about that place,…but yes, I want to go. Besides." She said, turning on her side to face him. "It will be good to get away for a while,… and this time, we'll be together."

"Okay then,… we'll go, and I'll show you th' mountain,…but there ain't no way into that valley…So what are you gonna do, take Willy out of school before it's out?"

"We won't need to, school lets out in less than a month, and we have to wait for the baby to come anyway,…and for Melissa to get her strength back."

"Well then," Sighed Billy. "I guess we can use that time to think about what we'll need for th' trip."

"You do know that Rodney believes there's another way into that valley, don't you?"

"Rod's a dreamer, honey,…don't forget, I know th' man that sealed th' mountain up,…and he wouldn't have been that careless."

"Well then, where do you think the Pterodactyl came from, it could fly out of that valley you know?"

"He's got you believing that, too, has he?"

"I don't know, Billy, but that was definitely a Pterodactyl,…no doubt about it. I only wish I could have seen it for real, and maybe preserved it, it would have been worth so much to History and antiquity….Oh, well." She sighed. "It'll be an adventure anyway,…and you'll be able to teach Willy a lot about survival,…and me, too." She giggled then. "As long as it's not in the desert,…I never want to see another desert."

"Yeah, well, a desert, it ain't,…believe me."

"Good, then I'm looking forward to it….I'll get Alicia to run the Café for a couple of weeks and,…oh, yes,…how do you feel about a woman wearing pants?"

"Never seen one in pants, I don't know…. You sure it's fitten?"

"Well fitten or not, you're going to see it,…Melissa and I are going shopping for pants tomorrow afternoon."

"No need for that,…if it's pants you want, you can wear some of mine."

"That'll be the day." She sniffed. "They make pants just for women now,… and they're not made from that scratchy old Denim!"

"Better buy you a pair of high-top boot, then,…to stuff the pant-legs in."

"Now that's a first." She remarked. "You agree with me on something,… first time for everything, I guess.…Now, tell me about the country up there again,…is it really that dangerous?"

"You'll need to keep a good presence of mind, first off, and be prepared for anything and everything that might happen,…because it usually will.… There's mountains with nothing but sharp rocks, shifting shale and giant Pine Trees on 'em,… hundreds of deep canyons and narrow ravines,… and those pines up there are so old and tall, you can't see the tops of 'em. Then there's Mesquite brush and Juniper, both with thorns on 'em three inches long,… and to top it off, there's Rattlesnakes by the thousands.…Watch out for all these things and you've got your adventure."

"Good,…I love a challenge."

"It's th' boys I'll worry about up there, they'll want to investigate everything."

"Tell you what, you keep Willy in check, and me and Melissa will watch after Benny,…how's that?"

"Benny,… what about Angela and Chris?"

"I'm going to leave them with Mattie and Doc,…they'll love having them, and we'll have two less to worry about. So don't worry, honey, I'm not!…I know what you're capable of, remember?…Good night dear."

"Good night." He turned over and stared at the pale walls of the moonlit room, his thoughts returning to the monstrous bird in the picture. What was something like that doing here,…and how the hell did it really get here? Everything Rodney had said, made sense,…if more of those things got out, they could be in trouble of a magnitude that would be unbelievable. If it did come from the mountain, then it was going to be up to him and Rodney to plug the hole it came out of.…Because there was nobody else left to do it.

He fell asleep wondering how they could ever hope to fight such creatures, especially if they were as big as Rodney said they were. It could be worse than the war ever was.

CHAPTER TWELVE

"You bring enough supplies?" Grinned Billy, eying the two, heavily loaded pack-mules.

"Can't be too careful." Grinned Rodney as he dismounted. "My Father-in-law insisted we bring along a large tent, so we could all sleep in it,…it just might come in handy, too." He went to help Melissa dismount and watched her run up the steps and into the house,… and he was grinning widely when he looked at Billy. "She looks good in pants, don't she?"

"I could get used to it." Nodded Billy, also grinning.

"She's excited about this trip, too,…almost as much as me."

"That won't last long." Sighed Billy as he tightened the cinches on the Roan. He re-checked those on Connie's Bay then turned as Ross led the ponies to the porch.

"Two ponies, saddled and ready, Boss." Grinned Ross. "Think they'll be able to keep up?"

"They'll do, Ross." He grinned then reached to pat the Roan on the neck. "But this one is still th' best around,…besides, we'll be takin' our time on this trip."

"Well,…I sort a wish me and th' Missus was goin' with ya."

Billy nodded. "I might wish you had, before we get back."

"Maybe next time." Grinned the new Foreman. "You got everything you need?"

"Well, I've been thinkin' on buyin' me a bigger Rifle, but nev.....

"Oh," Said Ross quickly. "Sam left his Henry here for you yesterday, I'll be right back!"

"Speaking of rifles." Said Rodney, going to pull a long-barreled gun from the boot. "Check out this one."

"Another gift from your Father-in-law?" Grinned Billy as he took the rifle from him. "What kind is it?"

"Bolt-action Springfield,...But the working parts are from Krag Arms in Norway. It's chambered for a forty-five-seventy round, check out the scope on that thing.... It's accurate for up to a thousand yards they say,... and probably kicks like a mule."

"It looks powerful enough...Think it'll bring down one a them big as a house, monsters?" He grinned and raised it to his shoulder. "I never seen a bolt-action rifle before,...how many rounds does it hold?"

"Seven, they go in that clip stuck in the bottom there....The action is foreign made, at least the schematic was. Springfield is trying to sell it to the military, before Krag does. I smell a law-suit, too, the plans had to have been stolen." He took the gun and shoved it back into the boot. "Is Will excited yet?" Grinned Rodney as he looked toward the house.

"I don't think he slept all night."

"Yeah,...Benny, neither,...and I think I know how they feel."

"Here you go, Boss." Grinned Ross as he gave Billy the rifle. "Any last minute jobs you want done?"

"Just one, Ross....Thank Sam for me if you see 'im. Other than that, you're in charge." He gave Ross his Winchester then shoved the long-barreled Henry into the boot. "The men all look to you for their orders now, anyway,... and you know what needs doin'." He shook Ross's hand and watched him walk away, then turned as he heard the screened-door slam, and grinning widely as Willy leaped over the steps to the ground, with Benny close on his heels.

"Uncle Rodney!" Yelled Willy, and threw himself into the lawman's arms.

"Whoa, here, big man,...you're getting too heavy for all of this. He swung him around then put him down and hugged them both against him.

"You ready for this trip, Will?"

"Yeah, it's gonna be fun." They yelled together.

"Better get mounted, boys." Said Billy. "Here comes th' women-folk." He hefted Benny to the back of his pony then watched as Willy pulled himself astride his Spirit Pony and grinning, went to help Connie mount.

"My, Lord,...this saddle is hard." She smiled down at him then. "It's just been a long time,...I'll get used to it."

"Don't count on it." He grinned. "It's gonna get a lot harder before nightfall." He glanced at Rodney then nodded at the boys. "Rod, I think we ought a tie Benny in th' saddle, don't you?...This is a little new to him."

Rodney nodded and went to the pack-mule, where he pulled a long length of rope from beneath the tarp. "Got your knife?"

Billy cut the rope into lengths and together they roped Benny securely to his saddle, and then nodding, gathered up the reins and mounted the Roan. He leaned and grabbed one of the mule's lead-ropes and looped it around the saddle-horn before looking at everyone. "We ready?" And when they all chorused a yes, he nodded again.

"Me and Rod will take th' lead with th' pack animals, th' boys'll be behind them…You gals keep an eye on these packs, and them, okay? If them packs start getting loose, give us a yell." He reined in beside Rodney then waved back at Ross before leading off down the dusty road.

They followed the main road for almost an hour, then turned due north to skirt the cotton-fields east of the house and then into the heavily-wooded timberline at the north end of Rodney's land, to eventually turn northeast toward the Goodland road and the new bridge that now spanned the Red River.

Traffic on the road was semi-constant and sometimes forced then to ride single-file when passing the large, bulky and heavily loaded freight wagons. But by late afternoon, they were exiting the quarter-mile long stretch of wood and iron and into the red sand of the Choctaw Nation. The lay of the land began to change almost immediately, from prairie grass and timber, to deep gullies and rugged foothills that were spotted with heavy thickets of Mesquite and wild Pecan trees. They had been passing shack after shack along both sides of the deeply rutted road since leaving the bridge, waving at the silent Choctaw that stared at them, and the children as they laughed and came to run alongside the horses for a ways.

Most all of the cabins sported a front and back yard that was a maze of iron plows and wagon parts. Some had wagons under repair, and most of the houses were in dire need of the same thing…Late that afternoon, they left the road when it began to veer toward the west and continued northeast through the rock-infested grass and Fir trees,…and the rest of the day was spent working their way farther into the elevating foothills.

The ragged peaks of the Seven Devils were visible in the distance east of them when Billy began looking for a place to stop for the night, settling on a spot with large rocks and a scarcity of trees. He clucked the Roan into a grouping of rocks and slowly circled the area before dismounting in the waist-high grass. He turned a rock over on the pack animal's lead rope then went to help Connie down.

"We camping here?" She asked as she stepped into the grass.

"Be a perfect place once you and th' boys tromp down th' grass."

"What?"

He grinned and went to help Rodney with the packs.

Unloading the pack animals was time consuming, but they soon had them picketed close to the campsite. The women already had the meal on the fire by the time they dropped all the bedding by the rocks, and that's when Connie hugged herself and verbally shivered as she went to the horses for their coats, leaving Melissa to dish the food into tin plates. When she returned, they both donned the light jackets before passing the food around.

Billy watched them, as well as Benny as the four year old picked at his food, but smiled when he saw that Willy was having no trouble at all with his. He wondered, though, if it had been such a good decision to bring them along? Because, even though the Nations were friendly again, it was a very unfriendly country,...and they were not used to the hardship it could offer up. He could tell that the boys were enjoying themselves, however, but were tired, and not their usual selves,...both looked about ready to turn in. It had been a tiring first day in the saddle for all of them and the women were already grunting from the ache in their backsides. He grinned again then looked across at Rodney.

"Th' army know we're here, Rod?"

Rodney nodded as he swallowed. "Got a wire day before yesterday from a Captain Ashworth in Washington. We'll be okay as long as we don't intimidate the Choctaw....Said if we do any fishing, or prospecting too close to one of the farms,...it would be wise to get permission first." He filled his mouth again as Billy began eating.

"How far is our mountain from here, honey?" Asked Connie. "Three days,...four?"

Billy nodded. "Maybe five, th' way we're goin'. It's rough country up there."

"Hey, that's no joke!" Commented Rodney.

"We'll turn north sometime late tomorrow." Continued Billy, turning slightly to look at the mountains in the distance. "We'll just catch the outer edge of them Seven Devils yonder,...and it might save us some time,...I hope."

"We couldn't be so choosy, the last time." Grinned Rodney. "You gals couldn't even imagine how bad it was."

"What are the Seven Devils?" Queried Connie.

"Yeah," Chimed Melissa. "What sort of mountains are they?"

He grinned at them and pointed. "That's th' Seven Devils Mountains right there,...you can just see one of 'em 'em over th' treetops yonder....

They're rougher than a cob, too....You remember th' gullies and creeks I told you about?...Well them Seven Devils are mostly shale-rock and its damn tricky to ride over.... If your horse slips on that stuff, its all over, but th' cryin'."

" Shouldn't we have stayed on the road then? It would have been easier."

"We would have, but th' road turned West on us,...we have to go North."

"If I remember right." Grinned Rodney. "This whole country is nothing but shale, no matter which way you go." He looked at the women then and grinned. "Don't worry, girls,...let the horses pick their way, you'll be okay."

"Main thing to remember." Added Billy. "And I'm mostly talkin' to you boys when I say this, stay close together....If you think its far down when you fall off your pony,... well,... just don't fall off your horse up here. Stay alert and your horse will take care of you." He grinned when he saw the wide-eyed expression on Connie's face then shrugged. "You wanted adventure."

"Don't be quite so graphic,...you'll scare the boys."

"This is serious everybody." Added Rodney. "There's wolves and panthers up in them mountains,...some down here, too, so we'll all have to watch our surroundings. It don't take much to spook a horse anyway, especially if it hears a rattler,...so be very alert, okay?...If someone gets hurt, we're gonna be a long ways from a Doctor"

"My, God, Rodney, we get the picture!" Gasped Melissa. "Okay?"

"Fore-warned is fore-armed." Grinned the lawman.

"Well." Sighed Connie, looking across at Melissa. "We'll just have to keep our eyes open, then. We can't let something like a few wolves and snakes ruin our vacation, now, can we?"

"That's right." Laughed Melissa. "I'm still very excited, aren't you, Connie?"

"Yes,...I am." She nodded, looking across at Billy. "Don't worry about us and the boys, we'll be just fine."

"I know you will." Grinned Billy. "Just remember that its not th' desert,... th' desert was easier."

CHAPTER THIRTEEN

It had been a trying three days, so far, and they were all exhausted as camping in the mountains had not been easy on the women, and especially the boys. They didn't sleep well the first night out, due to the night noises and being afraid the wolves might decide to come into camp. Willy had fared pretty well, however, he was just too excited to sleep, he said,... and whatever Benny's problem was, he made up for it during the day,...and it was good that he was tied to his saddle.

Late that afternoon found Billy leading the way out of a deep, cluttered ravine. He urged the mare up the last few feet to level ground then led the pack animal off to the side a ways while the rest of them climbed out. Then sighing, he shifted his weight in the saddle and looked up through the branches of the giant Pines at the tree-studded heights of the Winding-stair Mountain, and then shivered as he remembered the storm of three years ago. Shaking off the feeling, he sighed and scanned the surrounding thickets and trees. He had not looked forward to seeing these mountains again, and now that he was here, he felt even worse about it. He shook those thoughts from his mind then as Rodney pulled alongside.

"Where are we?" Grunted the lawman as he shifted his weight in the saddle.

Billy looked up through the branches again. "That's Winding-stair Mountain, right over there."

"I thought it might be." Breathed Rodney. "Big as life, too,…and that means, what,… one more day to the mountain?"

"About." Nodded Billy then raised himself out of the saddle to study the trees behind him again.

"You looking for something?"

"Yeah, Peter,…ain't like him not to be here already."

"Well I couldn't tell him where to meet us, and I didn't know his whole name….So he might not have even gotten the wire."

"In that case." Sighed Billy, easing himself back into the saddle. "If he got it, he'll find us, I guess,…that little Choctaw's got more savvy than any man I know." He grunted from the pain in his legs then dismounted and walked to where the women were sitting their horses and gazing up at the mountain. "You okay, Honey?" He said as he reached to squeeze her upper leg.

"Owww!" She gasped, looking down at him. "That hurt!" She fussed, but then smiled. "That's a scary mountain off there, Billy,…what's it called?"

"That's th' Winding-stair." He grinned. "Come on." He coaxed, reaching up for her. "We'll camp here tonight,…you'll feel better in th' morning."

She nodded and painfully lifted her leg over the rump of the horse and allowed him to lift her down.

"Thank, God!" She moaned, testing the weight on her legs. "My entire body aches….I wish I'd thought to bring the liniment."

"Walk around a bit while we make camp." She nodded and he watched her walk slowly around her horse toward Melissa as Rodney was helping her down, then grinned and went to help Willy with his spirit pony. "You okay, son?"

"Yes, sir! He beamed, "I don't hurt at all."

"Yeah, well a man's a lot tougher than a woman….Now go gather some dry wood for a fire, okay,…we're gonna camp here tonight." He waited for Rodney to untie Benny, letting him slide off into his arms before gently placing him on the ground at Melissa's feet, then went to help him with the pack animals.

"That boy won't wake up till tomorrow morning." He grinned.

"Th' way I feel, I won't, neither." Yawned Billy. "But I'm hungry, too."

"I'm almost too tired to eat,…but not quite. I'm still excited just being here,…and not being shot at."

Billy nodded and they both set about relieving the mules of their heavy packs.

"This is a lot a canvass to lug around." Grunted Billy as he toppled the baled-up tent from the packhorse onto the ground. "When you plannin' on usin' this thing?

"At the mountain,…I figure we'll be there a couple of days."

Once the animals were picketed, they grabbed the supplies and bedding and went back to camp. Rodney unrolled Benny's bedroll, then gently placed him in it and tucked the blankets around him.

"He's going to sleep tonight." Grinned the lawman as he stood up.

"If I weren't so hungry, I'd go to bed, too." Yawned Melissa on her way to help Connie with the meal.

Willy was adding more wood to the fire as Rodney squatted down beside Melissa and took the knife from her hand. "Thank you, Honey." She said tiredly then watched him open the canned beans. She handed him the salt-pork to slice, then yawned. "I've never been so tired, Rodney."

"You'll be a top-hand at this sort of thing by the time we get home, Baby." He returned, placing the strips of meat in the skillet with the beans. He looked at Billy then. "Any bread left, Billy?"

"All we got's in th' sack there." Said Billy as he eased himself down against one of the rocks to roll a smoke. "We'll whip up some Pone tomorrow once we set your tent up." He licked the cigarette and lit it, then stared back at the mountain.

"What's wrong, Billy." Asked Connie from her place at the fire. "You keep watching that mountain like you're expecting something to happen?"

Billy smiled at her. "Nothin's wrong,… I've just got me one too many bad memories….These mountains tried to kill me once."

"That didn't bother you the last time we was here." Grinned Rodney."

"I didn't have much time to think about it then,…and my wife and son weren't with me."

"I know." Sighed Rodney. "But this is a new set of circumstances,…the only thing we've got to worry about now is a few outlaws and critters. Of which, I suspect these mountains are still quite full of….And that reminds me,…you might want to consider putting on your guns, it ain't that tame up here, yet."

Billy nodded. "I'll put 'em on in th' mornin'….Hell, I ain't give 'em a thought." He grinned then. "It's been three years, you know."

"I know, but I always feel better when you wear 'em."

"Well, I wish he would never wear them again." Commented Connie as she dumped the sliced potatoes in with the pork and beans to fry.

"I know you do." Sighed Rodney. "And believe me, Connie,…if I could use a gun the way he can, I'd wish that, too…. But, if he hadn't worn 'em three years ago, we wouldn't be here now….Unfortunately, the times we live in calls for a man's ability to use one,….because it's the only way justice can be served sometimes. A gun is truly an equalizer when it comes to justice, or protection." He saw Billy frown at him then and nodded his head. "I'm sorry, Connie." He grinned. "I wasn't trying to argue with you or take sides, honest….I just got carried away."

"I know, Rodney." She smiled. "I'm proud of his abilities, too….Now let's eat, I'm starved."

"The meal was good, and the strong, hot coffee even better. Connie poured their cups full again, and Billy leaned back against the rock then rolled and lit a smoke as he watched them clean up. He drew smoke into his lungs and watched Willy as he crawled atop one of the rocks beside him. "How you makin' it, son?"

"Good,…I like it up here, Daddy."

"You remember being up here, Will?" Asked Rodney, holding a lighted twig to his cigar.

Willy nodded. "Yeah,…it was cold, and I was scared most of the time."

"Must have been hard on you,…being up here alone like that."

"Mister Lance took care of me, I remember that. I liked him, too,…he wouldn't let those other men hurt me when they wanted to."

"Billy!" Gasped Connie as she was spreading the blankets out. "Don't make him remember all that, he's just a child?"

"No, I'm not, Mama,…I'm not scared anymore.."

"Are you sure, Baby?"

"Yes, ma'am." He looked back at Rodney then. "The other bad men were all scared of Mister Lance, Uncle Rodney, cause he was a gunfighter."

"You remember all that, son?" Frowned Billy. "Even their names?"

"Not all of 'em,…but, I remember the man that wanted to hurt me, his name was Sam.,…he was real mean, and ugly,…and I remember Mister Tiny, he wanted to hurt me, too."

"What about White Buffalo, you remember him, too?"."

"Yeah, I liked him, too, Daddy."

"It's time for bed now, William." Called Connie, come on."

"Awww, gosh, mama….I want to stay up with Daddy." He slumped his shoulders and slid off the rock then walked to his bedroll.

"That man, Lance." Mused Rodney. "Did he really take care of him like that?"

"I believe he did." Nodded Billy. "At least, that's th' feelin' I got when I talked to him."

"You actually held a conversation with th; man?"

Billy nodded again. "Briefly,…before I killed him."

"He was the one that shot me, right?"

"He was fast!" Nodded Billy….. "I didn't want to fight 'im, Rod, I even offered to let him walk away,…but he wouldn't do it."

"The challenge wouldn't let him." Sighed the lawman. "I guess I'll never understand that part of it."

"If you'd lived that life, you would."

"You felt it, too, then?"

Billy nodded. "It's almost like a tremendous surge of excitement,…it puts every nerve in your body on edge, and you've never felt so focused before… It's like nothin' else matters but th' man in front of you, him, and the gun on your hip." He shrugged then. "I always hated th' feelin', too, because at th' same time, I'm usually scared to death."

"That's the difference between them and you, Billy,…they like it."

"I guess,…but I don't think Lance Ashley was all that different. But then again,…that damn challenge stood between us,…that, and th' knowledge, that if we did walk away,… we'd always wonder?"

"That must have been a bad time for both of you then." Sighed Rodney. "Will being lost, and sick, and feared dead…. I guess that's why I never pushed you to talk much about it."

"It would have been too hard to talk about it back then." Admitted Billy. "But it don't bother me now." He stiffened then as the distinct sound of the Roan's snorting came to him, and they both stared in the direction that she was looking. Rodney pulled his pistol as they got to their feet, and their sudden movements caused the women to stand also, and Willy to sit up in his blankets. They stared intently at the darkened trees as the lawman thumbed back the hammer on the new Colt pistol.

"Hello, the camp!" Came the muffled, yet recognizable voice of a Choctaw Indian.

"Is that Peter?"

"No,…I don't know who that might be. But he's Choctaw." They watched as the short, stocky Indian walked out of the trees and came toward them, hands away from his sides to show then he wasn't armed.

The Indian grinned widely as he approached. "I am Elijah, Two-rains, Wilson,…are you Mister Upshur?"

"That I am." Nodded Billy. "But I was expectin' Peter to meet us?"

Peter is in the Cherokee Nation working as tracker for Marshal Books." He shrugged then. "He says he is sorry, and will join us if he returns in time."

"Th' Marshal keep 'im pretty busy, does he?"

"Sometimes,…I think." He shrugged again then came on into the rocks.

Rodney poured coffee into one of the cups and held it out to the Choctaw who accepted it happily before sitting down on the ground.

"You walking?" Grinned Billy as he looked toward the trees.

145

"I have my mule in the trees there." He smiled. "I was not sure it was you,…the mountains are sometimes a hideout for bad men." He stopped to sip at the strong coffee.

"Peter said I was to guide you to a good place for fish,…but he also grinned when he said this….Do you wish to go fishing?"

Billy grinned. "Peter knows me too well, I think….We came because of the giant bird, your people killed…..We're tryin' to find where it came from, and my friend here thinks it came from th' Devil Mountain." He immediately saw the fear in Elijah's dark eyes as the Choctaw began shaking his head.

"I will not go there, Mister Upshur,…the mountain is forbidden."

"That's okay." Said Billy quickly. "We plan to set up camp outside of th' mountain somewhere….All we'd like you to do, is stay in camp,…sort a watch over things while we look around,…will you do that?"

"Yes." Nodded Elijah,…I will do that for you, Mister Upshur, but I will not go near the mountain."

"That's good enough." Nodded Billy. "Now,…we'd like to know more about that bird, Elijah,…did you see it?"

"It was somethin' straight from hell." Nodded the Choctaw. "It was brought to Winchester Station, where a man from the railroad took a picture of it." He shook his head then. "This bird was an evil warning of bad things to come, I think."

"And you don't have a clue to where it came from?"

Elijah nodded. "Yes,…the farmer told me that he saw it come from the Devil mountain….And if you go there, Mister Upshur,… you might not return."

Billy quickly looked at the women when he heard their sharp intakes of breath, and motioned them to come forward. Elijah got to his feet as they approached, Billy took Connie's arm then nodded at the Indian.

"Honey, this is Elijah, a friend of Peters',…Elijah, I'd like you to meet my wife, Connie here,…and my friend's wife, Melissa."

I am pleased to meet you both." Smiled Elijah.

"And this young man, is my son, William." He grinned as Willy reached to shake the Choctaw's hand.

"Ahhhhh,…Little Wolf." He grinned then vigorously shook the smaller hand.

"How did you know that?" Smiled Willy, his eyes wide and awe-struck.

Elijah shrugged. "All Choctaws know you, as well as your father,…and this man, too, I think." He looked at Rodney then. "But I do not know your name?"

Rodney shook his hand and grinned. "Call me Rodney."

"Now that that's settled." Said Billy, "You do agree to stay in camp to watch our supplies and pack animals?"

"I have given my word." He nodded.

"Fair enough,…go get your mule, you can bed down here by th' fire with us."

— —

Devil Mountain towered eerily above them as they stopped the tired horses, then Billy and Rodney sat in their saddles for a time staring at the battlefield where they had infiltrated the ranks of the treasure hunters.

"It ain't changed much." Commented the lawman.

"Nope." Said Billy as he stared up at the mountain. "And neither has that." Pine and ancient Fir almost totally surrounded the base of the mountain, hiding some of the scars left by the shelling.

"It almost scares me to look at it." Breathed the lawman.

"Is this the mountain?" Asked Connie as they all reined in closer to them.

"This is it." He nodded.

"It almost has a,…supernatural feel about it, doesn't it?" Added Melissa to no one in particular.

Billy grinned and shook his head. "We'll put your tent up right here, Rod,…we could be here a spell." He looked at Elijah then. "This far enough away for you, Elijah?" And when the Choctaw nodded. "Then lets picket th' horses and unload them supplies." He dismounted and helped Connie down before helping Elijah with the animals, wanting to get the tent up before dark.

It took the better part of an hour to clear the area of grass and debris and to set up the large canvass tent,… and when it was done they all stepped back to look at it.

"Well lets stop gawking and get a fire started." Said Rodney, shaking his head.

"What?"

"Nothing, Billy." He grinned. "I was just thinking we could hold services in this thing, a revival even, its so big."

"Your father in law was right, though." Commented Billy. "Its plenty big enough for everybody."

"Well, come on,…somebody I know has to make biscuits tonight,…and it ain't me."

It was well after dark by the time they finished eating. Billy scooted back and rolled his smoke, then fished a burning twig from the fire and lit it as he gazed up at the dark mass of the mountain. He then looked across the fire at the Choctaw. "You ever been this close to th' mountain, Elijah?"

"I have never seen the mountain so close, no."

"Where do we start looking?" Grunted Rodney as he sat down beside him.

"On this side,…where we went in before. We'll work our way around it from there,,,,How far does this mountain go, Elijah,…you got any idea?"

"For several miles,…into Arkansas, I think."

"Well it sure is quiet." Said Connie as she put away the food. "Not even any birds singing." She shivered and took the bundle of food into the tent.

"Evil spirits are about." Commented the Choctaw. "The animals and birds know this."

"Not even th' Crows." Grinned Billy. "But I think I know where they went." He looked at Rodney then. "They're at th' farm."

Rodney laughed. "You're a skeptic, Billy,…a real non-believer."

Billy shrugged. "Well, you know me,…If…."

"If you can't see it, it ain't real." Laughed the lawman. "I know,…but you have to admit, there's something at work here….I can feel it,…and I'll bet you can, too."

"Every question has an answer, Rod,…even this one,…that's what I believe."

"Then why don't you think there's another way into this mountain?"

"Because I know th' man that closed it."

"You made my point." Grinned the lawman, causing all of them to laugh. "Say, Elijah." He said, changing the subject. "We saw a lot of farms between here and the Red River,…but not a single one in the last ten miles or so of here, why is that?"

"That is why." Said Elijah, looking toward the mountain again. "There are many new farms in the wilderness, but there will never be one here."

"Elijah." Said Billy, exhaling the strong smoke. "Th' Ancient Ones protected your people against outlaws, and th' like,…am I right?" And when the Choctaw nodded. "Then why is this a forbidden place,…why are you afraid of it?"

The Choctaw shrugged. "When I was a boy, the ancient warriors came to our farm,…we never saw them come, they just came,… like spirits on the wind. They spoke to my father in the ancient language of the Choctaw, and he was so afraid, that he went to his knees before them. After he agreed to furnish them with some of our food each month,…they told him that, to come near the mountain would mean death to all of us." He looked back at the mountain then. "Many farms were already giving them food,…but our farm was new, just cleared for planting. We did not know of them before then, only rumors that they existed in the mountains….My father was very frightened,…and when they left,…the same thing. We never saw them go. All Choctaw believes that they are the spirits of our ancestors, and even though we believe they are gone now,…we also believe they are still here."

"Did you see them anymore after that?"

He shook his head. "Peter has seen them,…many times."

"Then, if I was to tell you that they were real, and not spirits at all,…you wouldn't believe me, would you?"

Elijah shook his head. "Peter told me that you are friend to White Buffalo,…he also told me they are no longer in the mountain. But Peter is wrong,…they are still here,…but they are angry with us and have released the evil against us."

"What evil is that?" Queried Rodney.

"An ancient evil, even older than the ancient Ones,… this was told to Peter by a warrior….The devil-bird came from here."

Rodney looked at Billy and shrugged, then all seven of them stared at the dark shape of the mountain.

"My, God, Billy." Whispered Connie as she ran her arm through his. "What if he's right?...Suddenly, I'm not so sure about finding a way inside."

"That's fine, honey,…you and Melissa can stay here with Elijah tomorrow while me and Rodney look around….If we find a way in, we'll let you know what we found."

"Don't even think about leaving us here, Billy Upshur." She scolded,… "And don't forget to wear your guns, all right?"

"What?...I don't understand you, woman….First you say don't wear your guns, now you say wear 'em?"

"I'm going to bed." She scolded again, then turned and went into the tent.

"Is mama mad at you, Daddy?"

"Course not,…why?"

"Oh, nothing,…sometimes I don't understand her."

Billy grinned and slapped him on the backside. "You're growing up, my boy….No man fully understands a woman, he's not supposed to, I think….. Now, I think we all better turn in."

"I will sleep here tonight." Said Elijah. "It is best to keep a fire burning, and I must watch the animals."

"Maybe you ought a stake 'em in closer to th' fire, then." Said Billy getting to his feet. "Good night, Elijah."

The morning dawned cool and damp as they prepared to search the mountain's outside perimeter. Connie suggested they leave the boys in the Choctaw's care, as they were still sleeping.

"No, I'm not!" Said Willy excitedly as he ran from the tent. "I'm going, too." He quickly buttoned his jacket and mounted his pony.

Billy and Connie both smiled, as did Rodney and Melissa, then they pulled themselves into the saddle as Billy led the way toward the dark mountain. It was dreary-looking in the half-light of day, with its high, uneven walls of protruding rock formations. They rode through the tall, lush grass of the prairie then across the shallow gully and into the tall trees and rocks along the base of the mountain, in and out of the twisting ditches and around large stands of Mesquite and giant Firs, having to skirt around the rotting trunks of felled timber and sharp-edged boulders. But at last, they were in the area where the Choctaw had led him and Rodney into the mountain.

Falling rock had completely blocked the entrance when the yellow sand had allowed the mountain to shift. The cavern was permanently sealed, and it was from that point, they began their search eastward.

The pace was very slow, having to search behind every Fir tree and large boulder, even dismounting at times to investigate areas of interest. In places, brush and trees were so thick that it was almost impossible to see the gray rock of the mountain behind them, and those towering heights of sheer cliffs seemed endless.

It was late afternoon when Billy finally halted the mare to sit staring up at the forbidden heights. "We must have come a couple a miles by now," He said as he turned to look at them. "And th' valley in there ain't that long,...I think its about time we started back."

"I guess you're right. "Sighed Rodney. "We can try along the other side tomorrow." He shook his head and stared longingly up at the mountain. "There just has to be another way in."

"Why?"

"Cause I hate to fish,...I can't catch 'em."

"Oh, my God, look!" Gasped Melissa and pointed up at the mountain. "What on God's earth are those?"

"Where, Honey?" Urged Rodney as he looked up through the trees.

"They're bats, Daddy,...look!" Shouted Willy. "Real bats!"

"My, God, they are bats!" Cried Connie excitedly. "Thousands of them!"

It looked as if a dark cloud of smoke was erupting from of the mountain as the night hunters swarmed out of the opening. They were coming from a large, dark hole in the cliffs, almost completely hidden atop the thick, timbered slope,… and the swarm was endless as they flowed out of the pines in search of food.

"That could be our way in." Said Rodney as he watched them. "What do you think?"

"You might be right." Mused Billy, and suddenly felt a tingle of excitement. "Won't hurt to look, that's for sure….I wouldn't get too excited, though. Chances are, it don't go all th' way through."

"Well, I've got a feeling it does,…and we wouldn't have seen it at all if not for the bats,…look how well hidden it is."

"We'll find out tomorrow." Said Billy as he turned the Roan around and clucked her down through the rocks. "Let's get on back to camp."

They filed in behind him and had just made the bottom of the grade when the distinct sounds of shod horses on hard rock came to them and Billy quickly held his hand up for them to stop before reining the mare around to face the valley's floor.

They sat and strained their eyes down the uneven valley of rocks and timber southeast of them, but the shadows of the oncoming evening made it difficult to see anything at all. The clinking sounds came to them again, somewhat muffled by distance and was followed by the faint squeal of a horse.

"There they are." Pointed Rodney. The clearing was a good half-mile away from them. He pulled the long-glass from his saddlebag and trained it on the riders.

"Can you make 'em out?" Breathed Billy as he stared at the faint images.

"Ten or eleven men, looks like." Said Rodney lowering the glass. "Hard-cases all, and riding single-file…. I heard where Belle Starr and her bunch were holed up in Arkansas somewhere, could be them." He sighed and put the glass away. "We're okay, though,…they're headed away from us."

"Good." Breathed Billy. "We'll leave them alone, if they'll leave us alone."

— —

They were back in the saddle bright and early the next morning, but this time Benny refused to be left behind, so he was securely tied to his saddle again.

"We ready?" Came Billy as Rodney tied the small rope securely. "Yeah." Grinned Benny,…I want to see the bats."

"I want to see them again, too." Grinned Willy.

He smiled at Connie and shook his head then climbed aboard the sidestepping Roan to rein her back toward the Choctaw. "This might take a while, Elijah, you be here when we get back?"

"I will watch the camp." He nodded.

"Be back as soon as we can, then." He turned the mare and led off toward the mountain again.

They were able to gallop their horses on the return trip, but the sun was still well up by the time they reached the spot where they had seen the bats, and that's where they dismounted and tied the horses, making sure they were hidden from the sight of anyone riding by below them.

Both men pulled yellow slickers from behind their saddles and put them on.

"What are those for." Queried Melissa.

"The bats." Grinned Rodney. We don't want to get rained on in there." He grinned at Billy as Connie leaned close to Melissa and whispered, causing her to nod her head and smile.

"We won't be gone too long." Said Billy as he untied the torches, Elijah had made for them last night. Giving one of the long sticks to Rodney, he walked over to Connie. "Stay in th' trees here and out a sight,…if we find a way through, we'll come back for you. The rifle's in th' boot there, if you need it, we'll hear th' shots and remember,… there's snakes out here, watch th' boys." He kissed her on the mouth then nodded at Rodney, who was just lifting Benny from his saddle, and the two of them began the climb to the cavern above them.

Fifteen minutes later, they were staring into the darkness of a large, cavern-like cave, where they immediately were forced to cover their faces with bandanas. The smell was enough to gag them as they fired up the torches and entered the large opening, the flames throwing a dim, flickering light on the uneven, rank-smelling walls.

"Keep your torch high, Billy." Said Rodney as they ventured inside. "This stuff could ignite, it ain't nothing but gas."

Raising the torches higher, they could just make out the roof and its inhabitants. Billy shook his head and led off over the thick, mushy blanket of bat droppings. They walked slowly, careful not to slip on the greasy dung, or into one of the numerous holes or cracks beneath the nauseating debris atop the rocky floor. There were deep pools of the droppings in the lower areas, and more being dropped at regular intervals to spatter dully into those pools. The floor itself was like walking on axle-grease and still, they moved ever deeper into the winding tunnel, hearing the occasional flapping of wings and shrill squeals from the ceiling overhead.

They had covered a good, one-eighth of a mile before the narrowing cave began to veer west, and that's where Billy suddenly stopped as the dim light glinted on metal in a crevice of the wall, and holding the torch closer, they could see the armor, as well as the polished bones.

"Looks like eight or ten men died in here." Gagged Rodney.

"Spanish soldiers." Nodded Billy.

"Yeah,…look how preserved th' armor is, no rust on it at all!…I wonder how they came to be in here?"

"I'd say they was hidin' from them Aztecs."

"Looks like they found 'em!"

They continued on down the tunnel and then, Billy noticed the flame of the torch as it began to flutter and bend in the direction they were going.

"There's air comin' in from somewhere." He commented and then continued on down the tunnel. They had been on dry rock since before they found the bones in the crevice, but the stench was still overpowering.

"Thank, God." Gagged Rodney.

They could see the cracks of daylight a short time later and when they approached, found themselves confronted by a huge, massive slab of rock that seemed to be blocking any exit from the cavern, and both of them placed their faces to the cracks and breathed deeply of the fresh air.

Billy held the flames higher, guessing the rock to be at least ten feet in height, and with no way to determine how thick it might be, looked at Rodney and shook his head.

"Dead-end!" Gasped Rodney. "What now, it's hard as hell to breath in here?"

"We got two choices. "Returned Billy, still looking at the rock. "We can try to move it,…or go back to camp and go fishing."

"How do we move it,…the damn thing must weigh a ton?"

"Pry-bars." Gagged Billy as he placed his face against the crack around the rock again. He breathed deeply then looked along the floor of the tunnel. "A good, strong pole might work.…We could move one a them rocks there in place and use it for leverage."

"There's plenty of saplings where we came in." Returned the lawman.

"Let's go get one." Nodded Billy. "We're too close to quit now."

The women were eagerly watching as they emerged from the cavern to make their way down the grade, and it was all Connie could do to keep Willy from bolting up to meet them.

"Did you see the bats, Daddy,…are they in there?"

"Yeah, did you see 'em?" Repeated Benny.

Billy grinned and waved as they neared the bottom, then nodded. "We sure did, boys."

"We smelled them, too." Grinned Rodney as he quickly went to untie the hatchets from his saddle. "I'm sure glad we brought these axes along."

"What are you doing?" Asked Connie. "Did you find a way in?"

"Don't know." Sighed Billy as he stopped beside her. "There's a very large rock blocking the exit at the other end, we're gonna try to pry it loose. We also found th' bones and armor of Spanish soldiers in there."

Her eyes went wide as he said that. "Really? And when he nodded. "My, God, Billy, what's that awful smell,…what's that all over your boots?"

"Bat-Dookie." Grinned Rodney and gave Billy one of the hatchets. "It's three or four inches deep on the floor in there."

"My Lord!"

"Which reminds me." Said Billy. "You women best get your slickers out, we're gonna need your help this time, th' boys, too, we got a pry that rock loose." He followed Rodney toward one of the tall saplings then as she grabbed the slicker from behind her saddle and hurried after him..

"Does it lead into the valley?" She asked as she donned the rain-cape.

"Maybe,…it goes through th' mountain all right, but whether or not it opens into our valley is another question….Oh, I stuffed th' boys' ponchos in my saddlebags, Honey." He bent down on one knee then and began hacking at the base of a good-sized sapling while Rodney chopped at it from the other side.

"We can help, too, Daddy." Said Willy at his elbow.

"Yeah, we can help." Voiced Benny.

"I tell you what, boys….If you'll stand back off a ways and watch for snakes while we fell this tree, you'll be helpin' a lot,…and don't let th' tree hit you when it falls, okay?"

The women also moved back while the tree was cut down.

— ~ —

They were finally at the end of the winding tunnel, gagging and staring at the massive boulder in front of them. Billy found a good, large rock and with the lawman's help, moved it in front of the boulder.

Connie gave the lighted torch to Willy and moved him back against the side of the cave with Benny as Billy fitted the long pole beneath the boulder and then across the rock.

"Okay all,…grab a hold a th' pole and pull down hard on it when I tell you….Ready?…Pull!"

They strained mightily at the pole for several seconds, then suddenly felt the slight movement as the huge rock began to shift on the powdery grit beneath it,… and then they rested.

"We moved it." Breathed Billy, shoving the pole further beneath the rock. "One more time now,…Go!"

They strained aching muscles for several more seconds and then, with a deep rubbing groan, the giant rock suddenly gave way and tumbled down the steep grade toward the lush floor of the valley to crash into the trunks of ancient Pine Trees before finally coming to rest.

They stared in awe at the valley's splendor as they gasped for breath in the fresh air. They were at least fifty yards up the inner side of the mountain, with large rocks littering the downward slope, and that slant closely followed the wall of the mountain, giving them a clue to its origin.

"Somebody built this grade, Billy." Said Rodney, "Its too even."

Billy nodded. "This is prob'ly th' way them Spaniards got in,...likely th' only way in back then."

"It's so beautiful." Said Connie as she took Billy's arm. "So lush, and untouched,...it's unbelievable, just like you said it was."

"We'll need the horses, Billy." Said Rodney. "This is a big place."

Nodding, Billy gripped Willy's shoulder. "Me and Uncle Rodney are goin' back for th' horses,...you and Benny keep an eye on th' women, okay?...And don't go down that grade, none of you, we'll be back in a little while."

They were back in what seemed like an hour to the women, and Rodney immediately lifted Benny to his saddle and roped him down as Billy and the women shrugged out of their rain-slickers.

"I can't get over how beautiful this place is." Sighed Connie as Billy helped her to her saddle. "It looks untouched by time,...like time has stood still, or something."

"I know." He said as he looked down at the trees. "Them trees could be well over a thousand years old, and I doubt if any of 'em has ever been cut.,... and I doubt the ground beneath 'em has ever seen th' sunlight."

"It's a paradise,...I love it already!"

"Yes it is." He nodded. "But you ain't seen nothin' yet." He smiled and mounted the skittish mare then nodded at Rodney to lead the way and watched as they started down the steep grade, then he took the spirit-pony's reins from Willy and followed Connie down behind the others.

They made level ground and rode out into the belly-deep grass where he then took the lead again, staying close to the sheer walls of the mountain as they skirted the ageless Pines and Giant Fir Trees. The Fir and Juniper were solid along the base of the cliffs and as they passed the pony-corral, he pointed out the natural cavern behind it before continuing on along the cliffs,...and it wasn't long until they saw the tall, rock doorway with its Aztec markings and stopped, once again to marvel at it.

"My, God." Gasped Connie. "It is real....Melissa and I have read everything, we could find about the Aztecs since you told us about this."

"And according to the books." Added Melissa. "They were only believed to have migrated to Arizona, and possibly Utah….So, how in the world did they wind up here?"

"Wait till you see what's inside." Grinned Rodney. "That cave is chock-full of treasure,… you couldn't dream that much treasure."

"Rodney's got it bad, doesn't he?" Grinned Connie.

"Yes, he does." Nodded Billy in return.

"What can I say?" Grinned the lawman. "I was born to be rich!" He looked at the scowl on Melissa's face then added. "If I'm rich, you're rich, honey.…Want to show them, Billy?"

"Lets check out th' main cavern, first." He led off through the grass toward the opposite end of the valley and a half-hour later, they were stopping at the polished rock floor of the gigantic cavern,…and there was nothing left that even suggested that anyone had ever been there, nothing but darkened splotches on the surface of the smooth, rock floor from the hundreds of cooking fires, that and the crimson blotches where the wounded had bled.

They dismounted and slowly walked across the length of the cavern floor and into the Council Chamber of the Ancient ones, where he immediately struck a match and touched it to the oil in one of the several rock columns along the walls.

"Oh, Billy!" Gasped Connie as the chamber was thrown into light. "Oh, my God!" She exclaimed when she saw the painted walls. "It's so tragically magnificent.…Look at it, Lisa,…can you believe it, it's just like they described it?"

Billy steered her toward the rear wall where the events of three years ago had been recorded. Suddenly, she gasped loudly. "That's where they found my baby, Isn't it?" Tears came to her eyes when he nodded.

"I remember this place, Daddy." Said Willy then. "But where'd the Indians go?"

"They left, Son."

"Where to?"

"I wish I knew." He took the boy's hand and Connie's arm then. "Come on, I want to show you somethin' else." They all left the chamber and followed him along the smooth outer walls, and after entering a much darker part of the cavern he turned through another doorway into the water-room. The lighting was very dim in the large cave, and the noise from cascading water very loud as they stared in awe at it. He steered her to yet another wall and an even darker doorway, where he picked up the ancient torch, lit it and then led the way into the Old Spanish mine. The tunnel was instantly thrown into brilliant color as the rich veins of solid gold in the walls and ceiling reflected the light.

The sudden introduction to the reflections were almost blinding as they stared at the tunnels contents. There were large nuggets everywhere, huge chunks of pure gold, all sizes of the precious metal,… and the floor was literally covered with it.

"It takes my breath away." Gasped Melissa as she stooped to pick up a large nugget. "God, its so heavy!" She gave the nugget to Rodney and stared at the walls again. "The walls are all solid gold, Rodney,…is this where ours came from?"

"Yes,…and this nugget right here is worth at least five hundred dollars,… the things that dreams are made of, Darlin'"

"Bring her back here, Rod." Echoed Billy's voice from deeper in the tunnel where him, Connie and the boys were waiting. "These are th' tools th' Spanish used to work th' mine." He said as he pointed at the spot. "There's picks, shovels and even a few breast-plates.…You can find their bones a little farther in a ways."

"They all died in here, didn't they?" Sighed Connie. "I wonder how many there were?"

"A couple of dozen judging by the bones." Said Rodney. "And they prob'ly didn't even know the Indians were attacking."

"Dear, God." She shuddered. "All of this, the tools, the armor,…I can't believe the history that's here. It should all be in a museum somewhere."

"Maybe someday it will be." Said Billy. "But not yet,…and maybe never if we don't want to see this place destroyed. Lets go back to th' cavern now.… And if you gals can find somethin' to do for a while, I'd like to take a good look around the valley." He steered them back to the water-room where the boys were skipping stones across the dark, sparkling water.

"My word!" Gasped Connie when she saw them. "I never saw them leave the mine."

"Me, neither." Exclaimed Melissa.

"No harm done." Said Billy. "Lets go, boys,…and stay together from now on, Son." He snuffed out the torch and they left the room.

"What now?" Asked Rodney as they walked toward the horses.

"I want to look for their bodies,…they have to be here someplace."

"And if they're not?"

"Then I'll accept your explanation."

They tightened the animal's cinches while the others caught up to them, then left their saddlebags on the rock floor.

"That's all th' food we brought with us." Nodded Billy. "You all can eat now, or wait for us,…we won't be gone too long." With that, they mounted and headed off through the trees.

The floor of the valley was in shadows as the sun sank behind the mountain, and was totally dark by the time they returned. They dismounted tiredly and pulled the saddles from the horse's sore backs, then did the same for the other animals before staking them out to graze. The women already had a fire going and that was a welcome sight as they stepped onto the cavern's floor.

"Fire feels good." He said, sitting down on one of the saddles.

"I thought it might." Smiled Connie. "Did you find anything?"

"No,...and it don't make any sense.. We went all th' way around th' perimeter of th' mountain,...there was no graves, no bones, no nothin',... they just disappeared."

"Maybe Rodney was right, and they left?"

He cut his eyes at Rodney then nodded. "It does look that way, as much as I hate to admit it. But where to?...we circled th' inside cliffs completely, and except for th' way we came in, there was no other way out, not even a landslide that might tell us they closed off an escape route. And they didn't leave th' way we came in, neither,...that rock's been there forever."

"I wonder how that rock got there?" Came Rodney. "We were damn lucky to have moved it."

"A slide, likely." Said Billy. "But it would have been a freak one for that rock to fall in just th' right place like that,...and without rollin' down that grade."

"Well, it could have been a slide." Said Rodney. "Or a quake, maybe,... or just another mystery we'll never solve."

"I don't know about that." Added Connie. "According to what we read about the Aztecs,...they were master stone-masons, experts at carving and even moving large rocks."

"That's right,...you should see the pyramids they built in Mexico." Said Melissa.

"I guess it could have been them at that." Said Billy as he accepted the slice of salt pork from Connie and bit into it. "Because it happened after them Spanish soldiers were killed. Anyway,... we're gonna have another look tomorrow."

"Why?" Asked Rodney. "Do you think we missed something?"

He shook his head. "I just want to be sure, because if we don't find some kind of an opening somewhere, your theory about that giant bird is also shot down. I know I'm a skeptic, Rod,...but that damn thing had to come from somewhere, and you're right about one thing,...this is the only logical place. We find where White Buffalo left th' valley and we'll find where that bird came in."

"The Pterodactyl." Sighed the lawman. "I'd almost forgotten our reason for being here. We'll look for as long as it takes....What finally convinced you they left, anyway?"

"Their horses." Shrugged Billy. "They would have survived here if they'd been left to fend for themselves,...and we found no bones to show they'd been killed." He stuffed the rest of the meat and bread into his mouth and chewed vigorously then reached for his canteen as he swallowed. "To tell you th' truth." He said, as he washed down the food with the cold water. "I'm some relieved we didn't find anything,…I didn't want to find anything."

"I know." Said Connie, touching his shoulder. "Anyway,…this whole thing is exciting,…isn't it? Even if we don't find anything, I'm glad we came."

"Yeah, and not only are we gonna sleep with ancient ghosts tonight." Grinned Rodney as he hugged Melissa. "Tonight, we are the richest people in the world."

"Not so loud, Rodney." Fussed Melissa. "You'll wake the boys."

"Okay. " He laughed. "Goodnight all."

"Come on, Billy." Urged Connie. "Let's get some sleep." She pulled him down off the saddle to lie beside her and pulled the blankets over them. But as tired as he was, he was still wide-awake. Connie was asleep in seconds, and he had to grin as he listened to her snoring.

His mind was a jumble of frustrating thoughts, and questions with no answers. He raised himself to lean against the saddle then rolled and lit a smoke as he watched the fire and listened to the night sounds in the valley. He inhaled the relaxant and stared intently at the domed roof of the cavern.

He could almost hear the ancient tribe of Choctaw as they moved about in their wickiups, could almost feel the presence of White Buffalo. Where could they have gone, he wondered? There was definitely a mystery here that he may never understand, and if there was no way to explain their disappearance,… there'd be no way to explain the Pterodactyl. The bird had to come from somewhere in this valley, but they had seen nothing that even gave a hint as to where it might have escaped from, or where the Ancient Ones had escaped to,…nothing at all. Aside from the council chamber, and the blackened floor of the cavern, there was no trace of them ever being here.

How could White Buffalo have survived the wound in his side? At the time, he had thought he could not, but now, he wasn't so sure,…because they had vanished without a trace, and had taken their horses with them. He shuddered then, almost able to feel the unnatural powers that controlled the valley,…like a shroud of mist was hiding the mystery and leaving no clues to be discovered. Were there other caverns in the valley somewhere? A cave, or tunnel that they hadn't found? There had to be something that they missed. He sighed and thumped the butt at the fire, then listened to the soft moaning of the wind in the trees as he fell asleep.

CHAPTER FIFTEEN

THEY WERE UP EARLY AND eating what food they had left, and when they were done, the men saddled their horses and again rode off through the tall grass toward the opposite end of the valley. The women and boys watched them leave, then quickly crossed the polished rock to the Council Chamber and went inside. Striking matches, they began lighting fires in the granite bowls atop the columns of rock along the walls. Then, while the boys sat on the floor, they began reading the history of the ancient people, having both developed a fascination for the primitive writings. Connie believed that the answer to their disappearance was hidden somewhere on the walls, and she so wanted to help Billy find the answers he needed.

Billy stopped the Roan as they came in sight of the treasure vault and sat staring at the thick stand of drooping Firs along the cliff leading up to it.

"We've been by here twice now, Billy." Sighed the lawman as he scanned the tree-lined cliffs.. "But I guess we could dismount and walk along the cliffs for a closer look,…what do you think?"

"Maybe,…but I think we got a be missin' somethin', Rod,… and it's right here someplace."

"I know, Billy, but what?…We've been over every foot of this mountain."

"They had dead to bury, Rod,… there was more than a dozen killed that night,…and we saw no graves. Why would they take th' bodies with 'em?"

"Beats hell out of me!"

"Okay,…lets make one more circle,…if we don't find anything, we'll try walkin'. If that don't work, we'll call it quits." He sighed and nudged the mare into motion again.

The sun had risen well above the top of the mountain as they came abreast of the treasure cave and here, they stopped once again to stare at the ancient painting of the winged serpent.

"You think there could be another exit in there?" Mused the lawman. "I could take a look, it don't look like they closed it all the way?

"Check it out then." Nodded Billy.

Rodney dismounted and tried forcing himself through the narrow opening, but couldn't and came to mount his horse again. "Can't get through. Now, what are you thinkin'?"

"Th' day we saw that treasure….I keep thinkin' it was my fault they had to leave, Rod. If I'd killed Snake way back when, none of this would have happened."

"Billy!" Said the lawman sternly.

"I know, Rod,…it wasn't my fault." He reined the mare past the cave and along the base of the cliff and that's when he saw what appeared to be a disturbance in the, otherwise, uniform grass and reined the mare toward the spot, only to stop abruptly when he saw the eggs. "Rod!" He breathed as the lawman pulled alongside of him. "Looks like I owe you an apology."

"Holy shit!" Gasped Rodney as he stared at three of the largest eggs he'd ever seen. "Pterodactyl eggs, by God!" He dismounted and pulled the rifle from its boot, took it by the barrel and smashed the eggs with the butt of it. "If these things had hatched out in here?" He shook his head and returned the gun to the boot. "Thank God, we found them."

"Yeah,…thank God we found th' way in here."

"I don't even want to think what might have happened if we hadn't." Breathed the lawman.

"Listen." Said Billy, quickly raising his hand for silence. They heard the crow then and began looking at the trees. They saw the large bird then as it glided to one of the sagging branches of a large Fir, not far from them. "It's an old friend of ours, Rod,…recognize it?."

Rodney grinned as he stared at the white-headed bird. "You think it's the same one?"

"I'd say so." The Crow cawed shrilly then and swooped down over the grass toward a thick stand of Fir at the base of the mountain, coming to rest on one of the thick branches there. When they didn't move, it suddenly flew toward them, cawing loudly, then lifted up and returned to the Fir again.

"What's he up to?" Grinned Rodney.

"It wants to show us something, Rod, come on." He urged the mare to the trees and dismounted as the Crow flew off across the prairie, then stooping, he moved the heavy limbs aside and went in beneath them, immediately seeing the large, dark opening in the wall of the cliff. His heart began to race as he swept away the cobwebs across the entrance. The opening was a good seven feet high, and as wide as a large horse. This had to be what they were looking for, he thought as he moved just inside of the cool, dark tunnel.

"Well, I'll be damned!" Exclaimed Rodney from behind him. "Remind me to thank that Crow!"

Billy came out of the tunnel grinning. "You mean you didn't hear it sayin', follow me?...Hell, it was plain as day to me."

"Sure I heard it,...I just didn't understand the language. But I'm learning!... Think this is it?"

"That Crow was pretty insistent on us finding it, so I'd say this is it, yeah. So why don't you go get th' boys and women-folk, they'll want a be in on this?...And bring that torch back with you."

Hearing him gallop away, he turned back to stare down the dark tunnel. They had to have gone this way, he thought, then grinned when he saw the petrified droppings in the rotted grass at the entrance. The next question, however, was where did it lead,...Arkansas somewhere? The Ozark Mountains were a wilderness, and could offer them safe haven for a long time. But that wouldn't explain the Pterodactyl being here. He walked back from under the branches into the sunlight and rolled a smoke, more confused than ever about the whole thing.

He was on his second smoke when they got back and was sitting against the wall beside the tunnel as Rodney held the branches up for the women to crowd in under them, leaving Willy and Benny to shove their way in beside them.

"Is this it, Billy?" Asked Connie excitedly. "My God, did they go in there?"

"We won't know till we look, Honey."

"Well lets go, Daddy." Yelled Willy.

"Yeah, lets go!" Echoed Benny, bringing laughter from all of them.

"Take it easy, boys,...we got a talk about this before we go anywhere." He looked into the tunnel then. "It's plenty big enough for a horse, and I did find old horse droppings just inside there,... so I'd say this is where they went, right enough....But this is also how that flesh-eating bird got out. We don't know what we'll be walkin' into in there,...it could be a nightmare. Now,...

you girls can come with us, or keep th' boys up here where you'll know it's safe, it's up to you."

"Not on your life, William Upshur!" Stated Connie. "We go where you go!"

"The same goes for me, too!" Voiced Melissa. "If anything happens to Rodney, it's going to happen to me, too."

Me, too." Shouted Willy, followed by his echo again.

It's settled then, I guess." Sighed Billy. "I don't know what we'll find in there, but each of you better damn well do what I tell you to do when we get there, cause we might have to do some fightin' before we get back....And I got a say that none of this makes any sense whatever to me."

"Maybe it ain't supposed to." Breathed the lawman. "Hell, nothing else does."

"I know that's right." Added Melissa.

"Okay then." Sighed Billy, grunting to his knees. "Lets unsaddle th' horses and stake 'em out in th' grass there."

They made quick work of picketing the animals then rejoined the women beneath the Firs. "Okay." Said Billy again. "We don't know what's in there, or where this tunnel's gonna take us, so stay close, keep your hand on the person in front of you at all times....I'll go first with th' torch, honey, you and Lisa bring th' boys in behind me, and Rod, you bring up th' rear,... you okay with that?"

"I've got my rifle, what can go wrong?...Lets go."

Nodding, Billy struck a match to the torch then looked at each of them before stepping into the tunnel. Almost immediately they were on a downward slant and the tunnel began to widen slightly as they walked. They continued ever downward in the twisting catacomb of the ages, and that tunnel seemed to have no end to it as for more than an hour, they moved ever deeper under the mountain, and the damp air was also turning colder. He felt Connie's hand squeeze his arm then and stopped. "What's wrong, honey?"

"I'm scared, Billy,... maybe we should turn back. If anything should happen down here, we might never get out."

"You'd be feelin' a lot worse if you'd stayed in th' valley, honey,...we're all together, and we're all gonna be okay,...trust me, it's gonna be okay."

Another hour passed before the tunnel finally leveled out, and still they moved along the winding corridor of sharp, uneven walls until at last, they finally found themselves in a massive room with nowhere else to go. Billy held the torch high and stared at the polished, smooth walls that surrounded them, and thought it to be at least a hundred feet long, and almost as wide. "Guess this is it." He said, his voice echoing around the room. "At least, it's as far as we go, looks like." He sighed a dejected breath of air and watched Connie go toward one of the walls.

"That can't be right, Billy." Breathed Rodney, coming to stand beside him.

I've found something here." Said Connie as she looked at one of the walls. "Here's more of those picture drawings with that same plumed serpent we saw on the rock up there."

"You boys stay close, you hear me?"

"Okay, Daddy, we will." Nodded Willy.

Billy held the torch above his head and joined Connie at the wall,... it was totally covered with pictographs and strange markings.

"These are Aztec writings, Billy." Said Connie as she moved along the wall in front of him. "And look at this one." She touched part of the strange drawing and studied it. It showed what could represent a yellow light with long and short streaks of yellow emitting from it, and in the midst of the streaks was a horseshoe-shaped, arch-looking object that appeared to be floating between the light and the ground below it. There were figures with strange headdress on the ground, their arms reaching upward toward the arch.

"What th' hell is this?" Muttered Billy.

"I have no earthly idea." Returned Connie, still staring at it. "But that yellow spot there could represent the sun with rays of light coming from it. But why is that horseshoe object just floating there in space?"

"Horseshoe?"

"That thing right there., see it?...And those are people below it there,... and they're either worshipping the arch, or trying to catch it for some reason.... But why would it be just hanging there like that?"

"Here's another sun over here." He held the torch closer so she could see it.

"Now that looks more like a sun than the first one, see how different the rays look, and look, some of the rays touch the arch on one side,...Lord, I wish I knew what this means?"

" What about those other marks?" He held the torch closer as he spoke, causing her to peer at the gray lines.

"They could represent rock, or the top of a mountain, maybe this mountain,...see,...that looks like a tunnel right there, or a shaft for the sun's rays to touch the arch,...but if that's the sun, then what's that other light, a star, the moon...or what?"

"There's hieroglyphics on that other wall there, too." Said Melissa from behind them. "Looks Egyptian to me."

"What the hell is this place anyway?" Breathed Rodney. "And why is it here?"

"A dead-end, Rod." Sighed Billy. "That's what it is."

"It can't be a dead-end." returned Connie "I think this all means something we can't even start to imagine,…and you know what else I think? I think that somewhere above us, there's a hole in the mountain, and when the sun is just right, something happens right here in this room….And you know what else?…I think that arch might be hidden somewhere right here in these walls."

"Well, at least one of us has some notions about it,…then what's that other yellow spot?"

"I don' know, Billy!." She sighed. "But whatever it is, it's lowering the thing into the hands of those people on the ground,…that's all it it can be doing?"

"Well,….I'm not sayin' you're wrong, honey,… but I don't see nothin' like that." Sighed Billy…. "All I see is what could be an ancient game of horse shoes." He pulled his watch from his pocket. "It's a little after ten,…how long do you think it'll be before somethin' happens?"

"God, I don't know, Billy!…I'm just telling you what I think it means."

"Bring the torch back here, Billy." Called Rodney, from the far side of the room. "There's more torches in the wall here,…they'll give us some more light."

Billy walked across the room and held his torch to the others, and one by one the ancient lengths of wood came to life, flooding the room with yellow, flickering light and illuminating the hundreds of pictographs and ancient writings on the walls.

"Can you believe all this?" Muttered the lawman.

"There's a whole city on this wall over here." Said Melissa. "Pyramids and all."

"I see them." Said Connie. "Look, Billy,…see the tower on that larger building, and the painting on it. That's the Aztec calendar, and it's just like the pictures in the book."

There's that arch again, too." Said Billy, moving farther down the wall. "And this one's got that feathered snake floating down with it."

"That's Quetzalcoatal." Said Melissa. "It's one of their Gods."

"I remember that." Said Connie. "The plumed serpent that could change it's self into a man at will. The legend says it came to earth on a chariot of fire several hundred years ago to teach the Mayans, and then the Aztecs…. It's magnificent, isn't it?"

Billy nodded then looked along the wall at the boys, they were laughing and kicking at something on the floor. "What's that you're kicking, Willy?"

"Horse-hockey!" He giggled.

Yeah, horse-hockey." Repeated Benny.

"They were here, Billy." Said Rodney. "You were right."

"Yeah." He sighed then looked at his watch again. He was beginning to tighten up inside and he didn't like it. Only a few minutes had passed since the last time he looked, and he was beginning to wonder if they should have turned back when Connie wanted to. There was nothing here but speculations, and nothing to tell them what it all meant. And, just what was supposed to happen when the sun's rays hit that arch?...If there really was one in the wall somewhere? He walked back across the room then.

Just what was the light above that arch, he wondered? Connie was right about one thing, there was a lot of history here,...but whose history? He stared at the yellow sun and the rays shooting from it. If those rays were representing the time of day, then maybe the longer ones could be the hours, and the shorter ones, half-hours and quarter-hours. He opened his watch again and looked at it, and then at the drawings. If he pictured the face of his watch on the wall just under the sun, with that arch in the very center of it, and then, if he lined everything up with the gray marks that Connie had said were holes in the mountain?...What he pictured then made his pulse quicken."

He got Connie's attention and pointed it out to her, and she came to the same conclusion by using the method. Whatever was going to happen, would happen at approximately eleven forty-five, give or take a minute or two.

"Come over here, Rod,...you, too, Melissa. I want a show you somethin'" He called the boys over also and once they were all there, he opened his watch and pointed at the wall again.

"Okay,...now, picture th' face of this watch, right here." He used his hand to circle the area beneath the sun. "And put this arch here right in th' center of it....Twelve o'clock would be straight up, right?... So that would put this streak of sunlight hittin' somewhere between eleven-thirty and twelve o'clock....We think that whatever's gonna happen in here, is gonna happen at about eleven, forty-five."

"Like what?" Queried Rodney. "All I see here is a room with no doors."

"Well, from what Connie's figured out,...that arch is in the walls of this room somewhere....And wherever it is, there's a hole leadin' from it, right up through th' top of this mountain,...and when th' sun's rays are just right, they'll touch the arch and trigger whatever's gonna happen in here."

"Good, Lord." Voiced Melissa.

"Well, I'll ask again,...like what?" Returned Rodney.

"It will open a door to,...somewhere,...I think." Returned Connie. "That's all that can happen....Of course, it's all speculation, Rodney, but we all know this room was created for a reason....There's just no way to know for sure what the reason is,...but logically speaking, something will happen here at about eleven, forty-five this morning."

"You mean,...a door will open up in these walls somewhere at eleven, forty-five,...is that what you're saying?"

"Yeah, Rod, it is." Said Billy. "And I don't think I want a know what it is, neither. So,... what we are gonna do, right now, is pack up and get th' hell out of this hole in th' ground!"

"We're not gonna wait to see what happens, ...what about the Pterodactyl?"

"Rod,...I don't give a damn about what's gonna happen down here,...and I care even less about that damn bird.... What I do know, is that we could all die down here. All we know right now,...is that th' Choctaw came down here, and that bird came out a here,...and I ain't got a clue as to th' wheres and hows of none of it.... If it was just you and me, it might be different, we could wait and see what happens,...but our family is with us, and I'm not gonna chance anything happening to them.... I thought this tunnel was gonna lead us out into another valley somewhere, maybe in th' Ozarks,...but this,...just look at these walls,... this whole room looks like its been carved out with a sharp knife or somethin', and then sanded smooth....No ordinary man could a done that. And th' drawins',...all of 'em weren't made by the Aztecs,...Connie and Melissa both said that....So who did make 'em?" He looked around at the smooth walls again.

"There's somethin' goin' on here, that we are a hell of a lot better off not knowin' about....And I want a show you why I think that,... come over here." He led them back to the wall and pointed. "This ball of light right here, th' one Connie said was th' sun?...Well Lisa got me to thinkin' about it.... See them lines that look like rays of sunshine?...Well one of 'em runs all th' way down th' wall here, and then all th' way up to th' ceilin',...see it?...See all them yellow dots up there?... You know what I think they are?"

"No." Said Connie. "We don't."

"I do." Exclaimed Melissa. "They're stars, and that line goes right to one of them,...see there!...I'm right, aren't I, Billy?"

"We've got no way of knowing that, Honey." Exclaimed Rodney. "Is that really what you're thinking, Billy?"

Billy shrugged. "I got no reason not to,...in fact, I'd say it's highly possible."

"My, God." Muttered Connie. "In a weird sort of way, it does make sense. And if its true, that larger light could be some sort of machine,...a flying machine."

"Oh, God, I'm dying!" Groaned the lawman. "There ain't no such thing as a flying machine,...here, or in space!"

"How little you know, dear husband of mine." Returned Melissa. "They have giant balloons that fly by using steam,...and they are experimenting with winged gliders....Even Leonardo DeVinci believed men could fly by using machines."

"And whoever carved out this room was a hell of a lot smarter than those people." Added Billy. "So lets go, we can block this tunnel when we get out."

Rodney nodded. "I can't argue with that, Billy,...But I do wish you could argue something without using all that logic....Now lets go, I can't stand anymore of this."

"What say you gals,...you ready?"

"I was ready to turn back before we got here." Returned Connie. "I only wish we had time to write down some of these symbols...oh, well,...lets go, come on, boys."

"Grab one of them torches from th' wall there, Rod" Said Billy as he led the way back into the tunnel.

CHAPTER SIXTEEN

"I DON'T THINK THIS PLACE has been used in centuries, at least not till th' Ancient Ones came down here." Said Billy from the front of the line. "I think its all just somebody's toy,…a means of recreation that they eventually got tired of."

"It's a very dangerous toy, if it is." Returned Connie, from behind him.

"Yeah,…but whose toy?" Came Rodney. "We didn't see anything, but pictures on th' wall,…and don't tell me its people in flying machines. Anyway," He sighed. " Lets just pray nothing else gets out of here, we might have to come back to fix it."

"Don't jump th' gun, Rod." Returned Billy. "This one ain't fixed yet."

"We will,…I hope." Muttered the lawman, and then in a louder tone. "Hey, Will,…you like to write,… if you ever decide to write a book about this when you grow up,…I've just thought of a title for it,…how's this?…"The Guardians of time",…pretty catchy, ain't it?"

"You're funny, Uncle Rodney."

"Yeah, you're funny, Uncle Rodney." Repeated Benny.

"What?…Is there an echo in here?"

It took them more than two long hours to make their way up the tunnel's steep incline but at last, they were once again in the bright sunlight of the hidden valley, and hearing the greeting snorts from the animals as they pushed their way out from beneath the sagging branches of the giant Fir and into the lush grass. Billy stopped then to look around, then turned to look back at the tunnel.

"We have to block it up, Rod,...make it look like it ain't there at all."

Rodney nodded and they both studied the walls of the mountain until Billy finally pointed at a tall slab of solid rock that stood against the cliff.

"Think we could pull that over?"

"Yeah, maybe,...if its not part of th' cliff....all we'd need to do is topple it sideways....That should cover it up nicely,... if we can do it."

"Lets saddle up then, maybe we can loop our ropes over th' top of it." He said, and between the two of them, managed to saddle up the four riding horses and lead them back to the Fir.

"You think you can do it?" Asked Connie as she came to walk beside him.

He nodded. "If its not attached to th' mountain, we can....We're gonna try and rope th' top of it and pull it down sideways."

"Good luck." She sighed, then stopped to watch them.

"Connie?' Said Melissa, from behind her. "Do you really think that could have been a space-machine?"

"Of course not, Lisa,...that's just what it could have represented...If there was life on other worlds, the Bible would speak of it, don't you think?...And nowhere in my Bible does it even reference life on other planets."

"Then how do you explain those markings,...they're not Egyptian hieroglyphics, at least not like those in the books?"

"I can't, Lisa,...maybe they're older than that."

"But if it is alien writing,...it would mean there is life on other planets, wouldn't it?...And if it was them who made that room and wrote those things,...they could come back any time they wanted,...even right now,... couldn't they?"

"I guess they could, but if they did come here right now, we would probably be able to see them. But if it was say, five minutes ago when they got here, we couldn't see them. Because right now is our present,... our past would be five minutes ago,...But then, they couldn't see us either, because they'd always be that far behind us."

"Five minutes behind us? Connie, I'm not talking about going back in time,...now, that would be impossible. But I do see what you mean,...I guess....Time doesn't wait for anyone....But still, if they showed up right now, we might not be surprised at all,...because they might look just like us."

"Don't be so sure, they'd probably be a lot different,,...they could have three eyes or something, or maybe only three fingers....But seriously, Lisa,...if there really is alien life in space, they're probably already here….We may have already seen them and just don't know it.,…and I'm only saying that because of what we've seen down there, and I'm not back-tracking, either,…I'm just widening my beliefs a bit. Who knows, maybe those who wrote the scriptures didn't know, or chose not to write about such things….Maybe, for our own good."

Billy and the lawman stopped just in front of the Fir Trees and shook out their loops. "Its going to be real tricky, Billy,…we'll have to throw over this tree,…so make a big loop and throw it high….I want you to know, too,… that I was never real good with a rope."

"That's still better than I am with one."

The ropes flew true, however, and settled around the top of the rock, then they mounted and looped the ropes around the saddle-horns of all four horses, then urged them to pull.

The horses strained at the task, and after several re-starts, and several minutes, the massive slab of rock began to lean and then, Suddenly, it toppled sideways, scraping the side of the mountain as it crashed through the branches of the Fir to cover the tunnel's large opening completely.

Dismounting, they took the hatchets and chopped away the broken limbs so that over time, new branches would grow over the disturbance.

"That ought a do it." Sighed Billy. "Now I'm gonna take these horses to water, there's a creek in th' corral yonder." He looked at Willy then, "Mount up, son, and bring Benny's pony with you." He waited while Rodney boosted Willy up then led off.

"God, I'm glad we're back." Sighed Melissa as she took Rodney's hand. "Um,…we'll be right back, honey, we're going to walk over to those trees, Connie and I need a little privacy, if you know what I mean….Keep an eye on Benny for me, okay?"

"Watch out for Rattlers." He grinned. "Could be some big ones here." He watched Billy and the horses until they dismounted at the creek, then looked back at the slab of rock and hoped it would be enough to hold back whatever else might try to escape the past. The large rock was at least two feet thick and weighed a ton or more…. He knew the present had nothing to fear from something as large as a dinosaur, but an animal the size of a horse could enter the tunnel, and if it was aggressive enough, might even succeed in breaking through the barrier. He sighed then. They would have to come back to make sure, he was sure of that. He felt Benny take his hand then and looked down at him. "What's wrong, little-man?...You got to go pee, too?" And when he nodded. "Well then go right there in th' grass, ain't nobody here but you and me." He grinned and idly watched the trees for the women.,…his thoughts, once again returning to the tunnel.

What if they were not doing enough to stop more of those creatures from getting loose? Even if that rock was enough to contain them, what if that Pterodactyl picture was to make it all the way to Washington? Would it trigger another investigation? He shook his head in confusion, knowing there was a possibility they might not be able to keep the valley a secret. He saw the women then, and taking Benny's hand walked toward the trees to meet them. "Come on," He grinned. "I want to show you gals something."

They were all standing around the remains of the Pterodactyl's nest when Billy and Willy got back and dismounted. "You boys stay close now, okay?"

"Come on, Willy." Shouted Benny. "Look what we found."

"Look at how thick this shell is, Billy." Remarked Connie as she showed it to him and Rodney. "The eggs must have been enormous."

"They was." Returned Billy. "You girls ready for that bath you wanted.?"

"I'm dying for it." She smiled. "But I want to see the treasure first."

"I thought you might,…if we can find them pry-poles, we'll do it….You remember where th' warriors threw 'em, Rod,…I don't."

"Yeah, I think they're under them trees,…if they didn't move 'em"

"Willy." Said Billy. "Go back to th' Fir and grab them torches, will ya, Son?" And when he left, helped Rodney insert the long, dry pole into the opening of the cave and finally managed to move the huge rock out enough to get into the treasure room.

"Here's the torches, Daddy." Puffed Willy as he slid to a stop beside him.

"Thanks, son,…but one's enough." He struck a match to the ancient wood. "Follow me, ladies." He grinned. "I'll give you th' grand tour."

Connie stopped to stare up at the large stone door. "Just look at that drawing, Billy, the colors have hardly faded at all,…isn't it wonderful?"

"I'm about to show you something even more wonderful, come on in." He took her hand and led her around the great, stone door and through the opening. The ancient treasure was immediately thrown into a glaring brilliance as the pale light touched it, and both men grinned widely at the women's astonishment.

"Oh, my." Gasped Melissa as she came forward. "Just look at that!…It's,… magnificent!"

The women, as well as the boys, were mesmerized by the tall, clay jars with their Aztec symbols, and the fact that they were overflowing with minted Spanish coins and rope-chains of solid gold. There were bracelets and neckwear of braided gold, some inlaid with Jade and large Emeralds. Coins and loose Gems partially covered the stone floor around the jars, along with large pieces of Jade, emeralds and rare Rubies.

Golden statues of Aztec Gods stood behind the jars, and were also inlaid with gems. Golden masks were hung from pegs of ancient wood along the walls,...and a tall pyramid of gold ingots had been placed against one side of the cave, and it was as tall as the roof of the room.

"Be careful where you walk." Warned Billy. "Especially you boys, rattlers could have crawled in here."

"Does all of this belong to us now?" Gasped Connie as she held up a magnificently adorned necklace.

"In a way,...I guess it does." Said Billy. "But, legally, it would belong to the Choctaw,...and th' Federal government. But,...as long as we're th' only ones who know about it, it belongs to us. But, we can't take any of it out a here."

"Why not?" Gasped Melissa. "This is worth a fortune."

The Government would just take it away from us, once they found out about it,...somethin' to do with th' historical value, and th' like. Then we'd be forced to tell 'em where it came from."

"And we know what would happen then." Sighed Melissa.

Connie nodded. "And it's a shame, too."

"It's not all that bad." Grinned Billy. "We still got us a gold mine,...and I think that'll do just nicely. But I'll tell you what,...Both of you can pick out one piece of jewelry to take home,...sort of an heirloom....But just one."

He grinned as they painstakingly made their choice and then ushered everyone outside, then him and Rodney used the pry-pole to completely close up the vault.

"How on earth can we keep this a secret, Billy?" Asked Connie as he was saddling Willy's pony.

"We forget that its here, Honey." He lowered the stirrup then looked back at the giant door. "It won't take long for th' vines to cover that paint there,... and after that,...who knows."

"What a shame, too." Sighed the lawman.

"Why don't we buy the mountain, Billy?" Cried Connie suddenly. "Why not buy it all,...even the land around it....We could build a home here in the valley,...we could all go in together and do it, the four of us,...I would love that!"

"What about your Café,...and th' farm?"

"We wouldn't have to completely move up here,...it could be a home away from home?'

"I sort of like that idea." Grinned Rodney as he pulled himself into the saddle. "We both know that somebody's gonna find this place,...there's a way in now. And it might be the only way we can ever hope to protect it."

Billy helped Connie and Willy to their saddles then mounted the Roan before grinning at the lawman. "You ready to hang up your gun and badge, Rod?"

"Nope,…but I could request a Federal Marshals appointment, with this area as my jurisdiction….After all, they're still minus one marshal in these parts."

"It is something to think about at that," Shrugged Billy." "Now come on, th' ladies need a bath,…and so do I."

The boys filled the canteens with the sparkling cold water and they all drank thirstily of it, then Connie began to rummage through the knap-sack for the bar of lye-soap.

"Now." She beamed. "If you Gentlemen will excuse us, you can go outside and wait your turns."

"Yeah, okay." Laughed Rodney. "Just don't use all the water."

"I just hope I don't freeze." Shuddered Melissa.

Once the men were back on the cavern's polished floor and getting dressed, Connie and Melissa exited out of the Council Chamber and came toward them.

"What were you two doin' in there?" Grinned Billy.

"There's some fascinating reading in there." Smiled Connie.

"Now." Grinned the lawman, after he buckled on his gun-belt. "Lets go get what we came for."

"How do you suggest we carry it, Rod?" Returned Billy. "We didn't bring anything strong enough to hold that much weight."

"There you go again with that damn logic….What do you suggest we do then? I'm not going home without it."

"We go back to camp and eat a good meal,…then, after Elijah leaves, we cut up th' tarp and come back for th' gold in th' mornin',… we can bring th' mules back to tote it out."

"That sounds good." Sighed Connie. "I'd like to spend another day or so here anyway….It's so peaceful."

"Yeah." Nodded Melissa. "That would be nice, although I miss my baby."

"Its settled then." Nodded Billy. "We'll come back tomorrow and load up what we can carry."

"Well, if we're leaving now, me and Lisa will be right back." She smiled as they walked off toward the trees.

"Look out for snakes!" Yelled Rodney.

— —

They covered the length of the valley at a slow walk through the tall grass, and once the grade to the bat-cave came into sight, Rodney nudged his horse up beside Billy.

"What's up, Rod?"

"Still thinking, I guess…. But if White Buffalo and his people did go back to the past, somehow…where do you think they went?"

"Someplace compatible with their way of life." Said Connie.

"They could be right here in th' valley, too." Said Billy, looking around at the ageless Pines. "And still protecting th' mountain….But then again,…who knows where they went,…hell, they could a gone anywhere?"

"Okay, then why would the Spanish build this grade when there was another way out of here?"

"Oh, I'm sure this bat-cave was th' only way in when th' Spaniards came….Aztecs probably dug th' other two,…remember th' sand? They would a had to have a way to take th' gold out"

"Speaking of that sand." Returned Connie. "The Aztecs would have been the only ones with the knowledge to use it like that."

"Makes sense to me,…I guess." Nodded Rodney and dropped back beside Melissa and the boys as they started the climb to the cavern's tall entrance. They dismounted there and led the animals into the darkness,…and a half-hour later were walking out of the grotto onto the downward slope of tall pines, and trying to rid their boots of the bat-dung in the process. That's when they saw the thin man get up from one of the rocks he had been sitting on.

"You see 'im, Billy?" Queried Rodney, from behind him. "You know him?"

"That would be Peter." Nodded Billy.

"He just saw us come out of that cavern, too,…is that a good thing?"

"You couldn't make him go in there, Rod,…don't worry about that."

They mounted and rode down the last several yards of the slope, where they dismounted again in front of the slender tracker, and smiling, Billy shook the outstretched hand of the little Choctaw.

"It's damn good to see you, Peter,…how've you been?"

"I am well." He nodded. "I became worried when Elijah said you had been gone for more than a day,…so I tracked you here and waited."

"To tell you the truth." Said Rodney at Billy's elbow. "We were worried. Too….Hi, Peter, I'm Rodney Taylor, and I'm glad I'm getting the chance to thank you for saving our bacon."

Peter looked at him a little puzzled, then suddenly nodded. "Ah,…in the canyon,…you are much welcome."

"I'd like you to meet part of my family, Peter." Grinned Billy. "This is my wife, Connie, and my son, Willy."

"This one must be Little Wolf." He grinned and shook Willy's hand. "And I am very glad to meet you miss Upshur."

"And this one is my very good friend, and City Marshal." He waited as Peter and Rodney shook hands again. "And this is Rodney's wife and his Nephew, Benny." He grinned then and moved slightly to one side as the two of them talked, then stared back up at the mountain, wondering just how long the valley's secrets would stay hidden? Rodney was right, sooner or later someone would stumble onto that bat-cave and inevitably, the valley and its contents. And he had a gnawing feeling that it would not be too awfully long in coming. These hills were still harboring some of the country's worst outlaws, and that valley would make an ideal hideout.

Maybe he should try to buy the mountain. Like Rodney said,…it might be the only way to protect it, as well as their newly acquired gold mine. And private property would be somewhat of a deterrent to other treasure hunters, outlaws, too,…maybe,… the outlaws would have to be handled differently. But, if he owned the entire mountain, and its mineral rights, the law would be on their side and then the treasure, as well as the gold mine would belong exclusively to them.

He thought of the drawings in the underground room and wondered if there really could be another world up there in the stars somewhere? A power that could cut a room that large from solid rock, like that, would never be known to ordinary humans, because they could never conceive it,…and they damn sure couldn't control it,…and that just might be a good thing, too. It was a fragile world anyway, and he couldn't fathom what might have happened if those eggs had been left alone to hatch,…and believable or not,… that Pterodactyl and its eggs, as well as that room with its strange drawings, were all anchored in a very true possibility of there being people out there in space somewhere. He was sure the answers to it all was on those walls down there, too,…and he was also sure they were better off not knowing those answers.

He caught Connie looking at him then and smiled at her as he walked over and placed a hand on Peter's shoulder. "You're a big hit with th' family, Peter,…I haven't seen Connie laugh so much in weeks,"

"You have a very nice family, Mister Upshur,…and I like your friends very much also."

"So do I, Peter….What do you think of Little Wolf, now?"

"Little Wolf is growing tall and strong, like his father."

"That brings us to you now." Said Billy. "Elijah said you was workin',… did you get your man?"

Peter shook his head. "Marshal Books had word that the Jesse James gang may have robbed the bank in Poteau, up in the Cherokee Nation, and his brave Osage tracker was too afraid to track them. But we lost the trail at Eufaula…. I think maybe his information was wrong anyway."

"This Marshal any better than your Marshal Thompson was?" Queried Rodney.

"Not so much." Grinned Peter. "You might have to shoot this one also."

"How'd you know about that?"

Peter shrugged. "I saw him with the others before that day,…and I saw the sun on his badge when you killed him."

"Tommy Thompson?"

"Yes." Nodded Peter. "He was never a man to be trusted."

"How did you know we were there, anyway,…the Crows tell you?"

Peter shook his head. "I followed you from the mountain, but at a distance,…I was worried you might be attacked."

"Then you saw th' fight at th' mountain?" Returned Billy.

Peter nodded. "I see it from a distance." He looked at Billy then, and nodded at the mountain. "Did you find what you seek here?"

Billy shook his head. "Its like they were never there at all."

"Perhaps the legends are true. Maybe they are spirits."

"No,…they were real, Peter,…we found where they went, we just didn't find them, and I'll say this…. You were right in being afraid to come here. Your people, and everybody else must not go in there."

"Yet, you went inside."

"We had no choice,…that monster bird came from here. This mountain is guarding some terrible secrets, Peter,…and I think that bird was only one of them."

"The Devil-bird." Nodded Peter. "You speak the truth, I see it in your eyes."

"This mountain must be protected, Peter,…and we need your people to help."

Peter shook his head. "The Choctaw will not fight to protect the mountain."

"Would they,… if they was legally trained and paid to do it?"

"I do not understand, Mister Upshur."

"I'm talkin' about a couple dozen men, paid and trained to police th' Choctaw Nation….Trained men that are armed and able to do th' same job th' Ancient Ones did,…seein' that justice is served for every Choctaw."

"My, God, Billy." Grinned Rodney. "What a great idea….Peter here could be Chief of Police, in charge of the whole shebang. He could do the recruiting, the training, all of it."

"We'll talk about it at supper tonight, Peter." Grinned Billy. "Besides, there's something else I want to talk to you about anyway." He grinned and gripped the Choctaw's thin shoulder again. "Rod gets a mite exci…"

"Billy!" Interrupted Rodney suddenly.

Hearing the caution in the lawman's voice, he looked at him, then quickly in the direction he was looking, seeing the two men on horseback, and with two more on foot as they came up the incline toward them.

"Be ready, Rod." He whispered. "Peter, you best move back, there could be trouble here." He turned to Connie then. "Take th' kids and horses back up in th' rocks, and stay there, all of you, no matter what happens,…do you understand?" And when Connie tearfully nodded. "Th' Rifle's in th' boot, remember that."

"I'm scared, Billy,…what are you going to do?"

"I don't know, now go! Son, you take Benny,… go,…use th' rifle if it comes to it,…but stay there!" He watched as they hurriedly led the animals up the hill into the rocks, then he turned back to watch the men approach.

The men were almost there when he nodded at Rodney, who then moved several feet to one side of him, while Peter had backed away a few paces then slowly moved to the right of Rodney.

The men were still some thirty feet down the grade when the man with the rifle raised his arm and waved at them, then he said something to the other men and continued on up the rise toward them.

Billy studied them intently, noting that they were heavily armed. They had shaggy beards and their clothes were filthy, and he knew them instantly for what they were,…and also hoped he was prepared for them. He continued to watch them, studying their hard-eyed faces as they drew closer, noticing that one of the men on horseback was an Indian, a narrow-eyed Indian with an unsmiling face, and even at that distance, the eyes were what held his attention. They were cold and dead looking, and they sent a chill through him.

"Didn't expect to find anybody way up here." Grinned the man with the rifle. "But I'm damn glad we did." His eyes flicked up the hill to the women and horses, causing him to flash tobacco-stained teeth in a lop-sided smile as he looked back at Billy.

"What happened to your horses?" Asked Billy.

"Huh?,…oh,…I guess we rode 'em to death. Anyways, they dropped dead on us." He shrugged then. "That's why we're so glad to see you fellers."

Billy dropped his arm to his side as he spoke, causing the man to stare at the double-gun rig. "And why is that?" He drawled.

"Cause you got horses." He grinned. "And we don't."

"And they're also not for sale." Grated Billy, his eyes darting from him, to the cold face of the Indian on the horse.

"Truth is." Continued the rifleman, also turning to look at the Indian. "We had to leave Mena, uh,…that's a town over in Arkansas, east a here a ways.…Anyway, we left in a bit of a hurry, and that's why we need your horses."

The Indian dismounted as the rifleman was talking and slowly came to stand beside him.

"You running from the law?" Asked Rodney dryly.

"You might say so,…yes'ir. Leastwise, they was a good-sized posse chasin' us."

"Well, I'm the law up here, Mister." Rodney moved his vest aside to reveal the badge. "And whatever it is, you've got a mind to do, you'd best forget it and move on."

The rifleman sized him up for a moment and then, with a sidelong glance at the Indian, he shrugged. "Ain't nothin' we'd like better, Marshal, but we need them horses,…look." He waved his hand in the air and sighed mightily. "I,…we could'a shot all a you from behind a rock down yonder,…but I wanted to be neighborly about this."

"The answer is still no!" Interrupted Billy tightly, his eyes still engaging those of the Indian. He knew this man was dangerous, and probably very fast, but it was the eyes that still held his fascination. They were lifeless, pale and evil looking, and seemed to bore right into his mind. This was the man he would have to fight.

The rifleman glanced again at the Indian, then at Billy. "I am real sorry you said that." He grinned then jerked his head at the Indian.

"This here is Mister Kiowa Joe Christmas,…you ever hear of 'im?" And when Billy shook his head. "Well, its no matter,…ye see, he's still a youngster, and not known too good yet,…but he will be. He is deathly fast with that gun, too,…that's what he is. He don't say too much, neither, but he'll shoot you real sudden like,…as you're about to see. Now, Joe needs all th' practice he can get,…and that's why I let 'im talk me out a shootin' you good old boys a while ago."

"Mister." Said Rodney suddenly. "You need to re-think all of this, because no matter what happens here, you're a dead man,…both of you." He nodded his head at Billy then. "Because I take it, you don't know who this is, neither."

The rifleman looked Billy up and down. "Can't say that I do,…no."

"Well, they call him, the Farmer." Said Rodney as he tried desperately to change their situation peacefully. "Ever hear of Black-Jack Slade?"

The rifleman stared at him blankly, then back at Billy. "He kill Slade, did he?"

Rodney nodded. "Slade and the men with him,...they wanted our horses, too."

By this time, the fourth man had dismounted and joined the third man, both of them moving several paces to the left, and this prompted Peter to move to face him.

"The way I see it." Continued Rodney. "You men don't fit any wanted posters here,...so why don't you save us all a lot of trouble and move on?"

"Unless you're tired a livin'." Said Billy evenly. "That's damn good advice."

The rifleman nervously scratched at his beard and looked at the Indian. "Know what I think?" He grinned, looking back at Billy. "I think Joe, here is gonna kill th' both of ye. And don't you worry none about them purty little gals off yonder, neither,...we'll take real good care a them."

"Rod?" gritted Billy. "Whatever happens on this side,... I want you to kill that son of a Bitch!"

"Pleasure's all mine." Breathed the lawman.

Billy nodded and continued to stare at the Indian. "Then I guess it's your move, Mister Kiowa Joe Christmas." Grated Billy, still watching the pale eyes intently. "Or do you need to do a war-dance first?" He saw the blink then and made his draw, the Colt fairly leaping into his hand, and he fired in almost the same instant as the Indian, his slug literally lifting the slender Kiowa off his feet as he was hit, and the impact was such that it slammed him backward under the hoofs of the rearing horses, some several yards down the grade.

It had happened in the slightest of heartbeats, and in the space of that same heartbeat, he turned the gun on the rifleman, his bullet and Rodney's striking the ashen-faced killer at almost the same time. He quickly turned the gun on the third man as he was thumbing back the hammer of his pistol and shooting him before he could pull the trigger. They both moved to shoot the fourth man then, but stopped when they saw Peter stoop and pull his long-bladed hunting knife from the dead man's chest.

Letting the air out of his lungs, Billy half stumbled as he quickly sat down on a large rock behind him, then placed his head in his hands and breathed deeply for a time. He could hear Connie and Melissa screaming then and raised his head to watch as they all ran down the slope toward them.

"Oh my, God, Billy!" Screamed Connie as she ran. "Oh my, God!"

"Are you all right?" Asked Rodney as he squatted down in front of him. "You ain't hit, are you?"

He looked at the lawman and nodded. "He almost beat me, Rod." He breathed. "Scared th' hell out a me." He holstered the pistol then and looked at his arm.

"It was close all right." Sighed the lawman, tugging at the bloody hole in the sleeve. "He nicked you, man." He moved away as Connie got there then went to take Melissa in his arms, consoling her and a screaming Benny.

"Oh, Billy!" Cried Connie as she dropped to her knees and wrapped her arms around his neck to silently cry.

Billy hugged her to him with his right arm and pulled Willy against him with the other. "I love you both." He said and hugged them even tighter. "But I'm okay,…everything's all right."

"I've never been so scared, honey." She sobbed.

"I'm okay." He said again. "Now come on, it's over….I'm sorry you and Willy had to see that,…it just couldn't be avoided."

"My, God, Billy, you're hurt!" Gasped Connie suddenly.

"It's just a scratch, honey,…it's okay." He held her away from him and looked at her concerned face, then grinned at the wide-eyed expression there. "Are you okay?"

She nodded. "I,…think so." She stammered.

He looked at Willy then. "Are you okay, son?"

Connie tore a strip of cloth from her blouse to use as a bandage then quickly rolled his sleeve up above the wound,

"I saw it all, Daddy." Said Willy excitedly. "You're a gunfighter, just like Mister Lance was, aren't you?"

"Don't think about that, son,…I had to protect you and mama, that's all….I'm sorry you had to see it,…and, son,…I'm gonna have to ask you not tell anybody about what you saw here today, okay?...nobody at all."

"But, why, daddy, it was great?

"No, it ain't great, son. Just don't tell anybody about it, you hear?"

"Gosh Darn it,…I can't tell anybody anythin' about this trip!"

"I'll explain it all to you one day, son."He shook his head and watched him walk up the grade toward the horses to sulk, then looked up to see Peter watching him and grinned. "You're damn good with that knife, my friend,… thanks for th' help."

"You did not need me, I think." Shrugged the Choctaw. "I have never seen a fight like that before,…even in Winchester Station." He looked at the crumpled body of the Kiowa some thirty feet below them. "This Kiowa was much faster than the dark man." He nodded. "You are truly a man to be respected, Mister Upshur."

"Thanks, Peter,…did you know him?"

"No,…but I have seen him kill before….He was a man with no soul. Even his own people scorned him."

"How'd he come by a name like Joe Christmas?" Grinned Rodney.

Peter shrugged. "An Indian only has one name,…but sometimes it takes two words to make the one. The Indian's name most times comes from a vision that his mother, or father sees during birth. But I think this Kiowa chose his own name, or it was given to him by a white family when he was very young,…because the name carries no meaning to the Indian….I think maybe this one chose it so he might live as an equal to the white man,…I think because it was part of the white man's celebration."

"What's yours, Peter?" Queried Billy.

"Birdsong….My father's white name was Wilson." He shrugged. "I chose to live in the old ways when I became older"

"And Elijah?…How'd he come by Two-Rains?"

Peter grinned. "It rained twice as he was born."

"And where does Wilson come from?"

"A white man, is all I know….The Choctaw try to live as equals also."

"There." Sighed Connie, tugging the sleeve over the bandage. "That will do till we get back to camp."

Rodney laughed and placed Benny on the ground, then the three of them walked to where the men had died and picked up their weapons, Rodney pulled the gun-belts from their waists and brought them all back to drop them beside Billy. "These are for your police force, Peter,…when you decide." He grinned. "Horses and saddles, too,…after I bury these gents….Oh, I've got a lot more guns in my office I can bring you, too."

"I will help you to bury them." Grinned Peter, and they walked back to the bodies where he helped the lawman drag the bodies over, and they soon had the four men draped across the backs of both horses.

"I'll bring the shovel down." Said Rodney then started up the hill to the horses.

Peter walked back to where the guns lay and stared at them.

"What are you thinkin', Peter?" Asked Billy.

"I think a police force is needed here." He nodded. "We have had one in place for many years, but they have became lazy, and too afraid of White Buffalo and the Ancient Ones to do their jobs,…they have become a joke. They are still in place, I think, but in name only. They were ordered to apprehend a gang of horsethieves before the Devil Mountain was attacked." He looked up at the mountain and sighed before looking back at Billy. "Chief Bryant controls the police force,… how can I convince him that I am the one that should control them?"

"We, Peter." He grinned. "We will convince him,…we'll work it out over supper tonight." They watched then, as Rodney brought the animals down and gave Melissa the reins,…then he untied the shovel and grinned at them. "You ready, Peter?"

"Where you gonna bury 'em, Rod?"

"Down the valley a ways, why? You don't think I want to bury 'em too close, do you?"

"Too close to what?"

Rodney shrugged then grinned. "My Trading Post, of course."

"Your Tradin' Post?"

"Yeah,…right here on this very spot, I think. The Choctaw will need a place they can buy and trade goods at a fair price. And you know what else?… I'm gonna build the Marshal's office right beside it."

"And I will help you to build it." Grinned Peter.

"You see, Billy." Grinned the lawman. "We've made our plans,…it's time you made yours." He grinned widely, then him and Peter went toward the loaded horses.

"How do you feel about all this, Lisa?" Asked Billy as they walked away with the bodies. "Think you could live way off up here away from your folks?"

"He's serious about it." She nodded. "So,…sure, I guess so. It's not that too awful far to Paris,…and we can visit."

"And what about us?" Sighed Connie. "You know how I feel about it."

He nodded then. "We'll see what happens….It'll be up to us to convince th' Choctaw Chief to sell it to us. But I think you and Rodney are both right,…buyin' th' mountain is th' only way to protect it. We've got th' gold to buy it with,…but we're still gonna need a lot a help, and even more luck,… and we're gonna need Peter and his cousin, Joseph to stand up for us. We'll lay it all out in front of Peter tonight, and if he agrees,…we'll go on from there. We may have to deal with th' Indian Agent, too"

"Doesn't the land belong to the Choctaw?" Shrugged Connie. "I thought the Government gave them the land, by treaty?"

"I guess we'll find out about all that in Fort Towson. Anyway,… if we can swing it, we'll buy th' mountain."

"Wonderful!" Giggled Connie. "Then we can build the school adjacent to the trading post."

"School???…What about th' Café?"

"I'm just kidding, silly, I'm not a teacher!"

CHAPTER SEVENTEEN

BILLY LED THE WAY OUT of the cavern and down the grade to the valley's floor, and once again was awed by its majestic beauty and untamed appearance.

"Where do you think we should build the house?" Asked Connie as she pulled up beside him.

He grinned widely at her then shook his head.

"What?" She smiled. "It's a good question."

"You're jumpin' th' gun a mite, ain't ya,…we got a long way to go before we can build a house?"

"I know,…but tell me anyhow."

"Well,…there's two or three choice spots. One would be next to th' corral there,…another would be at th' cavern,…but I think I'd likely build in front a that treasure cave,…that way we could keep an eye on everything, including that tunnel."

"You're still worried about that, aren't you?"

"Yeah," He nodded and clucked the Roan toward the forest of ancient Pines separating them from the main cavern, and a half-hour later they were dismounting at the polished rock floor again.

"Son, you and Bennie stay close now, you hear?"

"Yes, Sir." Nodded Willy as he slid from the back of his pony.

Rodney helped Benny down and he immediately chased after Willy across the smooth rock. "Be careful boys!" Shaking his head, he went to help Billy with the bundles of canvass then both of them walked the length of the cavern toward the mine. Both turned to watch as the boys chased after the women, who had just entered the council chamber then Billy began spreading the large pieces of canvass on the rock floor outside of the water-room.

"I guess you're right at that." Sighed the lawman. "It would be hard to tote them bags out of the mine."

"Yeah, it'll take a little longer." Nodded Billy. "We can fill a canvass in th' mine, then we both can carry it out and dump it."

"It would go a little faster with some help." Came Rodney, looking toward the council room. "I'll go get the gals."

"Leave 'em be, Rod, we got plenty a time." Said Billy. "But we will need one a them torches we left at th' cave."

"I'll go get 'em." Said Rodney and started back across the cavern's floor. "Be back in a few, Billy."

Early afternoon found them sitting around a fire on the rock floor of the cavern. The women were preparing food, as they all wanted to eat before the return trip to camp again. The women were discussing the historic drawings of the council chamber as they worked, while the boys sat at the feet of the men while they discussed the gold.

"How much you think we got, Billy?"

"Another four hundred pounds, at least." He grinned "Enough to buy this mountain, maybe."

"Peter was pretty much for that idea, wasn't he?

"I just hope it works out." Sighed Billy. "Th' hard work is still ahead of us."

"Yeah, wish I knew what to expect from that Choctaw Chief,...think we'll have time to make it home before the meeting?"

"Depends on when, and if Joseph can set one up,...he's th' one with th' education. But if anybody can pull it off, he can,...he's one smart Choctaw. Anyway, by th' time we get to Towson, he'll have wired us about that meetin', one way or th' other"

"Well, once we get that part of it behind us, I'll contact th' army,...cause right now, I don't have a clue who we'll need to talk to?"

"Th' man in charge of Indian affairs, I'd expect." Returned Billy as he reached for the makings. "That Chief'll know who he is. But, we'd better wait on that, too, it might be all in th' hands a that Chief."

"Didn't think of that." Sighed Rodney. "I wasn't looking forward to dealing with th' Government anyhow,...so let's hope that's th' way it pans out."

Billy licked the smoke and lit it, taking the acrid relaxant deep into his lungs. "We only got one problem that I can see,...if we do get th' okay."

"And what's that?"

Billy shrugged. "How to explain th' gold, for one thing,...and for another,...once we do,... how to get 'em to grant us th' mineral-rights?"

Rodney nodded. "Then why tell them? We'll pay off the Chief, and if he has to, he can pay off th' Government, they should own th' mineral-rights, if they own th' land...don't you think?"

"I hope so, Rod,...I sort a dread th' whole thing, to tell ya th' truth."

"Me, too." Sighed the lawman. "Just one more bridge to cross, I guess." He looked off toward the valley then and smiled. "Be worth it though."

"Supper's ready, boys." Said Connie, prompting them to get to their feet.

The meal went fairly quick, made better with discussions about the valley and the mine. But at last it was over and the women gathered up the tins and started off toward the water room to wash them.

"That was good," Sighed Rodney. "But now I'm bushed. Lugging that gold plumb wore me out."

"Guess we could wait till mornin' to leave." Said Billy as he rolled his after-dinner smoke, then held the match to the lawman's thin cigar before lighting his own. "We got about everything from camp with us, except for your tent."

"I'm afraid that tent will have to stay behind, Billy, th' mules'll have about all they can carry, as it is....How long will it take Peter and Elijah to get back to Winchester Station?"

"Couple a more days at least." Breathed Billy then reached to rub his arm.

"That Kiowa had been a fraction faster, we'd a been in trouble, Billy."

"Yeah, well he should a beat me,...I never seen anybody that fast before."

"Then, I guess you were right?..You're only as fast as you have to be, to win."

"I've always believed that was th' case. Anyway,...it's over and done. It's time to worry about that meetin'."

"You're right about that." Sighed the lawman. "I guess when Peter gets back, it'll take him another day to convince Joseph, right?"

"Maybe not." Sighed Billy. "I think Joseph will go for th' idea pretty quick,...what with him havin' to guard his family like he did." He got to his feet then to gaze at the valley, then sighing, looked down at the lawman. "If we're gonna stay th' night, we best unsaddle th' horses."

"Can we help, Daddy?" Voiced Willy, closely followed by his echo.

"Yeah." Laughed Billy. "You both can help,…come on."

Billy heard the Roan's low whinny and was instantly awake and searching the expanse of darkness inside the cavern, his eyes flicking toward the animals then as he reached to pull on the eyeglasses. There seemed to be nothing out of sorts at first glance, but if something wasn't wrong, why were the animals so restless? The mules, usually passive, were now pacing back and forth the length of the picket line, and the four horses were very restless as well. Something was wrong, he thought, and strained his eyes at the moonlit valley again before staring at the dark expanse of giant Pines,…but he saw nothing, not even a breeze in the trees.

He got slowly to his feet and walked the few scant yards to the horses where he moved among them, reassuring them with a pat on the rump as he continued to gaze at the valley. What had spooked them, he wondered? Then sighing, realized they were quiet again and walked back to the rock floor and sat down. He was shivering from the cold as he reached for tobacco and papers, then rolled and lit his smoke before getting up again to work his long coat from atop the bedroll behind the Roan's saddle.

He was pulling on the coat when the mare suddenly snorted again, and was closely followed by the nervous snorting from the other animals. He heard the faint rumble then, and a second later felt the slight tremble in the ground. Instantly alert, and afraid of what he thought was happening, he went back to quickly shake the others awake. "Get up!" He said gruffly,…we got a problem!"

"Billy, what's wrong?' Gasped Connie as she reached to pull Willy against her, and at that moment, both her and Melissa screamed as the polished rock floor began to shake beneath them.

Billy quickly grabbed her and Willy by the arm and ushered them off the rock and into the grass alongside the rearing horses. He released Connie and grabbed the reins of both horses as they tried to break free of the picket. Rodney was grappling with the other animals as Melissa and Bennie rushed to Connie's side and all four of them held on to each other as the rumbling grew steadily louder.

Both women were crying and holding on to the boys as the men subdued the animals and held them in check. And then suddenly it was over, leaving all of them breathless and trembling from fright.

"My dear God, Billy, what was that?" Gasped Connie loudly.

"Earthquake!" He whispered and then pulled her against him. "Either that, or an avalanche."

"Didn't feel like no avalanche." Puffed Rodney as he hugged Melissa. "No rocks falling anywhere, that I could see. Could be on the other side of the valley somewhere."

"Oh, God!" Gasped Melissa. "Maybe it was the cavern we came through,… we could be trapped in here!"

"Dear God, Billy!" Said Connie quickly. "What if she's right?"

"We'll have to go see,…let's saddled up, Rod."

The horses were all saddled in short order and then, leaving the mules picketed, they mounted and headed off through the darkened forest of pines to finally ride out in view of the tall bat-cave,… stopping just at the bottom of the grade.

"It looks okay to me." Sighed Rodney. "I don't see a thing out of place."

"Stay with th' women, Rod." Said Billy and urged the Roan up the grade to the cavern and rode inside, then re-emerged to slowly descend the grade again. "No dust up there, couldn't see inside." He said as he scanned the inner wall of the cliffs. "Come on, we'll check out the cliffs on the way back, maybe we'll find somethin'." He led the way toward the natural corral, and when Connie and Willy pulled alongside, continued to search the cliff's heights,… while the others searched at ground-level.

He was worried. If it wasn't an avalanche, it had to have been an earthquake, but how,…and why, He wondered? And where was the damage? There was no visible sign of any,…at least not in the valley. But maybe the damage wasn't in the valley, he thought as they came abreast of the large Fir and the blocked tunnel. He stopped the Roan to stare at the spot and after a few seconds, looked at Connie and dismounted. "Stay on your horse, Honey, I'll be right back." He walked to the Fir and bent to go beneath the heavy branches.

"What is it Billy?" Breathed Rodney as he pushed in beside him. "What are you lookin' for?"

"I don't know, Rod." He said as he squatted to run his hand over the surface of the massive slab of rock. "Feels like it might be cracked." He said as he fished a match from his shirt and struck it. The crack was quite distinct in the light of the flaring match.

"It's busted all right." Sighed Rodney. "Billy, are you thinking what I am?"

Billy grunted. "It was an earthquake all right,…and I think it came from down there. This is th' only damage in th' valley, by th' looks of it."

He turned in the darkness to peer at the lawman. "We have to go back down there, Rod."

"I know." Breathed the lawman. "But what if th' tunnel's blocked?"

"Then we'll leave,…but we got a try and find whatever's wrong down there,… th' next quake could open up another cave,… and maybe that one'll be large enough for one a them big as a house monsters to crawl out of."

"When do we go?"

"In th' mornin',…I figure it'll be light in another couple hours. Come on, let's get back to th' cavern."

What is it, Billy?" Urged Connie as he mounted.

"Quake busted that rock we pulled down." He put his hand on her leg and squeezed slightly. "We have to go back down there, honey."

"Why, for God sakes?"

"Cause that's where th' quake started,…and I got a be sure no more holes open up to let another monster out. We got a try and fix what's wrong,…if that's possible. You girls'll stay here with th' boys this time, too."

"Like hell we will! We're going where you go, Billy,…if you die, we die with you, and that's that! If you say no, we'll follow you anyway."

Billy opened his mouth to speak, but instead turned and mounted the skittish Roan and led the way back toward the large cavern.

— ⁓

They were silently watching the boys play tag in the light of the fire, each deep in their own thoughts as they waited for dawn to break. The women were nestled snugly in the arms of the men as they waited, and fear and worry was evident on all their faces.

"You sure you won't stay here, honey," Asked Billy suddenly. "You got Willy, Chris and Angie to think about, you know, and it could get dangerous this time?"

"Billy," She sighed. "Christopher and the baby are in very good hands,… loving hands,…and I will die before I'll go home without you. Okay?"

He hugged her tighter and continued to watch the energetic romping of the boys. "Better pack th' rest of th' supplies then." He said, looking back at her. "We might need 'em."

She nodded and moved away from him, then began gathering up the rest of the food.

"What are you doing, Connie?" Asked Melissa as she pushed away from Rodney.

"Billy thinks we should carry all the food with us,…think you and I can carry it?"

"Of coarse we can,…we can cut a blanket in half."

Rodney moved across to sit beside Billy. "I sure wish they'd stay here."

"That makes two of us,…but I can't argue with the logic."

"I guess not. What's th' plan when we get there?"

"No plan." Sighed Billy. "If we don't find sign of a cave-in, we wait and see what happens in that room…. If another tunnel does open up, we'll likely find th' problem."

"And what if we can't fix it,…you thought about that?"

Billy shook his head. "Rod, I'm findin' it hard enough to think at all right now. This whole damn thing is impossible,…oh, I know it's real,…but it goes against everything I believe in. God,…people from other worlds, monsters from th' past?…I thought I had bad dreams before, but this,…"

"I don't know what to think about it anymore, neither!" Voiced Rodney. "But we'd better find a way to fix it, else we might not be able to survive!… Sure changes my way of thinking, too,…about a lot of things…. But I still draw the line at flying machines!"

"Rod,…whoever put them contraptions down there, was not from here,… and they had to fly to get here!…And that's th' facts as I see 'em."

"Yeah, well,…I guess there's things we don't know about our world, that's for sure." He sighed. "I'm not sure I want to know, to tell you the truth."

"Well, I wouldn't draw th' line too quick, it's comin' daylight. We best get everybody mounted, we still got a move that slab a rock. When we get there, you go get that pry pole while I take th' animals to th' corral."

"You got it,…guess I'm ready if you are."

— ‿ —

It took them both to topple the broken end of the rock away from the tunnel, leaving them just enough room to squeeze through the opening.

"Have you wondered why this was the only rock that was busted in that quake?"

"Just one a them things, I reckon." Returned Billy as he helped the lawman slide the long pry-pole alongside the massive rock. "It might a happened for a reason, too,…who knows." He moved back beneath the sagging branches and nodded at the women. "You can come in now." He said, holding the branches up to let them through, and when they were all beneath the Fir, he looked at them soberly.

"Okay,…were usin' th' same rules as before. Rod will bring up th' rear. Honey, you and Lisa hang on to th' boys,…and stay close." He turned as Rodney gave him the lighted torch then entered the tunnel.

The return trip was somewhat slower than the first, as Billy continuously searched the tunnel's narrow walls for structural damage along the way, but at long last he spotted the dim light ahead of them. "Torches are still lit down there." He said, his voice echoing eerily in the tunnel,…and several minutes later they were back in the large, stone room. Billy placed the torch in the wall with the others then came to the center of the room as he scanned the ancient pictographs again.

The women were already walking along the walls and trying to decipher more of the alien text,…and discussing it between themselves.

"Don't seem to be anything out of place in here." Commented Rodney as he took his watch out. "Quarter past ten already,…took us more than two hours to get down here, is that thing still gonna open at eleven forty-five?"

"If we're right, it will." Sighed Billy. "And when it does, be ready to use that Buffalo gun." He looked down at the wide-eyed boys then. "What's wrong, boys?"

"We're scared, Daddy. Are we gonna die?"

Billy squatted and hugged Willy against him. "No, Son,…we are not gonna die. All we're doin' is tryin' to find out what caused that earthquake."

"What's a earthquake?" Questioned Benny.

"It's like when two mountains rub against each other." Explained Rodney. "And when they do that, it makes the ground shake and groan."

"And sometimes it makes cracks in th' ground and rocks." Added Billy. "And that can be dangerous. So, don't be afraid, cause I need you to help take care a Mama and Lisa, you know,…sort a keep them from bein' so scared."

"Yeah,…okay." Nodded Willy. "Cause they're women, right, Daddy?"

"That's right." He grinned.

"I want a take care of the womans, too." Voiced Benny.

"Course you will." Said Rodney quickly. "Uncle Billy was talking to you, too."

The next hour was spent discussing the alien text and pictographs in the room, especially those they thought suggested that whoever created all of this, was from another planet, because the strange writing on that section of wall was nothing like anything they'd ever seen in a book, totally different than the Egyptian, or Aztec symbols.

But after making several rounds of the large room, and several Smokes later, Billy shook his head and took out his watch as him and Rodney left the women to their discussions. "It's eleven twenty-five, Rod," He sighed. "I think we ought a all be in th' center of this room here when it happens, cause we ain't got a clue where it'll open. And we ought a do that now, I think,… in case we're wrong about th' time."

"I'll get the girls." Nodded the lawman and went to bring them back.

Billy explained his reasons when they gathered around him. "Now, I think it's best we all sit down and try to get comfortable. Just be ready to go when that tunnel opens, wherever that might be?"

"It's going to be right there, I think" Said Connie and pointed at part of the wall. "That's the only place without any markings."

"Seems logical to me." Grinned Billy. "Now, I want a say this again,…this is different than th' last time we was here, because we're goin' in this time, and we don't know what we'll find. When that tunnel opens, we'll have to move fast, okay? We don't know how much time we'll have before it closes,…and that's when it might get dangerous…. If one a them animals is on th' other side a this wall when we start through, we'll have to keep goin', cause there won't be enough time to turn back before it closes up again."

"Then we'd best go in first." Sighed Rodney.

"Yeah, and once we're in, move to one side so th' rest can get by you,… and keep that cannon off safety, all right?"

"How'd you know about the safety?"

"You showed me th' gun, remember?" He shook his head and looked at the watch again. "Almost eleven thirty-five, we best get ready." He smiled as Connie hugged his arm then leaned to kiss her.

"I love you, Billy."

"I love you, too, Daddy." Said Willy and wrapped his arms around them both.

"I don't know how to tell you how much I love th' both of you." He said with passion. "But I swear I won't let anything happen to you."

"We know." Breathed Connie.

Billy looked across at Rodney then and nodded. "It could happen any time now, let's get up and be ready." He got to his feet then helped Connie to hers before reaching to pull Willy against him. "We ready?"

"Ready as we're gonna be." Nodded the lawman as he put Bennie's hand in Melissas' and kissed her.

"Listen!" Billy raised his hand for silence, and they all could hear the low hum emitting from within the wall in front of them,…and it was growing louder with each passing second. Billy raised the Henry rifle and breached a cartridge into the chamber, then moved Connie and Willy behind him as Rodney stepped up beside him to stare at the wall.

It was subtle at first, but then they began seeing a movement in the rock, almost like ripples on water at first, then more like a flag in a stiff breeze as the wall began slowly to fade away,…creating an opening through a dozen-foot expanse of solid rock, that appeared to be an archway into yet another room.

"Dear heavenly Father!" Gasped Connie. "What is this thing?"

It was glowing brighter as she spoke and emitting a constant drone as the opening suddenly stopped shimmering and the walls of the tunnel became solid rock again.

"Let's go!" Shouted Billy. "Hurry!"

They moved quickly, but cautiously through the expanse of tunnel, and could feel the strong magnetic pull of the arch as they passed and soon, they were all in the inner room and watching the tunnel close up behind them.

Billy quickly reached to touch the wall's surface, but felt nothing but cold, solid rock. "I expected it." He sighed. "But I'd still like to know just what th' hell happened?"

"That probably makes four of us." Breathed Rodney.

"My, God!" Gasped Melissa. ":Are we trapped in here now?" She grabbed Rodney and turned him around. "How do we get out of here, Rodney?"

"Let's everyone calm down here." Said Billy harshly. "We knew this would happen,...we'll get out a here tomorrow at eleven forty-five. Now,... just remember what we came here for,... we find th' problem, we fix it if we can, and tomorrow mornin', we go home." He looked into the eyes of each one of them then nodded. "Now come on, I can see daylight in that tunnel over there,...let's check it out. Keep your rifle ready, Rod."

Keeping the women and kids behind them, him and the lawman led the way into the narrow fissure, and once around a bend in the open tunnel were confronted with the brightness of day as they moved on to the cave's ragged opening. Connie and Melissa pushed their way between them, and all of them stared in astonishment at the strange new world before them.

They were standing at the threshold of what appeared to be an ancient world, and as they stared aghast at the jungle below them, they saw a dense growth of monstrous trees and vines of a species that none of them had ever seen before. There were ferns so large that a man could walk beneath the overhanging stalks of leaves. Everything was huge, the plants, flowers with giant blooms, huge, twisted vines with odd-shaped leaves and runners as thick as a man's arm,...and those runners had wrapped themselves around the giant trees, along the ground and even the face of the mountain where they stood.

Giant, palm-like trees grew tall and sprawling, and were thick amid the rocks and tall waving reed-like grass. They were standing at the top of a downward slope of lush grass that ended at the valley's luscious floor and there the foliage was so thick and dense that travel looked impossible.

Billy pushed aside the thick vines and stepped out into the light. Everything was damp and green, and the red clay of the earth was barely visible through the grass at his feet. Literally everything was covered in greenery of some kind.

"It looks so,...prehistoric!" Gasped Connie, as she was still in awe of the untouched wilderness. "Do you think it is,…prehistoric, I mean, I've never seen plants like this before?"

"Dear God," Voiced Melissa. "What have we done?"

"We didn't do anything." Said Billy and looked back at them. "Look at the tunnel there,…it's completely caved off, see all the rocks out there? This has to be from that earthquake,…and that's why th' tunnel never closed up."

"And that's also how the Pterodactyl got out." Commented Rodney.

"This ain't no million years ago, Rod." Said Billy as he looked up at the mountain's towering height. "It's got a be some kind a trick."

"Then how do you explain it?" Returned Rodney.

"My God, Look!" Cried Connie and pointed at the yellow sky, and the giant bird that soared above them.

"Is that Pterodactyl a trick, Billy?" Grinned Rodney.

Billy slowly shook his head. "I guess it ain't so impossible at that…. It appears we just stepped back to a million years ago,…and I think we're gonna regret it."

"I already regret it, so let's find out why this tunnel didn't close, and fix it." Sighed Rodney.

"How do we do that?" shuddered Connie. "If there was an arch here at all, it's gone now!... But it must have been right here,… see how the mouth of the tunnel has widened out? It could have dislodged,… because it looks like several feet of the mountain was caved away."

"Then where is it?" Breathed Melissa."

"We have to find it, Billy." Said Connie. "It could be the only way to repair the mountain."

"Where do you suggest we look,…It could a tumbled all th' way to th' valley down there?...It could a shattered in a hundred pieces, too."

"Maybe it didn't too!...We've got to try, honey."

"Yeah," He sighed. "I know we do."

"We're hungry, Daddy." Voiced Willy, his eyes still a little wide with fear.

"Me, too!" Echoed Benny.

"First things first I guess, huh, Billy?"

Billy nodded as he scanned the trees in the valley below them then sighing, turned back to the women. "What kind a vittles we got?"

Connie shrugged. "Biscuits, salt, a couple potatoes,…I don't know, we just brought what we had, and it isn't much."

"You up to goin' huntin'?" Sighed Billy.

"Oh no, Rodney," Cried Melissa. "You're not going out there!"

"We've got guns, honey, it'll be okay. It shouldn't take long to find some game in this wilderness,…and maybe you gals can spot us some fruit or something,…go pretty good with supper, wouldn't it?" Melissa tearfully nodded then allowed Connie to lead her back into the tunnel with the boys.

"Think they'll be okay if we go,…this is one scary looking place?

"I hope so." Sighed Billy. "I'll leave my rifle here, Connie knows how to use it. We need meat, and besides,… I'd like to look around a little."

"God only knows how safe it's gonna be once it gets dark." Sighed Rodney as he watched the soaring Pterodactyl.

"All we can do is wait and see." Returned Billy, also looking at the monstrous bird. "If anything does happen, we'll just have to deal with it."

"Like we'll have a choice." Sighed the lawman as he swung the Krag off his shoulder. "Looks like I'll get to shoot this thing after all….I just hope the caliber's big enough." He gave Billy the gun and pulled the long-bladed hunting knife from his belt. "While we're waiting, I'm gonna track down some firewood for the night,…it's damp in that cave."

Billy nodded and stared back at the yellow sky, and felt a chill enter his body at the same time. How could all of this be real? It was against every law of nature, and everything else he ever believed in,… yet it was real. As impossible as it was, they were here, and he was looking at a prehistoric world. Was this the Choctaw Nation, the way it was millions of years ago? He shook his head in disbelief again, realizing that a million years ago, was somehow,… right now.

He stared out over the large valley again, watching as the Pterodactyl floated over the tops of the rainforest, but then was completely startled as the giant bird was suddenly caught in mid-flight by something very large. The giant animal had literally leaped from out of the trees to grab the bird in its jaws. Mesmerized, he continued to stare at the spot, then caught the movement of the swaying trees as they were pushed aside, even hearing the sharp cracking sounds as some of them snapped in half, the massive trunks crackling like splinters of dry wood,…and then he saw the creature itself.

In gut-wrenching awe, he saw the animal's very large head emerge from out of the tangled foliage, only to open its huge jaws and emit a low, guttural sound that progressed into an awesome, ear-shattering roar that echoed across the length of the valley,…and then it disappeared back into the trees,…and still breathless, he turned around as Connie, Melissa and the boys ran out of the tunnel.

"What in God's name was that?" Yelled Connie as she clutched his arm.

"Rodney??" Screamed Melissa.

"I'm here, baby." He gasped, pushing past them with his armload of firewood. "God Damn it, Billy,...what was that thing?"

"Animal of some kind." He breathed. "All I saw was it's head,...but it was big!"

"A Dinosaur." Nodded the lawman. "And it sounded like a mean one. Told ya they was big as a house,...damn noise almost made me ruin my jeans, too!" He continued on into the cave with the firewood, and with Melissa and Benny close behind him.

Billy continued to watch the jungle of moving trees as the beast moved on down the valley. Could still hear the grunting until it finally faded into the distance.

"What in the name of God have we gotten ourselves into?" Gasped Connie as she pulled a tearful Willy against her. "What have we done, Billy,... my, God!"

"We didn't nothin', honey,...this place was already here,...at least it was here a million years ago. And so was God, I think,...but it is kind a hard to believe God had a hand in it....Anyway,...I'd sure like to know th' hows and whys of it, because common sense tells me it ain't possible,...yet here we are,...and it's very real!"

"That's what scares me....Are we going to be all right, Billy? I mean,..I have more faith in you than anyone else in the world, and if you say we'll live through this, I'll believe you."

He sighed and pulled her against him. "Honey,...all we can do is wait for that wall to open up again,...we'll be okay till then, I promise."

"You're not really going hunting with that thing on the loose, are you?"

"Why not,...we need fresh meat? Besides,...I planned this whole thing, I wanted to make sure you had your adventure." They both laughed halfheartedly then and stared back at the valley.

"Is this where your Indian friends came?"

"There's no way of knowin' that, I think. But I doubt it, White Buffalo would never bring his people to a place like this, besides,...all this happened three years after they left th' valley."

"I thought I smelled sulfur in the air before that thing roared." Commented Rodney as the three of them came back through the tunnel. "Anybody else smell it?"

Billy nodded. "Saw some smoke down th' valley there, too."

"As yellow as that sky is, it has to be a volcanic cloud." Returned Connie. "They're loaded with sulfur. I'd guess there's a very active volcano somewhere in this valley,...and that's probably what caused the quake."

"And that's why the sky is like that?" Gasped Melissa.

Connie nodded. "We'll probably be able to see the glow when it gets dark."

"Well, I know we're a million years in the past right now,...but where are we, I wonder?" Voiced the lawman. "Is this the Choctaw Nation the way it was,...or another part of th' world completely?"

"That's a good question." Said Billy. "Who knows, maybe this don't even exist,...maybe that arch thing made it all up!"

"Do me a favor, Billy,...if I ever try to convince you of anything again,... just shoot me, will ya? Because the more we talk about this, the more it confuses me."

"Be my pleasure, Rod." He grinned and squeezed the lawman's shoulder.

"Thank you,...now, about that hunting trip, are you ready,...we still have to look for that busted arch-thing, you know?"

Connie sucked her breath in again. "Please don't go, Billy,...not with that beast out there?"

"We need th' meat, honey, it'll be okay. Besides, I want a look around a bit. I'll leave my rifle with you, just in case, and don't worry,...we ought a be able to hide from somethin' that big."

"Believe me," Breathed Rodney. "If I see it, it'll never be able to catch me."

"And why is that?" Frowned Billy.

Rodney grinned at him then. "The ground will be too slick!"

"My God, Rodney!" Cried Melissa. "Be serious,...this is no time for your jokes. This happens to be real!"

He laughed and hugged her. "I'm sorry, honey,...I know it's real. We'll be careful, okay?"

"Damn it, Billy, you saw that thing!" Sniffed Connie. "No one can fight something that big,...aren't you the least bit afraid, for god sakes?"

"Yes, Ma'am." He nodded. "I'm plenty scared."

"Then let's stay inside until tomorrow and leave this God-forsaken place? What'll happen to us if you don't come back?"

"Guess I'll just have to come back. Look,...Honey, you and Lisa take th' boys on back in th' cave, okay,...they're scared, too!" He took her by the shoulders and held her away from him.

"That Pterodactyl came from here. It somehow made its way through that tunnel, all th' way up to th' valley. What if somethin' even worse than that bird was to get through?...How many people would it kill before it was stopped?"

"If they could stop it at all." Agreed Rodney.

"That's right. And we need to keep our strength up if we're gonna find that Arch and fix th' tunnel. We need th' meat, Honey. Trust me,…we'll be careful,…now here." He gave her the Henry-rifle and turned her around. "Go on back in th' tunnel now, we have to go."

"You are a bull-headed man, Billy Upshur,…both of you!" She took Willy's hand and started into the tunnel. "Be careful, you hear me?"

"Rodney, please?"" Sniffed Melissa.

He hugged her to him. "Honey, if we're gonna eat tonight, we got a go hunting. Like I said earlier, see if you can find some fruit or something while we're gone,…but don't stray too far, okay? And if you don't want a look for any, that's okay, too,…just try not to worry about me." He kissed her mouth then. "It'll take more than that thing to keep me from coming back!" She smiled half-heartedly then took Bennie's hand and followed after Connie.

"I sure wish we hadn't brought 'em down here." Sighed Billy.

"We didn't have a choice, when you think about it."

"That's true." Said Billy as he looked back at the valley.

"You said you wanted to look around, Billy,…are you thinking White Buffalo might have come here?"

Billy shook his head. "He wouldn't a come to a hell-hole like this,…but I do think there's people here."

"How would you know that?"

'I don't know. A gut-feelin', I guess,…anyway, I want a look around some while we hunt…Won't hurt to look!"

"Let's go then." Sighed Rodney as he looked at his pocket-watch. "It's already nearly twelve-thirty." He reached and took the Krag from Billy and slung it onto his own shoulder. "I'm ready if you are."

━ ━

They moved cautiously down through the tall grass toward the valley's heavily foliaged and debris strewn floor, through the large leaves of primeval plants, pushing aside vines as thick as their arms. Once there, they found themselves immediately in damp, shoulder high grass. They were in the mist-covered, densely foliaged jungle of a world, that in all appearances, was millions of years old.

The terrain was broken into deep crevices, cracks in the ground that could swallow up a man,…they pushed past giant palm-like trees with bark like none they had ever seen and had been constantly in a mist-like fog since making lower ground. And for most of that time, they had been aware of movement in the thick underbrush.

They heard the sound again, and this time it was definite. Something was moving in the grass and shrubbery behind them, the rustling sounds were distinctly audible. Billy gripped Rodney's arm, and both of them crouched in the thick foliage to silently search the trail behind them.

"Whatever it is, it ain't very big." Whispered the lawman with a noticeable quiver in his voice.

"No,…but it could still be mean as hell. I don't hear it now, though."

"That don't mean it's gone!…What do you want a do?"

"We go on." He whispered They cautiously stood then moved back into the thickest part of the valley, occasionally hearing the grunts and roars of large animals from somewhere in the jungle, and stopping from time to time when the ground would seem to vibrate beneath their feet,…and when it stopped, would continue on through the darkness beneath the monstrous plants and trees.

Rodney was gripping the large-bore rifle tightly as he led the way through a thick tangle of branches and vines, and had just pushed aside a giant rope-like tangle of vines when he stopped abruptly to stare through an opening in the trees.

"What is it, Rod?" Breathed Billy as he moved in beside him. "What do you see?"

Rodney shook his head. "I don't really know!…Just don't tell me I see a pyramid, way off yonder."

Billy worked the telescope from beneath his long coat and raised it to his eyes. "That's exactly what it is,…and there's two more behind that one."

"The Aztecs must have come here."

"Somebody did, that's for sure. But it looks older than th' Aztecs."

"You thinking alien beings again?"

"Why not,…after what we've seen so far?"

"Yeah,…don't guess you see any activity about?"

Billy shook his head. "Too far away and too many trees."

"Well, we ain't got time to go see." Sighed the lawman. "Be dark in a few hours,…and I don't know about you, but I don't want a be caught out here in the dark."

Billy was about to say something when he heard the faint rattle of raspy breathing behind them, and instantly felt the chill at the back of his neck,… and when he turned around, he saw the hair-covered, ape-like man as he was raising a sharpened spear. He drew and fired, hearing the guttural scream as the furry creature was thrown backward into the heavy foliage. Both of them were shaking badly as they stared at the spot where the ape-man had fallen, their ears ringing from the sudden explosion of gunfire as it echoed down the valley.

"What in hell you shooting at?" Gasped Rodney.

"Some kind a ape!" He said as he went to pick up the sharpened length of timber. "He was about to stick me with this thing." He used the spear to move the foliage aside, revealing the body of the man-animal.

"A cave-man!" Gasped Rodney. "A fucking sixty million year old cave-man, by God!"

Billy dropped the spear and cocked the Colt again. "They're still animals, Rod, cave-man or not,...and they prob'ly hunt in packs."

"I don't hear anything."

"We didn't hear this one till he tried to kill me!...Keep your eyes open." At that moment, they did hear the roar,...an ear-popping sound that seemed to shake the very ground they stood on, and terrified, they dropped to the ground in the underbrush and watched as the twenty-foot tall reptile rumbled past them. The creature seemed cumbersome as it swung its head from side to side in searched of its prey. Suddenly it stopped and roared again, showing rows of long, pointed teeth, and the noise it made was unbearable. They scarcely breathed as the monster lizard moved on into the thickest part of the jungle, again feeling the ground tremble as it walked.

"Good God'a-mighty!" Groaned Billy, almost breathless. "That Son of a Bitch was big!" He looked at the ashen-faced lawman then. "You okay, Rod?"

Rodney nodded. "I just pissed my pants, is all."

Billy managed a weak grin as he fought his own nerves. "Let's get out a here."

"What about the meat,...not that I give a shit anymore?"

"We can hunt on th' way back,...we don't find anything, we'll do without." He looked around at the ever-clutching underbrush. "If there was any more cave-men out and about, that thing scared 'em off,...might a saved our bacon ta-boot."

"Yeah, well you can bet your ass on that!...But he didn't save much,...I probably won't be able to have any more kids after this!"

Billy grinned again and stepped over the body in the grass as he led the way back down the valley. Two hours of fighting the thick foliage finally found them back at the grassy slope and climbing out of the valley toward the cave,...and that's when they heard the animal grunt. They stopped in the tall reeds until they could locate it, finally seeing the large, hog-like head of the animal as it rooted in the soft loam beneath the giant ferns.

"Meat on the table." Grunted the lawman. "Look at it, I never seen a pig with horns before,...and the son of a Bitch must weigh a thousand pounds!" He raised the Krag to his shoulder and fired then suddenly yelped as his shoulder went numb.

"Oh, damn, that hurt!" He lowered the gun and grabbed his arm. "Where is it,...did I hit it?"

"You got 'im,…come on." Making their way slowly through the reeds and brush, they found the dead animal beneath the thick growth of ferns.

"That's some big pig!" Panted the lawman. "If that's what it is?" He gave the rifle to Billy and pulled the knife from his belt. "Keep watch while I slice us off a chunk of hindquarter."

Billy nodded and stared up at the cave where Connie was just lowering the rifle, then grinned as they all came out into the grass. He waved reassuringly then turned to watch the surrounding jungle.

The lawman made short work of carving the meat from the animal's haunches, then cleaned the knife on the furry carcass and put it away. Billy helped him lift the slab of meat to his shoulder, and they had just started the upward climb when Rodney suddenly grunted and fell to his knees in the rocky grass,…causing Billy to quickly move to his aid, and that's when he saw the length of yellow metal. "Here's what tripped you, Rod,…hold up." He bent and worked the object free of the matted grass.

"What is it?"

"Beats me,…but I know what it reminds me of,…damn thing is four-feet long, at least,…and it don't weigh a pound."

"What's it remind you of?"

"This is a piece a that arch, Rod,…it's got a be. I'm gonna bring it with us,…you ready?"

"Oh, hell, yeah!…This thing is heavy." With Billy's help, he got to his feet again and continued slowly up the grade.

"Rodney, are you okay?" Cried Melissa as she came to meet them.

"I'm okay, baby,…I tripped, that's all." He grunted the last few yards to the cave and waved her away from him. "This thing is bleeding all over me, honey, don't get too close."

"You scared the life out of me, Rodney,…my heart almost stopped when I heard that shot."

"Mine, too." He grunted as he moved past her. "Damn gun kicks like a mule!" He entered the cave and continued on toward the inner room, with Melissa and Bennie close behind him.

"Are you okay, Billy?" Asked Connie as she looked at the strange piece of metal. "My God, Billy,…that's a piece of the arch!"

"Yeah,…Rod tripped on it down there." He pulled Willy against him then and grinned. "Thatk's, son,…you did a great job, I'm proud of ya,… here, carry this to th' cave for me." He placed the length of metal in the boy's arms.

"Billy!" Gasped Connie. "He can't carry that thing, my Lord!" Then she gasped when she watched him holding the four-foot object in one arm.

"That's th' lightest piece a metal you'll ever see." Commented Billy. "take it on into th' cave, son,…we got a cut up that meat."

"We'll have to find the rest of it, Billy,…it's got to be out here somewhere."

He pulled out the pocket-watch and sighed. "It's four-thirty now,…let me help Rod carve up that hindquarter, and we'll look for it while you gals cook supper, how's that?…Hope you brought salt,…I hate meat without any salt."

"It's in your knap-sack." She sighed then followed him inside the cave. He leaned the Krag against the wall then pulled his own knife as he squatted to help the lawman peel the thick hide from the slab of meat.

"Hope th' meat ain't this tough." Grunted Billy as he tossed the piece of pelt aside then helped slice the stringy meat into strips.

"Ugh!" Grimaced Willy as he squatted down beside them.

"What's ugh?" Grinned the lawman. "Ain't you boys hungry?"

"It's nasty, Uncle Rodney."

"Yeah, it's nasty!" Voiced Benny.

"It won't be nasty in a little while." Grinned Billy. "By th' way,…did you help Willy protect th' women?"

"Yeah!" He said loudly. "We ain't afraid, are we Willy?"

"Guess what we seen while you was gone, Daddy?" Said Willy with a glint in his eye. "You'll never guess."

"Willy!" Shushed Connie. "Let Daddy get through with the meat first, okay?…then I'll tell him."

"Awww, Mama!"

"Tell me what?' Frowned Billy. "What happened, honey?"

"We saw some more tunnels!" Blurted Melissa as she looked at Connie. "I'm sorry, Connie, it slipped out."

By now both him and Rodney were frowning at them. "Well, one of you tell us what happened?" Sighed the lawman.

"Connie?" Urged Billy. "What about th' tunnels?"

"There were four of them." She sighed. "One at the back of the room there." She pointed as she spoke. "Another one there, there and there."

"When?" Asked Rodney as he scanned the walls of the cave.

"About an hour after you left." Returned Melissa. "It scared us to death, too!"

"What did you see?" Insisted Billy.

"The one back there opened on a desert somewhere." Said Connie. "There were dunes of sand,…we felt the heat all the way in here. Another one opened in the mountains, we could see the snow-caps, and there was a lot of trees."

"One was all dark and scary!" Blurted Willy. "It was a cave, and it had a lot of spider-webs in it."

"Rattlesnakes, too." Sighed Melissa. "We could hear them."

"And the fourth one?"

"An Island, maybe." Sighed Connie. "I don't know. We could see the ocean, I think, and there was what looked like a huge stone statue of some kind. They opened one after the other, too, and not two minutes apart,…and that tells me there were five arches in the walls of this room, counting the broken one. And I've been thinking about that, Billy. The tunnels seem to open when one of the arches is touched by sunlight,…and when the sun no longer touches it,… it turns back to solid stone."

"We know that, honey,…what are you gettin' at?"

"If we put that broken arch back together in that tunnel, there won't be any sunlight touching it and,…well, if it works, we might not have time to get out of the tunnel before it closes."

"Then we'll just have to put it at the opening in here."

"But it could turn this whole room back to solid rock!…No, I think it will have to go closer to the end of the tunnel, Billy."

"Why not compromise then?" Came Rodney, looking at each of them. "Put it half-way." He shrugged.

"Works for me." Sighed Billy. "But we got a find th' rest of it first. Rod, you, me and th' boys'll look for it while th' girls cook supper, okay?" And when the lawman nodded, he looked back at the wall and ceiling. "I'd have to say this room was some kind of a waitin' room, maybe a depot of some kind,…look up there next to th' ceilin'"

"My God, we didn't see those before." Remarked Melissa, "And look, they're all in blue colors,…but you barely can see them."

"And we'll never know what they mean, neither." Said Rodney.

"If this is a way-station of sorts." Mused Connie as she got up to go look at the strange markings. "Then these things must tell you where and how to get to where you want to go,…sort of like instructions." She looked back at their puzzled expressions. "Well, it could be,…couldn't it?"

"I'm getting dizzy." Groaned Rodney. "Run that by me again?"

"I don't know what I'm saying, Rodney,…I have no idea what they mean."

"Well," Muttered Billy. "I'm pretty sure of one thing. These different doorways must open to different time periods in our past, and not th' same one every time, neither,…or in th' same place."

Rodney grunted to his feet and stared at the wall. "If this place is what you said, it could be a long wait just to go where you want a go. But if you're right, then whoever put these things here would have some way to make the tunnels open wherever they wanted them to,…and without the sunlight." He looked at them then. "Does that make any sense,…it don't to me?"

"Nothin' makes any sense here, Rod,...you know that!"

"Then we'd best go find th' rest of that arch,...I'm tired of this vacation."

"Let's go." Said Billy. "Come on boys. You girls build up that fire a little and put th' meat on, okay,...then one of you can bring th' rifle and watch our backs while we look." He turned and followed Rodney and the boys back through the tunnel.

— ~

It was almost dark by the time they found the larger portion of the arch, and they both carried it back to the tunnel, as it was light, but cumbersome, and finally placed it against the dark wall of the tunnel close to the slight bend of the shaft. Willy had gone to bring the shorter piece while Melissa followed him back with the torch and they watched as Billy placed that piece against the wall as well.

"Damn it, it's still too short!"

"But not by much." Voiced Rodney, pushing his hat back onto his head. "But where could it be, we've been all over that grade out there?"

"Maybe it's covered up." Sighed Billy. "We'll look again in the mornin'. But we had better bring in some more firewood, it could get real cold in here tonight."

"We've got the torch, Billy." Said Connie quickly. "Couldn't we look for it tonight,...this place scares me to death?"

"We could,...But a movin' light could attract animals."

"And ape-men." Nodded the lawman.

"Ape men?"

Billy sighed. "We was attacked by what Rod said was a cave man. Anyway, whatever he was, he was covered with hair and looked like an ape,...we had to shoot it."

"My God!" Gasped Connie. "There weren't supposed to be human-life here in the age of dynasaurs. Not what I've read about it anyway."

"Whatever he was, he knew about weapons." Said Rodney. "He had a long pole with a sharp point on it. Let's get that wood, Billy."

"Well, you better take a little water and wash that blood off your hands, that'll attract animals, too." The lawman nodded and went back into the cave.

Billy laid the broken arch on the stone floor and hugged both Connie and Willy, holding them close while he stared back at the tunnel's opening. He couldn't let them know how worried he was. The sky had now turned a bright orange as night was unfolding, and he knew that once it was full dark, there would still be a faint light from the fire in the inner room,…and that could be seen from quite a ways off, by both ape men, and animals. He would need to stand guard at the opening tonight.

"What if we don't find the rest of the arch, Billy?" Said Connie as she also looked out at the reddening sky. "It could be under a ton of rock."

"We'll find it, Honey. We have to! If we don't fix this thing now, our world might never be safe again."

"I bet I can find it, Daddy." Said Willy, "Can I help you look?"

"You sure can,…it might take all of us. I'm real proud of you, Son,…How are you makin' it anyway,…you feel okay?"

"I'm sceered."

"We all are, bud, but it'll be okay. Here comes Uncle Rodney now,…you and mama go back inside, we're gonna find some firewood for tonight. Go on." He kissed Connie as Rodney shouldered the Krag, then followed the lawman back out into the tall grass.

— —

They ate the seasoned prehistoric meat hungrily, all of them casting furtive glances at the tunnel's darkness from time to time.

"We're living just like the cave men did, Benny." Grinned Melissa as she suddenly broke the silence. "In a cave, how about that?"

"What's a cave man?" He returned with a serious expression on his face.

"Well,…they were the first people on earth a long, long time ago, and they lived in caves just like this one. You'll read all about them when you start to school."

"I wonder if they were as scared as I am back then?" Breathed Rodney.

"I'm sure they felt something." Said Connie. "But I'm not sure they even knew what fear was. It was a way of life for them. If it was fear, they learned to accept it."

"Well I still don't understand how there could be cave men here?' Sighed Melissa. "They're not supposed to be here."

"Maybe th' history books are wrong." Said Billy. "Because, if they weren't already here back then,…they was put here by them that built this,…contraption."

"Hunters." Voiced Connie suddenly.

"What?

"The aliens,…maybe they were hunters. They could have brought Neanderthals here,… for their own sport, maybe. But then again, I agree, history was probably wrong"

"Well, at any rate it's obvious they ain't been here in a few hundred years,…must a got tired a th' sport."

"Then why leave it all in place?" Asked Rodney. "They must a known this might happen."

"Maybe they're like people are everywhere,… we don't put away our toys neither."

"Well I will from now on!"

Billy grinned. "I keep rememberin' what White Buffalo said about th' evil in this mountain, and I think he was right. If we don't stop this right now, it will eventually destroy our world,…or at least, everybody in it.!...Who knows what these doorways can do, or where they might open up at?...There could be things ten times worse than this out there."

"Like what?? Gasped Connie. "How could anything be worse than this?"

"Yeah." Came Melissa. "If there is, I'd as soon not know about it."

"We can't ignore it, neither." Said Billy. "This whole thing, this place here, it's like an explosion, just waitin' to happen. Anything could come through one a them tunnels when it opens up."

"And we're caught right in the middle of it all." Sighed the lawman. "That's why we got a find th' rest a that arch, and pray that it works when we do. Cause I looked, and I couldn't tell where the thing might have been standing, the way the tunnel was broke off out there. It must have destroyed the hole through the mountain as well."

"That's a good thing, I think." Said Billy as he rolled and lit a Durham. "If th' sun can't hit it, this'll be one tunnel that'll never open again." He drew deeply of the acrid relaxant and exhaled smoke at the ceiling. "I just wish we could do th' same with the other four."

"Nothing less than dynamite could do that." Breathed the lawman. "And it would take a hell of a long fuse."

"And it could bring down th' whole mountain."

"Maybe that would be worth it." Said Connie as she stared back at the blue markings on the ceiling.

"It could start a massive earthquake," returned Billy. " And could destroy a whole lot more than th' mountain. But what we could do,… is plant just enough explosive to cave in th' tunnel when we get back,…that would keep anything from comin' through again, at least in th' valley."

"Couldn't one of these other tunnels open up in our time?" Queried Melissa. "They open everywhere else."

Billy nodded. "We been livin' with that all along, Lisa, and I can't see there's anything we can do about it. No,…we close this one off and go home."

"Wouldn't it be great if one of them opened up on another planet somewhere?"

"Tell you what?" Said Billy. "You and Connie are into this pretty good, and that long piece of arch has got some strange markings on it." He took the picture of the Pterodactyl from his shirt and gave it back to Rodney, then went back into the tunnel to retrieve the long, curved piece of yellow metal. He brought it back and sat down again.

"We might have us some answers if we could decipher th' markin's on this thing. You got a pencil, Rod?"

"A piece of one, why?"

"Think you can draw, or trace over th' writin' on this thing?"

"Billy, you're a genius." Smiled Connie. "I know of some people who may be able to decipher it,…if we ever get out of here."

"Who are these people?" Quizzed Rodney as he laid the metal across his lap. "What's their specialty?"

"Well, I don't actually know them,…I read about them. One is a professor in Chicago, a Doctor Richard Henry, Professor of Egyptology. He deciphers hieroglyphics, even Aztec and Mayan pictographs. There's also a professor of antiquity in New York."

"And what if these are not any of those?" Grinned Rodney as he looked back at the wall of the cave. "If this room was a depot, then what was that other room used for?"

"Draw th' pictures, Rod,…th' bucket's overflowin' on that one."

"All I'm saying is, that other room's bound to serve a special purpose, it's too big not to."

"Maybe there's more archways out there." Added Melissa. "Besides the one we came through, I mean. Maybe it's a receiving room for whoever put the arches here?"

"I think you may be right on th' money there, Lisa." Said Billy.

"Thank you. Did you hear that, Rodney,…I'm right!"

"One problem at a time, Lisa." Grinned the lawman as he began to sketch the alien text. "I just hope our arch opens back at the same place every time."

"Amen to that." Grinned Billy as he speared a piece of the charred meat and passed it across to Willy. "You ain't had much to say about this, Son,… tell us what you think?"

"I don't know." Shrugged Willy. "Daddy,…did a man from the sky really do this?"

"Yeah," He grinned. "Maybe he did." He looked up at Connie and shrugged, then got to his feet again. "You two best get some sleep now,… or try to,…and keep plenty a wood on th' fire," He kissed her then looked down at the lawman. "I'll take first watch, Rod, I'll wake you in a few hours. Good night all." He retrieved the Henry and headed off down the tunnel to the opening where he stood for a minute to stare at the orange-red sky, then rolled and lit his smoke before sliding down the wall to squat on his heels.

The sounds from the valley were un-nerving, and loud at times, and caused him to shudder inwardly when he heard them. He was trying not to think about the trouble they were in, and blowing smoke from his lungs he stared at the dark wall of the tunnel thinking that Rodney was right, there wasn't anything to indicate where that arch had been embedded. He sighed and picked up the shorter piece of metal that, even in the semi darkness, somehow seemed to reflect light from some hidden source and wondered what kind of metal it could be? Where did it really come from, he wondered again, and what makes it work? There had to be a greater source of power, something other than the sun to activate it, maybe something built into the arch itself, and only turned on by the sun,…but how? He looked up then as he heard someone coming down the tunnel.

"Billy?"

"What is it, Honey?" He got to his feet as she and Melissa approached.

"Watch for a minute while we go outside, okay?"

"Don't go too far." He blew smoke from his lungs and stared at the pinkish glow of the sky again as the women moved out into the darkness, and was thinking about the volcano as he inhaled again. He couldn't get that arch off his mind somehow. What if it didn't work after they put it together, there wouldn't be anything to stop the creatures of the past from infiltrating throughout history. Because if this here was truly earth's past, and that was to happen, it could very well change the history of mankind, because none of it would have happened the way it did. So, what could they possibly do to stop such a chain of events from taking place,… other than blowing up the room in there?

He also knew they couldn't chance blowing it up, because what Rodney said about being trapped in solid rock made too much sense. An explosion here could change everything back to the way it was before the arches were installed. Sighing, he thumped the spent butt back inside the tunnel just as the women returned.

"Billy, did you happen to find any water close by out there?"

"I'm afraid not, honey,…why?"

"We wanted a bath, it's been a while, and we're down to one canteen of water."

"Get some sleep, honey." He grinned. "We'll all take a bath tomorrow." He watched them disappear up the tunnel before squatting down again to watch the giant birds soar over the treetops in the ancient valley, then sighing, settled down and leaned against the cold rock of the tunnel to watch the night unfold.

CHAPTER EIGHTEEN

BILLY AWOKE WITH A JERK as Connie shook him again, and as he opened his eyes, she unfolded the bandana on the cave's rock floor in front of him and he nodded his thanks, then picked up the warm piece of meat and ate it.

"Where is everybody?" He asked, taking the watch from his pocket. "It's eight o'clock, why didn't you wake me?"

"You needed rest, so relax,...they've been out looking for that piece of metal for over an hour now."

"But it's dangerous out there, honey,...you should a woke me!" He kissed her quickly and got to his feet, and with her close behind him headed for the tunnel.

The sky was gray and had a reddish tint to it. Heavy fog completely covered the valley's heavily wooded floor, and the purplish mist reached halfway up the slope. The whole area looked as if it had rained since he'd gone to sleep, because water was dripping from every leaf and blade of grass as the boys waved at him from the rocks below.

"Mornin', Lisa." He said as he moved past her. "You do know how to use that thing, I hope." He grinned as he eyed the Henry rifle in her small hands.

"I hope I don't have to." She smiled. "I'm just holding it for Connie."

"I'll take it now." Said Connie and took the rifle from her. "And thanks."

Melissa nodded and followed Billy down through the waist-high grass to help in the search.

"Everything quiet?" He asked as she came alongside.

"Yeah,…can't see anything in all that fog, but there's been some terribly wicked sounds coming from that jungle!"

"No tellin' what's watchin' us." He said as he watched the boys hunting through grass that was taller than Benny was. "But we can bet somethin' is." He sighed, then shivered in the morning's dampness as he looked toward the valley then bent and began pushing the grass aside as he joined the hunt. He was frowning, however, suddenly thinking that he'd seen movement in mist and straightened to look down the slope again. A shadow stirred in the fog then, causing him to stare hard at the purplish haze, and at that moment, his heart almost stopped. The shaggy head of an apeman appeared through the haze, then another, and yet another.

"Look out, Rod!" He yelled as he drew the Colt, and immediately saw the lawman begin climbing toward the boys. He shot one of the early men as he emerged from the fog, knocking the hairy half-animal out of sight, then shot a second one before he also started the climb back toward the cave. He saw Connie helping Melissa back into the tunnel and looked behind him in time to duck the sharpened length of wood. He saw another hurl a spear toward Rodney and the boys and shot him as he released the slender shaft. Rodney had grabbed the boys by this time and was pushing them up the grade ahead of him as other lengths of sharpened wood were hurled out of the fog at them.

Connie began firing then, felling another as Billy climbed toward Rodney and the boys. She fired again as an early man lobbed a heavy, gnarled club at him, missing his head by inches. He saw Rodney tuck Benny under his arm as he climbed, and was pulling Willy along by the arm, when the boy suddenly pulled away from him and ducked out of sight in the tall grass.

"Don't stop, Will!" Yelled the lawman. He started back for him just as Connie shot another of the attackers, hearing the apeman scream as he disappeared back into the fog,…and the shooting had become like sounds of thunder as the noise echoed eerily across the valley.

Billy was almost there as Rodney reached to grab Willy, but saw the boy pull away again and continue to struggle with a large rock.

"I got 'im, Rod, get Benny to th' cave!" He turned as he spoke and shot another apeman before reaching for Willy."What's wrong with you, son,… let's go!" He panted and quickly swept the boy into his arms.

"No, Daddy!" Yelled Willy as he tried to wriggle free. "I found it, look!"

He saw the yellow metal, then looked toward the cave as Rodney took the rifle from Connie and began firing into the fog. Billy looked back at the mist, then back at the polished metal. "I'll get it, Son, you go on to th' cave,...run!" He bent and worked the broken metal from beneath the rock, then looked back again as more of the prehistoric apes emerged from the fog.

"God damn it, Billy, get on up here!" Yelled the lawman, shooting another attacker as he was raising a stone axe, tumbling him back out of sight.

Billy half-crawled up the slope, firing as he went,...and footing on the loose rocks was not the best. But he managed to catch up to Willy as he fell again and scooped him into his arms and at last, pushed past Rodney and into the tunnel. He put Willy down and leaned weakly against the smooth wall of the cave. "Go on inside, Son," He breathed. "Get out a here." He gave Connie the piece of metal and sent her back before moving in beside Rodney.

"Shit!" Gasped the lawman. "That damn fog's crawling with 'em,...and I just ran out of bullets!"

"Load it from my belt!" Urged Billy as he continued to fire. "Watch out!" He yelled, throwing himself back into the lawman to escape the spear. Rodney levered the rifle and shot the creature as he charged at the tunnel, stone axe waving above his shaggy head. Both had to duck then as several spears were heaved up the slope at them.

"Jesus,...how many of 'em are out there?" Rodney fired again as one of the apes got too close, then quickly worked bullets from Billy's belt and reloaded.

Billy shot another as he hurled his war-club at the tunnel, but then his heart seemed to suddenly stop as he saw the reptile's massive head emerge from the fog in front of them. Breathlessly, he grabbed the lawman's arm as he fired again and pulled him back out of the opening.

The women and both boys had come back down the tunnel as Billy pulled him back, and he heard them scream when they saw the monster. "Get them kids back in the cave!" He shouted then looked back. "Holy God!" He shouted as he watched the giant animal lumber up the slope toward the unsuspecting cavedwellers.

The animal's massive head and upper body was almost touching the tall grass as it continued up the slope, its heavily muscled legs bringing it up the rise with deadly purpose and then without warning, the large head dipped downward to snare a screaming apeman in its powerful jaws, biting him in half as if he was nothing, only to drop him and snap up another.

The reptile's attack was methodical and deadly, and the beast quickly murdered another before the apemen even realized it was there, causing them to scream shrilly, and as the other apes realized the danger, they hurled their spears at the beast and quickly disappeared back into the fog.

The monster shook its ponderous head from side to side then suddenly threw back its head and roared, blood streaming from its open mouth. It then planted a large foot on one of the bodies and tore at it, devouring the fresh meat of the prehistoric man.

Not daring to breathe, the two men pressed themselves against the wall of the tunnel to watch in horrified awe as the animal fed. The beast would raise its monstrous head from time to time to search for intruders, and after it had eaten from one carcass, it would move to another and tear at the flesh of that one.

They watched in terror as the reptile devoured one after another of the bodies, and after what seemed like a long time, it appeared sated then threw back its head again and roared loud and long, making the earth tremble with the intensity. Then it suddenly swung its ugly head around until it appeared to be looking right into the tunnel at them.

"Oh, God damn, Rod, don't move!" Whispered Billy, and used his arm to hold the lawman against the wall. Both of them had totally stopped breathing as the monster stared into the dark opening at them,...then it suddenly huffed loudly and turned away, to move clumsily back down the slope toward the floor of the valley. They sucked large gulps of air into their lungs as they watched it enter the fog again, and it was then that both women ran back down the tunnel toward them, followed by two screaming boys,...and both of them reached to hold their family against them. After a minute, Billy turned Connie around and gently urged her back to the inner room.

"It's gone now." Calmed Billy softly as he looked at her ashen face. "Get hold of yourself now, we got work to do,...we'll be okay now."

"No we won"t,...it knows we're here now, Billy, it'll be back!"

"Hopfully we'll be gone by th' time that thing gets hungry again."

"You don't understand, Billy!" She gasped. "That was a Tyrannosaurus Rex,...they kill just to be killing, it's what they do! It won't stop,...they're very cunning hunters!" She began to cry then, causing Willy to cry also and to clutch at her even tighter.

"Okay, Honey,...we'll just have to work faster, that's all." He glanced at Rodney, seeing him nod then looked back at the bloodless face of his wife. "You okay now?" And when she nodded. "Then let's put that arch together." She nodded and he moved her along the tunnel back into the inner cave, where he grabbed the lengths of yellow metal and carried them back, then, with his arm still around her shoulder, instructed her and Melissa to stand guard at the opening.

After studying the tunnel's walls, Billy judged the distance in from the opening, then placed the eight-foot length of metal against the smooth wall of the tunnel, telling Willy to fetch one of the cavemen's spears to hold it in place while Rodney placed the shortest piece against the other wall. The lawman was about to insert the longer section when the women suddenly screamed again and ran back toward them.

The tunnel suddenly grew dark as the opening was blocked and in that instance, an ear-piercing roar shattered the stillness to echo through the tunnel like thunder, and still shrieking, the women threw themselves into their arms as the beast roared again and shoved its monstrous head into the tunnel as far as it could, only to tear more loose rock from the cliff as it withdrew.

"Get back in th'cave!" Shouted Billy and pushed Connie and Willy toward the inner room, then sent Melissa and Benny in pursuit. He grabbed the Henry and levered a cartridge into the chamber as the massive head was shoved into the opening again. He levered three quick shots at the reptile's open mouth, causing the startled beast to back out of the tunnel and stop a few feet down the grade where it roared again, loud enough to jar the rock beneath their feet. Aiming again at the gaping mouth, he levered several more rounds, seeing fragments of teeth fly from the beast's open jaws. The reptile backed farther down the grade, and then he was out of ammunition. But suddenly, the louder explosion of the Krag vibrated the stillness.

"Where you been?" He gasped as he quickly reloaded the Henry.

"Had to go get my gun." He raised the large bore rifle and fired again, but only caused the beast to shake its head and roar again. "Shit!" Voiced the lawman. "Damn thing just shook it off!"

"Hamstring 'im!" Shouted Billy as he levered and quickly fired at the reptile's huge rear leg, and then both of them concentrated their fire at the bend in the creature's leg, firing round after round into the large tendons until suddenly, the monster roared again, but this time in pain as the massive tendon was severed. The leg slowly gave way beneath the enormous weight, toppling the monster down with a crash, then to tumble end over end back into the fog.

They sucked air into their lungs as they both squatted on their heels in the tunnel's opening, listening to the reptile's insistant roaring from somewhere on the valley's floor.

"I just lost ten years of my life!" Breathed Rodney as they stood up again.

"Billy?" Screamed Connie from the inner room. "Are you all right?... Damn it, answer me!"

"Stay where you are!" He shouted back. "We're okay,...it's gone!...Let's get that arch in place, Rod, I'm sick to my stomach of this." He sighed and glanced at the yellow sky, and was about to look away, then quickly looked again. "What th' hell is that?"

"What, Billy?" Gasped the lawman, also looking upward. "Jesus Christ!" He stammered. "That's a fucking meteor,…look at the size of that thing!"

The massive chunk of alien ice and rock seemed to stand still in the prehistoric sky, and was emitting a long, wide trail of fire that stretched as far across the sky as they could see,…and the sound it made was akin to a tornadic wind.

"Th' thing's barely movin'." Commented Billy.

"Hell it ain't,…it's so big it looks that way! Must be five miles across!"

"Yeah," Muttered Billy. "And it's bound to hit th' ground, too!…Let's get that arch in place!"

"Amen to that!" Returned the lawman and followed Billy back into the tunnel.

The women and boys had come back as they got there and Rodney gave Melissa the heavy rifle before stooping to pick up the length of metal.

"You girls need to take th' boys back to th' cave right now!" Said Billy giving Connie his rifle. "If this thing works, the tunnel's gonna turn to stone pretty quick without that sunlight. Go on now,…we might have to move fast!" They grabbed the boys and moved back to the cave as Billy watched Rodney set the length of metal in place.

The arch was intact now, and they both moved back a step to watch it intently, as after a few seconds, it began emitting a low vibrating hum, and then to glow dimly, growing brighter as the hum finally increased to a constant drone.

In awe, they watched as the broken sections of alien metal mended, welding each into one solid piece again. "Time to go!" Shouted Billy, and both of them scampered for the safety of the inner room, and almost immediately felt the vibrations as the open tunnel began to shimmer, then to shudder with a rippling movement,…and then the tunnel was gone, leaving nothing but solid rock where it had been.

Rodney moved quickly to the polished wall and placed both hands on the surface. "We did it, by God!" He grinned and turned to face the others. "We did it!" He grabbed Melissa in a bearhug then shook Billy's hand vigorously. "We may of just saved the whole world, Billy!"

"Thank you, God." Sighed Connie, and made the sign of the cross, before pressing herself against Billy. "Thank God we're alive to talk about it, too."

"Amen." Whispered Melissa.

"Thank God we won't be there when that meteor hits, huh, Billy?"

"Meteor?" Gasped Connie. "What meteor?"

"We saw it while we watched that,…rex thing tumble down th' mountain out there."

"Damn thing must a been five, six miles across!" Added Rodney. "God, it was huge! We're okay now though, that all happened sixty-five million years ago! We're back in our time now." He bent to pick up Benny as he spoke.

"All that's left to do now,…is wait." Sighed Billy as he slowly sat down beside the fire. "Ya know,…we might need to put out this fire, might not be a vent in here."

"You're right." Said Rodney and quickly kicked the burning wood apart and stamped out the flames. "What about th' torch?"

"We need that." Said Billy as he took out his watch. "We got an hour to wait, might as well sit down and relax,…and I don't know about th' rest of ya,…but all this has made me weak as hell,…got any a that meat left?"

"Yeah," Came Rodney. "Let's eat, I'm starved."

"Hope nobody's gotta go for a while." Grinned Billy as Connie unwrapped the rest of the cooked meat.

"Hell, that's a minor problem." Said Rodney. "I just pray that other tunnel opens up on time." He looked around at the room's interior then. "Has any a them other tunnels opened up yet?"

"No, Sighed Melissa. "They won't open till sometime after we're gone, thank God,…and you know what,…nobody will believe what we've been through this week."

"And we can't tell anybody, neither." Warned Billy."Maybe one of us can write about it someday,…one of th' kids, maybe."

"Yeah!" Voiced Willy, excitedly. "I will, daddy, I know th' title, too,… don't I Uncle Rodney?"."

"I sort a think you might." He grinned at the lawman and shook his head..

"It'll have to be a fiction, Will." Added Rodney. "And that's a shame,… cause someday mankind is gonna get a scary awakening. And it just might be our great grand-kids,…or theirs. At any rate, it's coming!"

"Speaking of kids,…I can't wait to see my baby." Sighed Melissa. "Seems like a year since we left."

"Seems like sixty-five million to me." Laughed Rodney. "And it feels a little strange in here now, too,… don't it?…There's air coming in from somewhere, …I can feel it."

"Guess they thought a that, too." Sighed Billy as he swallowed the meat and reached for the makings. "Must a put air-holes in here someplace." He rolled and lit his after-dinner smoke, then picked up the Henry and levered the cartridges from it before taking a rag and stout cord from his pack.

They cleaned their weapons while the women talked, and had just finished when they heard the droning sound, and pulling their guns watched as yet another section of the large cave opened into a tunnel. They got to their feet and moved to cautiously peer down the long passageway, seeing the rays of sunlight through openings at the other end, and then watched as it slowly began to ripple again.

"It's either boarded up down there or caved in." Breathed the lawman as the tunnel closed. He looked at Billy and holstered the gun. "Wonder where it'll open up at tomorrow?"

Billy shrugged. "A hundred years ago, a thousand,...who knows? They open in different time periods, and in different places every time." He looked back at the wall behind him then. "All except that one,...it'll never open anywhere again."

— —

They passed the remaining time by rehashing the many theories about the arches until at last Billy checked his watch again and nodded. "It's about time." He grunted to his feet and took the torch from the hole in the rock, and they were all breathless when they heard the droning. Once again, they watched in awe as the wall slowly faded away and then suddenly, it was open. They could see the large room, and the torches along the wall.

"That's it!" Said Billy,...let's get out a here!" They moved quickly through the long tunnel and into the outer chamber, then turned to watch the wall close up behind them.

Billy hugged Connie against him. "Enough adventure for you?"

"Oh, yes!" She shuddered.

"You'll never get me back in there again." Sighed Melissa.

"Me neither!" Voiced Benny.

Connie sighed again. "I still wish we had some way to record all these symbols."

"But we don't." Grinned Billy. "So, let's us go get our gold and go home, okay?"

"You haven't changed your mind about buying the mountain, have you?"

"No,... we still have to keep folks out a here. No,... we're gonna go to Fort Towson first, to wait on Peter's wire,...and if he's got that meetin' set, we'll go home when it's over."

"Amen!" Sighed Rodney. "Let's get the hell out of here."

Billy grinned and led the way into the tunnel.

CHAPTER NINETEEN

LEAVING THE CAMPSITE BEFORE DAWN the following day, Billy led them back into the rough terrain of the wilderness in a southerly direction, and the way back had not lessened the arduous journey. They were constantly jabbed by dead branches, slapped in the face by lowhanging Pine branches and pricked by the thorns of brambles, and it was like that for the next ten hours. By late in the day, they were all ready for a break.

Billy pulled aside in a small clearing of rocks and tall prairie grass and dismounted, grinning when he heard the audible sighs of relief from the women and quickly unsaddled the Roan and staking her out in the luscious grass. He went to help Connie down and smiled again as she began rubbing briskly at her backside. Thought you was used to it by now?"

She turned to glare at him. "I was used to it, we're not going back the same way, that's all. And I feel like a pincushion, besides!"

"Be more of th' same tomorrow, till we hit one a th' roads, anyway."

"Yeah, well I should hope we do." She moaned then went to join Melissa and the boys as they surveyed the campsite, then all four set about tramping down the grass for the fire.

Grinning, Billy unsaddled her mare and Willy's pony before staking them out with the Roan, then grabbed the halter ropes of the two mules and led them to the edge of the clearing to wait for Rodney.

"Kind of grumpy tonight, ain't they?" Grinned the lawman as he came to slap the rump of one of the mules, and then helped Billy lift the heavy sacks from the animal's backs. "Got some blood over here, Billy." He commented as he inspected the animal's sore back.

"This side, too,…rubbed the hair plumb off."

"Guess we better rig up a couple of them racks, huh?"

"Looks like." Sighed Billy. "We best get at it, too."

They found the dead wood needed and began rigging the makeshift racks, tying them together with strips of rope.

"Think they'll work?" Sighed Rodney as he grunted to his feet.

"It worked before." Returned Billy. "It ought a work again,…guess we should a done it to start with." He got to his feet then placed both hands on his hips and shook his head.

"What?" Came Rodney when he saw him.

"Just watchin' th' women there,…they're plumb tuckered."

"They're not alone,…th' boys are, too."

Billy nodded and watched as the boys piled more dry wood by the fire. "What say we drag th' gold in next to th' fire, and get somethin' to eat, Rod, I'm hungry."

"Right behind ya." He nodded and reached down to grab one of the sacks.

It took them only a few minutes, but they were both groaning when they finally straightened and moved toward the crackling fire.

"You're just in time." Smiled Connie, and quickly spooned the hot, prehistoric meat into tin plates for them while Melissa poured their coffee. "And you better be glad Lisa thought to bring the rest of this meat with us."

"As long as we got salt." Grinned Billy. "And thanks, Lisa, one of us had to have some sense." He took the plate and found a place against one of the large rocks and sat down against it, then grinned widely as Connie placed the tin cup of hot coffee on the ground beside him. "Thanks, Honey,…at least we brought plenty a coffee."

"How far are we from the fort?" Grunted Rodney as he sat down.

"Three days, I guess,… maybe four."

"And another week to get home after that."

"Depends on that meetin', you anxious?" Grinned Billy as he forked food into his mouth.

"Well,…yeah, some. I want to see my daughter, for one thing, and for another,…not knowing what's going on in town sort a worries me."

"Thought you said Jim could handle it?"

"He can,…but we were only gonna be gone a couple of weeks,…and next week will be three."

221

"There's a telegraph at Towson, you can wire Jim when we check on Peter's wire.. Now,… what else is botherin' you?"

Rodney swallowed the meat he was chewing then shrugged. "Nothing, really. Gose got a wire from the Sheriff over in Dennison, the day before we left, saying they had Kinch West in custody. He wanted us to come take him off their hands. Got me and Gose a little excited when we read it,…and well,… since I couldn't go, he agreed to accompany Jim to go bring him back."

"What's to worry, then,…both Jim, and Gose are capable? Who is Kinch West, anyway? With a name like that, you'd think I would a heard of 'im."

"That's right,…I never told you about that, did I? Well, you and nobody else around these parts ever heard of him. Lang got his name from one of the men that rode with him."

"Lang?…What th' story on that?"

"That's why I probably never told you about it, what with the trouble you and Lang were having at the time. Anyway, we were having a problem with a certain gang of horsethieves back in sixty-seven, in fact, just a few weeks before you got home. Anyway, we looked high and low for 'em, all over the county, and couldn't find 'em. Then one day, a farmer came in and told us about seeing riders pass his place on several occasions, said they'd always cut across his cornfield heading for the breaks in the Sulfur River Bottoms. He was complaining about them trampling down his corn and wanted something done about it."

Billy grinned and took a swallow of his coffee. "Knowin' Lang, I bet that's all he needed."

"Bet your butt on that. We'd had complaints from folks all up and down Red River about losing their stock to rustlers, and me, for one, was glad Risinger came in that day. Lang was getting awful hard to live with, what with the town council riding his ass. And us doing everything we could to catch the bunch, too,…that's mostly what was pissing him off. All we knew was that they were working out of Lamar County somewhere. We knew this because a lot of folks were reporting seeing men driving horses across their land, and well,…we just couldn't find 'em. I think Lang was about to call it quits till John came in."

"And this, Kinch West was bossin' th' outfit?"

Rodney nodded. "Only one that got away, too. Anyway, all we had was another man's word that it was even West, he was last known to be somewhere in Indian Territory."

"Maybe somebody was usin' his name."

"That's possible, too, I guess. But whoever he was, that fella also told us, West was the one that shot Mister Parish the week before."

"Well, you got most of 'em anyway."

"Yeah, all but West,... and two others that were killed. Lang was fit to be tied, too, he wanted all of 'em,...real bad.."

"How about this man, Parish, who was he?"

"You never heard of Garland Parish?"

Billy shook his head. "All before my time, I guess. I never met too many folks before I left."

"I know." Chuckled the lawman. "I didn't know 'im, neither. But West supposedly shot 'im down in his own front yard. The killin' had the town in an uproar, too, I hope to tell ya,... me, Lang and some of the Melitia looked the county over for a whole week. Course it would a helped if we'd known what he looked like,... hell, I still don't! Lang managed later, to get a wanted poster on 'im from somewhere in the Nations. But some idiot must have drawn his likeness, it was God-awful. I couldn't have identified the man with the picture in front of me." He shook his head and sipped at the hot coffee, then sighed.

"Mister Parish had a place out past Doc's a ways. In fact, Connie bought his place after that. Anyway, Parish and Orin Lassiter were partners in what's now, Lassiter's wagon yard. They were good friends, I think,... even Lang liked 'im. I'm surprised Lang didn't insist on hanging the whole outfit right on the spot that day, might have, too, if it hadn't been for Sam Rucker. You know him, don't you?"

"His daughter's gonna marry Sheriff Gose, ain't she?"

"That's the one. Lang would have gotten away with mass murder that day, if not for Sam, because Judge Bonner had given us warrants for the whole bunch, dead or alive."

"He stop lookin' for West, after that?"

Rodney shook his head. "Not till we heard that West had been killed down in Mexico somewhere. But, evidently,... that wasn't true, neither."

"Well." Sighed Billy. "You'll know how it turned out when you send that wire,...they ought a be back by now."

"Bar any trouble." Nodded the lawman and began eating again as the boys and women joined them with their supper.

The meal went quickly after that as their idle discussions were on home and their children, and what they might have been doing in their absense, and then it was over and the women collected the plates to clean them. Rodney went to retrieve the blackened pot from the fire and poured fresh coffee in their cups while Billy rolled and lit his after meal smoke.

"Think we'll make the fort ahead of Peter, Billy?"

"Well,... they're still a couple days from home yet, and its three more days from there to Towson, so yeah, I'd say we will,...if he's even comin'. They might not a set th' meetin'."

Rodney placed the pot between them and sat down again. "Peter liked the idea of heading up a police force, didn't he?"

"Yeah, but that might not happen, neither. You heard 'im say there was already one in place, and has been for several years. So, don't bank on it too much"

"Then we'll just have to convince that Chief, what's his name,…Bryant, that Peter can do a better job at it. Besides, they were nowhere around to help White Buffalo."

"They was too scared to do that. Don't forget, to th' Choctaw, the Ancient Ones didn't exist, they was ghosts. They knew they was there, and knew they protected them, but only a few ever seen 'em.. To them, they was ghosts, plain and simple,…and somethin' to be feared."

"White Buffalo ain't no ghost, Daddy." Blurted Willy suddenly. "He was real, we seen him."

"We know that, son, but the Choctaw don't. And we can't talk about 'em,…we can't tell anybody, not at home, or in school. You do understand that, don't you?"

"Yes, sir,…but it's gonna be hard."

"Look at it this way,…you'll always know somethin' nobody else knows and besides, White Buffalo wouldn't want anybody else to know, not even where he lived."

"I won't tell anybody, Daddy."

"Me neither." Voiced Benny. "I won't never tell!"

"Good boy, Benny." Laughed Rodney.

"Why don't the other Indians believe White Buffalo is real, Daddy?"

"I don't know,…Superstitious, I guess. Nobody knows why."

"Well I hope this Chief Bryant is superstitious." Sighed Rodney. "It'll make it a lot easier to sway him."

"And maybe not, too. Peter said he's only about a quarter Choctaw, his old man was white."

"That figures?"

"And not only that, we'll have to convince Chiefs from all three districts, as well as a man named Walker. He's th' President of the Choctaw Senate,… Bryant is only th' head Chief."

"This gets better all the time, don't it?"

"All of 'em know about th' Ancient Ones and all th' years they've been afraid of 'em, and I'm sure both Walker, and Bryant was likely afraid, too. And they sure knew about th' attack on th' mountain, and th' rapes and murders in th' wilderness,…they had to. And because of that, we just might do okay at that meetin. We just got a say th' right things at th' right time,…and we got a follow Peter and Joseph's lead."

"You mean, back 'em up on what they say, or what?"

Billy shook his head. "So we'll know when, and what to say when it's our turn."

Rodney grinned and then scratched his head. "I tell ya, Billy,…this thing's already got me worried."

"I hear ya. It's somethin' new to me, too."

"Daddy?" Said Willy suddenly, and when Billy didn't answer him, he turned and tugged at his sleeve. "Daddy?"

"Yeah, Son, what is it."

"Is that one of them outer space machines?" He pointed up at the darkening sky as he spoke.

Billy looked at him narrowly before looking skyward. "Where, Son?"

"Right there, Daddy, see?"

The tiny light was moving in a straight line from West to East across the darkening sky, and Billy shook his head. "I don't know what that might be."

"Well I do." Returned Rodney. "It's a shooting star."

"Mama!" Called Willy, and when he got the women's attention, he pointed again. "Look up there, Mama,…see it?"

"Yes, I do!…Look Lisa, what do you think that is?"

"It's a shooting star!" Repeated Rodney. "There ain't no such thing as a flying machine!"

"Rodney!" Scolded Melissa. "It doesn't have a tail, shooting stars and Comets have tails behind them!"

"I'm getting another headache." Mumbled the lawman and looked back at the object,… just in time to see it disappear. "Where the hell did it go?"

"Would a shooting star do that, Rodney?" Giggled Melissa.

"I don't see nothin'!" Complained Benny, causing all of them to laugh.

"Don't worry about it, honey." Soothed Melissa. "It's gone now."

"I bet it was a flyin' machine, Uncle Rodney." Said Willy excitedly. "I really bet it was."

"Well," He sighed. "It was something, all right, I'll grant ya that. But it wasn't a flying machine, Will,…trust me on that."

"Rodney Taylor, you are hopeless!" Scolded Melissa again.

"It is a hard thing to believe all right." Said Billy as he reached for tobacco and papers again. "Th' jury's still out on it, too." He rolled and lit the Durham and inhaled deeply of the smoke. "But,… I don't think I believe it's impossible, neither, considerin' what we seen down there."

"I'll admit to that, my self." Nodded Rodney. "After going through it, I'd have to say nothing's impossible, anymore. But I still don't believe in machines that can fly."

"That coffee still hot, Rod?" Grinned Billy.

— ‑

They were in the saddle early, and for the next two days were in some of the worst country yet. They were forced to endure deep gouges from the hundreds of dead limbs and protruding branches that grabbed at them from out of the waist-high grass, and if that wasn't enough, pricking thorns of Mesquite thickets were taking their toll as well. But the worst was the festering heat in the lower areas of thick Pines and swamp-like marshes where swarming mosquitoes plagued them, and the horses.

Footing for the animals was also something to guess at on the tall, wooded slopes with their shifting rocks,...and fallen timber was a nightmare. Billy had known they were in for a rough time, when they were forced to make last night's camp in the bed of a debris-laden ravine, as the trees and brush were so dense on level ground, it was impossible,...and as usual, they were in unfamiliar country.

The morning was passing slowly as they maneuvered the horses up yet another steep, tree-infested hillside, and between the insects, and the nagging complaints from Connie and Melissa, he was thinking he should have gone back the way they had come. It would have thrown them another day away from Fort Towson, but it might have been worth it. He was constantly forced to break off Pine branches that might have slapped at them, and all the time, desperately hoping they would come across one of the old army roads that crisscrossed the mountains. Windingstair Mountain was to the far Northwest of them now, and he knew, within reason, they were in the vicinity of one of those roads,...and as it turned out, he was right, because he could see it as they started their descent, just visible through the trees below them.

Relieved, he urged the Roan down through the tangle of trees, then through a large grove of wild Pecan, and a half hour later, was leading the way into yet another steep-sided, twisting ravine, with the road just on the other side. Once on the bottom, he reined the Roan between the large rocks to stop against the high embankment on the opposite side, wanting to rest the horses, and sighing, he pushed his hat back on his head and watched the others descend.

"There's a road up there on th' other side." He said when they pulled up in front of him.

"That's a relief." Breathed Rodney as he stared up the tall wall. "How do we get to it?"

"By findin' a way out a here, come on,...it won't take long." He clucked the mare into motion again and led the way along the cluttered gully for another dozen yards before finding what he was looking for,…and stopping again, he twisted in the saddle. "We ought a be able to climb out here, but you gals best hold on, it could get tricky,…that goes for you, too, Son. Benny, you lean forward and hold on to th' saddlehorn, okay?" And satisfied, he glanced at the mule and gave its load the once-over before urging the Roan up the crumbling, clay embankment,…and a few slips, and breathtaking seconds later, was crossing the dozen grass-covered yards to the deep-rutted wagon roan. He crossed the hard-packed ruts then stopped to wait on Connie and the others again.

"Thatk, God!" Gasped Connie as she came through the tall grass and onto the road. "That country is God awful." She began to briskly rub at the bloody snags in the legs of her jeans then. "Look at this, Billy, I'm bleeding,… and my clothes are ruined!"

"It couldn't be helped, honey, it would a cost us another whole day to go back th' other way. We'll make better time now." He shifted his aching backside in the groaning leather and dismounted with a grunt before reaching up for her. "Come on, honey, we'll stretch our legs a bit,…and I know you got a go, too,… cause I do."

"Oh, God, yes!" She moaned and allowed him to help her down. "I've been in pain for an hour."

"You should a said something'"

"Billy,…you can't just blurt out something like that,…really!" She moved under the horse's head as Rodney helped Melissa down. "You need to go with me, Lisa?"

"Yes, Ma'am!" She moaned, and quickly followed Connie into the trees.

"Don't go too far!" Said Billy loudly.

"And watch out for Snakes!" Shouted Rodney with a grin.

"I got a go, too, Daddy." Said Willy as he dismounted.

"Me, too!" Voiced his echo.

Rodney grinned and went to untie Benny. "You boys can do it right on the road here, ain't nobody here but us."

Billy sighed his relief and shifted the double-gun rig back into place before reaching for the Durham sack. "We'll make some good time, if this road goes all th' way South?"

"Yeah," Agreed the lawman, buttoning up his jeans. "If, is the question." He came to stand with Billy as he pulled a slender cigar from his shirt pocket and bit off the end. "Wonder if this is the road we used three years ago?"

"Could be." He licked the thin smoke and struck a match to it, then held the flame to Rodney's cigar. "If it is, it ought a take us all th' way to Wheelock,…won't be far to th' fort from there."

Rodney nodded. "We still got a ways to go, though. You plan on making camp again tonight,…or riding on to the fort?"

"Depends on th' boys,…and th' women, too, I guess. But I ain't up to stoppin' in Wheelock, don't know about you."

"Me, neither. There'll probably be soldiers there, river-rats, too, now that Jonesboro's drying up,…and some of them yay-hoos could get a little salty."

"And too nosey, ta-boot. Might take a hankerin' to know what's on them mules,…amd me, for one, can do without any gun-play this close to our meetin' place. How far is that fort from Wheelock, anyway?"

"Ain't got a clue,…but it's got a be ten miles, at least. But you know what?…We're gonna have th' same problem there. The town will be over run with that scum,…hotels, too. We can't camp anywhere close to that fort, Billy."

Billy inhaled more of the acrid smoke and blew it skyward. "Then maybe we can find out where that Council Lodge is and camp there,…maybe you can get that information from the telegrapher when you send your wire."

"Good idea."

"I been thinkin', too, that we might run across some unwanted company before we get there, this stretch of road looks well used." Commented Billy absently as he stared along the rutted trail. "So here's what I think we'll do. We'll tie your mule to Connie's saddle. That way, we can keep th' gold, them, and th' boys between us. I can watch th' road ahead, while you keep watch behind us."

"That sounds like a plan, let's do it!"

They quickly made the changes, and after checking all the saddle-girths, Rodney hefted Benny back to his saddle and strapped him down.

"Here come th' gals, Son,…better get mounted." He went to help Connie up while Willy mounted, and after explaining their plan of travel, mounted the mare, and when the rest were settled in and ready, he turned the Roan and led off down the hard-packed clay of the road.

It was still quite warm on the mud-clodded road, even in the shade of the towering pines, and those ageless trees were thick along both sides,…and the mosquitoes were still a problem. Connie and Melissa were discussing the events at the mountain as they continuously slapped at the pesky invaders,… and even the boys were conversing,…but no one was complaining, and that was a relief in it's self.

Their discussions of the mountain, however, led to his thinking about it, also,…and that caused him to shudder when thinking of that ancient world and the monsters that inhabited it. But along with the thoughts came the unrest again, and he tried to think of other things. For one thing, he knew he would be glad when the meeting with Chief Bryant was behind him, because the anticipation was beginning to wear on his nerves,...and to top it off, he wasn't sure the Chief would see them at all on such short notice. The whole thing would depend on Peter and Joseph, and whether or not they had managed to wire Bryant for a meeting,...and that was the dilimma. He would much rather forget the whole thing and go home, back to a normal life on the farm. But he also knew, that after what he had seen at the mountain, their lives would never be normal again.

He sighed heavily and reached for the makings, then painstakingly rolled and lit the brown-paper smoke, taking the acrid relaxant deep into his lungs as his thoughts returned to the metallic light they'd seen in the sky, and thinking that Melissa was right,...the thing didn't look like a shooting star. It wasn't a light, either, but more like the sun's reflection on metal. Because, even though it was dark where they were, the sun would still hit something that high up,...and whatever it was, there didn't seem to be any kind of a visible trail behind it.

He knew that this way of thinking was only because of what he'd seen in the tunnels,...but there was just no other reasonable explanation. What if that object in the sky was a flying machine? It could have been, for all they knew, and if it was, it was almost a dead, mortal cinch that people from another world were already here. Everything pointed to his being right, when he thought that White Buffalo might be one of them,...maybe the whole tribe was. Could they have been placed there centuries ago to protect their toy?

Sighing again, he took another pull at the acrid smoke. There was no explanation for the time-portals, other than that, and if it was true, whoever, or whatever had put the portals in place, were still here,...or very able to come and go at will. They may not be using the portals anymore,...but in that respect, they could be like most people on earth, and just got bored with it,...but with that kind of power on hand...? He shuddered again, and knew that life, from now on, wouldn't be the same. Because somehow, whether it had been planned, or otherwise, they had been chosen to protect the secret, and the treasure,...well, maybe that was the incentive. But whatever it was, it scared him.

"Guess it's out of our hands, right girl?" He grinned when he saw the Roan's ears flick back at him, then reached down to slap her on the neck as his thoughts turned back to the meeting.

'Wonder what this Chief Bryant will be like' he wondered? Will he be a logical man, like Peter, or Joseph? Or would he be more like some polition, set in his ways and hard to convince? After all, according to Peter, he was more white, than Choctaw,...and what about that man, Walker,...he was mostly white, too, and somewhat of a polition, anyway,... his being President of the Choctaw Senate.

He thumped the spent butt onto the road and scanned the trees along both sides before looking along the darkening shadows ahead of them. They had been at a steady, but fast walk for hours now, and had not passed a cabin,...and if this was the road to Wheelock, they should have already seen the burned-out remains of the cabin with its graves. But then suddenly, there it was, and not much past his wondering about it. They came abreast of the ashen remains a short time after that, and the memory of what him and Rodney had seen there three years ago was still quite gory.

"What happened here, Billy?" Called out Connie, from behind him.

He stopped and reined the mare around to face her. "A Choctaw family was killed by Comanches three years ago. Me and Rod found 'em right after it happened,...their graves are right over yonder."

"Dear God!" She whispered. "That must have been an awful sight."

"It wasn't the only one, neither." Added the lawman as he nudged his horse up alongside the women. "Some were even worse than this one."

"How horrible that must have been for these people." Said Melissa as she gazed at the debris.

"That don't quite describe it, honey." Nodded Rodney.

"What's a Comanche, Daddy?" Asked Willy, quisically.

"Yeah, what is it?" Came his echo.

"They're Indians, too, Son. A pretty bad bunch." He looked at the rest of them then and nodded. "We best move on now." With a last look at the graves, Billy turned back just as Connie was making the sign of the cross on her breast, and clucked the Roan into motion again,...and it was at that instant that she uttered a low whinny, causing him to immediately stop again and stare down at her head,...and when her ears pricked forward, he raised his hand as a gesture for the rest of them.

"What is it, Billy?" Blurted Connie.

"Somebody comin',...don't talk anymore." He reached down and worked the tie-down loop of leather from the hammer of the Colt and, once more, strained his eyes along the shadowy roadway ahead of them. No one was in sight yet, so he twisted in the saddle to look at her. "We'll wait here till they pass, so let me do what talkin' there might be, okay?" And when they nodded, he looked past them at Rodney, and saw him pull his pistol and hold it across the saddle out of sight, then turned back to watch the road. He saw the riders a couple of minutes later, just as the Roan snorted again. He watched the dark shapes of four men as they rounded a bend of the road and rode toward them.

As the four came closer, he could tell they were all heavily bearded and unkempt, as their clothing appeared soiled and baggy looking in the shadows. 'A filthy lot' he thought as they drew closer,...and though he couldn't yet see their faces beneath the floppy hats they wore, he knew they would be hard-eyed and mean. They all four were wearing sidearms, and rifle-butts protruded from boots beneath their legs. They stopped their horses as they came abreast of him.

"Howdy there, Pilgrim." Nodded the man closest to him. "You folks out for a ride, are ye?"

Billy watched as the man beside the first one gigged his horse slightly forward to stare somewhat hungrily at the women, then raise himself in the stirrups to peer at the loaded mules before leaning across to speak to the man who had spoken. That man also, raised up for a look before settling back to look at him again.

"What's in th' packs, Pilgrim,…you don't mind me askin'?"

Billy stared back at him, then grinned. "But, I do mind. What's your interest?"

"Why nothin' a'toll, Pilgrim." Replied the man gruffly. "Curious be all,… where you good folk headed?"

"Th' way you come in,…and I'll say it again. What's your interest?"

The man glared at him momentarily, then shrugged his wide shoulders,… and in the heat of the road, the odor from unwashed sweat and grime became strong in the heat of the road. "Now, don't you go bust a gut on us, Pilgrim, I'm jest bein' na'borly."

Billy nodded. "Okay,…then be neighborly and move on,…because what's in them sacks is nothing but granit rock for my fireplace, and it belongs to me."

The man leaned from the saddle to spit a stream of tobacco juice at the road, then straightened and showed broken, yellowed teeth in a smirking grin, his eyes darting from Billy to the pack mules and back again,…and in that fleeting moment, Billy could see the intent in the man's beady eyes. And when he suddenly turned to look at the other three, he knew what was going to happen.

The Colt came out in a whisper, seeming to suddenly appear out of nowhere, and causing all four men to stare at the weapon in disbelief.

"Whut th' fuck's that for?" Gasped the large man.

"I don't know if you gent'll understand this, but I got a feelin' I just saved your miserable lives." He waved the gun at them then. "Now, I want your gunbelts, and I want 'em now,…and do it slow and easy."

"Now, looky here, Pilgrim!" Blurted the big man as he reluctantly unbuckled the belt. "What th' fuck's th' meanin' a this, we didn't mean you folks no harm?"

"Yeah you did." Gritted Billy. "And I'd a killed you, too. Now make a loop out a them belts and pass 'em to me,…and be real gentle about it."

"God damn you, you Fuck,…I'll remember you fer this!" He angrily buckled the belt together and passed it across to Billy, then cursed some more as he took the other three and passed them to him, then bitterly watched as Billy looped them over his saddlehorn. "You're gonna regret this, Pilgrim!"

"I already do. Now, pull them rifles and grab 'em by th' barrels." Once the men complied, he nodded. "You can be on your way now, Neighbor,… and give them rifles to th' Maeshal back there on your way by…. And then, you'd best keep goin'."

"I'll see you again, you Fuck!"

"And watch your mouth, neighbor, there's ladies present!"

Still glaring hatefully at him, the four moved sullenly past him and the women to where Rodney was waiting with drawn pistol, and one by one gave up their saddleguns, then, cursing loudly, spurred their squeeling mounts into a hard run along the rutted road.

Rifles under his arm, Rodney dismounted as Billy holstered the Colt, then came forward to lash them to Connie's pack animal before moving beneath the necks of the boy's ponies to stand in the middle of the road and look the way the men had gone.

"Think they'll keep going?" He sighed as he turned to face Billy.

"If they're smart, they will."

"Why did you do that, Billy," Asked Connie. "They didn't threaten us?"

"Oh, yes they did." Sighed Rodney. "They just didn't say so."

"Once they got past us, honey, they'd a turned on us,…thinkin' they'd get th' upper hand."

"How do you know that?"

"I just know, honey. Get mounted Rod, let's go." He smiled at Connie then. "Would you rather somebody got shot?"

"Don't be ridiculous, Billy, of course not!"

"Then trust me, honey,…we would a had to kill 'em." He turned the mare and tugged on the mule's leadrope, then led off down the road again,…and wondering if he'd been wrong? But then again, he knew he wasn't wrong, the men were dregs of humanity. They had no consideration for anyone, other than themselves. He also knew, with some probability, that they came from the settlement of Wheelock. And it would be just his luck, he thought, for there to be even more of them.

It was an hour later, and almost full dark on the road when the mare snorted again, causing him to once again raise his hand to stop,…and with his hand resting on the grip of the Colt, he sat and watched the mule-drawn wagon approach. He turned in the saddle and told Connie to wait there, then urged the Roan forward to intercept the wagon.

An aging Choctaw farmer, along with a younger man were sitting on the seat, and they stopped the team as he approached, then sat in silence to stare warily at him as he stopped beside the wagon. "Howdy." He said with a grin, and pushed the hat back on his head.

"Howdy." Returned the Choctaw, his tired eyes flicking from Billy, to the other riders behind him.

"What'll you take for th' wagon, friend?"

The Choctaw peered curiously up at him, then shrugged and picked up the drivelines.

"Hey, old fella, I'm serious. I'm here to buy your wagon, not to hurt you.... Tell you what I'll do, I'll give you fifty dollars in gold coin for it, I'll even swap mules with ya,...how about it?"

The old man looked at the young one, then turned to look at the wagonbed.

"I'll throw in a Winchester Rifle ta-boot, how's that?"

The old man thought for a minute longer, then grinned toothily at him. "Make that seventy dollars in gold, and you make a deal."

Billy grinned and shook his head. "You drive a hard bargain, my friend." He leaned to open the flap of the saddlebag, then took out a few coins and counted them. "You're pretty smart, old timer." He grinned as he dropped the access coins back into the pocket. "You knew right off, that I needed this wagon, didn't ya?" And when the old Indian grinned, he leaned and counted the coins into his outstretched hand, then reached to shake on the deal. The two Choctaw quickly climbed to the ground as Billy waved the others in.

"What did you do, Billy?" Asked Connie, curiously.

"I bought a wagon,...we can tie your horses to th' tailgate, and you all can ride for a while." He grinned and helped her and Melissa down, then turned to Rodney. "Let's off-load these packs to th' wagon, Rod." Nodding, the lawman quickly helped him heave the heavy sacks of gold into the wagon and cover them with the remains of a ragged tarp that was there. Then they cut the bindings that held the wooden racks in place on the animal's backs and tossed them off the side of the road. Rodney untied Benny from his saddle, and after him and Willy relieved themselves again, lifted him into the bed of the wagon.

Once the animals were tied snugly to the tailgate, and everyone was in the wagon, Billy turned to grin at the old Choctaw, who was still waiting patiently beside his new mules, then reached into the wagon for one of the confiscated rifles and gave it him. "Just like I promised, my friend, seventy dollars, two mules and one rifle,...Many thanks, and good luck to you." He gripped both their hands warmly. "Yokoke." He said sincerely. He grinned at the surprise on their faces, then mounted the mare and pulled alongside the wagon to watch the two men swing onto the mule's backs and continue into the shadows.

"How we gonna work this?" Came Rodney, still leaning against the bed of the wagon.

Billy reached down and took the reins from his hand. "I'll take your horse, you drive th' wagon. I'll bring up th' rear and keep watch." Rodney nodded and climbed to the driver's seat as Billy looked down at Connie and th' boys. "Them sacks don't leave too much room for sleepin in there, but you best try and get some, cause we ain't stoppin' till we get to th' fort, and I don't know when that'll be. We got a little town to go through a ways up th' road, and we'll have to do it quietly,...th' place'll likely be full a men like them other four was, and we don't want any trouble." He nodded at Rodney and reined the horses aside as the lawman turned the wagon around on the narrow road, then fell in behind the trailing horses.

It was hot and muggy, and not yet sundown, but because of the mountains and heavily timbered slopes, it was pitch-dark on the road. The old wagon creaked and groaned as it's narrow wheels bounced in and out of the deep, uneven trail of ruts, and Billy had to grin at the dim images of the girls as they held onto the loose-fitting sideboards for support. The boys, however, had fallen almost instantly fast asleep.

He was satisfied with the wagon. It was a good alternative to the highly visible packs on the mules, and was hardly noticeable in the wagon at all, especially under the old tarp. They were making better time as well, he noted, in spite of the road's condition, and sighing, he turned for a look behind them before settling back in the saddle. They were still a long way from Wheelock, and he was already bone-weary,...tired from so many days on the back of a horse. He concentrated idly on the barely visible rumps of the trailing horses and began passing the time with thoughts of the upcoming meeting and wondering, for the umpteenth time, if what they had to do was even possible, considering the fact that almost the whole of the Choctaw Nation didn't believe the Ancient Ones ever existed. And those that did know the truth, were too afraid to admit it, even to each other,...and especially that they had been donating food to help feed them all these years. Because even those farmers believed they were ghosts, and that the mountain was forbidden, and evil,...that is, all but Peter and Joseph, but even they would not enter the mountain it's self. Because superstition had been instilled in them for generations, and its impact was a strong and everlasting influence.

They were able to make good time, in spite of not being able to see the road, but they had no further encounters with unwanted travelers as the hours progressed and so, were able make it to the settlement of Wheelock in just a little after midnight. They began passing the remote, and rundown shacks about a mile before reaching the settlement, and all of them were dark, and obviously sleeping,...all save the mongrel dogs that ran out to greet them. The sightly moonlit yards in front, were almost totally littered with farming equipment, wagon parts and the like. Rodney held the team to a squeaking walk past the shanties, and the noise from the wagon seemed louder to them, than that of the barking dogs.

They could hear the laughter of drunken men, and the shrieking of saloon women by the time Rodney stopped the wagon. They were within sight of the sagging structure now, and he sat the seat to watch the activity in the narrow, dimly lighted street.

"What's th' holdup?" Urged Billy as he pulled up alongside.

"There's fighting in the street up there,...in front of the saloon there."

"Yeah, well,...they prob'ly been doin' that all night. Prob'ly won't even notice us. To them, we'll be just another wagon comin' through."

"Maybe,...but there's several more standing along the front stoop,... taking a piss, looks like. And I don't see any cavalry horses at the hitchrails. There ain't no law here, Billy, and that worries me some."

"I'm worried a little, too, Rod,...you got any options?"

"All I'm saying is, we're only two men, and there could be twenty drunks still inside there. And with no soldiers around, them pukes could get away with anything!"

"You're right, but we can't stay here. Can't go around, neither, th' wagon wouldn't make it. To me, straight ahead is our only option." He reared back on the reins to back the mare up, then looked down at Connie. "You girls okay, Honey?"

"No,...I'm like Rodney. This place scares me."

"Me, too!" Whispered Melissa.

Rodney turned around on the seat then to look at her. "You all right, Sweetheart?"

"Yes, I'm just worried, Rodney,...we're okay."

"Th' boys asleep?" Queried Billy.

"Dead to the world." Nodded Connie.

Billy nodded. "I think we'll be all right. But I want you and Lisa to stay down and out a sight. We have to go through here to get to th' fort, and I don't want them Bums to see you."

Both women quickly lay down in the wagon's splintering bed, and satisfied they wouldn't be seen, he nodded at Rodney. "Take it slow, Rod, and try not to look at them,...just don't stop. You'll know what to do if we get in trouble."

Rodney nodded, and with a last look at the women, turned and slapped the reins to the mules' backs and continued on into the heart of the activity. Dozens of drooping horses lined the street on both sides of them, some tied to brush and rocks, and others to the porch posts of the shacks across from the saloon.

The bar was full, too, and very loud. The yelling and cursing of both men, and women, was ugly in their drunken stupors,...and the men in the alley stopped their fighting to gape at them as the wagon lumbered into the dim light reflecting onto the street, and then only to shout curses at them, or to throw empty whiskey bottles in their direction, but no attempt was made to hinder them in passing. Then they were finally out of earshot from the trading post and passing more of the darkened cabins where, once again, several mange-ridden mongrel dogs greeted them, barking and nipping at the legs of the animals, but at last, even the dogs turned back, and that's when Rodney whipped the team to a faster pace along the, now, moonlit road,...and another two miles farther on, was turning them onto the road to Fort Towson.

— —

It was a tiring ten miles, and when the town of Fort Towson came into sight, Rodney urged the team off the well traveled road and into some trees a dozen yards away,...where he once more pulled them to a stop.

"Looks peaceable enough, don't it?" Commented Billy as he dismounted stiffly beside the wagon.

"Yeah,...but you can bet there's still a bar open somewhere in town. And to be on the safe side, I'll ride on in alone, come daylight."

"You been here before?"

"With Lang once,...the Fort's on the other side of town yonder, closer to the river,...but the telegraph office is smack-dab in the middle of town there."

Billy nodded. "Then we best get a couple hours sleep."

"I'm all for that, I'm dead tired. But you know,...I was here that one time, but I don't recall ever seeing that Council Lodge anywhere."

"Well, th' Choctaw wouldn't put their Government building too close to town, I don't think. We'll find it....Go ahead and curl up on th' seat there, Rod,...I'm gonna stake out th' horses in th' grass back there."

"You don't have to tell me twice!"

— —

It was mid-morning when Rodney left the road and galloped his horse back toward the campsite, where he walked the animal into the cover of trees and dismounted. "Everybody's up and at 'em, I see." He grinned at them, not understanding their silence, then shrugged and hefted one of the two floursacks of supplies from around the saddlehorn and placed it in the bed of the wagon. "What did I do,...ain't none of you speaking to me this morning?...After I went to the trouble to fetch breakfast?"

Billy looked up at him from his seat on the tailgate, and shrugged. "What'r you talkin' about,...you been gone, Rod?"

Rodney pushed his hat to the back of his head and gazed searchingly at each one of them. "What am I missing here?" He looked at the boys then, they were both staring at the ground in front of them, but then he saw the grin appear on Benny's face. "Okay people, what's going on here?...Come on, Benny just gave you up."

"Awww, Benny!" Chastised Willy, and they all busted out laughing.

Melissa got to her feet and came to hug him. "I'm sorry, honey." She giggled. "We had it made up to do that when you got back. Had you frustrated, didn't it?"

He grinned sheepishly then, and nodded. "I will remember this, you know,...and I will get even." He leaned down and kissed Melissa on the mouth. "Was this your idea, woman?" And when she shook her head, between giggles, he looked at the rest of them. "I'd best get some breakfast out a this."

"I think we can manage that!" Laughed Connie, getting up from the log they were sitting on. "Besides, Billy and the boys are the culprits."

"But it was worth it." Grinned Billy. "You should a seen th' look on your face."

"Well, you got a understand. After what we've been through these two weeks, I was expecting anything."

"That's what made it so funny." Snickered Connie as she shooed Billy from his seat and tugged open the sack. "What all did you bring?"

Rodney retrieved the other sack from the saddle and placed it in the wagon. "Well,...I got a slab of salt pork, some jerky, flour, coffee, canned beans, spuds and, oh yeah,...some Crow,...which all of you will be eating come payback time." This caused another round of laughter. "There's also a bag of straw in that other sack, Connie,...got a dozen large eggs in it, so be careful." He grinned again at Melissa as she retrieved skillet and eating utencils from the pack.

"Bring the salt, too, Lisa," Reminded Connie.

Rodney moved to where Billy had sat down on the log, and gave him a fresh sack of Durham Tobacco before sitting down beside him.

"Hey,...thanks, Rod, I was about out."

"What about us, Uncle Rodney?" Whispered Willy from beside him. "You bring us anything?"

"Yeah, you bring us anything?" Echoed Benny in a much louder tone.

"You don't need anything, William!" Scolded Connie.

Rodney grinned. "You know what, boys. I don't know,…but I might have just accidentally dropped a sack of gumdrops in one a them sacks."

"Yeaaaa!" Yelled the boys in unison, and they both rushed the wagon, only to be stopped by Connie's stern voice.

"Oh, no you don't!…If there's any candy in there, it'll keep till after you've eaten. But since you're so full of energy, you can build the fire to cook on, William,…get matches from your daddy."

"You help him, Benny." Grinned Melissa.

"You hear from Peter, Rod?"

"Yeah,…the wire came in yesterday. We're all set, they ought a be here late tomorrow, or sometime the next day. Said Chief Bryant was leaving Boggy Depot that same morning,…he should be here sometime tomorrow."

"That's a relief." Nodded Billy as he reached the near-empty sack of tobacco from his shirt. "Jim get his prisoner back?"

Rodney placed the stub of a half-smoked cigar in his mouth and lit it before shaking his head. "Turned out it wasn't Kinch West at all,…just some drifter that matched the description. Jim checked out the man's story by sending a few wires, and what have ya,…then told the Sheriff to let him go."

"Long ride for nothin'."

"Hundred miles, more or less, round trip. That Dennison Sheriff thought sure he had West in custody."

"Sounds more like a madeup name to me. anyway"

Rodney pulled another paper from his shirt and unfolded it. "Got this one, too."

"Another one?"

"Yeah, he forgot, and had to send two. Do you know a bounty hunter by the name of Gus Thornton?"

Billy turned to peer at him. "Why,…he lookin' for me?"

"That's what crossed my mind when I read the first couple a lines,…but, according to Jim, he's not. Tom Stone told him who Thornton was, and where to find 'im."

"That'd be th' bartender at th' Dollar Saloon?"

Rodney nodded. "Jim found Thornton at the Lamar Hotel and questioned him, but he wouldn't say who he was looking for, only that he had followed a cold trail here from Alabama….And that the man was wanted by the army."

"It could be me, then, except for one thing. I never been to Alabama."

"I don't think it's you. Gose thinks it's John Risinger."

"Risinger, ain't he....?"

"One and the same. Jim said Thornton's been looking the County over, but as yet, ain't found 'im. Said Gose even asked him not to offer Thornton any help in finding him."

"Maybe him and Gose are friends.... Jim check Thornton out?"

Rodded nodded again. "He's a real bad one. According to the High Sheriff in New Orleans, Thornton's a fast gun, and he doesn't bring anybody in alive."

"Jim could have his hands full then. What did you tell 'im to do about it?"

"I told him the war was over, and to leave it that way.... He'll handle it okay. Maybe if Thornton don't find his man, he'll give up and leave."

"Not likely,... he'll try to recruit some help first."

"You think so?"

"Depends on th' reward." Nodded Billy. "But if it's worth his while, he'll tell Jim who he's after and ask for help."

"Why ain't he done that already?"

"Beats me,...maybe he thinks he could lose th' bounty if he tells th' law."

Rodney sighed then. "Well,...using that logic, he could become a problem for Jim. You always do that to me,...you know that?"

"I don't mean to, Rod. But I've learned that nothin' ever happens like it ought to,...there's too many twists and turns. I'm just guilty of tryin' to think of all of 'em before I do anything."

"Guess I'll just have to trust Jim's judgement. Anyway, I told 'im we'd be home in a few days. I didn't think to ask that telegrapher if the ferry was still operating at Jonesboro."

"We're likely as close to a bridge as we are to Jonesboro. You didn't forget to ask about th' Council Lodge, I hope."

"I remembered that. We're about three miles from it,...I passed the road on the way back."

"Good,...and I hope there's water there somewhere,...I don't want a see that Chief, smellin' like th' last four men we met."

"A shave wouldn't hurt, neither."

"Come and get it, boys." Voiced Connie.

＊ ＊

The Council Lodge turned out to be a long structure, built of logs and milled lumber. A wrap-around, railing porch was built across the entire length of the front, and down both sides, with bannistered wood steps, one in front, and a set at the rear of the porch on both sides. The building was anchored atop large, hewn blocks and was at least three feet off the ground. The roof was also of logs, and gabled. A large rack of Elk horns adorned the mid-area of the front gable, and to the right of the porch, at few feet out, stood a thirty-foot, slender pole displaying a rust-colored flag depicting the Great Seal of the Choctaw Nation. In the middle of the flag was a blue circle, and inside that, a yellow circle with an unstrung bow and three arrows. Behind the bow was a combination Peace-pipe and tomahawk, the pipe bowl on top with smoke coming from it, and the tomahawk blade below it, with the pipestem handle protruding behind the arrows. Along the top of the porch, about midway, was a carved sign that read, CHOCTAW COUNCIL LODGE.

Having found their way to the meeting place, Billy led the way into the trees, pitching camp along a fast-running creek that paralleled the lodge grounds, and in full view of the lodge itself.

Rodney climbed down from the wagon's backless seat as Billy dismounted, and then went to help him untie the horses from the tailgate and lower it, before staking the animals out along the creek's grassy banks.

"Isn't someone supposed to be here?" Asked Connie as they returned.

"Chief's on his way, honey,...be here tomorrow. We'll just have to wait, I guess. Anyway, we got soap, and a creek full a runnin' water. We best get ready for whoever does show up."

" "If he don't show up, we could still be up that old familiar creek."

"Let's hope not." Grinned Billy. "At any rate, Peter and Joseph ought a be here tomorrow."

"Tomorrow, or the next day." Sighed Rodney. They've got fifty miles or more of rough country to ride through before they get here."

"They'll take th' roads all th' way,...and if they don't stop, and ride hard, they'll be here. This meetin's important to them, too. They likely left yesterday mornin' sometime"

"I know that,...I just can't help thinking something's gonna go wrong."

"Well!" Sighed Connie, finally taking her eyes away from the lodge. "If you two will keep watch,...I'm going to have a bath in yon creek. You coming, Lisa?"

"I can't wait."

"Then I'll get the soap and a towel. William, you and Benny are next, so stay close, you hear?"

Rodney looked back at the lodge as they left. "Good, solid building, ain't it?"

"Yeah,...but I'm wonderin' why nobody's here?"

"I guess the Chief travels a lot. You said there was three Choctaw districts."

"According to Peter." Nodded Billy.

"Then there you go. We'll just have to wait. According to th' wire, I assume they'll be coming straight here from Boggy Depot"

"That, Rod, is a logical assumption. Come on, let's get a fire going."

＿ ＿

It was late the next day, and they had just finished the night's meal when they heard the wagon,…and all of them quickly moved out of the trees to watch the covered, horse-drawn Surrey cross the open, grass-covered meadow and stop at the lodge. Nine blue-coated, armed Choctaw escorted the coach, two in front, and six in back. Number nine was driving the carriage.

"This must be Mister Bryant." Commented Billy, as he watched the driver jump to the ground and quickly open the side gate to the rear seat.

A medium built, stately looking and middleaged man stepped to the ground to stare at them for a moment, then he removed his black top-hat to reveal a narrow face behind an almost totally white mustach and beard. His hair was neatly trimmed, as was his beard, and he wore a white shirt beneath a gray vest and long, black coat. His pants were creased, and as black as his shoes. He studied them for another moment, then said something to his driver, who quickly led the way up the steps to hold open the door for him. Another of the escorts led the carriage around the building and out of sight, while the rest dismounted and tied their mounts to the porch then went up the steps and sat down on the several straight-backed chairs that lined the wall.

"Important man, ain't he." Breathed Rodney. "I guess this answers one of our questions."

"Now, what?" Uttered Billy, and both of them watched the carriage driver come down the steps and walk toward them. "Maybe we're about to learn somethin'." He turned to look at Connie then. "Stay back there with th' boys, honey."

"Halito." Greeted the Choctaw as he stopped in front of them, and then in English. "Are you those who wait to meet with Chief Bryant?" And when Billy nodded. "Chief Bryant has said the meeting will take place tomorrow, but only after Peter Birdsong arrives. Until then, he wishes you comfort and well-being,… goodnight." He bowed at the waist and immediately walked back to the lodge.

"That's that, I guess." Grinned Rodney. These must be the Lighthorse Police Force, Peter talked about. No wonder they can't police the wilderness,… Bryant's using them as bodyguards."

CHAPTER TWENTY

THEY FOLLOWED PETER AND JOSEPH through the heavy door of the Council Lodge, and the carriage driver closed it behind them as they walked toward the seated Chief. Chief Bryant sat in a tall-backed armchair mid way of the long chair-lined table in the center of the large room, and silently gestured with his hands for them to take a seat.

Billy took those few seconds to appraise their benefactor, noting that the Chief was as well-groomed as when they first saw him, and he was wearing his black coat. The vest, however, was also black, but it was the eyes that held his attention the most, the pupils, themselves were almost black, and the eyes appeared to bulge slightly out from the sockets, and the eyelids covered the eyes almost half way, giving him a sleepy appearance. But the sparkle in his eyes told him the man was anything, but.

The Chief took his time to study each one of them, as if trying to read their minds, and when he finally spoke, it was in a soft, but forceful voice.

"I am William Bryant, High Chief of the Choctaw Nation. Which one of you is Peter Birdsong?"

"I am Peter Birdsong, Sir." Peter stood as he spoke, and faced the Chief from across the table.

"I've heard good things about you, Peter. There are many, who say you are the best tracker in all the Nations, and I've heard this from Indian and white men alike. Your reputation is commendable. Now,…with that being said, please introduce these other gentlemen."

Peter nodded. "Next to me, is my cousin, Joseph. The next man is Mister Upshur,…he is also known by many Choctaw as, Man with Glass eyes. The man with him is Marshal Taylor." With that, Peter sat down again as the Chief continued to study both Billy, and Rodney.

"Marshal Taylor." He repeated thoughtfully. "Are you a law man, or is that your name?"

"I'm a Marshal, Sir." Returned Rodney. "In Texas. I have no jurisdiction here,…as yet."

"As yet." Nodded the Chief. "Does that mean, you will have jurisdiction here?"

"It might, yes, sir."

Bryant nodded, then looked at Billy "I've heard the name, Man with glass eyes before, on several different occasions. Seems to me, it came from your son being kidnapped,…during a robbery, I believe?"

"That's right." Nodded Billy. "It was."

"It seems you have earned the respect of a great many Choctaw,…I commend you as well, Sir." He looked back at Peter then. "Your wire said something like, this meeting concerned the sale of a mountain. I believe you called it, Devil Mountain, is that correct?"

"Yes, Sir,…The mountain of the Devil."

"I've heard of that, also,…though I have no idea where it is. I've heard the mysterious legends that surround it as well. And I even know of the attack on it by treasure hunters, an attack that left over a hundred white men and Comanches dead, of which, I believe,… is still unresolved. I've heard stories of men saying they were attacked by Ghost Indians there,… so therefore, no one really knows what happened. The army's conclusion was that the White men and Comanche killed each other, which to me is a logical conclusion,… and regrettable. But, before we get into the sale of this,…Devil Mountain,…I want to say up front, that I do not believe the stories of ancient ghosts living there. I think it to be preposterous that Choctaw of the old ways, have been hidden in a mountain fortress, undetected for generations. And as far as I know, no Choctaw has ever seen them."

"I have seen,… and talked with them, Sir." Said Peter sternly. "Mister Upshur, and Marshal Taylor have also seen, and talked with them. They have spoken with White Buffalo himself."

The Chief quickly looked back at Billy and Rodney. "Is this true,…you have talked with this magical Chief?" And when they both nodded, he stared at the table for a moment, then sighed heavily. "I will have to be convinced of this before further discussion of the mountain can continue."

Billy stood up then and reached inside his shirt, bringing out the gold medallion White Buffalo had given him. He held it up, then placed it on the table and pushed it toward the Chief.

Chief Bryant picked it up and meticulously examined it. "This is remarkable, to say the least,...very unusual,...where did it come from?"

"White Buffalo.... He gave one to me, and one to my son. I can't read the symbols on it, but I was told, by White Buffalo, that no Choctaw would refuse me food, rest, or passage on his land as long as I have it."

The Chief nodded, then slid the piece across to Peter. "Can you read ancient Choctaw pictographs, Peter?...Because I can not."

Peter picked it up and got to his feet. "It says that he who harms the wearer of this token, will pay with his life." He slid it back across to the Chief and sat down again.

"It's hard for me to believe something so unbelievably impossible,...when it has been such a laughable subject for so very long." He looked back at Billy and sighed again. "I believe you, Sir. As of now, I believe the Ancient Ones do exist,...I've no other choice, it seems. So,...if these ancient Choctaw live in this,...Devil Mountain. Why do you wish to purchase it,...would they not resist such a sale?"

Billy got to his feet again. "Chief Bryant, Sir,...th' only way I can answer that, is by tellin' you th' whole story,...and just between us, I'd rather th' army didn't know about it.... It's gonna take a while, too, but when I'm through, you'll understand a lot a things you didn't before."

"Then we'd best get some hot coffee in here.... But I have to tell you, Mister Upshur,... that not only do you have to sell me on this idea of yours, Chiefs from all three districts have to agree to the sale,...as well as Tandy Walker, President of our Senate, none of which were able to attend todays meeting on such short notice. What it means, is that I will have to take your proposal to them for approval before anything can be done. However, I will say this. You convince me,...and I will convince the others. Now, let's get that coffee in here, if this is going to take a while."

Rodney pulled the heavy door shut behind him and followed the other three down the steps, catching up as they walked through the almost waist-high prairie grass toward the camp. They were each lost in their own thoughts as they entered the trees.

Both Connie, and Melissa came forward to place their arms around their man's waist, then walked with them back to the wagon. Billy sat down on the tailgate and Connie stopped beside him. Rodney and Melissa sat down on the old log with the boys, while Peter and Joseph sat cross-legged on the ground. None of them had as yet spoken a word.

"Billy,... don't keep us waiting like this!" Burst out Connie with anticipation. "What happened in there?"

Billy sighed, then reached to his shirt for tobacco and papers. "Nothin' happened,...yet." He rolled and lit the smoke, inhaling the strong smoke gratefully. "We layed out everything for 'im,...but I don't know what he really thought about any of it. According to him, he's gonna run it by th' other Chiefs and let us know." He looked down at Peter then. "What's your take on it, Peter?"

The little Choctaw reached and broke off a blade of grass and placed it in his mouth. "I think you will buy the mountain. I think he understands that good will come from it."

"I got that feeling too." Voiced Rodney. "He was real attentive to the whole story, Billy, and he did have some good questions for you."

Billy nodded. "what about you, Joseph?"

The hotel owner grinned and shook his head. "I'm still going over the story you told. I had no idea most of that even happened. But when Peter told me the Ancient Ones were gone, and that you wanted to buy the mountain,... well,...that was all I needed to know. Peter told me on the way here, about what you did to help them with the outlaw gang up there,...I spent a lot of nights with a rifle in my hands because of that. But, yes,...I think the way Peter does,... I believe the Chief was sold on the idea."

"I was under the impression you knew Chief Bryant, Joseph?"

"I have met him, but only once, briefly....however, I do know Tandy Walker quite well, I've spoken with him several times. Chief Bryant spends most of his time at Boggy Depot, and at times, so does Walker. I do know that Chief Bryant means what he says,...he will meet with the other Chiefs, and I believe he will convince them to sell the mountain. None of them want another massacre in the wilderness."

"He looked surprised when we told him our plans for a police force,... didn't he, Peter?"

The little Choctaw shrugged again. "No man likes to hear that his creation is not as effective as he would want,...the Lighthorse Brigade was his idea. But he knows it is so,...they are useless for anything but to escort his carriage. We will have our police force, Marshal Taylor,...I believe that."

"I hope you're right."

"What do we do now?" Broke in Connie.

"We go home and wait." Sighed Billy. "We'll leave in the morning."

"Good." She smiled, then looked at the others. "Joseph, you and Peter will take supper with us tonight."

"You'll stay th' night, too." Added Billy. "We still got some talkin' to do."

— —

Once they were back at the main road, Rodney reined the team into some trees alongside it, and after Peter and his cousin said their goodbyes and left, he mounted his horse and rode off toward Fort Towson again, wanting to send another wire to his chief Deputy. He returned an hour later to find Billy and the rest fanning themselves in the shade of the tree's sultry heat.

"How'd it go?" Asked Billy as Rodney tied his horse to the wagon. "Thornton still in town?"

"No,…as a matter of fact, he left last night, didn't say a word to anyone. Jim said Seth followed him all the way to the Jonesboro cut-off,…said he rode on toward Clarksville."

"That'll make th' ride home a little easier,…you ready?

"Ready and willing." He grinned, then leaned to kiss Melissa before climbing back to the wagonseat. He slapped the lines across the team's backs and reined them onto the road again before sending them westward.

After rolling and lighting another smoke, Billy mounted the skittish mare and galloped after them, still thinking of yesterday's meeting, and not at all fully convinced they had sold the Chief on his proposal. This Choctaw head-Chief was obviously blessed with a sack full of horse savvy, he thought,… because he was pretty good at reading a man's eyes and body language. But not this man, and that left him a little uneasy.

What if Bryant goes to the army with the story? And that thought made him glad he had omitted his and Rodney's involvement of three years ago, or, where the pterodactyl actually came from. But then again, Bryant might have no choice, but to consult with the Indian Bureau on the matter. He hoped not, because they could be a much harder sell, than Walker and the other Chiefs. In fact, He thought worriedly,…because of the trouble three years ago, the Bureau of Indian Affairs could stop the sale completely, for whatever reason they wanted. But if the Chocktaw were actually the sole owners of their land, the government could be excluded. But, if that was the case,…why is there an Indian Agent? It was confusing, to say the least. He should have brought that up last night with Joseph, He thought, but concluded that he couldn't think of everything. And to think about it at all, was beginning to give him a headache and that, he thought wryly, was something else he could do without.

Sighing heavily, he worked the bandana from around his neck, found a dry corner, then removed the wire-frame glasses and cleaned them before wiping his face and forehead then sighing, worked them over his eyes and ears again. Twisting in the saddle, he quickly scanned the empty road behind them and thought it strange there was no traffic, then sighed again as he turned back to watch the women tug the ragged tarp up enough to shade them from the sun. He nodded his approval at them, then tried to relax in the swaying saddle for the trip ahead.

Traffic picked up on the old road toward mid-afternoon, and they were forced to pull aside a dozen times to make room for overloaded freight wagons, and other wagons conveying Choctaw families with their boisterous children and barking dogs. But they endured, and late afternoon found the road turning more to the South, and soon had them traveling almost paraelle to the Red River. Traffic had also picked up considerably as they began passing groups of hardeyed men on horseback, men that eyed them and the women in passing. There were also a few that were traveling alone, and others in pairs, or in threes, and it was these they were most wary of. Most of them were bearded and shaggy-headed, and the clothes they wore, soiled with sweat and red dust from the road. They were all hard-eyed and armed, and stared at them as they passed, especially at the women and horses. Billy knew them for what they were and watched them closely when they passed, and then behind him after they passed.

Men like them were everywhere in the Nations, he thought, and that was likely why Snake had no trouble signing up his army three years ago. And now, what with the Territories wide open again, it was not a safe place to travel,…and if the army couldn't control men like these, the Choctaw were in for even more trouble. As it is now, he thought sadly, even Rodney's police force would have it cut out for them,…but it was sorely needed, and Chief Bryant, of all people, should know that.

He twisted around to watch three more hardcases after they passed and at the same time, thinking that a good police force just might make a difference. 'At any rate,' He thought as he faced forward again. 'It couldn't hurt none.' He shook his head then, there wouldn't be one at all if his proposal was turned down. What would he do, if that happened? Not only that, what would happen to the mountain? Sooner, or later, somebody was bound to find that bat-cave, and ultimately, the valley and its secrets,…and there would be nothing he could do about it. Except maybe, get there first and take what they could of the Gold and Aztec treasure out of there, which in itself, could present them with even more problems. 'But we'll do it, if we have to, he vowed.

At that moment, he was jerked from his thoughts by a long, drawn-out whistle, and quickly looked up as the two horsemen were passing. The burly, bearded man closest to the wagon was the whistler, while the Dapper-dan, gambler-type on his right leaned forward over his saddle and spoke.

"Hello-o-o-o, ladies." Grinned the gambler, and both men stopped their horses to smile at them. By this time, Rodney had stopped the wagon and gotten to his feet.

"Keep riding, assholes!" Said the lawman loudly, causing both men to stare angrily at him.

"What did you say, Lame-brain?" Snarled the bearded man.

"He said, keep ridin', assholes!" Grated Billy. "Get th' shit out a your ears and you can hear!"

Both men jerked their attention to Billy then, and the bearded one leaned over and crossed his arms on the animal's neck as he looked Billy over. "And you think we ought a leave just cause you said so,…is 'at right?"

"That's about it!" Grinned Billy, and then dropped his arm at his side when he saw the Dandy doing the same.

"Well, now," Continued Whiskers. "What if I was to tell you that this man here beside me, could kill th' both a you in th' blink of an eye,…what then?"

Billy returned the stare for a moment, then shrugged. "Then all I can say, is that you're either lyin', big-time, or Mister Dapper there wants to be dead." This caused Whiskers to straighten in the saddle and glare hatefully at him.

"And if either one a you goes for your gun, I'll kill you." Added Billy.

"And I'll kill the one that's left!" Stated Rodney.

The gambler's face was a blank as he stared at Billy, but his eyes were hard, and deadly as he judged his chances.

"What'll it be, Gents?" Grinned Billy. "And be quick about it, will ya, there's more folks comin' down th' road,…wouldn't want them to get hurt now, would we?"

The gambler chose that time to relax in the saddle for a moment, his eyes still on Billy. Then he leaned closer to Whiskers. "Let's go, Wade."

"What,…Go? Why?" He Growled, but in the same blink of an eye, his mouth fell open in disbelief. Billy's draw was so quick, that neither man had time to even think of reacting to the movement.

"I think that's why, Wade." Drawled the Dapper.

Whiskers nodded, somewhat reluctantly.

"But now that it's gone this far." Said Billy. "I'm gonna insist that you throw your hardware into th' wagon there."

"What?" Gaped Whiskers. "Fuck you, too, Jack!"

Billy cocked back the pistol's hammer. "Gunbelts, guns and all, Gents,… and that includes your saddleguns. And don't get me wrong, I got nothin' agin' either of you, I'm just makin' sure you don't try to double back and bushwhack us.….It's do or die time now,… what's it gonna be?"

The two men silently did as they were told, then sat to stare at him until he holstered the Colt. Whiskers immediately spurred the startled animal into a hard run down the clay road.

Dapper watched him steadily for another moment, then smiled. "Till we meet again, Sir."

"You better hope we don't, Sir. And just so you know,...I know you got a hide-out tucked under your arm there, and I'll kill you before you can touch it....And another thing, you ought a think about changin' partners,... Whiskers there could get you killed."

Dapper smiled slightly, then slowly nodded. "Are you that good, my friend?"

"He's better than that good!" Said Rodney angrily. "Now, get moving, Mister."

Dapper looked back at the lawman, then bowed slightly and tipped his hat to the women before spurring his horse in the wake of Whiskers.

Rodney nodded at the family of Choctaw as the wagon passed, then watched Billy ride up beside the wheel. "Why is it that when we go somewhere, we always come back with a wagonload of guns?"

"Beats me." He grinned, then looked down at Connie. "Why don't you break out that Jerky, hon,...it's a long time to breakfast?"

"I'm hungry, too, Mama." Said Willy getting to his knees.

"Me, too!" Voiced Benny.

"I'll get it." Laughed Melissa. "Looks like we're all hungry."

"Billy," Voiced Connie as she looked back down the road.. "Will those men try to come back, you think?"

"They're not fool enough to do that, they're both unarmed. Let me worry about it." He accepted the stick of Jerky and waved it at Rodney. "We can go when you're ready, Rod."

"Yeah, okay,...but I'm already wishing we'd tried for a crossing at Jonesboro. We didn't have these kind a problems, a few weeks ago. What's going on here, anyway?"

"Less populated th' way we went in, I guess.... Besides, th' Goodland road bridge ain't that far now"

"Well, it's beginning make me nervous. Sooner or later, we ain't gonna have the upper hand in one a these encounters,...what then?" He sighed and accepted the stick of Jerky, then slapped the team into motion again.

━ ▬

It was a couple of hours shy of midnight when they turned onto the bridge and crossed into Texas again, and from there, the road was quite deserted all the way to Paris,…and they were entering the square in town at close to three o'clock in the morning.

Rodney spotted Seth as he was rattling doors along the boardwalk and stopped the wagon at the hitchrail.

"Hey, Marshal." Laughed the Deputy as he stepped down to the street and shook Rodney's extended hand. "Glad you're home, Sir. How was th' vacation?"

"Vacation was good, Seth. Looks like everything's quiet tonight." He yawned mightily, and then quickly scanned the silent buildings. "Just the way we like it."

"Yes, Sir,…like a church-mouse. Saloons closed about an hour ago. Adam's gone now to jail about a dozen drunks,…Judge Bonner'll be busy, come Monday"

"Sounds like a usual Friday night." Nodded Rodney and climbed down from the wagon. "Jim at the office?"

"Oh, Yes, Sir. He's practic'ly lived there while you was gone." He looked up at Billy then. "Howdy, Mister Upshur, Missus Upshur."

Billy nodded at him, then dismounted and tied the Roan to the tailgate before untying the lawman's horses and letting it down, he then led Rodney's three mounts to the front of the wagon and gave him the reins.

"You going on home tonight, Billy?" Questioned the lawman.

"I want a get our cargo home." He nodded. "You go get some sleep, though, you're all three wore out."

"Sounds good to me,…what about the wagon?"

"I'll lock it in th' grain-shed, it'll be okay." He turned and took the sleeping Benny from Melissa, then held him while Rodney pulled astride his horse before hefting the boy to th' Lawman's arms. He went back to help Melissa from the wagon, then helped her to mount before giving her the reins to Benny's pony. He walked back in beside Rodney then. "We'll weigh everything and put it away when you get there, we'll expect you for supper on Sunday. You hear anything from that Chief, you'll let me know quick, won't you?"

"Yeah, don't worry about that. It's gonna keep me awake till I do."

"Thank you, Billy." Broke in Melissa, and leaned to touch his shoulder. She turned to say goodnight to Connie. "Have a safe trip home, see ya."

"You bet," Nodded Billy. "see you on Sunday." He climbed aboard the wagon and took the reins. "See you later, Rod,…you take care, Seth." He clucked the mules into motion down the Bonham Road toward Doc Bailey's house.

Willy was still sound asleep when Connie crawled over the gold-sacks and onto the wagon seat. "It's so good to be home again, Billy. And I've missed the Restaurant, too." They both looked the dark café over in passing, and she sighed and snuggled up against him.

"Well,…did you have enough adventure this trip?" He grinned, looking down at her as she cut her eyes up at him.

"I'll say,…but it was worth every minute. I've seen things that no one else will ever see. I've been sixty million years in the past, seen tyrannosarus Rex, and cave men, and I've discovered we're not alone in the universe. Who could ask for any more than that?" She shuddered then. "I think that's what worries me the most, too,… not knowing if they're friendly."

"We could go back and find out!"

"That's okay,…I'll be seeing it in my sleep, anyway. That'll do just fine, for now."

"Speakin' a sleep, why don't you and Willy stay in town tonight,…it's too early to wake th' kids up…. I'll take th' wagon on to th' farm and be back in th' mornin'"

"I'm not gonna argue with you on that one." She yawned. "A bed will be a luxury. But, you get some sleep before you come back, okay?…If we're not at Doc's, we'll be at the café."

— ⁓

"Thanks, Reba." Grinned Billy after he wiped his mouth. "I ain't had a breakfast like that in three weeks. Ross, you married yourself a great cook here."

The foreman grinned and patted his protruding midsection. "You think I don't know that?" They all laughed, and she got up and poured them fresh coffee before cleaning off the table. "What say, we go out on th' porch, Boss, might catch a breese out there."

"Breeze sounds good to me, it's been one hot summer so far."

"Everything points to a cold, wet Winter, though." Grunted Ross as he sat down.

"How do you know that?"

"Don't rightly know. Lumbago, I guess,…but it proves to be right, more times than naught."

"From what I could see of th' cotton on th' way in, it's lookin' good. Is this bad weather gonna give us time to pick it?"

"Yes, Sir,…I think we'll have time, and it's gonna be a good year, I think…. So, how was th' vacation,…have any trouble up there?"

"A little more than I wanted, but all in all,…it was okay, I guess. No fish though. Panned a little gold, and discouraged a few bad guys here and there. Never got to use Sam's rifle neither,… how is he, by th' way,…you seen 'im?"

"Ain't seen 'im since you left, Boss."

"Well." Sighed Billy, draining his cup. I got a get me a little nap before goin' back to town,…it's been a while, too. You got everything lined out for th' day?"

"Pretty much. Gonna be thinnin' cotton along th' road today, weedin' th' corn, too…. We got plenty to do."

"Good," Yawned Billy, getting to his feet. "Let 'em all knock off at noon today,…they may want a go to town."

"Sure thing, Boss."

Billy gave him the cup and stepped off the porch. See ya, Ross,…thank Reba again for me, will ya?"

"Sure thing. Oh, th' mails on th' kitchen table, Boss."

Billy waved at him and continued on to the darkened house.

It was lunchtime at the restaurant when he walked through the door, and the place was crowded. He hung his hat on the rack and threaded his way through the tables, speaking to people he knew along the way to the kitchen, which was also busy. Connie and the Mexican woman were in a rush, loading plates with food, bringing bread from the oven, and almost running him down as they carried out the trays. He shook his head and made his way back to the only empty table by the window, of which he knew was always empty and reserved for him and family. He pulled out the chair and sat down, then reached for the makings to deftly roll and light a smoke as he watched the paying customers,…and they were loud, as all seemed to be talking at once, and trying to be heard over the noise around them.

He watched the street traffic for a while as he smoked, seeing people stop to pass the time of day as wagons and other riders veered to go around them. People with nothing else to do, he thought, then shook his head and grinned. There was nothing else to do on a Saturday. It was all work during the week, from sunup to sundown, buying supplies, or shopping on Saturday,…and Church on Sunday, only to start over again on Monday. The same routine every day, with nothing to look forward to, but more of the same. 'If only they knew what else was out there' He thought?

And he thought again of the meeting with Chief Bryant, once again going over all that was said there. What more could they have said, or done, he wondered? He had told him everything,…well, almost. There was no way he could tell anyone about the alien tunnels, the treasure, either. The

Government would be all over that mountain if he'd done that. They'd tear it to shreds. He knew that if his offer failed, there'd be a hell of a gold rush in Indian Territory once it was discovered,…and that thought caused him to grit his teeth and vow, that if it did fall through, him and Rodney would do their best to strip that mine and treasure cave. He would bury it on the farm someplace, if necessary. He saw Rodney coming up the steps then and shook the thoughts from his head.

"Morning, Billy." Grinned the lawman as he sat down. "That your rig outside?"

"Didn't feel much like sittin' a saddle today." He nodded.

"That makes two of us. You get any sleep?"

"Four, five hours, maybe,…you?"

"The same,…wanted to check on things at the office. Had to make Jim go home."

"Th' man's dedicated."

"He is, that. Everything all right at the farm?" And when Billy nodded, he scanned the noisy room. "Sort a crowded for a Saturday, ain't it?"

They looked up then as Connie placed coffee in front of them. "You two want lunch, or breakfast?"

"Lunch." Grinned Rodney. "Whatever you got."

"I'll wait a while." Smiled Billy. "Had breakfast with Ross this mornin'"

"Be back shortly then." She nodded. "Hectic around here today." She hurried away to take money from several customers, then reached through the serving window for the pot of coffee and began filling cups.

Rodney watched her leave, then sighed and looked at Billy. "The waiting got you impatient yet,…I'm nervous as a whore in Church?"

"Yeah,…me, too. Seems like a week since we left there already. Hell, it'll take Bryant a week to call a meetin, and another week to hem and haw before we hear anything."

"And probably a couple more to set a price." Sighed the lawman.

Just then the door opened and the Telegrapher came in, looked the room over and spotting them, came on to the table. "Wire for you, Marshal."

"Thanks, Cletus,…but you didn't have to come all the way here to bring it to me."

"Oh, that's okay, I was comin' to dinner anyway. Hello, Mister Upshur, nice to see ya. Later, Marshal."

"Cletus." Nodded Rodney and watched him go to the counter. "Hey." He grinned when he opened the wire. "It's from Joseph."

"Already, what's he say?"

"Winchester Station has a new Telegraph Office,…Also a new spur and railroad depot. How about that? Course, I never been to Winchester Station, so I wouldn't know how important that is."

"It's important." Grinned Billy. "That all he said?"

"No,…he says Peter's jumping the gun, already recruiting men to build a road to the mountain…. He says to keep in touch."

"Always good for a man to be sure of his self." Grinned Billy as he rolled and lit another smoke. "Wish I was."

"Here you are, Rodney." Smiled Connie, sitting the heaping plate in front of him. "How's Lisa feeling this morning?"

"Don't know, she was still asleep when I left."

Connie nodded and left for the cash drawer again, leaving him to eat his lunch.

Billy watched the street's activity again while the lawman ate, and thought of the little Choctaw. He never ceased to amaze him. But, if he's that sure of himself, things just might work out after all,…and that road would be one of the first things they'd have to build. But that's still weeks away, he thought sadly, and it might as well be a year. He saw a man running up the middle of the the street then, and narrowed his eyes as he watched him weave in and out of the street's traffic.

It wasn't until he veered toward the café that he saw the sun's glint on the badge. "Here comes one a your Deputies, Rod,…in a bit of a hurry, too."

Rodney wiped his mouth with the table linen and leaned to peer out of the window. "That's Glenn, wonder what's going on?" He scraped back his chair and got up, as did Billy, at about the time Glenn burst through the door.

"Marshal Taylor?" He gasped loudly as he searched the room. "Where's th' Marshal?"

"Over here, Glenn,…what's wrong?"

The deputy came to confront him. "M,…Marshal, he's back,…you got a do somethin'!"

"Hold on, Glenn!" Rodney grabbed his shoulders and shook him. "Slow down and tell me what happened?"

"He's back, Marshal! And he's got some men with him!"

"Who's back, Glenn?"

"Th,…Thornton! Seth's in jail at th' office. I was, too, but Thornton let me out to find you. He's got Sheriff Gose in jail, too."

"Gus Thornton, the Bounty Hunter?"

"Yes, Sir,…Gus Thornton."

Rodney looked at Billy then. "Funny way to ask for my help, ain't it?" He turned back to Glenn then. "Come over here and sit down, Glenn, I want the whole story. Come on, it's okay." Once the ashen-faced Deputy was seated,

Rodney looked around the room and saw that everyone was either standing to stare at them, or turned around in their chairs to watch. "There's nothing to get excited about folks, go ahead with your meal,…please." He turned back to the Deputy then.

"Okay, Glenn,…start from the beginning and tell me about Thornton."

"Well,…me and Seth got back to th' office with food for th' inmates, and,…and while we was doin' that, Thornton kicked open th' office door and pushed Sheriff Gose into th' room. He had three men with 'im, and they all had guns pointed at us. Anyway, he didn't say a word, he jest pushed th' Sheriff into the cell-block and threw 'im into a cell, then threw Seth in there with 'im. Well,…one a th' other men took me back to th' office, and when Thornton came back, he wanted to know where you was. I,…I told 'im I didn't know, and,…and he told me to find you and give you a message."

Rodney and Billy both eased themselves back into their seats at that point. "What did he say, Glenn?"

"He said to tell you, that he knows you're hidin' John Risinger somewhere,…and he wants you to turn 'im over to 'im by nightfall, or,…or he might be forced to hurt somebody. He says if you warn th' Melitia about this, he'll kill Seth."

""Son of a Bitch!" Sighed the lawman. "Wonder why he thinks I have Risinger?"

"It's called confidence." Said Billy. "To him, he's already looked everywhere there is to look, and if Risinger was anywhere in th' county, he would have found 'im. And since Jim's th' one that went to see 'im, it has to be you that's hidin' 'im…. He'll never make himself admit he just couldn't find his man, he won't admit it to anybody else, neither, because he's th' best,…in his mind anyway."

"Billy?" Broke in Connie as she came to the table. "What's wrong?"

"Gus Thornton's at th' jail, and he's got Seth and th' Sheriff locked up there."

"Oh, my God, Rodney, what are you going to do?"

"What do you want me to do, Marshal?" Breathed Glenn, still somewhat out of breath.

He looked from Connie, back to the Deputy. "I want you to get Clem, Tatum and Rufe, and clear the street around the courthouse. Clear the whole block, and keep it that way…. Does Jim know about this?"

"I sent Rufe to tell 'im when I came here. I seen Judge Bonner when I come down th' stairs, he knows, too. But there's guards at th' front door, and th' Judge can't get out. Thornton said you, th' Sheriff and everbody else here was interferrin' with th' Federal Law, and he was authorized to bring Thornton in dead or alive, and to do whatever he had to, to do it."

"Well I can send for help, Marshal." Said the Telegrapher from his stool. He stood and dropped a coin on the counter. "I'll wire th' Sheriff in Clarksville, he'll send you some help."

"Thanks, Cletus. You might give John Rucker a headsup, too, we might need the melitia before this is over. But tell John not to go near the Courthouse till he hears from me, or Billy."

"Sure thing, Marshal." He quickl;y left the café, and that's when almost everyone in the room dropped money on their tables and started to leave.

"Wait a minute, Folks." Said Rodney, getting to his feet. "Take another way home when you leave, okay, stay clear of the court building,…let me handle this." They all nodded and filed out onto the porch.

"Go ahead, Glenn." He sighed. "Get everybody away from there,…and you stay there to keep it that way. Tell Rufe and the other men to stay in the square, and away from the Courthouse."

"Okay, but what about th' guards out front there?"

"They won't start anything, gunfire might ruin Thornto's plans. Just keep your hands away from your gun.." He looked at both Connie and Billy as the Deputy left.

"What are you going to do, Rodney?" Asked Connie again.

"I ain't got a clue…. But I'd better think of something by sundown."

"Might be a good idea to go get Risinger." Said Billy.

"I can't turn that man over to Thornton, Billy,…he'd kill 'im as soon as he got out of town, he won't have a chance!"

"Then don't turn 'im over to Thornton,…bring 'im here. If it comes to it, you can use him to bargain Thornton down to the street, be easier to deal with 'im there."

"You're right. It's about the only thing I can do." He got up and pulled on his hat. "You keep an eye on things till I get back?"

Billy nodded. "Ride hard, Rod, from what you told me, it's quite a ways out there."

"You going to help him, Billy?" Asked Connie when Rodney left.

"If it comes to it." He nodded, and then suddenly, his eyes widened. "Rodney!" He gasped loudly, as the shot rebounded up the empty street..

"Stay here!" He blurted, then got to his feet, donned his hat and quickly left the café. People were running away from the direction of the square, as he jumped from the porch to the rutted street in a hard run toward the courthouse.

He slowed to a walk as he came abreast of the gunmen on the boardwalk, eying them closely as he walked toward the fallen Deputy.

"We didn't want a shoot 'im." Drawled one of the men as he came to the edge of the walkway. "But he drew on me…. I could a killed 'im."

"Yeah,...I just bet you could!" Snapped Billy as he squatted next to Jim. "You hit bad,?"

"Shoulder,...I'll be okay. Thanks, Mister Upshur."

"Come on, I'll help you to Docs."

"I'm a Doctor, young man." Called a middleaged man from a doorway on the opposite side of the street. "Bring him in here."

Nodding, Billy helped Jim to the Doctor's office, and then inside to a table, where they both helped him to lay down. "I heard there was another Doctor in town. I'm Bill Upshur, nice to meet you, Sir."

The Doctor shook his hand. "Tom Lovejoy,... I'm a surgeon. You're Doctor Bailey's adopted son, aren't you?"

"Well, yes, sir,...I guess I am, thanks." He looked down at the Deputy then.

"I need your gun belt, Jim." And when Jim nodded, he unbuckled the belt and slid it from beneath him, then took the gun from his belt and jammed it in the holster before buckling the rig around his own waist.

"I ain't no gunfighter, Mister Upshur,... I just lost my head out there."

"Nothin' wrong with that, Jim,...you did your best."

"Where's th' Marshal,...he okay?"

"Rod's fine,...He's busy right now. You relax and let th' Doctor tend that wound." He nodded at the Medic and walked back out on the boardwalk to stare at the two men across the street, and both of them had moved to the edge of the porch as he came out. He turned to scan the square and the three deputies there, and they were staying out of pistol range. 'At least they're being smarter than Jim was' he thought, and then started down the walkway.

"Deputy gonna live?" Voiced the gunman loudly.

He stopped to stare at the man. "No thanks to you." He nodded.

"You gonna take up th' fight?" This, from the other man.

"You'll be th' first to know." He heard them chuckling as he walked back toward the café. He was both scared, and angry as he walked,...but he knew there was nothing he could do at the moment, Thornton was fortified on the top floor, and he had hostages. They had to get him out of there if they were gonna stop him. And they would need John Risinger to pull it off. He was sure of that.

"Is Jim okay, Mister Upshur?"

He looked to see Glenn standing in the alcove of one of the shops, and nodded. "Shoulder wound, Glenn, he'll make it."

"That's good news. Say, I seen th' Marshal runnin' down th' alley up yonder a ways. Where's he goin'?"

"He's workin' on somethin', you just keep folks away from th' courthouse like he said, it'll be okay."

"Yes, Sir."

He nodded at the Deputy and continued on to the café, where Doc Bailey was just climbing out of his surrey. The old Doctor worked his way up the steps and was standing beside Connie when he got there.

"What's goin' on down there, son,...a cowboy stopped and told me somebody was shot. Is Rodney all right?"

"He's okay, Doc. It was Jim Stockwell,...he's over at Doctor Lovejoy's office."

"That's good. Tom's a good Surgeon."

"You've got a gun on, Billy." Gasped Connie. "What are you going to do?"

"Wait on Rodney to get back, Honey, after that,...we'll think of something. Want some coffee, Doc?"

"I think I need some." Sighed the old man, and slowly followed them inside. "Who's doing this, William?" He voiced as he sat down at the counter.

"Bounty Hunter, name of Thornton. He thinks Rod is hidin' a man he's after, and he's got Seth and Sheriff Gose in jail. He says he'll kill 'em if Rod don't turn John Risinger over to 'im by sundown."

"I know John Risinger,...I delivered his youngest son. They're nice people, too. What's John done, anyway?"

"I don't know, Doc. Thornton says th' army wants 'im. Must a happened durin' th' war. Anyway, Rod's gone out to bring 'im in."

"You're not gonna turn him over to this man, are you?"

"Not if we can help it. But with Risinger here, we might use 'im to get Thornton in th' street."

Doc accepted the hot coffee, and she poured Billy a fresh cup. "God, why does this sort of thing have to happen?" She sighed. "Why can't people realize how precious life is, and stop this useless killing?"

"That, my darlin'" Breathed Doc. "Is somethin' folks will be asking themselves a hundred years from now. It'll never end,...not as long as hate rules the world. It's what keeps the Devil alive."

Startled then, as the door was suddenly opened, Billy whirled instinctively, and in a whisper, the borrowed pistol was cocked and covering the ashen-faced Telegrapher.

"Oh, ho, wait, don't shoot!" He yelled, crossing his arms in front of his face as he cowered in the doorway.

Catching himself in time, Billy released his breath in a gush of air and shakily holstered the weapon.

"Jesus Christ!" Gasped Cletus...."I never seen anything that fast before!"

"I'm sorry, Cletus,...this mess has got me upset,...come on in, man, have some coffee." He got up and went to help the trembling man to the counter. "I wasn't expectin' anybody to come in right now, Cletus,...are you okay?"

I think so, Mister Upshur." He nodded. "But I'm not so sure I didn't,... soil my britches." He grinned then. "I didn't know you could handle a gun like that,...I never saw anything like it." They all breathed a sigh of relief then as Cletus eased himself onto one of the stools.

"Would you like some coffee, Mister Benjiman?"

"Oh, god, yes!" He stammered. "Thank you."

"What brought you back here, Cletus,...you get word to Clarksville?"

"Oh, that's what I came to tell you. Somebody got in and smashed my equipment while I was here,...I can't send, or receive."

"Thornton's men." Sighed Billy. "Son of a Bitch thought a just about everything, didn't he?... Have you got a horse?"

"No, sorry. I never had much use for one."

No problem. Can you drive a team?"

"Yeah, I can do that all right,...but why?"

"I was thinkin' they had a telegraph office in Honey Grove,...and if somebody could get there, they could wire Clarksville, as well as alert th' Sheriff there to what's goin' on here."

"Sure, I can do that,...but how do I get there?"

"My buckboard is tied out front there, a longside a Doc's. You can be there in little over an hour, if you use th' whip. Tell 'em we'd appreciate help to bottle up th' town here,...and if they can't send anybody, just tell 'em to watch for 'em in case they get away from us. You got all that?"

"Don't worry, I got it." He took a drink of his coffee and hurriedly left.

Billy went to the window to watch as Cletus turned the team and whipped them into a run. "There goes a man with a strong sense of civic duty. A damn good man." He sighed and came back to his stool, then looked at the frowning face of Doc. "What's wrong, Doc?"

"Son, a long time ago, Lang told me something....He said you was a natural with a handgun,...said he'd never seen anything like it before. I never knew what he really meant by that, till now.... I'm impressed, Son, I truly am."

"Thanks, Doc,...but sometimes I think it's a curse."

"Well I don't." Smiled Connie. "His ability is the only reason we made it home, at all. But I'm like you, too, Doc. I didn't understand either,...until we took this trip and now, I thank God for that ability."

"Come on now,...stop it, will ya?...I get no pleasure from killin' a man,... even when I found my folk's killers, I didn't like it.... I'm not a killer, Doc, no matter what anybody might say."

"I know that, son. But, being what you are, let you come home to us. And for that, we're all thankful."

"Thanks, Doc."

"Now then." Grinned the Doctor. "Daughter in law of mine, would you like to tell me what happened up there, to make you say what you just said?"

"Some other time, Doc." She smiled. "I promise. Now, let's change the subject, please? Are the kids running you crazy,…I know you must be tired of them, especially Mattie?"

"Awww, honey, don't you worry none about our grand kids, far as we're concerned, they're at home."

Connie smiled and squeezed his arm. "Thank you."

"It's the truth." He looked back at Billy then. "When do you expect Rodney back with John?"

"Before sundown, I hope, he's gonna be cuttin' it awful thin. He could have a hard time convincin' Risinger to come in with 'im, too, especially if he is th' one Thornton's after. But he'll bring 'im back, one way or th' other, I'm sure a that…..And I got till then to figure out how we're gonna use 'im to get Thornton to come out,…and without shootin' anybody else, doin' it."

"How many Deputies has Rodney got, for pete's sake?"

"I don't really know." Sighed Billy. "Five or six, and Gose's got two or three. But where they are is anybody's guess. Anyway, we couldn't get to Thornton if they was here. That office ain't even got a window in it. And it'd be auicide to climb them stairs."

"Well, you'll think of something, son. Anyway, I'm gonna hang around here till this is all over,…I might be needed." He turned to Connie then. "You got any vittles left in the pot back there, my dear, I forgot to eat before I left?"

"Of course, I do. Is steak and potatoes all right."

"That's exactly what the Doctor ordered."

"Steak and potatoes it is,…coming up." She was about to leave when she saw a man step up to the boardwalk. "Someone's coming in, Billy."

Both him and Doc turned toward the door as the man entered.

"Hello, Doctor." He nodded. "Mister Upshur."

"Come on in, John,…join us." Urged Doc.

"What brings you here, Mister Rucker?" Asked Billy, going to shake his hand. "Didn't expect to see ya."

"Cletus Benjiman told me what was going on at the Marshal's office,… but he left before I could get any information from him….What's the situation down there?"

"You come in that way?"

"No,no,…I took another route to get here. How can I help?"

"Sit down over here, sir,…have some coffee." He ushered the Militiaman to a stool beside Doc just as Connie placed his cup in front of him.

"Thank you, ma'am." He nodded, then looked at Billy. "This is a grave situation, Mister Upshur,…you got a plan of action?"

Billy eased himself on the stool beside him, then nodded. "Yes, sir, I'm thinkin' on it. Cletus is on his way to Honey Grove right now,…he'll alert Clarksville, and maybe Bonham. Th' man holdin' Sheriff Gose and Rodney's deputy blames Rodney for his not findin' th' man he's lookin' for…."

"Well,…John Risinger's not an outlaw, I've known the man since the war. I did some checking on Gus Thornton, too,…he was a lawman in Nacogdoches, Texas, at one time,…and also in New Oleans, till he discovered there was more money in collecting bounty. The man's a killer now, and he uses the law to do it. And it's sad, he was a good lawman."

"Evidently, not anymore." Broke in Doc.

"He's right about that." Continued Billy. "Th' Sheriff in New Orleans told Jim Stockwell he was a gunman, and a bad one at that, fast on th' draw, too, I hear."

"It's hard to believe it!" Rucker shook his head sadly.

"Anyway, he's accusin' Rodney of hidin' Mister Risinger,…and he says, if he don't deliver th' man to him by sundown today, he'll kill Rodney's Deputy."

Rucker nodded. "Go on, I'm listening."

"Rodney's gone now to bring Risinger in. We're gonna try to use 'im as bait to get Thornton to come down to th' street,…but here's th' problem. Thornton's got two men on th' boardwalk in front, and three more with him in th' Marshal's office. And Judge Bonner is in his office, and likely his woman secretary, too. They can't leave with them men out front."

"That's a problem, all right." Breathed Rucker as he took a swallow of coffee.

"How many men do you have, Sir?"

"A dozen men will be at my office within the hour."

"I'd like you to meet 'em. In no way let them do anything to start a fight, instead,…put all of 'em down there in th' square with Rodney's deputies,… arm 'em with rifles and sidearms. I want th' men on that boardwalk to see what they're up against."

"What are you gonna do, sounds like you got a plan?"

"I do, and it just hit me. I'm gonna get th' Judge and his secretary out a that buildin', it'll be less for Rod to worry about."

"How, if you don't mind my asking?"

"I figure they'll need to relieve themselves before long,…and when they do, I'll take 'em out, quietly, one by one."

"Whewww,…I hope it works."

"Me, too. Now, if you would, Sir,…go back to your office th' way you came,…be there to intercept your men."

Rucker nodded. "It's you're show, Mister Upshur. But I have to tell you,… if it don't work, we may have to rush the place."

"This is th' Marshal's show, Mister Rucker. He'll take care a Thornton when th' time comes. He'll let you know if he needs you."

"Good enough." Nodded Rucker and got up to leave.

"Mister Rucker?" Said Billy, and after he stopped at the door. "Thanks." Rucker nodded and left.

"How are you gonna take out those two, William?"

"I don't rightly know, Doc. But right now, I'm goin' down and talk with Glenn, he's watchin' things from a storefront down there. I'll be back in a bit."

"Be careful, Billy." Urged Connie.

He nodded and left,…and both her and Doc went to the window to watch him walk down the street.

Billy walked slowly toward the court building, and when he came to the boardwalk where Glenn was hiding, he stepped up to the planking and walked to the alcove.

"Anything happening, Glenn?"

"No, sir,…they're just leaning against th' wall there, smokin'"

"Have they been to take a leak yet?"

"What?"

"Has either one of 'em had to go piss, yet?"

"Oh,…yeah. One of 'em has."

"Where'd he go?"

"In th' alley of th' Gun shop there. He walked down between th' buildin's there, why?"

"Okay,…now listen. John Rucker's Men will be joinin' Clem and Rufe down there in th' square, and I want you to watch for 'em. When you see 'em, I want you to step out on th' boardwalk here and take your hat off. That will be th' signal for me to go th' back way to that alley over there."

"Yeah," Grinned the Deputy.…."I get it, Mister Upshur. Seeing all those men will make 'em nervous,…and when they're nervous, they'll…"

"Have to go piss." Nodded Billy. "And I'll be waitin' on whoever it is."

"Yeah, but they're not gonna go at th' same time."

"No, but th' other one might go look for 'im. If he don't, I'll take 'im out anyway. Now, when you see that second man go into that alley, I want you to go get Judge Bonner and th' woman out a th' buildin', get 'em to safety. And Glenn,...do it quietly,...no screwups, okay?"

"I'll do my best,...but Missus, Littlejohn ain't in th' buildin'."

Billy nodded. "That'll make it easier. Remember, walk out there and take your hat off." When Glenn nodded, he looked toward the square where a large number of civilians were still gathered behind Rodney's deputies and that worried him, because several of those in front were dressed as cowboys, and they all wore guns.

"Glenn,...some of those men in th' square there, are ranchhands, and that means there could be a couple a hotheads among 'em, so, watch 'em. If one of 'em starts somethin', we're gonna have to rush th' place. If you think there's a chance that might happen, take off your hat and wave it at me. Now don't forget, man,...if one of 'em goes to piss, just take your hat off, nothin' else." He turned and walked away then, and with one last look at the gunmen, stepped off the boardwalk and made his way back to the café.

— —

Rodney slid his horse to a stop just outside John Risinger's white-picket fence and dismounted, then waved at the boy on the porch as he opened the gate. "Is your Daddy home, son?"

The boy nodded and went into the house, and a minute or two later, John Risinger stepped out on the porch with a shotgun. "What can I do for you, Sir?"

"It's me, Mister Risinger, Rodney Taylor. I'm Town Marshal in Paris."

"I recognize you now, Marshal,...what brings you out this way?"

"We've got a situation in town, that I need to talk with you about."

Risinger stared at him for a moment, then nodded. "Come up on th' porch then, it's cooler here."

"Thanks." He walked to the porch and climbed the steps to shake Risinger's beefy hand. "Mind if we sit down, I've got a story to tell you?"

Risinger eyed him narrowly, then gestured to one of the rocking chairs. "This got to do with me?" He asked as he sat down.

"Yes, sir, I'm afraid so,...and I'm gonna have to talk fast, cause I ain't got a whole lot a time. Now I have to ask you,...are you wanted by the army?" He knew the answer when Risinger looked down to stare at the porch. "I'm not here to arrest you, Sir,...but I do have to ask you to come back to town with me, at least three people's lives depend on it."

Risinger frowned at him, then slowly nodded. "You mind tellin' me why?"

— ‐

They were sitting at the table by the window, when Billy saw the deputy remove his hat. "There's th' signal." He said, getting to his feet. "Th' melitia's in th' square. Now both a you stay out a sight here, you hear me? I'll be back long before Rod is." He kissed Connie on the mouth and left, dropping off the end of the porch into the alleyway, then made a sharp left turn behind the Boot store and half-ran down the cluttered alley, having to pass a half dozen business places before he got to the alley between the gun shop and Court Building.

Breathing heavily, he stared at the end of the gun shop's rear wall, but saw nothing and wondered if the gunman would come all the way down the alley when he relieved himself. 'Bad luck, if he don't', he thought nervously and moved slowly toward the side of the building and once there, peered cautiously around the corner, almost giving himself away. The gunman was already in the alleyway.

The guard was turned toward him as he buttoned up his pants, and Billy slowly pulled the pistol from the holster, and then, just as the gunman adjusted his gun back in place and turned to leave, stepped into the alley. "Hey." He whispered, and when the startled guard whirled around, he raised the pistol and laid the barrel across the side of his head, felling him like a side of beef.

Holstering the weapon, he stared along the Court building's rock wall, and when the other one didn't show himself, bent and grabbed the gunman's arms and pulled his body around the corner and into the old woodshed, that was attached to the rear of the Gun shop, once there, he quickly removed the man's gunbelt, then tore the shirt open and removed it, using it to tie his hands behind his back. He then used the man's bandana to stuff in his mouth before tugging the pants down around his boot-tops.

Still breathing heavily, he moved back out to the alley and peered along the building again. 'I got away with that one' he thought. 'Now for the other one,...but how do I get 'im back here?' He bent and picked up two rusted tin cans, thinking it might work, and then lobbed them up the alley, and they did make a very audible noise when hitting the hard dirt. He jerked back out of the way then to wait, and was soon rewarded.

"Hey, Randal." Called the gunman loudly. "What'r you doin' back there, man?...hurry up, will ya, I got a go, too." And when he got no answer. "God damn it, Randal, what's goin' on back there?...You okay?"

The gunman waited another few seconds and then, with another long look at the square and along the street, pulled his pistol and stepped down into the alley, where he slowly began to walk towrd the end of the building.

264

Billy moved back inside the woodshed and flattened himself against the wall, just inside the open door. He could see the man as he peered around the corner, and then watched him cautiously come toward the shed.

"Randal, where th' fuck are you, man?" He saw the body then and rushed to kneel beside the fallen guard. "What th' f…"

Billy clubbed him hard with the pistol, then followed the same procedure as with the first man. He then looped the holstered guns over his shoulder and worked his way back toward the restaurant. "Okay, Glenn," He muttered. "Get th' Judge out a there."

He hung the confiscated guns on the coatrack as he came inside.

"My, God, Billy!" gasped Connie. "I was so worried." She went into his arms and clung to his wiry frame."

"I'm okay, honey." He soothed, and moved her away from him. "I'm okay, I'm back now."

"You got their guns, I see." Nodded Doc in satisfaction, then turned to look out of the open door. "And here comes Glenn and the Judge,…on th' run, too."

Billy turned as the two men climbed the steps and crossed the porch. "Come on in, Judge. Glenn, you best get back to your post, okay. If anybody tries to come out, fire a shot at 'em, keep 'em inside,…Rod'll be back before long, and he'll handle it….and Glenn,…good job. Glenn,…If one a them Bastards so much as opens that front door, put a shot in it. Pass th' word, keep 'em inside that building."

"There's a back door." Said the Judge quickly.

Glenn nodded. "We'll cover it, Your Honor." And with that, quickly leaped from the high porch and trotted back down the street.

"Who are those men up there, anyway?" Growled the Judge.

"Bounty Hunters, Judge." Said Billy as he took Bonner's arm. "Sit at th' counter there and have some coffee. I'll tell you all about it." He told the Judge everything that had taken place so far, beginning with Rodney's telegram to Jim,…and when he finished, the Judge shook his head in wonder.

"My, God." He breathed, and then smiled at Billy. "Son, I want to thank you for getting me out of there,…I'm very grateful, and I won't forget it. That being said, I authorize you and the Marshal to do whatever it takes to rid us of this scum. And as far as John Risinger is concerned, he's a free man, Government be damned!"

"Thanks, Judge." Grinned Billy, and looked at his Sam Colt pocket watch. "Th' Marshal ought a be back with 'im in an hour or so,…and I think you ought a stay here till he does, Thornton's not goin' anywhere."

The Judge nodded and reached for his coffee, but saw Doc instead and grinned. "I'll be damned, Walter,…it's good to see you." He clamped the old Doctor's hand in a firm grip. "Fat and sassy as ever, I see."

"Don't know about Sassy, Your Honor,…but I'm fat, and I'm here."

"That's all that counts, my old friend."

— ·

Rodney ushered Risinger quickly up the steps and inside, and after a long look down the darkening street, followed him in. "Billy, what was that shooting all about as I left?"

"Jim threw down on one a them gunnies,…he's at Doc Lovejoys."

"Hurt bad?"

"Shoulder,…he'll be okay."

"That's good news." Breathed the lawman, then spotted Bonner. "Judge Bonner,…I thought you were in the Court Room, how'd you get out?"

"I've got your Deputy and Mister Upshur here, to thank for that."

Rodney nodded and looked at Billy. "It's almost sundown."

"What's your plan, Rod,…remember, there's still four of 'em up there?"

The lawman nodded again. "Okay. The only thing I can do, is go down there and call 'em out. Mister Risinger, I'd like you out there in the street with Billy when I call 'em down. And, Billy, keep him about twenty yards away from that boardwalk." He puled the conversion Colt and checked the loads, holstered it again and nodded at Billy. "This is my job,…just keep it even for me."

Billy nodded. "Let's get it done."

The three of them quickly crossed the porch and went down the steps to the street, and no one spoke at all as they covered the three blocks to the Courthouse. Billy and Risinger stopped in front of the boardwalk across from the building, as Rodney Pulled his gun and stepped up to the porch.

Breathing nervously, Rodney moved slowly to the large, oaken door and peered through the plate glass insert, and seeing no movement in the darkening hallway, opened the door and stepped inside, cocking the pistol as he went. The hall was dark, but he could see well enough as he quietly checked the doors along the hall, finding all but the Judge's chambers locked,…and taking a deep breath, he exhaled and moved to the stairwell to slowly climb up to the second floor level.

He could see the light from his office on the floor above him, and knew that Thornton had left the door open. Then, staying in the shadows of the stairwell, he called to him. "Hey,…Thornton!…Gus Thornton! It's Marshal Taylor,…and I've come to talk!" A few seconds passed, and then he could see the shadows of several men on the stairwell wall as they came out of his office.

"You just made it, Marshal." Growled the raspy voice of Thornton. "You got my prisoner?"

"I got 'im."

"Then bring 'im up."

"It ain't gonna be that easy, Thornton.... You bring my Deputy and th' Sheriff down to the street, and we'll trade out."

"You take me for a fool, man?...That weren't th' deal!"

"Maybe,...but it is now. You want Risinger, you come down and get 'im. Don't worry, I'll clear the street, except for Risinger, and a friend a mine." Several long seconds passed in silence, and he was beginning to think Thornton was calling his bluff.

"Tell you what I'm gonna do here, Marshal." Rasped Thornton. "You don't bring my prisoner up here, right now, I'm just gonna kill that deputy of yours,...how's that?"

"Before you do that,...think of this. I hear one shot, or even a yelp of pain from either one a those men,...you will never leave this building alive, and that's a promise. You bring my people down to the street, we make a trade,...you live. You don't,...you're a dead Son of a Bitch!...Now I heard you was a gunfighter, fast on the draw and all that. You gonna turn yellow, with a reputation like that?"

"You do know how to rub a man wrong, don't ya, Marshal?...Okay, hillbilly, we'll do it your way,...but hear this,...you try to trick me, I'll kill your fuckin' ass. You got that?"

"Bring 'em out, Thornton." Rodney quickly moved back down the stairs and out to the street.

"He's bringing 'em out." He panted as he rejoined Billy and hia prisoner "We're gonna swap you for the Sheriff and my deputy, Mister Risinger,...now listen to me. When it's time, I want you to start walkin' toward Thornton as soon as my people start toward us, and when you get even with them, with all your strength, move them out a my line of fire, you got that?"

"Yeah, sure,...but how?"

"I don't care, throw 'em down, tackle 'em down, push 'em,...just do it. And John,...you stay down with 'em!"

"You sure about this, Rod?"

"No, but it's got a be done, Billy. Paris is my town and this is my job. I have to know I can handle it."

"Okay," Sighed Billy. "Then here's my part a th' plan. I called in three of Rucker's best marksmen while you went in th' Courthouse,...I got two of 'em on the boardwalk behind us, and one in the alley at the gun shop. Now,

Thornton's men will come out ahead a him and his prisoners, and when they get to th' street, they'll spread out behind 'im. Now when Mister Risinger here makes his move out there, Rucker's men will stand up and lever their rifles,…that'll startle 'em long enough to get th' drop on 'em. If it works,… you'll have Thornton all to yourself."

"If it works." Sighed Rodney. "It won't be easy, as dark as it is. Okay, here they come!"

The courthouse door opened slowly, then one of the gunmen walked out onto the walkway to search the street and square before stepping aside to let the other two men pass. All three men came down the steps to the street and slowly spaced themselves several feet apart to stare hard at them in the fading light.

Gose and Seth were pushed through the door then, and as Thornton ordered them into the street, the gunman nearest to him said something that caused Thornton to look around at the darkened buildings. "Where's my men, Marshal?"

"They'll be released when this is over."

Thornton nodded. "One of my men is gonna go for our horses, now.… .When he gets back, we'll finish our business." He jerked his head at the man nearest him, and that man sprinted toward the square, and disappeared around the corner.

"Now, Marshal,… just so you'll know. I am fast on the draw,….I'm very fast. You might say, I've earned my reputation th' hard way. So, don't get any bright ideas here, cause I'll kill these men before they can get to ya,…and that's a fact." He chuckled then. "Somethin' else you should think about, too. Dark as it is, th' eyes can play tricks on a man,…chances are, you won't even see my draw."

"You talk a good gunfight, Thornton,…now just shut your face, why don't you, and send my men over here,…you don't need that other man for that?"

"Thornton looked at the two men on his right, then nodded. "You're right, I don't, here they come, Marshal,…and you best remember what I said." He said something to Gose, and they both started to slowly walk across the wide street.

"Go ahead, Mister Risinger,…and do this right, okay?"

Risinger started walking toward the two lawmen, and Rodney took a deep breath of the hot summer air and exhaled loudly as he waited, his hand still at his side and brushing against the butt of the Colt pistol. Risinger was almost even with the lawmen when the three melitiamen emerged from the shadows and levered their Winchesters. "Don't move!" Shouted one of them just as Risinger threw himself bodily into the two startled men, taking both of them to the hard-packed street.

Rodney drew and fired only a fleeting second before Thornton, the slug seeming to lift the gunman before pitching him into the courthouse steps behind him, and causing his slug to fly harmlessly into the night sky. And crouching, Rodney fired again as the third gunman spurred his horse toward them,… and missing, he fired again, this time knocking the man backward over the rump of his horse, to lay sprawled face down in the street.

As the echoes of gunfire faded away, Rodney placed both hands on his knees and sucked air noisily into his lungs a few times before straightening to holster the pistol.

"You did good, Rod," Breathed Billy…."Damn good!" He placed his hand on his friend's shoulder and squeezed, affectionately as he watched the militiamen disarm the two bounty hunters.

"Take them two upstairs and lock 'em up!" He shouted. "You'll find two more in th' woodshed behind th gun shop there."

"Rodney!" Screamed Melissa suddenly, causing Billy and Rodney both to look toward the square. And it wasn't until she screamed again that they saw her running across the now crowded expanse toward them. Rodney ran to intercept her just as Connie, Doc and the Judge arrived on the scene. Billy hugged her to him while she sobbed, and watched Doc go on to examine the fallen Thornton.

Doc Lovejoy opened his office door then, and with a lighted lantern in one hand, helped Jim Stockwell out to the boardwalk with the other, and then stepped into the street to examine the other gunman's body.

Judge Bonner watched as the two shirtless gunmen were herded up the boardwalk steps and into the courthouse. "Hanging these two is going to be a pleasure I haven't had in a long time."

"There's four of em, Judge." Grinned Billy. "Two's already upstairs."

"Even better, by God!" He walked quickly across the street and into the building, and it wasn't long until a dim light appeared in the window of his office.

"I was so scared, Billy." Sobbed Connie.

"Scared,…why?… I didn't even pull my gun. Rod did it all,…shot 'em both, big as you please."

▬ ▬

Billy helped Ross set the long table in place at the end of the other two, and his wife, Reba followed them with the tablecloth. Two of the field hands began bringing benches and chairs and placed then around the tables.

"Long table, Boss,…who all you got coming?"

"Well,…if they all show up, we got Rodney and his family, Doc and

Mattie, Jim Stockwell and his wife, then there's Sheriff Gose and his fiancé, John Rucker and his wife, you and yours, and th' hands and their families. Oh, yeah, I invited John Risinger and his family, Sam, too,...if they make it. By th' way, Ross, I appreciate all th' prepared food you and th' hands brought to th' table. But then again, I should be talkin' to your wife,...many thanks, Reba."

"Our pleasure, Mister Upshur." She smoothed out the large cloth and began laying the silverware, turning the bowls and plates upside down over the utensils to keep away the insects. Once she had placed table linen on top of each plate, she stepped back and scanned the tables for a minute before going back into the house to help Connie.

Billy pulled Ross to the wicker-chairs beneath the large oak and sat down. They each rolled and lit a brown-paper cigarette just as Willy, Chris and Angela burst around the end of the house, just barely ahead of eight more yelling kids.

"I used to love playin' tag, when I was a boy." Sighed Ross. "How about you, Boss?"

"I don't think I was ever a boy, Ross,...never had a chance to play games, kid's games anyway." He inhaled a large drag of acrid smoke and blew it skyward, as he listened to the large Crows that circled overhead.

Ross exhaled a cloud of smoke and watched them also. "Looks like they came to stay, don't it?"

"Th' Crows?...Yeah,...I've sort a gotten used to 'em. Them big, black birds got a lot a savvy, Ross. You wouldn't believe how much."

"I guess not." Ross turned to look toward the road then. "Wagon comin', Boss."

"That'll be Rodney." And they both got up to go greet him. "Got everybody with 'im, too." They waved as the buckboard came to a stop in the yard, and then he saw the black carriage come around the trees behind them. "Doc and Mattie, Too."

"You're early." Grinned Billy as he went to shake the lawman's hand.

"Had some news that couldn't wait, if you know what I mean?"

"Well, get on down and make yourself at home. Hi, Lisa,...and you, too, Benny." He reached to help the boy from the wagon. "Willy and th' others are behind th' house yonder." He watched him run toward the back yard, then reached to help Melissa and the baby down. "Connie's in th' kitchen, Lisa, go on in."

Doc stopped his buggy behind Rodney"s rig and climbed down, while Billy rushed to help Mattie.

"Thank you, William, honey." She grunted as she straightened her dress. "Where's my precious Daughter in law?"

"In th' kitchen, Mama, go on in." She pulled him down and kissed his cheek before waddling off toward the house.

"The old Darlin' is a little down in th' get alongs, these days, William." Grinned Doc as him and Rodney came around the back of the buggy. "But then again, so am I....How are you, son?"

Billy shook the old man's hand warmly. "We're very well, Doc,...now come on, there's chairs under th' trees back there,...you, too, Rod,...I want to hear your news." He took Doc's arm and ushered him toward the back yard, and once they were seated, reached for the makings again.

"Well,...it's been two weeks, Rod," "Said Billy as he licked the smoke. "things back to normal in town?"

"Finally,...I helped hang those four gunmen yesterday. That was the first hanging I ever actually took part in,...and I didn't like it!"

"Well, I never seen one, and don't want to." He touched the match to the cigarette and blew smoke up at the trees. "Now,... what's th' news, you hear from Peter?"

Rodney smiled and leaned forward in his chair. " No,...Joseph wired me, late yesterday,...said him and Peter had a meeting with Tandy Walker and Chief Bryant this week in Boggy Depot." He smiled widely. "It's gonna happen, Billy,...we are gonna buy a mountain, and a thousand acres surrounding it,... excluding the land that extends into Arkansas, of course."

"What about mineral rights?"

"Everything. Joseph said we're to meet in thirty days at Boggy Depot. All the Chiefs will be there to sign the deed,... and the bill of sale."

"Did he say how much it's gonna cost us?"

"Joseph gave me a figure of around fifty thousand dollars,...in gold."

Billy nodded. "At twenty dollars an ounce, that'll come close to two hundred pounds."

"Actually," Said Rodney," Shaking his head and grinning. "It's more like two hundred and ten pounds."

"Two hundred and ten pounds," Gasped Doc. "Of gold?...Where you gonna get two hundred and ten pounds of gold, William,...you hit a Mother load or something?"

Billy and Rodney burst out laughing, and that's when Billy leaned to grip the old Doctor's knee, and pointed. "Out a that grain shed over yonder, Doc."

"Out a that,...What?"

Billy grinned at Rodney then. "I think it's time we told Doc about our plans, since him and Mattie are a part of 'em."

"Think we got time," Grinned Rodney. "Folks will be showing up soon?"

"Well, you better damn well take the time!" Blurted Doc. "You two didn't do anything wrong, did you?"

"You know us better than that, Doc." Grinned Rodney. "By the way, Billy,…I sort a jumped the gun a bit this week,…I sent a letter of inquiry to Judge Parker, and he wired me back, saying he had planned on putting Bass Reeves in the area,…but that Reeves was sort of balking at the idea. At any rate, he said he'd make a decision on it in a few days."

"That's a start, Rod. But, speakin' a jumpin' th' gun,…Connie sent a copy of them markings we found to a professor of antiquity and science, at one a them Universaties in New York state somewhere…. Don't know what might come a that."

"Enough of this!" Interrupted Doc. "What about that gold?"

Rodney nodded at Billy, then shrugged. "Folks will be showing up in an hour, Billy,…and it's a long story."

"Then we'll have to cut it short….Doc," Grinned Billy. "Things are gonna change for you and Mattie before long,…as a matter of fact,…things are gonna change for all of us…. Okay, Doc. It all started after Willy was kidnapped,…well, actually, about three months after I brought him home. Anyway,…after we…….'

The end